Ebook ISBN: 978-1-956335-01-9

Audiobook ISBN: 978-1-956335-11-8

Paperback ISBN: 978-1-956335-10-1

Front cover design by Danielle Fine at Design by Definition.

Dragon, talisman, and ship drawings by Etheric Tales.

Luma map designed by Fictive Designs.

First published in 2022 by Ringtail Press.

www.melissajacksonbooks.com

 Created with Vellum

WICKED TREASURE

THE
CHARM
COLLECTOR

BOOK 2

MELISSA ERIN JACKSON

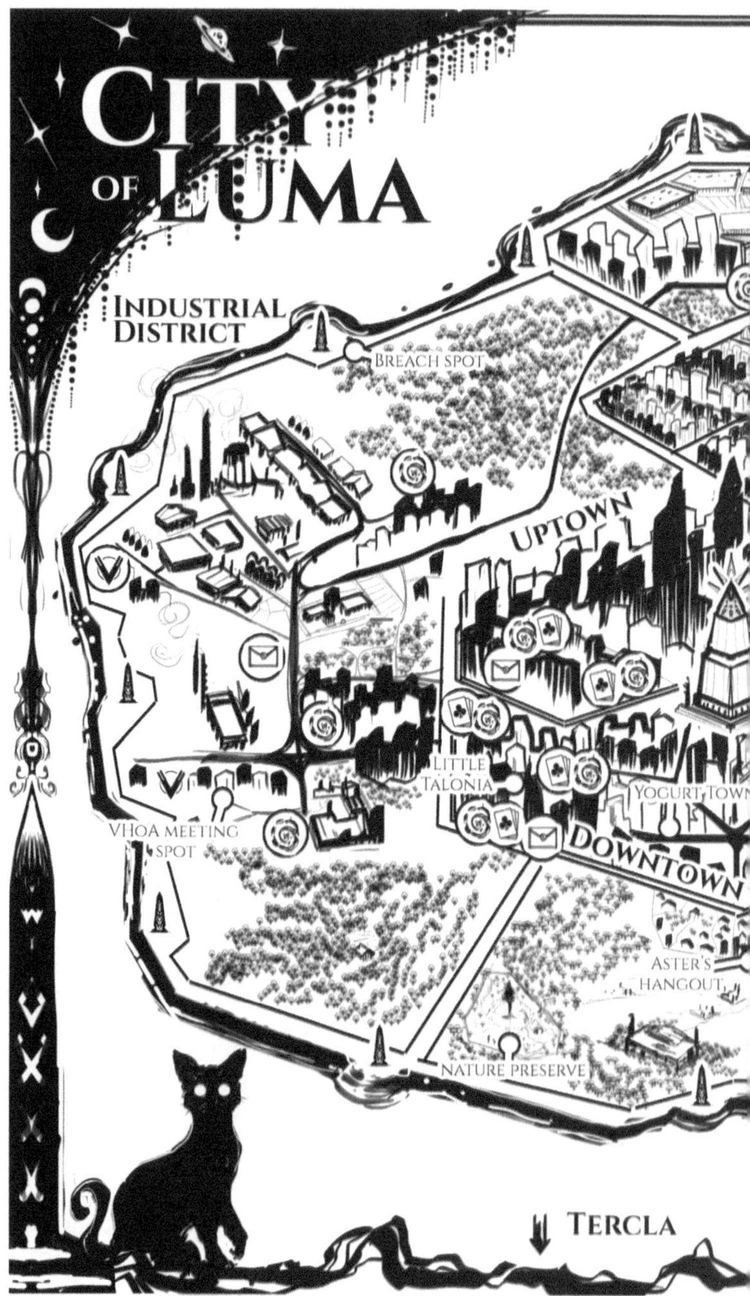

CITY OF LUMA
INDUSTRIAL DISTRICT
BREACH SPOT
UPTOWN
LITTLE TALONIA
YOGURT TOWN
DOWNTOWN
VHOA MEETING SPOT
ASTER'S HANGOUT
NATURE PRESERVE
TERCLA

WAREHOUSE DISTRICT
CALIFORNIA
SACRAMENTO
SAN FRANCISCO
LUMA
LOS ANGELES
SAN DIEGO
ARDMORE
KAYDA'S APARTMENT
HENRI'S APARTMENT
WORTH'S APARTMENT
AL'S BURGERS
MONTCLAIRE
'S APOTHECARY
THE GOLDEN MUSKRAT
VHOA HEADQUARTERS
NECROPOLIS
VEIL OBELISKS
TELEPAD STATION
CASINO
VISITOR'S CENTER
TELEPOST STATION
SORCERERS' COLLECTIVE HEADQUARTERS

Chapter 1
KAYDA

Kayda fastened her belt as she walked out of her bedroom, only to stop dead in her tracks in the doorway. Her gaze snapped to the left. A series of soft clicks sounded from her balcony. Body tense and eyes narrowed, she dropped her hands from her waist and curled her fingers into fists by her sides. She was sleep-deprived and punchy. Whatever in the hells was on her balcony had chosen the wrong day to mess with her. She had to get to work for her extra shift at the casino—she'd been working a lot of extra shifts lately.

Working meant she had somewhere productive to aim her frustration and concern about Harlow—specifically, at the drunken idiots wandering the casino floor. With any luck, she'd be able to bodily throw another teenage orc out the door by his tail. An underage orc kid had been trying to go unnoticed last night. He was young enough that his tusks hadn't started to protrude over his upper lip yet and his skin was a milky lime instead of a vibrant green—but his tail had given him away.

Unlike human men who could get self-conscious about certain appendages being too short, for orc men, the shorter your tail, the older and more virile you were. Insecure young orc

1

males like the oaf yesterday tucked or docked their tails to appear older. The tail on this one had busted out the back of his pants and had whipped a martini right out of a lady's hand. There weren't many orcs in Luma, mostly because once they were of age, if they hadn't gotten into a sport or profession that let them expel their genetically enhanced rage, they often wound up involved in enough criminal shenanigans that they were imprisoned or exiled before they were out of their twenties.

Kayda had delighted in tossing the orc kid out, but the delight had been a temporary balm to her lingering worry.

The clicking sounded again. It was faint, almost drowned out by the sea of voices outside thanks to rush-hour foot traffic from the telepad station down the street. Streams of people were leaving work, while others flooded into the area for the shops and restaurants. Sometimes Kayda cursed her heightened draken hearing—it took time, patience, and training to learn how to filter ambient noise.

A lady could go mad if she heard everything from a rumbling airplane overhead to a munching earthworm below, all at once. Kayda's sense of hearing was like adjusting the dials on a radio, instinctually turning up certain noises while dialing back others. When she was in an emotionally heightened state, however, as she had been for weeks, the dials were more like malfunctioning faucets that turned on full blast at inopportune times, causing confusion and debilitating headaches.

The fact that she could hear the soft sound outside told her she was, at least currently, in a steady frame of mind.

Squaring her shoulders, she stalked across her small living room—past the dining room table marred with angry scratches from Harlow's demented sword—and to the closed windows that overlooked the tiny balcony. The blinds were drawn shut.

Clink, clink.

If this damn apartment building had another pixie infestation, so help her ...

She reached up, grabbed hold of the drawstring on the blinds, and yanked the cord down in one fluid motion. Perhaps the quick movement would scare the winged monsters and give them simultaneous heart attacks. Kayda liked the idea of her balcony being littered with tiny petal garments, like potpourri.

What stood on the railing of her porch was neither startled nor a pixie. It was a bluebird the size of a house cat. Kayda cocked her head; the unruffled bird mirrored the action. When Kayda did nothing more than stare at it for ten long seconds, the bird walked a couple of inches to the right along the railing, and then to the left, never taking its eye off Kayda. Avian pacing.

Click, click, click, went the bird's talons.

Kayda unlatched the window and forced it up. A few flakes of white paint fluttered onto the worn wood of the windowsill. As Kayda stooped under the open window—the shattered glass, also thanks to Harlow's sword, had been replaced, at least—the bird did an about-face on the railing and tottered back the other way. The balcony gave a soft groan of protest under Kayda's weight, but held firm. Sunlight winked off a copper cap atop the black plastic tube affixed to the bird's leg. This was a courier bird.

Who in the hells would send Kayda a courier bird?

The bluebird stopped directly in front of Kayda and held out its leg, clearly wanting to speed up this process. Kayda reached for it tentatively, not because she feared the bird, but because she wasn't the best at handling small, delicate things with care. Her pinkie was bigger than the tube. She'd much rather snap the bird's leg off so she could take her time getting the tube open, but she figured the bird would take offense to that. She fiddled with the top of the small canister, accidentally poking the bird's chest. For her efforts, she got a sharp beak jabbed into the back of her hand.

"Ow!"

Squawk!

Growling, Kayda grabbed the bird with both hands and tucked it under her arm like a football, feet up. The bird offered a muted squawk from somewhere near her armpit. After some finagling, Kayda found the button to push on top of the plastic tube, which caused the bottom to pop open. A small scroll of paper was curled inside. She had no easy way to get it out, though, as her fingers were too wide. She turned the bird over and gave it a hard shake to dislodge the scroll. The bluebird shrieked and pecked its thick beak into Kayda's wrist. Yelping, she managed to release the bird *and* catch the message.

The bird dive-bombed Kayda's head a few times, narrowly missing swipes from Kayda's large hands, then squawked very loudly directly into Kayda's face.

"I don't like you much either!" Kayda shouted, though she supposed it wasn't the bird's fault Kayda wasn't blessed with fine motor skills.

The bird sailed over the top of the apartment building across the street and out of sight, presumably heading back to its rookery.

Kayda stared down at the scroll in her hand and cursed softly to herself, doing her best to unfurl it without tearing the thin paper.

Unlike the telepost message Kayda had received a week or so ago that had supposedly been from Harlow, yet written by someone else, this note was in Harlow's familiar scrawl.

I wish we could eat ramen until we burst. I hate that I haven't been able to call you. I promise I'm safe, but I've been scared to draw too much attention to you. I'm leaving the city, but not forever. Stabby,

Mr. Supervillain (yes, really!), and I are going on an adventure. Grayson will be jealous. I miss you.

Kayda reread the message five times before her brain let her accept what it said. Harlow had left Luma. Not only had she left, she'd done so with the sword and "Mr. Supervillain"? As in Caspian Blackthorn? There had been rumors spreading all over the city about what Harlow was actually up to, where she'd gotten the sword, and if she and Caspian Blackthorn were in cahoots. That last one had been the hardest for Kayda to believe. How could Harlow have been with *Caspian*? Up until a month or so ago, they hadn't known each other. Hells, Harlow hadn't even known what the guy looked like. Swapping theories on Caspian's identity had been one of Kayda and Harlow's pastimes.

And why would Grayson be jealous? The water elemental was only obsessed with one thing: pirates. Kayda supposed adding pirates into the mix wasn't out of the range of possibility at this point.

There was so much Harlow hadn't told Kayda—and now she was gone. Kayda squeezed her hand into a fist, crumpling the note. How dare Harlow keep Kayda in the dark just to protect her. That was the same bullshit Felix had pulled on Harlow, Kayda was sure of it. And now Harlow was doing it to her.

Kayda wanted Harlow back in Luma so Kayda could strangle her.

She heaved a sigh. Only Harlow and Henri could get her this riled up, and for two completely different reasons.

Being pissed off wasn't productive. And she still had to get to work.

Climbing back through her window, she tossed the crumbled note onto her kitchen counter. Her attention, as it often did, shifted to the shiny tower of black plastic by her TV. She'd had the newest iteration of this gaming console for a few weeks. A gift to herself to help her deal with the stress of not knowing what was going on with Harlow. She'd much rather resume her game from last night, to smash buttons and the heads of monsters alike, but she had to finish getting ready for work. On her way toward the door, she shot a furtive glance at the tiny ball of paper on her counter. It was currently her sole connection to Harlow. The paranoid lady refused to use a cell phone other than in dire emergencies and she *still* hadn't called Kayda during the mess of the last month. If getting accused of murder and being on the lam with a psychotic sword didn't equal an emergency, Kayda didn't know what would.

Kayda crossed the living room to her kitchen and tentatively picked up the note, smoothing out the paper. Her gentle efforts resulted in a corner being ripped off. She grabbed a can of coffee and clunked it on top of the paper. That would straighten it out. Later, she'd figure out what to do with the information it had given her.

Kayda had just finished putting her belongings in her locker at the start of her shift when she heard a commotion from the connected break room. She glanced at the clock on the wall above the door; she had five minutes before she had to be on the casino floor.

The break room didn't get much use. Most of the staff preferred to eat outside in the casino's outdoor pavilion area to get away from the constant noise and permeating smoke of the place—both of which traveled under the employee-only doors. Hardly anyone used the room with any frequency other than Julianne, who was obsessed with *Faet of the Heart,* a trashy soap opera that had a bunch of "will they, won't they?" romantic subplots between humans and fae. The answer was always, *yes, of course they will.* The true question was: will it end in tragedy? The answer was usually yes there, too. Boris was often in there with Julianne, claiming he was also a fan of the show. But everyone knew that what Boris was a fan of was Julianne. The irony? Boris was a draken and Julianne a human. Boris had it even worse for Julianne than Kayda had it for Henri.

When Kayda poked her head into the small room, though, *Faet of the Heart* wasn't on the TV mounted in the corner—a newscast was. Boris and Julianne were in the room, but so were five others. Henri wasn't, which Kayda was simultaneously glad about and disappointed by. She *was* actively avoiding him, after all.

"What's going on?" she asked.

The chatter from those assembled was even louder than the TV. A few of them turned to glance at her.

Boris said, "The Collective is going to have a press conference. Well, I mean, they're going to play their prerecorded press conference soon." He rolled his eyes, then faced the screen again when the familiar chime sounded, alerting viewers that a sorcerer, or one of their spokescats, had something important to say.

The Collective had been working very hard to paint themselves in a better light—holding press conferences on a nearly daily basis since Harlow and her new friends had hijacked the news. Kayda wasn't sure how effective these face-saving measures were. She figured most people tuned in because they secretly craved it would happen again—that someone would break into the curated newscast with another anti-Collective message. It had happened just the one time, though.

Instead of that newscast from weeks ago being about the Collective's diligent work to get the missing fae girls back home, the fae girls themselves had appeared on screen, telling all of Luma what had really happened to them: they'd been drugged with Bliss, trafficked out of Luma, and while in a drug-filled haze, had been working with a vampire who used the beautiful fae to lure his human food out of clubs and into his nest of waiting vampires. A goblin girl, Vian, had died while in captivity—which the Collective had tried to hide. Eight girls had been found alive, five of whom had been from Luma. The others had been trafficked out of hubs in the Pacific Northwest and were presumably home now.

At the end of the account from the fae girls and a couple of their parents, the screen had gone black. White letters had spelled out the question: *Whose side is the Collective on? What aren't they telling us?*

The girls hadn't outright accused the Collective of being aware of what was happening and ignoring it, but the implication had been undeniable. There had been protests in the streets almost immediately. People praised Harlow and her sword for bringing the girls home. Yet, the prevailing opinion seemed to be that Harlow had murdered those shifters. The majority of people who had been polled in the days since—if the polls could even be trusted—thought Harlow was a hero. But they also believed she needed to pay for her crimes. Kayda didn't blame her for skipping town. She took offense to learning about it in a Goddess-damned note.

One of the grim-faced sorcerers was on screen now, with the usual Sorcerers Collective logo—silhouettes of several hands all reaching upward toward a ball of glowing light—painted in gold on the black wall behind him. The logo was supposed to symbolize the power of many working to create a unifying force. Kayda had always more or less accepted the Collective for what it was: an almost faceless organization that kept Luma enclosed in its little sanctuary where in-the-know humans, magic, and the descendants of non-Earth natives could exist peacefully. The goings-on of the Collective rarely affected her daily life that much, so they didn't take up much space in her mind. What had happened with Harlow, though, made Kayda wonder if she'd been naïve all this time, thinking Harlow was too paranoid for her own good.

"Hello, citizens of Luma," the sorcerer intoned dryly. "We know there have been many reports out of Montclaire about mundanes and fae—goblins in particular—rioting and causing property damage. While this isn't a new event as of late, in light of what transpired recently, what *is* new is that the mundanes have been armed with charmed items. We, too, have the dynamic images of Harlow Fletcher burned into our minds, the dragon sword in her hand. This image might be emboldening to other mundanes who idolize her, but remember that she is not completely innocent."

Kayda's eyes narrowed. Two of her coworkers looked over, knowing Harlow was Kayda's best friend. Boris smiled at her sympathetically.

Davis, however, lacked sympathy and tact. "Hey, Kay. Psst."

She cut him a glare.

Davis was unfazed. Probably because he had a good six inches and a hundred pounds on her. And also because he was dumber than a sack of rocks. "You got any idea where your girl is? Think she'll kill again?"

"Shut up, Davis," she snapped.

"*Jeeez*," he said, hands up. "What I say?"

Rolling her eyes, she refocused her fury on the TV.

"Any charmed item imbued with more than Level 4 magic is quite detrimental to a mundane's well-being," the sorcerer droned. "Anyone caught selling such items to mundanes will be apprehended by the werecats or bounty hunters and brought before the Collective for judgment. These items are banned for a reason. Reporting information about mundanes using these banned goods that leads to an arrest will earn the Good Samaritan two thousand dollars.

"To those naysayers who believe these reckless mundanes will learn their lesson when they use magic beyond their means, may we remind you that regardless of their lack of magic, it was humans who were able to slay the few ancient beasts who wound up on Earth due to the Glitch. History books, as young as they are, written by the first generation of marooned fae tell grand stories of dragons, griffins, and chimeras from the fae home world. They spoke of how these great beasts ruled the land and skies. Though they were mighty, they were few on Earth. And those few were slain by humans who used the ancients' own magic against them."

Davis grumbled something under his breath.

"Those dark times are behind us now. We have reached a unity among fae and mundanes," the sorcerer said, awkwardly gesturing to the logo behind him as his disingenuous smile twitched. Powerful, emotion-provoking orators, sorcerers were not. "Instead of fae fearing what mundanes could do to us, we have built a society where we can live together as one people, magic-touched or not. Because we care deeply about the well-being of our mundane neighbors, it's up to all of you to help us keep everyone out of harm's way. We understand that emotions are running high, and we understand your frustrations. We hear them. We are listening. We will do better ... together."

The screen abruptly went black, and white text scrolled across it with the phone number to use to call in reports about humans wielding charmed weapons, as well as a large reminder of the amount of the cash reward. The flashing red "$2,000" made it feel like an infomercial.

Kayda honestly couldn't tell if the Collective meant to protect humans and had expressed it in a very backhanded way, or if they were truly trying to incite violence against humans. Depending on who you talked to, "mundanes" was a slur. The fact that the Collective used it might have been their precise way of speaking, or it could have been a way to stir up more unrest.

She didn't know about what was whispered among the other fae, but Kayda knew there was a subset of draken who resented humans because of the history on Earth. In school, everyone learned how the humans had managed to kill off the larger fae, armed with charmed weapons and their unflinching egotistical fervor to hunt the foreign beasts into extinction. Dragons had a choice back then: shift into their human form to hide among the bloodthirsty population of humans who vastly outnumbered them, or remain in dragon form and destroy the humans who might hold the key to getting them back home. Most chose to shift, to blend into the population until things grew steadier. The longer the shifted dragons stayed in human form, the more they lost their ability to shift at all, though they retained their heightened senses, speed, and strength. Shifted dragons mating with others of their kind, and some mating with humans, created offspring that gave rise to the draken. Heightened abilities were passed on, but the ability to shift was not. More and more draken were born with weaker abilities every generation. Some in the community shunned anyone who diluted their powers by being with a human—which was part of the reason why, Kayda guessed, Boris hadn't made the move on Julianne yet. If he had a family that was against it, he might pine away forever.

"So ... Kay," Davis said, smiling broadly. "Where'd Harlow get that sword anyway?"

He was trying to sound casual, but he was clearly fishing for information.

"She have, like, a stash or something? Think she might be loaning some of that stuff out to people?"

Clearly, the buffoon had no idea that "Harlow Fletcher" and "Fletch," the semi-infamous charm collector, were one and the same.

She rounded on him. "You want me to rat out my best friend and anyone she might know to ... *you?*"

Davis's expression lit up. He looked right and left, finding a couple of their coworkers eyeing them. He took a step closer and lowered his voice. Conspiratorially, he said, "We're totes on the same page, Kay! We could split the cash. You down?"

She stalked out of the room.

Chapter 2
KAYDA

The following morning, Kayda had a plan in place and Harlow's note in her pocket. As she walked up Tabbert Road, the area swarmed with tourists, shoppers, and hungry folks hoping to find a place without an hour-long wait, Kayda adjusted the mental dials on her hearing. For a human, the cacophony of Downtown Luma could be so loud, it was hard to hear one's own thoughts. Harlow had said as much on several occasions. But Kayda could reduce it all to background noise—a soft, persistent hum. What she looked for now among the ever-present din was if anyone was following her. Was anyone matching her footsteps? Stopping when she did? Quickly darting out of view when she glanced back?

She'd purposefully not done much snooping when Harlow was a fugitive in Luma. Harlow was paranoid at the best of times, but Kayda guessed Harlow's years of being suspicious of everyone had served her well once she actually had *reason* to be paranoid. Anyone who knew Harlow would know she and Kayda were close—that Kayda was one of Harlow's few contacts outside of her client list.

But so far, Kayda had only uncovered two people who had

been keeping tabs on her. One happened to be the partner of the werecat guard Harlow had been accused of murdering. His name was O'Neill, Kayda thought. The deep slash across one eye—the iris a milky white—was possibly courtesy of the sword, if O'Neill been in the vicinity when his partner was killed. O'Neill had had rage pouring off him like a fog, but he'd never approached Kayda. She figured her size had played the biggest role in that. O'Neill might have had shifter magic on his side, but Kayda was over seven feet of muscle and walked like she knew it. If Harlow had been best friends with a smaller woman, that woman probably wouldn't have fared as well.

Kayda hadn't seen O'Neill in a while. Instead, on occasion, Kayda would spot a young female werecat guard loitering suspiciously at the casino, or trailing far behind Kayda on her way to or from work. Kayda wasn't sure if the lackluster surveillance would increase or die down completely now that Harlow had fled Luma. Of course, it was possible the Collective didn't know she was gone yet.

Hopefully Kayda's outing now didn't tip anyone off, but so far, she hadn't noticed anyone tailing her.

As she pushed open the door to Jo's Apothecary, a pair of goblin kids raced out, each with what she presumed to be a mood-brightening lollipop, given the giggles that erupted from them after every lick of the bright red candy. The floors creaked under Kayda's boots. A trio of human women regarded Kayda's head-to-toe black ensemble warily. Kayda usually had two modes: sexy vixen or SWAT team. Today was a SWAT team kind of day: black long-sleeve shirt tucked into black cargo pants held up by a black belt, and black combat boots. She'd massaged gel into her short white hair to make it look extra spiky. She flashed a toothy smile at the ladies as she went past, and heard two of them audibly gulp, while the third dropped the bar of homemade soap she'd been holding. It hit her shoe, slid across the floor, and came to rest under a display case. The women scurried after it, clearly happy for any excuse to get away from the giant scary lady.

Kayda had an extra bounce to her step as she made her way to the counter. Maybe today wouldn't be so bad.

Behind the counter was a colorful arrangement of "freshly bewitched candies!" according to the sign. Lollipops, cellophane-wrapped caramels, vibrant pieces of rock candy affixed to sticks, and various sweets shaped like animals and insects that had been crafted out of thin lines of honey. Her grandmother used to love the candy insects, often asking Kayda for a bag of honey butterflies. They were one of the few things that had eased the near-constant ache in her grandmother's throat. She'd place one of those candy butterflies on her tongue and sigh contentedly as the honey and gentle magic melted, easing the pain—at least for a little while.

A man stood behind the counter with his back to Kayda, fussing with the candy display. When five full seconds went by without him turning around, Kayda rapped her knuckles on the wood. The man turned. He frowned. Kayda did, too.

Erik seemed to sense that Harlow and Jo had a special connection, so he tolerated Harlow. Kayda had always harbored a sneaking suspicion that Erik didn't feel a shred of respect for Kayda herself, but couldn't prove it since he was usually pleasant enough in Harlow's presence.

"Your awful human friend hasn't been in since days before her murderous rampage," he said, arms crossed. "You better believe I told the cops that."

Kayda stifled a sigh. "Hello to you, too, Erik."

He curled his lip, as though offended that his name crossed her lips. "What do you want? You always come in with *her* and she's obviously not here."

For all Erik knew, this could be Kayda's favorite shop and

she spent hours here specifically on days Erik didn't work—for Erik was an odious toad.

He was right, though. Kayda never came here without Harlow.

"Where's Jo?" Kayda asked.

"Right here, dear."

Kayda turned to find the fifty-year-old dark-skinned witch behind her. Jo was a good two feet shorter than Kayda, and was as outwardly soft as Kayda was hard, but Josephine Beliu was not a witch to trifle with.

"Hi, Jo," Kayda said, in a tone much gentler than the one she'd used with Erik. "Can we talk for a few minutes?"

Jo's sharp gaze roamed Kayda's face, then dropped to the pocket that Kayda currently had a hand stuffed inside, knuckles brushing against Harlow's note. "Of course. Follow me."

Erik muttered something under his breath, but Kayda didn't even offer him a backward glance.

As Jo had always done with Harlow when the two swapped information in exchange for the unique charmed items Harlow picked up on her raids, Jo led Kayda to the back of the shop, and then through a storage room door. As Kayda followed after Jo, the lock on the door snicked into place. Kayda didn't know if Jo always kept the room locked to keep out nosy customers, or because not even Erik was granted access. Kayda hoped it was the latter.

They passed rows of boxes lining the hallway and stepped into a more open area. Kayda hated it back here; it was too cramped. One false move and she'd send half a dozen boxes to the ground. The area they stood in now thankfully had a slightly higher ceiling, so Kayda didn't have to stoop as she did while walking down the hallway. The cloying, musty scent of dust and old cardboard made the claustrophobia a tick worse, but Kayda wouldn't be here long.

"You're even twitchier in here without Harlow's energy to calm you down," Jo said, head cocked slightly as she eyed Kayda. She reached out with both hands, got up on her tiptoes, and placed her palms on either of Kayda's shoulders. She applied gentle pressure. "Get these things away from your ears."

Kayda gusted a sigh and rolled her shoulders a couple of times.

"There we go," Jo said, then held out her hand. Gold rings decorated every finger. "Now, what did you bring me?"

Kayda took the note out of her pocket and handed it over. She waited for Jo to read it before speaking. "Is there any way to do a locator spell or something off that? It's her handwriting. She touched the paper. Can you tap into her essence or whatever?"

Jo hmmed. "Possibly." She headed for her messy desk. She rummaged in drawers and boxes until she found a paper map. She spread it out on the uneven surface of the desk. Small wooden boxes, glass vials, bundles of dried herbs, and a few talismans created peaks and valleys from below the well-worn map.

Kayda tucked her arms behind her back, willing her neck to stay loose while she waited. The sound of Jo's lilting spellwork relaxed her, like the soothing tones of a lullaby sung in a foreign tongue. Kayda's dragon ancestors had blessed her with many things, but magic-craft wasn't among her gifts. Harlow knew more about magic than Kayda did; she needed to for her work. Clients liked buying things from a woman who knew what she was selling. Kayda currently felt utterly helpless here, which was not an emotion she had much experience with, nor did she like it. Harlow was the closest thing to family Kayda had left, and now with her gone, Kayda felt adrift.

How annoying.

She wanted to punch something.

Jo glanced at her over her shoulder. "Why don't you go ask Erik for some mood-boosting candy, hmm? You're making my magic glitch with all that high-strung energy of yours."

"Erik hates me," Kayda said.

"Oh, he doesn't hate anyone," Jo said. "He's ... going through a lot. He's figuring out who he is and lashes out accordingly. His personality is all rough edges with people he doesn't know."

Kayda didn't care. Erik was a jerk, end of story. She blew out a long, deep breath, rolled her head from side to side, and shook out her arms, trying to expel all her "high-strung energy." She'd tried a meditation DVD once—Luma's tech could be so behind the times when compared to the mundane world beyond the veils—and the soft-voiced woman talking Kayda through the breathing exercises had annoyed her so much, she'd thrown the remote at the screen and broken the TV. She hadn't tried meditation since, but she'd do what she could now if it meant she didn't have to interact with Erik.

Ten minutes later, Jo let out an "I got her!"

Kayda crossed to Jo in two quick strides and peered down at the lumpy map. At first, Kayda didn't see anything but the West Coast of the United States snaked through with rivers and highways, and dotted with trees and a few circles marking the locations of hubs. This was no mundane map. Luma was drawn in the middle of California, the vampire hub of Tercla below it. To the north was the hub of Kensey in Washington, and Pinebough in Oregon. As Kayda's eyes started to drift toward the east, Jo pointed a dark finger back toward California.

And then Kayda saw it: a small black dot inching its way north out of the state. "That's them?"

"Yep," Jo said with a nod. "If you'd like, I can keep this going here, and I'll give you a call if the dot stops for any length of time. I can't say how long I'll be able to track her, as the energy of her on the paper will fade eventually. It doesn't require much magic on my end to keep the locator spell going, so it's no trouble."

"That would be great. Thanks, Jo."

"Not a problem."

Kayda helped Jo move a few cardboard boxes to clear a patch of wall so the map could be taped onto it. Once the map was in place, the two women stepped back and watched the slowly moving dot for a few seconds, arms crossed.

"Did you know she knew Caspian Blackthorn?" Kayda asked.

"That rumor is true, then? Two fugitives on the run together ..."

"Three, if you count the sword," Kayda said.

"I'm sure she's fine, dear," Jo said. "Harlow is resourceful. And I'm sure you'll hear from her once it's safe."

Kayda feared that time would never come.

After exchanging phone numbers with Jo and thanking her one last time, Kayda let herself out of the claustrophobic office and made her way to the exit. Suddenly changing her mind, she strolled to the counter instead. She waited while Erik laughed good-naturedly with a customer. When it was Kayda's turn, the smile slipped right off Erik's dumb mug.

"What do you want now?" he asked.

"Jo said I can have a happy-making lollipop. I'll take a grape one."

Erik pursed his thin lips. "Lady Josephine doesn't see you and Harlow for the criminals and thugs you are. She needs to be protected. She's too nice to see what's right in front of her face."

Kayda fought an eye roll. "*Lady Josephine* is a grown woman. She's smart and can make her own decisions about who she spends time with. She doesn't need you butting in." She held out a hand, opening and closing it twice. "Grape."

Erik turned a shade of red even darker than the cherry

candies behind him. He plucked a purple lollipop from the display and then whirled back to dramatically slap it into her palm.

Kayda yanked the cellophane wrapper off and popped the sweet into her mouth. She grinned around it at Erik, crumpled the wrapper, and dropped it on the counter. Words a bit impeded by the candy, she said, "I'd wish you a nice day, but I wouldn't mean it."

With that, she headed for the door.

"You've proven my point!" Erik called out. "Delinquent!"

Kayda didn't care. The mood-boosting sweet had kicked in, and the sound of her own laughter drowned out whatever Erik groused about next. Kayda happily moseyed out into the sunshine.

Chapter 3
HARLOW

I peeled my eyes open and stared up at the stark-white, unfamiliar ceiling. Yawning, I scrubbed a hand across my face. Something flaked off my chin, and I had a sneaking suspicion I had been drooling. Groggily, I propped myself up on my elbows and I tried to get oriented. I'd slept hard. I widely opened and closed my eyes a couple of times, attempting to make my eyelids feel less leaden.

The bed I was in was huge and covered in fluffy white pillows and a heavenly comforter that felt crafted from clouds. I noted that I wore jeans and a T-shirt, and I was on top of said heavenly comforter, rather than underneath it. I had taken my boots off, though, so at least I wasn't a total heathen.

Directly ahead of me stood a massive armoire with a flat-screen TV perched atop it on triangle-shaped legs. The screen was dark. Beside that was a pair of doors, one of which stood open. A living room lay beyond it. Details of where I was started to solidify as the last dregs of sleep ebbed away. I remembered that on the other side of the living room was a second bedroom. I didn't sense any movement in the suite. I supposed Caspian could be asleep, though I didn't even know what time it was.

Even still, sorcerers didn't usually sleep in. It wasn't efficient to while away the hours in bed when one could seize the day or whatever other nonsense responsible adults said.

I glanced to my left, where soft sunlight cascaded onto a round, wooden table. Windows flanked three sides of the seating alcove, the windowsills lined with plush bench seats. The soft white curtains were pulled open and tied into place on elegant hooks protruding from the walls in three places. Outside, sunlight glittered on the surface of a lake.

I got to my feet and padded across the soft beige carpet toward the door leading into the living room. Caspian sat on one of the four love seats, a leather-bound book in his lap. He glanced up as I stepped inside and offered me a slight nod.

I scanned the room for the sword, finding its preferred duffel bag lying on a table identical to the one in my room. The bag was unzipped, and sunlight bathed the blade's shiny steel surface. Was it dozing in the sun like a house cat?

"How'd you sleep?" Caspian asked, pulling my attention away from the sword.

"Like the dead," I said, rubbing the heel of my palm against an eye. I flopped into the love seat across from him and pulled my bare feet onto the cushion. "How long was I out?"

Caspian checked his watch. "Fourteen hours."

"Dang." I yawned again, stretching both arms above my head. My back gave a few muted pops in response. "Guess I was more tired than I thought."

"I practically had to carry you in here like a sack of potatoes last night." There was almost a hint of a smile as he said it.

His gaze quickly shifted down to his book again, as if he worried the words would be offended that he was no longer paying attention to them. I let him return to his reading, settling further into the chair and gazing out the nearest window. We were on the third floor, so most of what I could see from this vantage were the tops of the pine trees.

It had been two days since Caspian, the sword, and I fled Luma. Washington was our tentative destination, but we were moving slowly for now. If a message popped up on my pocket mirror that the bounty hunters were after Kayda, Grayson, or Jo for their close association with me, I'd hightail it back to Luma, even if I had to hitchhike to do it. I knew Caspian would drop everything to go back if we got word from Welsh that things had gone sideways back home. Or if one of Caspian's courier birds showed up with an urgent message. We'd gotten out of California as fast as we could but we were going to linger in Oregon for several days—just in case.

Things had been quiet on the home front save for the occasional "How's it going?" text from Felix—which I ignored. The whole Felix situation was ... messy. So I avoided it. Healthy, I know.

Caspian and I had stayed in a dinky motel off the highway the first night in Oregon. It had taken almost eight hours to get there, and we'd both been cranky by the time we arrived. While I hadn't complained about the sketchy accommodations—I wasn't paying for them, after all—Caspian's constant air of distaste about the state of the room had been hard to ignore. The sheets were too scratchy, the water in the very stained shower was too cold, the spider on his pillow was too large. Granted, I'd been dismayed about the spider, too, and had screamed so loudly that the sword had zipped across the room and skewered the poor spider to the pillow, slicing right through it and a couple of inches into the mattress.

We'd fled in the wee hours of the morning, Caspian leaving a hefty cash tip on the nightstand so we wouldn't have to answer any potential questions posed by the motel staff. Surely weirder shit than "overprotective murder sword antics" had happened in that place.

When he'd told me where we'd be staying the following night, I'd discreetly checked out the website on my phone while he drove. I'd balked at the price tag but had to remind myself that Caspian was rich and was used to living a life that reflected that. He wasn't flashy—because sorcerer—but he also liked nice things.

I believed Caspian when he said he was happy to foot the bill for this excursion, but I still felt bad about it. We both agreed that using either of my accounts—the Harlow one, or the one for my alias, Deanna Kyle—would leave a digital trail of breadcrumbs the Collective would be able to follow. They'd tracked my telepad movements last month while I'd been moonlighting as Deanna. The account had to be compromised by now. Caspian, bless his equally paranoid heart, had multiple aliases. For this trip, he was using one he'd been holding onto for emergencies. It was safer this way.

Once we were back in Luma, though, I'd pay him back. If he refused it, I'd hide cash all over his mansion so he'd find partial payments until the end of time.

When we'd arrived in Eugene last night, I'd been so exhausted, I no longer felt a shred of guilt about him paying for several nights in this giant suite. I'd fallen on the bed in all my clothes and passed out. Everything had finally caught up with me.

The stress of the past month had forced me to survive on adrenaline. Plus, I wasn't sure how much I'd healed from the sword's magic pouring into me. One day soon, I knew I'd be haunted by nightmares fueled by the reality that I'd killed vampires and draken alike. Several of them. First at the Steel Drum Bar & Grill in Fresno, and then later outside the veiled storage container where the stolen fae girls had been kept. Most of it had been the sword's doing, but I'd been holding it while it tore into flesh. Blood and gore had covered my skin just as much as they'd coated the sword's blade.

Would I have to pay for that eventually, in a legal sense? Murder was murder, even if the victims deserved it. The monsters the sword and I had cut down had been responsible for trafficking drugs and young girls. After the carnage, we'd rescued the girls—most of them, anyway. That fact had to work in my favor. Yet, it felt like another reason—to add to the long list of reasons—why the Collective wanted me strapped down in one of their interrogation rooms, truth serum dumped down my throat.

Stan's voice echoed in my head. *"My girls and I will leave, you walk out of here and never return, and I won't let the Collective know where you are. If you think you're safe from them in the mundane world, you're quite mistaken."*

A vampire's words could never be accepted at face value, and I didn't believe that he'd had a direct line to the Collective. Stan *had* gotten his information from someone inside Luma; he'd had to in order to keep his enterprise going. Stan provided Bliss to his contact in Luma, and in exchange, fae girls had been shuttled into the mundane world and Stan's necrotic clutches.

Yet, the possibility that there had been truth in what he said nagged at me: that even outside Luma, I wasn't protected from the Collective.

Last night, though, the sight of mundane security monitoring the lobby, the comforting, clean scent of the fresh flowers in vases in the hallway, and the peace and quiet of the room had overridden every anxiety. And I'd slept. The best sleep I'd had in ages.

I didn't know Caspian Blackthorn that well and knew the sentient sword with an anger management problem not that much better. But at this moment, I felt safe with them. Safe enough to sleep for fourteen hours and wake naturally. I watched Caspian, a slight crease to his brow as he read. It was probably some overly detailed manual about rune construction that would put most people to sleep. He was, at most, five years older than me, but he had the air of an old professor sometimes —okay, most of the time.

"Thank you," I said before I realized I was going to say it.

Caspian looked up from his book. "For what?"

I shrugged. "Everything."

He smiled softly. "You're welcome." After a beat, he asked, "Are you ... hungry? The restaurant downstairs has a creperie."

"Starved."

He closed his book. "Ready to go in ten?"

I climbed off the chair. "Make it twenty," I said, suspecting there was still dried drool on my chin. It was very possibly in my hair, too. I hadn't had the energy to put my sleep cap on last night, so it would take a few minutes to get the mass of curls under control.

"Are you okay to stay in here by yourself, cutlass?" I heard Caspian ask as I stepped into my room.

Tap.

"Good. Promise not to murder any of the housekeeping staff if they happen to come in. They might refresh the towels and bedding."

Tap ... tap.

The sword's equivalent to a maybe. Ugh. I begged the sword not to ruin this outing of fancy crepes with the discovery of dead maids.

It struck me then how casual that last exchange had been.

My life had gotten very strange.

By night three in the fancy hotel, I'd developed cabin fever. Caspian spent most of his days poring over his books, taking notes in his efficient handwriting on the crisp white pages of his notebook. He had uprooted his life to go on this side quest with me—and was funding most of it—so I hadn't wanted to disturb him. This was the kind of boring stuff he liked to do: studying ad nauseam even when he was long out of school. I figured he was learning as many new spells as he could in preparation for ... who knew what.

I had promised the sword early on that I would figure out where it had come from. It had woken up, for lack of a better term, when I'd stolen it out of Haskins's basement. It couldn't remember where it had come from. This was the problem with sentience—once you possessed rational thought, you inevitably had an existential crisis. The runes that had been etched along the sword's fuller had granted it a consciousness no inanimate object should have.

But it had memories, it seemed. It had a kind of amnesia and was working its way back to its origins.

The sword had saved my life on numerous occasions now, and I wanted to do this for it. It wasn't just a sense of obligation, though. I was doing this for myself, too. I harbored no suspicions that the sword would turn on me—it was loyal that way. Yet, it clearly had its own agenda. When that agenda ran counter to mine, it did whatever suited its purposes and I was left to deal with the consequences.

The murder of Oliver Randal by the sword had been the event that turned me into a fugitive. And while investigating Randal's murder had uncovered the trafficking scheme operating out of the Ghost Lily, I still had no idea why the sword had killed Randal in the first place. When Randal had grabbed hold of the sword's hilt during the auction that resulted in Haskins buying the sword, information had passed from Randal to the sword. Information that had upset the sword so much, it had taken off on its own to kill Randal.

I needed to figure out what those memories were, and what the sword's ultimate agenda was. If I didn't, I'd continue to be blindsided by its often-violent decisions. By association, I'd be the one arrested or exiled. Or, as was the case now, on the run with no clue if getting any semblance of my old life back was possible. And now Caspian was caught up in this mess with me.

We needed to find what the sword wanted in order to have any hope of being free of it.

My chest twinged at the idea. I'd grown so fond of the diabolical thing. I didn't want it gone, not really. I wanted to trust it not to murder people who had wronged it. It really put a damper on things.

So, for now, the tentative plan was to slowly make our way to Washington. A sunken pirate ship had been found off the coast there a year ago, and what few clues we had so far pointed to the sword having been on it. No one was sure where the ship and the majority of its cargo had ended up after it had been pulled from its watery grave. My best guess was Kensey, the state's magic hub. The current sticking point was that we didn't know if *our* Collective had issued warnings to the other hubs about us. We could be fugitives across the nation—across the world. If either of us passed through Kensey's veil, even if we were glamoured, it could potentially set off silent alarm bells. Or very loud ones. Or ones accompanied by poisoned darts.

I'd never been in a hub other than Luma's, and while Caspian had been to a few of them, he'd never been to Kensey.

Too much was unknown.

I knew taking our time was probably wise, but right now? Right now I was bored out of my skull. I'd watched TV for three straight days while Caspian read, and the sword spent most of its time in power-down mode, lying in the duffel bag as if it were just a mundane sword. We hardly left the room other than to eat, and half the time, Caspian preferred room service. I'd gotten so desperate yesterday that I'd gone down to the hotel gym and ran for five miles on the treadmill. Now I was sore on top of everything else.

I paced along the length of the living room now, toward the door to Caspian's room, before doing an about-face and walking back the other way. Maybe moving would get rid of the jitters. Not to mention loosening up my stiff quads.

After three round trips, Caspian let out a huff of air. "What are you doing?"

"Pacing," I said. "Obviously."

"Yes, but why?"

"Aren't you dreadfully bored? We've been in this suite for three days."

"We agreed we needed to lie low for a while, didn't we?"

"Well, yes. But this is too low. This is hibernating-bear low. Wanna go sightseeing or something? Or go get dessert somewhere?"

Caspian eyed the book in his lap, then the window nearest his chair. The world beyond the glass was dark. "Perhaps we can sightsee in the morning—you know, when it's daylight and we can *see* the sights. Why don't you find a movie?"

I slunk into the love seat across from him. "I can't watch anything else. I don't think there's anything left. I've watched all there is to watch, Caspian. All of it."

"You could ... read," he ventured, and the suggestion somehow sounded sensual. As if reading were akin to a strip-tease. Hell, maybe that was what got Caspian's rocks off: watching a lady read. Sounded like being studious was what had lit his fire for his ex.

I wasn't opposed to curling up with a good book, but it would still mean sitting in this damned suite. Silently.

Popping out of my chair, I crossed the room and resumed my pacing.

A muted thud sounded and I knew Caspian had clapped his book shut. On my trip back across the room, I glanced over to find him studying me. He had an elbow propped up on the armrest and his chin on his fist.

"Is this boredom or something else?" he finally asked.

I hit the end of the living room, turned on my heel, and paced back the other way. As I walked, I told him my concerns about Kensey—which wasn't a new topic for us, but one that had been discussed only in passing. Once the floodgates had opened, I couldn't seem to shut them off.

The sword emerged from the duffel bag sometime during my rambling session, perhaps stirred from sleep at the mention of itself. It hovered in the inverted position near the love seat I'd vacated earlier. I could see it in my peripheral vision, its blade following my progress across the room and back.

When I finally ran out of words, Caspian said, "This is related to what I've been studying, actually."

Legs warm and tired, I crossed back to the love seats and dropped into the one next to him. "Yeah?"

"Yeah." He perked up, grabbing the book off the side table between our chairs. Flipping to the page marked by his notebook, he said, "Getting through the Kensey veil, as you've said, runs quite a few risks. Glamours don't hold up to veil magic. Welsh is one of the best glamourers in Luma, if not beyond. I'm not being hyperbolic. His skill is ... exceptional. He's experimented with some of his strongest glamours to see if they'll hold up against the veil's magic. None of them do. Which is a comfort, honestly. If veil magic was easy to trick, a vampire with the right glamours could get in, for example. It would be chaos."

I nodded. "What are you looking up, then? Tricking the veil can't be it ..."

"No, but there are ways to test the strength of sections of a veil," he said.

An image of a metal obelisk covered in runes popped into my head. Veil magic ran between obelisks that circled each hub city—like fence posts.

"Veil maintenance is one of the key things the Collective is in charge of. There are hundreds of potential steps and troubleshooting techniques that go into maintaining the integrity of the veil," Caspian continued in his flat teacher voice. I knew this was a topic that greatly interested him, given how he leaned toward me in his chair, but his monotone belied that. "Certain areas of the veil—based on how much activity the spot might get due to everything from an approved tourist entrance to an area that is often crossed by animals—have different porosity levels. In Alaska, where my parents are, there are quite a few spots that are frequented by caribou in the winter months. My parents were part of the Collective team that had to restructure a section of the veil to accommodate their migration to keep the Collective's breach alarms from frequently pinging—and eventually failing—during key months. They even—"

I gave my head a light shake.

Lips pursed, Caspian sat back a fraction. "You have that same glazed-eye look that Welsh gets. Do I bore you?"

"I wouldn't say bore. You just tend to get ... uhh ... very wordy about things that aren't ... interesting?" I said, wincing.

To my relief, Caspian chuckled. Welsh entirely lacked tact, so I was sure Caspian had heard much worse from him.

"Anyway," Caspian said, clearing his throat, "what I'm trying to say is that if we find a weak part of the veil, I might be able to manipulate the magic enough that we could slip through. It wouldn't be tricking the magic of the veil so much as creating a blind spot. The veil won't register we passed through because it won't know."

"Oh ..." I said, nodding. "Is that easy to do?"

"Easy? No. And we don't know enough about Kensey to know where the weak spots are. If we got hold of an accurate map of the city, I could make some educated guesses, but even then, it would take a lot of trial and error. I would need to test parts of the veil from afar—like throwing pebbles at an electrified fence—and chart the data. It could take weeks, in all likelihood."

I deflated. The sword hummed softly across from us, which I took to mean it shared in my disappointment.

After a beat, Caspian asked, "Do you think it's possible your bounty hunter would have information about the layout of Kensey?"

I cocked a brow at him. "My" bounty hunter? Caspian wasn't the type to use anything other than proper names. He addressed the sword as "cutlass," because "sword" was too general. He knew "my" bounty hunter's name.

"Yeah, Felix might know someone there," I said. "He said he's got a few contacts in other hubs. Bounty hunters keep in contact across them—they're like jurisdictions—since it's easy enough for a criminal to jump in a telepad and end up on the other side of the country in a blink if they stayed enough steps ahead of the bounty hunters on their tail." I worried at the inside of my cheek. "Are you sure you're okay with me telling him we want to get into Kensey? The fewer people who know what we're up to, the better, right? You've said that roughly four million times now."

"You trust him, don't you?" he asked, ignoring my dramatic statement that I'd used solely to ruffle his drab feathers.

"Mostly," I muttered.

Caspian studied me, his expression unreadable. "Concerned he'll make more decisions in your best interest without consulting you first?"

I sighed. "Something like that. But I guess it's not a terrible idea. We're flying blind. We'll need the help. Plus, he's probably already guessed that Kensey is a possibility."

Oregon's hub was in the southeast of the state and well out of our northward path, so we hadn't considered paying that one a visit.

"Give him a call," Caspian said.

My excess energy had been spent from all the walking and talking, but the idea of calling Felix wore me out even more. I slipped off the love seat without a word and headed for my room where I'd left my cell phone in the front pouch of my backpack.

I was almost over the threshold when I heard a tap from the sword.

When I turned back, Caspian had returned to his book and the sword was drifting back to the duffel bag.

What had Caspian asked the sword? And why had he asked in a tone so soft I couldn't hear it?

Chapter 4
HARLOW

Felix answered the phone so quickly, I hadn't heard it ring. "Hey! You all right?"

"Yeah …" I said slowly, climbing onto one of the window bench seats and sitting cross-legged.

"It's just that I've checked up on you a bunch since you left and you haven't really replied. I started to worry."

I sighed. "Sorry. I'm fine."

"How is *Caspian*?"

I knew Felix well enough to know that was his jealous tone and I wasn't going there. "He's fine. I'm fine. The sword's fine. Are you?"

"Shit's a little hectic here," he said.

"I gathered that. The pocket mirror goes off several times a night lately."

He chuckled darkly. "I almost forgot you still had one of those."

"What code is oo?" I asked. "They use all the same ones from when I was training, but oo is new. Seen it come up at least twice in the last few days."

"Can't tell you."

I grunted. "Stupid Soul NDA."

"Deever's been on me like a tick. Most by-the-book nosy-ass partner I've ever had. I'm also twenty years younger than him and better at the job, which pisses him right the hell off. Once he figured out you and I have a history, he's been keeping tabs on me like he expects me to fuck up."

I chewed my bottom lip. "Does talking to me right now qualify as fucking up?"

"Oh, Low ..." he said softly, using my old nickname.

I closed my eyes, my chest constricting at the familiar sound. Bittersweet had never been such an accurate word to me before.

Felix was walking a dangerous line. He'd said himself that he was in the viper's den to better cut off their heads, but what if they cut off his first? The more he knew, the more danger he was in.

In that same gentle tone, he said, "I'm fully aware of the risks I'm taking. If I didn't want to be involved, I'd tell you."

Of course he'd be able to read my silent hesitations.

"If I get in too deep, or if Deever gets too close to figuring anything out, I'll back off. I promise."

"I don't want you to get in trouble because of me."

"I know," he said. "Talk to me."

So I told him all the same things I'd told Caspian, including our desire to get into Kensey.

"Getting you a map is no problem. We have access to a database of all the hubs—population numbers broken down by species, suspicious crimes, city layouts. It helps to know as much as possible in case a perp 'ports to another city."

"Have *you* been to Kensey?" I asked.

"Quite a bit," he said. "Mostly for the job, but there was a bounty hunter conference there last year. It was a first-time thing—probably a last-time thing, too. The Collective thought it might be good for *organizational unity*."

"So a bunch of hunters got very drunk and sloppy because they had a weekend off on the Collective's dime ..."

Felix laughed. "My hangover was so bad I swear I went blind in one eye for twenty-four hours."

Smiling, I asked, "Any chance you made any lasting friendships there during your nights of debauchery?"

"There's a couple I can call, yeah. They might have some better ideas on how to tackle this than I do. Roscoe and Fiona are both possibilities. I'll touch base, and if they can help you out, they'll call you directly," he said. "I trust both of them. Fiona saved my life once and I've saved Roscoe's at least twice. Just keep me in the loop."

"Thanks, Felix."

"You bet." He started to say something, then sighed. "Tell Caspian hi for me."

He disconnected the call before I could reply.

As I was getting out of the shower ten minutes later, my phone lying on the counter beeped. Felix had sent a picture attachment of Kensey's map, along with a text. *Hub maps are updated in the system every month. This is the most accurate one we've got in the system from two weeks ago.*

I got dressed in my pajamas like the homebody I was and padded across the suite. Hoping Caspian knew what to do with this information, I interrupted his reading once again by standing in front of his chair and then handing him my phone once he looked up. I couldn't say I was excited about a plan that amounted to "Caspian tests a lot of crap while Harlow tries not to die of boredom," but it was currently the only solid plan we had.

I said, "Let's get that practical, calculating sorcerer brain of yours going."

He took the phone and smiled softly up at me. "I thought it was a chaotically evil brain."

I waved that away. "That was back when you lived in my head as a supervillain. You're real now. And you're just ... neutral."

"You sound disappointed."

"I was expecting a middle-aged eccentric madman and I got a very normal thirty-something guy who wears tweed."

Caspian glanced down at his plain black T-shirt and jeans. I wasn't sure if he owned tweed. "And what are you, then?"

"Me?" I sat in the chair across from him. "I'm neutral good. I break the law when it's for a good reason."

Caspian snorted. The sword sailed over so it could tap twice on the end table next to me.

"What?" I asked, a touch indignant.

"If you were truly neutral, you would have liberated all those charmed items and then *given* them to your so-called clients," Caspian said, holding my phone but scrutinizing me. "Or you would have found a way to procure said items without committing home invasion. You were doing an arguably good thing by selling them to those missing a piece of their homeland, but you didn't do it altruistically. You did it, at least in part, to fill your bank account."

Tap, the sword said.

I glared at it. It was supposed to be on my side.

"Why did you take the cutlass?" Caspian asked.

I stared at the sword, the iridescent scales on the hilt glittering. My cheeks heated. "Because it was pretty."

Tap.

I rolled my eyes. "Of course you agree with that."

The sword hummed.

"And you took it even when you knew it was possibly a *dragon* cutlass?"

Sighing, I turned back to Caspian. "Yes."

He nodded once. "You might be aligned with good, but you're just as chaotic as Welsh."

Well, that was rude.

I glanced at the sword again, floating there all shiny and deadly. Wrinkling my nose, I decided Caspian was probably right.

The following day, we were on the road—me behind the wheel this time. Caspian and I were fighting over the radio. He wanted classical music and I wanted pop. We had access to music, TV shows, and movies in Luma, but we were always a few months behind the mundane world. Radio stations were iffy in the city, so all music had to be purchased and downloaded, or in some cases streamed. Because of some weird licensing issue, music showed up months after it first hit airwaves outside the hubs. Now that we were outside, I could hear music in real time, and not after it had presumably grown stale. I wanted to listen to the biggest hits of the summer *during* the summer. I did not want to listen to Bach's Concerto No. 87 or whatever this shit was. Nor did I want to hear Caspian wax poetic about how this or that particular piece was supposed to pull up images of majestic mountains in one's mind—mostly because his monotone was going to put me to sleep and we'd crash into a ditch.

My cell phone in the cup holder on the dash blissfully interrupted Caspian's incredibly mind-numbing history lesson on the Cascade Mountains. I glanced over at my cell long enough to see that the call was an unknown number—which wasn't that surprising, seeing as the only one currently programmed into it was Felix's.

"Oh! Can you answer that and put it on speaker?" I asked him.

Caspian sputtered to a stop in his monologue and gave his head a shake. I turned down Bach or Tchaikovsky or *whoever* as Caspian hit accept on the call. He tapped the screen a second time and the faint din of voices filled the car. "Hello," he said, sounding like a stuffy butler. "May I ask who's calling?"

"Uhh ..." said the female voice on the other line. "This is Fiona. I'm calling for Harlow?"

"I'm here!"

"Oh good. I thought Felix gave me the wrong number. So I hear you're heading into my neck of the woods from Luma?"

"Yeah," I said. "We're in Oregon but we should be crossing the state line in about an hour."

"I can't decide if hitting the open road and taking hours to get between states would be freeing or maddening," Fiona said. "Nothing beats a telepad ride."

Caspian chimed in. "It can be maddening when you're forced to listen to Burgundy Six every fifteen minutes."

"*Oh* my God." I shot him a venomous look. "I'm going to cut you, Blackthorn. You can't be mad about listening to a band whose name you can't even get right! You know what? No. Actually, I'll have the sword cut you."

"The cutlass would not choose sides in an argument so frivolous!"

The sword, which was in its duffel bag on the seat between us, hummed softly. I took that to mean it was staying out of this one.

"Traitor," I muttered.

"Oookay," Fiona said, and I flushed, having forgotten she was on the phone. "Felix told me you're looking into that pirate ship that was found a year ago, yeah? He said something about you two being weapons collectors and that, uhh, you, sir, own an auction house?"

I blinked, shooting Caspian a wide-eyed look. So Felix trusted Fiona, but not with the full truth. I could work with that.

"That's right. We've heard quite a few rumors about what came off that ship," I said, inexplicably taking on a more professional air. Now I sounded as stuffy as Caspian did naturally. "Some of the contents ended up being sold at an auction in Luma and we were very intrigued by what we saw. Yet another shipment was headed south a few months back, we heard, but I imagine there're some floating around Kensey."

The sword hummed beside me, and I got the distinct impression that it was amused by my "floating" comment. We were all curious if there were other sentient weapons like my sword.

"Yes, rumors suggest there are items from the wreck here," Fiona said a bit cryptically.

"There's something I've wondered about ..." Caspian said. "If I remember correctly, wasn't there a nationwide effort by the Collectives to scrub mundane minds and news of the discovery, and to seize all the treasure aboard? Part of the uproar from hub residents at large had been because we don't know what was on the ship. If the Collectives went through so much time and resources to make this discovery go away, how have *any* of the items ended up on auction blocks?"

I'd idly wondered this myself, but seeing how I'd been making my living the last few years, I'd figured well-informed thieves had snuck in under the Collective's nose and had made off with some of the goods. That, or someone in the Collective was ferreting the stuff out to black-market contacts in exchange for a cut of the sale.

Fiona tsked softly. "I'm going to be limited in what I can say. Felix said you know about a bounty hunter's, uh, restrictions?"

Caspian had a brow cocked in my direction when I glanced over at him.

"Soul NDA."

"Ah," he said, not nearly as alarmed by this news as I had been when Felix told me.

"Right." Fiona started and stopped saying something half a dozen times. I'd seen a Soul NDA in action before with Felix. When a person attempted to reveal something covered by the contract, their eyes glazed over and they lost track of what they'd been saying. Felix had said the contract made talking to noncontracted people ... challenging. Finally she asked, "You know how when you cook a really big dinner and have leftovers?"

Caspian and I side-eyed each other.

"Sure ..." I ventured.

"And you spend all day thinking about coming home to have those leftovers, but when you get there, there's only a small amount left because your roommate ate most of it?" Fiona sounded some combination of uncomfortable and frustrated. "Well, the pirate ship loot situation is like that. You can't believe everything you hear about leftover spaghetti."

"What on *earth*?" Caspian murmured.

But I thought I got it. "When the Collective finally got a hold of the ship and everything on it, not all of the loot was there. More of it ended up *out* of the Collective's hands than in it."

"Yes," Fiona breathed.

"But to keep face, they made it seem like they got all of it." I took a hand off the steering wheel and placed it on the duffel bag. "I found proof that their cleanup efforts hadn't worked, and revealed that this stuff is dangerous and might end up all over the country. They don't know the full extent of what was on the ship any more than we do."

The sword vibrated in response, but I could only guess what it meant.

"What *exactly* did you find that turned the Collective

against you?" Fiona asked, sounding intrigued—like a gossip-hungry teenager.

Were the roles reversed, I'd be overly curious too, but I didn't know how much I could trust her yet. The fact that Felix hadn't given her the whole truth kept me from telling her about the sword.

Fiona tried again. "Did you—"

"I'm quite interested in what *you've* encountered," Caspian said, interrupting her. "I would guess that these unique items have been popping up in Kensey with some regularity, given the proximity to the salvage site. Has the influx of these items caused any problems for you in your line of work?"

"For sure," Fiona said. "At least two black-market auctions have been raided by werecats in the last year, but based on some of the stuff we and police are seeing, it's obvious the public—mostly humans—have gotten hold of the more dangerous loot. Some guy bought a fire talisman, thinking it would be like a high-powered lighter. He busted it out during a company birthday party to light the candles for his coworker, melting the candles, cake, *and* his own arm. Level 5 magic."

The guy was lucky he hadn't melted more than an arm.

"We can't figure out where the stuff is coming from, though," Fiona said. "Either most of the loot from the ship is still in town, or it got moved out of Kensey and is being smuggled back in smaller quantities. The second one might sound like more work, but it's much harder for the Collective to regulate anything if it's happening outside the hubs. It's technically better for everyone if the items are kept beyond the veils.

"The mundane population is only in danger if they interact with the items, and since mundanes aren't the target buyers, the suppliers keep it all well-hidden until they find a willing customer or can set up an auction. It's a big world, though. That stuff could be anywhere, and we won't know it until someone else liquifies a limb."

"Have there been any hints about an upcoming auction?" Caspian asked. "I've run quite a few in Luma and would love to see how they're run elsewhere."

"Yes, but I'm reluctant to tell you about it, honestly," Fiona said. "Felix swears you're both more than capable of taking care of yourselves, but all I have is his word. I'd feel terrible if something I told you got either of you in more trouble than you already seem to be in."

"I'm a sorcerer," Caspian said. "I can protect us both."

Fiona whistled. "Felix apparently only told me the bare minimum."

"Kind of his MO," I said.

Chuckling, Fiona said, "So there's an orc who's got his fat sausage fingers in damn near every pie when it comes to these auctions lately. He's involved peripherally in the ones in Kensey, but he often hosts the ones in the mundane world. The guy is a brute and has a handful of troll minions. They've paid someone a lot of money to get them glamours that make them look human—but more like bodybuilders or wrestlers."

"What's his name?" I asked.

"Domino," Fiona said. "We know all about him, but since he keeps most of his illegal dealings outside of the hubs, it's technically out of our jurisdiction. When drugs like Bliss or skin-melting talismans make it into the hubs, we can crack down on it, but nine times out of ten, we trace it back to Domino. We can't touch him."

"Couldn't the Collective sic their cats on him?" I asked.

"Sure, but then what? To the mundane population, it'll look like a hit or a disappearance. If he's killed, his glamours will dissolve. Then they'll have to get rid of an eight-foot-tall beast with green skin and tusks. He lives in a mundane gated community surrounded by innocent humans. I can't say for certain, but it's likely Domino has contingencies in place for what his minions are supposed to do if he meets an untimely end—especially if they figure out the Collective put out the hit. His inner circle is made up of a bunch of powerful mafia-type fae that even the Collective seems scared of." Fiona huffed. "The Collective has taken down misbehaving fae outside the hubs before, but it's rare. Domino has grown too powerful and well connected. Now with this mystery cache of weapons and magical goods he seems to have gotten his hands on? We're worried. But all we can do is sit back and hope he gets himself killed handling one of these things and puts him out of our misery."

The sole sound in the car was that of tires rolling over the highway.

"I suppose I can understand why you're reluctant to send us information about one of these events ..." Caspian finally said.

Fiona's tone was subdued. "A pair of Kensey's best werecats went to an auction on a purely reconnaissance mission a few months ago. Three hunters went as backup. One of Domino's minions must have sniffed out the cats' shifter magic because, in the *middle* of the auction, the minions tackled them. They hauled the cats out, beat one to death in the parking lot, and assaulted the other one within an inch of his life, sending him off with a message to the Kensey Collective that their werecats aren't allowed in Domino's territory. Meanwhile, the auction went on as if nothing had happened. Domino himself came out on stage to assure the crowd everything was fine, so the attendees were nice and distracted while the cats were under attack."

"Shit," I said on an exhale. "Did all of the hunters make it out of there?"

"Yeah. They smartly stayed back in the auction hall to not give themselves away as being associated with the cats," Fiona said. "They waited until the trolls were back inside before they snuck out and helped get the shifters back to the hub—one went to the morgue, the other to intensive care. The second one was awake long enough to relay the message to the hunters, and has been in a medically induced coma since."

We slipped into more stunned silence.

Fiona let out a long sigh. "So, no, I don't want to be responsible for any of that happening to either of you. Felix said you could handle yourselves and to give you as much information on the auction scene here but ... it's bad. I get that rare item sales are your livelihood or passion—or both—but it very well could get you killed if it's one run by Domino."

I frowned.

"But a Domino auction is the most likely to have items from this ship, yes?" Caspian asked.

"Unfortunately, yes. Every time we get caught up in a case connected to something we think came off that ship, it's linked back to Domino."

"How do we get on the invite list?" he asked.

I shot him a sharp look. Was he insane? And he had the nerve to call *me* chaotic.

"I suck at dissuasion," Fiona muttered. "There are four intersections we've tracked down so far where Domino's people leave markers. They're usually WE BUY HOUSES signs. If there's a contact name on the sign, that's not one of his. The phone number is always different, and the area code varies, so we figure he gets new burners each time. If you're serious about attending, I can get in touch with a couple of my sources who can put an ear to the ground and get the latest password for you. You can't buy your way onto the list. You gotta know someone who knows someone. I'll text you the locations of the frequently used corners, and then you'll have to check them every day for a new sign. Call the number on the sign, give them the password, and they'll give you the address of where to go. Don't chat them up. Don't ask questions. Then, once you're there, you have to hope his troll minions can't sniff sorcerer magic and tear you to pieces."

Fiona sounded a hair away from pissed, and I wondered if she was going to call Felix after this to tell him she wasn't going to assist any more strangers.

"Thank you for your help," I said.

"I'll text you the locations and I'll be in touch once I have a password. Don't die, all right?" The call disconnected.

If our original plan sounded boring, this one sounded suicidal. Attending an auction run by an orc mob boss would be more fun, but one could argue there wouldn't be much fun to be had if we wound up as corpses.

I patted the duffel bag with my slightly shaking hand. "The things I do for friends."

The sword hummed.

Chapter 5
KAYDA

Kayda had just made her way out of the casino's employee-only door at the end of her shift when someone called her name. Her heart lurched into her throat. Only one person's voice could do that to her. She considered ignoring it and sprinting the three miles home. Since sprinting away would be dramatic and childish, she opted for walking very quickly.

She was halfway across the parking lot when she heard it again.

"K-Kayda?"

Ugh. That sweet stutter of his. It would be her undoing. Stopping, she steeled herself, then turned around.

Henri slowly loped toward her. His shift was starting soon. She'd purposefully altered her schedule to be busier *and* to avoid Henri as much as possible. Usually she could sneak out the back before he came in. No such luck tonight. With everything going on, she didn't need his ... Henri-ness ... messing with her already "high-strung energy."

"Hi, Henri," she said, unable to not sound reluctant.

"H-hi," he said as he stopped in front of her. He was a

couple of inches taller, and she had to tip her head back to look into his eyes. A rarity for her. Fae light from a lamppost glinted off his glasses. Even in the dim setting of the parking lot, she could make out the blue tinge that inched up his neck and colored the tips of his ears. She hoped her own skin wasn't showing any hints of green. Humans flushed red, pink, or darker brown, like Harlow did, when embarrassed. Draken's skin took on the hue of the scales their dominant dragon ancestors once had.

"I uhh ... I wanted to ask if you've h-h-heard from Harlow," Henri said. "I know you're worried about her. Y-your sister from another mister, as they say." He laughed at his joke and went so blue, he was nearly navy.

The other guys at work were still asking Kayda things like "Did that Harlow chick really murder those guards?" or "So you're, like, best friends with a serial killer?" Henri, though, never seemed to question Harlow's innocence. She wanted to kiss him squarely on his nerdy mouth for that alone.

"Yeah. She got out of Luma," Kayda said, not concerned in the slightest about sharing this information with Henri. "I just don't know where she's going."

Henri's bright green eyes studied Kayda's face. After a long, thoughtful pause, he said, "She didn't abandon you, you know. She'll be b-back."

Tightness squeezed her throat. "Thanks, Henri."

Silence descended on them. If this were any other guy, she would have said something like, "Are we going to do this, or what?" But Henri, despite being a giant teddy bear of a draken, got her all flustered. She had no idea why. A year later, here they remained, acting like awkward teenagers despite being well into their twenties.

She needed to leave.

"Umm ..." Henri wrung his hands, then pressed his glasses

back up his nose. "If you're not ... uhh ... if you're feeling s-sad this weekend and w-want some c-company, I'll be helping with my family's b-booth at the farmers m-market in Ardmore North. You could c-c-come by, if you'd like. We're there from eight to n-noon on Sundays."

Kayda wasn't sure when her mouth had dropped open. In all the time she and Henri had been friends—even though she'd been harboring the hugest crush on the guy for almost the entire time—he'd never come anywhere close to inviting her to anything.

"Y-y-you don't have t-t-to," Henri said, taking a step back. His skin had gone almost purple now. "I was th-thinking that you've seemed lonely without Harlow, but you p-probably already have p-plans. Of c-course you do." He added that last part with a furious shake of his head.

"That sounds great," Kayda blurted. "I always say I'm going to check out the market but never make it over there."

Complete and utter lie.

Henri stood straighter. "Y-yeah?"

"Yeah."

He nodded vigorously. "Good. Yeah. Okay. See you Sunday."

Kayda would see him at least twice more at work before then, but she kept her mouth shut as he trotted back to the building and disappeared through the employee door.

Bewildered, she started her walk home.

Her mind was still in overdrive twenty minutes later, the night air doing little to cool her warm face that had nothing to do with exertion and everything to do with a bespectacled draken.

She blamed her Henri-muddled thoughts on why she didn't hear the cadence of footsteps sooner. Footsteps that had fallen into the same cadence as her own. Footsteps that followed her even as she slunk into the alleyway between her apartment building and the one next to it. A hole-in-the-wall club was best accessed through this alley, frequented almost exclusively by neighborhood locals.

Turning her sense of hearing up a few dials, she assessed who this person could be—a person who was very loud to her ears now that she was properly paying attention. A witch would have used magic to deafen their approach, and a Collective guard would be better trained than this. The breathing and footwear were too loud and clunky respectively to be an elf, yet too even to be the hooves of a faun. They were taller than a goblin and shorter than a draken. Human. And male, if she had to guess.

She could deal with a human male. Especially if he was drunk and was stupid enough to think he could rob or accost her because she was alone.

When she was halfway down the alley, she spun. The man froze, hands up in placation.

Her night vision threw his features into sharp relief. She stared dumbly at him, wondering if she'd suffered a concussion at work somehow and hadn't realized it. First Henri asked her out, and now ... this?

"*Felix?*"

"Hey, Kayda," he said with unnerving calm. "Can we talk?"

Kayda stood in her living room, arms crossed, as she watched Felix Turner of all people slowly wandering her apartment. He'd never been to her new place. She hadn't seen hide nor hair of his scrawny ass since he'd broken Harlow's heart five years ago. Kayda's hands squeezed into fists below her armpits.

"What do you want, Turner?" she finally snapped, unable

to take his silence any longer. It had probably been fifteen seconds, tops, but it'd felt like an eternity.

He stopped his idle assessment of her apartment and faced her, crossing his arms, too. "You heard from Harlow lately?"

Kayda would punch him in his stupid face. She dropped her arms to her sides and rolled her neck. Nothing other than clocking him currently made any sense. If she threw him out the window like she'd done to the sword weeks ago, she didn't think he would fare as well.

Felix's gaze shifted to Kayda's hands and he took a step back, palms held out. "Easy, Kayda. Harlow and I didn't work things out or anything, but we've at least gotten to the point where she doesn't want to kill me on sight."

The fight leached out of Kayda in an instant. Harlow hadn't said a word to Kayda for weeks, yet she'd been in contact with *this* louse? Kayda wanted to punch him again, if only because she couldn't punch Harlow.

"*Oh*," Felix breathed, apparently reading the roller coaster of emotions playing out on Kayda's face despite barely uttering a word. "Look, if it helps, I tracked *her* down. She didn't come looking for me. And she looked even more pissed off than you do now when she saw me."

That *did* help. A little.

"She knee you in the jewels at least?" she asked.

"No, but the sword almost decapitated me."

She nodded. "That sword's all right."

Sighing, Felix said, "All I can tell you is that she's headed to Kensey. I don't know what she's got planned. I can barely get her to reply to my texts. I only hear from her if she needs something."

Kayda tried not to rankle at the idea of Harlow-freaking-Fletcher texting. She hated cell phones. "I don't know what she has planned either." Recalling the note, she added, "All I know is that she's with the sword and Caspian Blackthorn."

She waited for shock or confusion to cross his dark features, but clearly, this was information he'd already known.

"Right," Felix said, jaw tight. "I would feel better if I knew more. I got a friend in contact with her, but I haven't heard back on what they talked about."

"Desperate much?" she asked, but there wasn't much bite to it. All she could seem to focus on was how furious she was that her "sister from another mister" had left her out of ... all of it. She glared down at her boots.

She sensed Felix moving nearer to her, just by a step, and her head snapped up.

Felix threw his hands out in yet another placating gesture. "I know I haven't been around for the last five years, but I *do* know how she operates. If she left you out of this, it's because you mean too much to her to jeopardize your safety."

"She gets us into trouble all the time!"

Felix shook his head. "Not like this. She got herself in *deep*, Kay. It's honestly a miracle she's not in a Collective prison pumped full of truth serum, or exiled to the Arctic hub, or dead. That sword—as much as stealing it is what got her into this mess —is the main thing that kept her alive. Well, that, plus Caspian and Zander Welsh."

Welsh! Even that human-hating witch had gotten mixed up in this?

"She's protecting you because she cares what happens to you," Felix said. "Me? She's gotten me to risk my job more than once. I'm happy to do it, but still. I'm expendable. She'd rather you hate her and be alive than the alternative."

Kayda cocked a brow. "She learned from the best, I guess."

Felix scratched his teeth back and forth across his lower lip.

"Sometimes you have to make messed-up choices to protect the people you love."

Bullshit.

After a long beat of silence, she asked, "Can you give me her number?" She hated that she needed to ask *Felix* that.

He lightly shook his head. "I can't violate what minuscule amount of trust we have. She's keeping you out of it for a reason. If I piss her off, she might cut me off too, and then we'll lose another thread to her. She'll contact you when she thinks it's safe to do so."

Kayda was getting real fucking sick of hearing that.

The urge to punch him had resurfaced with a vengeance. "Well, you wasted your time coming here. I don't know anything more than you do and I'm not sure I'd tell you if I did."

"That's fair." He reached into his back pocket and pulled out his wallet. From that, he produced a crisp white business card and, after sighing very heavily, handed it to her.

Kayda took it from him warily, then blinked down at the card several times. This confirmed something she suspected already, but it was shocking to see it there in black and white. She scoffed. "You became a bounty hunter after all? Bet Harlow *loved* that."

Felix stuffed his wallet back into his pocket. "If you hear from her or think of anything I should know, call me. That's my personal line for the side cases I take on; only my clients call it. You wouldn't be calling my desk phone at Collective Headquarters or anything."

She resisted the urge to tear the card up and toss the pieces in his face.

"I'll see myself out," he said, offered her a tight smile, and headed for the door.

As he reached it, with her back facing him, she begrudgingly asked, "Can we trust Caspian?"

"Unfortunately. She's safer with him than she'd be with either of us." The door quietly closed behind him.

Kayda stared down at the card for a while. Instead of throwing it away or tearing it up, she placed it in her junk drawer in the kitchen—just in case. But she couldn't fathom ever needing to speak to Felix Turner again.

After a long hot shower that did nothing to ease her fury at her best friend, Kayda lay in bed, staring at her ceiling.

"She didn't abandon you, you know," echoed Henri's words from earlier.

Yet, that was exactly what it felt like.

Chapter 6

KAYDA

On Sunday, Kayda was wide awake by 4:30 a.m., thoughts of Henri lingering with the remnants of the rather racy dream she'd been having about him. The worst part of all this was that Harlow would have been delighted to learn that Kayda had officially turned into a hormonal ninny full of obnoxious feelings over this outing. And she needed wardrobe advice. Kayda lived for opportunities to wear dresses, but they usually had a leg-slit up to the thigh. If Kayda was going to dress to the nines, being eye-catching wasn't enough. She aimed for aggressively attractive. She liked turning heads. But Henri wasn't wowed by that kind of thing—in fact, "aggressively attractive" seemed to terrify the daylights out of him.

It was a farmers market, so leg-slits would probably give all the old grannies the vapors anyway. Today was a casual day, especially if his family was there. She imagined a gaggle of bespectacled, bookish Henris and considered bailing on the whole thing. She could tell him she had a stomach bug and be done with it. But knowing him, he'd show up with a container of homemade soup and she'd be so overwhelmed with lust that she'd accost him in the doorway and scare the poor guy off for good.

After going for a fifteen-mile run around her neighborhood in the near dark, she did her usual morning routine of push-ups, sit-ups, and stretches. She hadn't been in a boxing ring or on a wrestling mat in years, but she liked to stay fit. She'd missed the routine even if she didn't miss competing. After a scalding shower, she stood before her closet that was sixty percent black pants and shirts, and pushed aside the garment bags containing her "aggressively attractive" dresses until she found the last item hanging there. The dress still had its tags. Harlow had made her buy it. It was cream-colored, had soft ruffly sleeves, and was patterned with delicate pink and blue flowers.

Kayda frowned. It was such a cute, soft dress. Kayda was not cute and soft. It irked her to no end that she was too self-conscious to wear it. She, who didn't care what anyone thought of her. She, whose self-assuredness was one of her favorite things about herself. Intimidated by a dress.

When Kayda had stepped out of the dressing room with it on months ago, her skin flushed green, Harlow had clapped and cooed. She'd even gotten teary-eyed, telling Kayda how beautiful she looked. By the time Kayda had gotten home with it, though, her father's voice had wormed its way into her head, repeating all the things he'd said to her growing up.

"You don't need money for another dress. You'll get it dirty, like all the others."

"You're too bulky for dresses."

"Men don't like women who are stronger than them."

"Girls like you don't win beauty pageants. Stop trying to be what you're not."

She'd left her home and family behind to live with her maternal grandmother in Luma *because* of her father. To get away from his abuse. It had all been mental, which was a blessing in a way, but that just meant no one could see the scars he'd left her with.

She snatched the frilly dress off the hanger.

Ardmore North was a suburban neighborhood with a high draken population. Kayda hadn't been in the area in a while and had to consult a map on her phone before she'd left. The farmers market was situated in the middle of a large park about ten miles from her apartment. Her long draken stride got her there in an hour flat. The brisk walk had given her plenty of time to work through half a dozen conversation topics she could attempt to broach with Henri. Unless she couldn't get him away from his family. Goddess, what if she had to make friendly chitchat with his mother?

She followed behind a stream of people—draken, humans, and everything in between—making their way down the sidewalk and past the large wooden sign welcoming visitors to the park. A banner strung between two trees proclaiming, FARMERS MARKET TODAY! flapped softly in the light breeze.

Her small purse, the strap slung across her body, bounced against her hip as she walked. *I am a soft and delicate lady. I am a soft and delicate lady ...*

The path she was on led to one of the entrances to the market, where food trucks, pop-up tents, and tables lined the edge of the circular road that snaked through the middle of the park like a river. In the middle of the circle stood a wide island of grass dotted with picnic tables. A parking lot on the upper eastern edge of the park was crammed with trucks and vans. Anyone selling wares in the market today who didn't live in the immediate area probably would prefer to drive in, rather than pay the hefty large-vehicle telepad fee.

As Kayda slipped into the throng of milling people, she scanned the business names on the banners hung from the tables and carts lining the road. Up until his invite, she hadn't even known his family participated in the market. From idle conversation, she knew his mother made jewelry, and that his older sister was an artist, but that was it. He had three siblings—all sisters.

"Wigs made from human hair!" a draken woman behind a table called out, holding a foam head aloft with a stick-straight white wig perched on it at an unnatural angle. The woman made eye contact with Kayda over the top of several humans' heads. "You, pretty lady! You'd be stunning in this wig!"

Kayda idly rubbed the back of her head, where her inch-long white hair was the softest. Draken women living in human cities were probably single-handedly keeping the wig business alive. She shook her head at the woman, who immediately gave up on Kayda and shouted to someone else.

A few carts down, Kayda purchased a bag of freshly made caramel popcorn, the wax paper warm in her hand. She'd just popped a few pieces in her mouth, gazing this way and that, when a voice sounded close to her ear.

"What's a pretty little thing like you doing here all alone?"

Little? Her nostrils flared, but she willed herself to ignore the guy. She was cute and soft like the dress swishing around her knees. Cute and soft ladies didn't elbow creeps in the gut. She angled her chin up, trying to see the name on the banner across the way, several of the words hidden behind a goblin child who was perched on the shoulders of a human.

"Are you lost, sweetie?"

Kayda twisted and gazed up at a draken man who had to be at least nine feet tall. There weren't many in Luma who could make her feel small. Heat clawed up her neck and into her face.

The man regarded her—from her black sandals to her

cream-colored dress, and into her no-doubt unfriendly expression. "Mmm. You *are* a sight." He leaned forward, peering into her bag of popcorn. "Are those as sweet as you?" His eyes flicked back up to hers, a tactic that probably worked better for human men who had eyelashes.

Kayda smiled demurely at him, which made him grin wide and full.

She kneed him in the crotch so hard the veins on his shale-gray-tinted throat bulged, like fat worms. He coughed, hunched over. Which left him in the perfect position to also get a knee to the nose. There was a very satisfying crunch of bone before he hit the ground. Thankfully the gaggle of faun children who played nearby had darted out of the way in time, narrowly avoiding the falling tree of a man. He collapsed between two tables, not taking anyone's wares with him. Kayda had taken down enough lecherous scumbags at the casino that she'd gotten very good at timing her attacks to avoid the destruction of playing tables.

"I'm not your sweetie," Kayda added, then turned away, marveling at the fact that she'd managed to drop him without sacrificing a single piece of popcorn. She knew several onlookers watched her warily—mostly non-drakens—but that was a-okay with her.

Until she glanced to her left and spotted Henri standing in front of a table, a pair of young women sitting behind it. Henri's mouth hung open.

Ugh.

If she threw the popcorn at him, would he be distracted long enough for her to get away?

When neither Henri nor Kayda moved, the smaller of the women behind the table got up and rushed toward Kayda. She'd likely tell Kayda to leave her precious brother alone.

"Hi," the young woman said, stopping in front of her. Kayda

glanced down. She was a good foot shorter than Kayda, and not a day over sixteen. Her cheeks and neck were mottled with a smattering of navy-colored dots—a draken version of acne that plagued most teenagers. A black wig sat atop her head, the hair pulled up into a high ponytail. "Uh, hello? I said hi."

Kayda blinked. "Hi."

"You're Kayda, right? Henri said a lady he knows from work might show up and since he's staring at you like you're a bowl of tinka fish, I'm guessing you're her."

"Yeah, I'm Kayda."

The girl held out her hand. "Libby." Kayda shook it, and when the girl took her hand back, she propped her fists on her hips, staring at Kayda unflinchingly. "Can you teach me how to do that? Knee a guy in the junk?"

The knot of uncertainty unfurled in Kayda's chest. "Sure can."

Libby nodded. "Especially if I have to deal with that guy again," she said, pointing somewhere behind Kayda. "He hit on my friend last week. She's fifteen and kinda scrawny. I went looking for her 'cause she went to go pee but was gone for a long time and I found her backed into a tree with that guy standing *way* too close to her. I started throwing rocks at him to get him to back off and when he looked at me, she got away and we ran back over here. Henri talked with him but obviously it didn't work, 'cause he's back."

Henri was just as effective as a bouncer and security guard as Kayda was—he wouldn't have lasted at the job this long otherwise. He had a quietly commanding presence. Overgrown oafs like the one writhing on the ground behind Kayda needed ... a stronger hand.

Kayda shoved her bag of popcorn at Libby. "Hold this."

The crowd parted as Kayda stalked back toward the man who had his large hands cupping his "junk," as Libby had so eloquently put it. He must have sensed the change in the crowd's energy, because he picked up his head, his face ashen. The whites of his eyes stood out in sharp contrast to his dark irises. He scooted back a couple of inches, the heels of his boots ripping up chunks of grass.

"Stay away from me, you crazy bitch!"

There was a collective intake of breath.

Kayda turned on her draken speed and had him pinned in an instant, one sandaled foot pressed against his throat and the other holding a wrist in place. He squirmed, instinctively using his free hand to try and pry her foot from his neck, but she pressed down harder with both feet. She twisted the one that had his wrist held down and smiled to herself when she felt the glass face of his watch shatter under the pressure.

Turning to look out at the crowd, she loudly asked, "Does anyone know this jackass's name?"

"Reynard!" someone called out.

Kayda peered down at Reynard, who had finally stopped squirming and now just glared at her. In a voice loud enough for everyone in the vicinity to hear, she said, "Nice to meet you, Reynard. Now, it's bad enough that you were being a creep with me, but it's really terrible to learn you've pulled the same shit with girls as young as fifteen. Is that why you're here every weekend, Reynard? Looking for young girls to harass because no woman your age wants anything to do with you?"

His face went even grayer.

"I believe you were asked to leave last week," Kayda said. "You didn't listen. What's it going to take to get you to stay gone, hmm?"

A draken woman who couldn't have been younger than eighty marched over in Kayda's peripheral vision. She figured she must have been related to Reynard, here to tell Kayda to back off. Instead, she upended an entire cup of something very cold, given the ice cubes, onto his crotch, which didn't seem to soothe his mangled junk. Reynard hissed.

"That's for patting my backside!" she snapped. "You keep going after ladies who don't have the strength or years to fight back. You're a big old bully!" She swung her mammoth-sized purse and whacked him in the stomach. She might not have had youth on her side, but she packed a wallop with that bag.

Reynard's breath heaved out in a whoosh. Kayda felt his throat bob under her foot.

Ahead of her, more movement pulled her focus away from Reynard. A pair of human-looking officers walked her way, the crowd parting for them, too. But they were no humans; they moved with feline grace. The two women were five-eight or so, not much taller, and one of them was so pretty, Kayda thought she'd be a better fit for a magazine cover than on the staff of the Collective's guard.

"We got a call about a disturbance," the too-pretty one said, regarding Reynard's prone form, Kayda's foot on his neck, and then finally Kayda herself. "There a problem here?"

"Reynard has been getting too handsy with the women at the market and they feel uncomfortable," Kayda said.

"Did he get handsy with you as well?" the other guard asked.

"Didn't get the chance," Kayda said, then pressed harder on his wrist, causing him to suck in a sharp gasp. "He *did* call me 'sweetie,' though."

Kayda couldn't be sure, but she thought she saw one of the pretty one's eyes twitch.

Libby was suddenly by Kayda's side, talking a mile a minute. "We called the cops last time and regular human ones showed up but didn't do anything because that guy is too big even for them to handle. My friend is too scared to come back because of him."

The pretty one cocked her head at Reynard. "And what do you have to say for yourself?" He tried to talk, but struggled, what with Kayda's foot on his neck.

Pretty Cop arched a brow at Kayda in question, so Kayda let up on his throat so he could reply.

He wheezed in a gasp, using his free hand to rub at the tender skin. "It's not a crime to talk to a lady, is it? All I did was tell her she looked nice and then she assaulted me."

"That the truth?" the second guard asked.

"Goddess honest," Reynard croaked.

"All right," the guard said. "Get up."

Kayda bristled, her lips pursed. The werecat guards were supposed to help in cases where the human cops couldn't. They were going to let him go? Kayda took a few steps back, gently pushing Libby behind her. Reynard, clearly still in pain and the front of his jeans drenched, staggered to his feet. He stared onlookers down, using his size to cow many into looking away. Kayda refused to break eye contact with him, and when he realized it, his thin lips curled.

He took two quick steps toward her, crowding her space and looking down his nose at her. In a low tone he clearly meant solely for her, he said, "You looked better from behind anyway."

Libby started forward, but Kayda held her back.

A roar sounded. Reynard spun toward it.

One of the werecat guards had shifted—the pretty one, from the looks of it. Now she was a sleek black panther, her massive head level with Reynard's navel. Her snout bunched up as she hissed, saliva shining on her long canines.

The other officer, her voice calm and collected, said, "Since you've told us the truth, you have nothing to worry about. Follow Officer Magnan. She'll lead the way to the squad car. One teeny hit of serum, you tell us the truth, and then you'll be back here next weekend to enjoy the market, hmm?"

"Wait ... uhh ... wait," Reynard said, turning back to Kayda. "Tell them it was nothing, yeah? I won't come back. Promise."

Kayda smiled sweetly at him. "Better get going. Don't want to piss off the cats."

"You bitch," he snapped. "I didn't even *touch* you."

"You tried to touch Sera!" Libby said from behind Kayda. "You're old and gross!"

Reynard's pulse visibly pounded in his throat. "Why you—"

Another roar, and then Reynard was yanked off his feet and thrown several feet across the park, landing on a picnic bench that collapsed under his weight. Officer Magnan had heaved him as if he were a toy. Several onlookers gasped, while a few scattered to spy on the proceedings from a safer distance in case this got ugly.

The guard still in human form winked at Kayda. "We've got it from here. He won't be back to bother anyone."

When Reynard was finally on the move away from the market, the assembled crowd cheered at his departure. He attempted to shout something in response, but that earned him a headbutt from Magnan, and once he regained his footing, he continued his march of shame with his shoulders rounded.

Though several smiles, thumbs-up, and words of gratitude were aimed at Kayda, the crowd kept a wide berth, eventually peeling away to return to what they'd been doing before the commotion.

She sighed. It was like she'd told herself this morning: she was not cute and soft.

"That. Was. Amazing!" Libby crowed, darting to Kayda's front now that Reynard was out of sight. "You are such a *beast*!"

Kayda knew she meant it as a compliment, but it hit her hard. Her father had called her that. The beast who wanted to be a beauty. "Hey, uhh—" She cleared the catch in her throat. "Hey, can you tell Henri I had to be somewhere?"

"L-l-liar."

Kayda turned to find Henri standing a couple of feet away, hands in the pockets of his cargo pants. He pulled a hand free to unnecessarily push his glasses up his nose.

"When I a-a-asked you to come down here, I didn't mean you had to w-w-ork," he said, smiling softly.

"You can take the girl out of the casino, but you can't take the casino out of the girl," Kayda said.

Libby, who stood beside her brother now, wrinkled her nose. "What?"

Kayda snorted a laugh. "Nothing. I really should probably go ..."

"Go wh-where?"

"Yeah, where?" Libby asked. "You said you'd teach me how to smash a guy's junk."

Henri cocked a hairless brow at Kayda. "Are you trying to c-c-corrupt my little s-s-sister?"

"Yes," Kayda and Libby said at the same time, and they grinned at each other.

"Liberty ..." Henri started.

"Ugh! Don't call me that!" Libby said, stomping a foot.

Henri smiled down so warmly at her, Kayda's chest ached. "Can you go help M-Mom for a m-m-minute?"

"Why?"

Henri not so subtly tipped his head in Kayda's direction and Kayda flushed to her hairline.

"Oooh," Libby said. "You wanna put the moves on the coolest lady I've ever met. Got it." With that, she ran back toward their family's table.

"S-s-sorry," Henri said after several long seconds. "Libby can be ... a l-l-lot."

"I like her."

"Of course you d-d-do. She's a mini y-y-you," he said. "I

mean she reminds me of y-y-you. Or you remind me of h-h-her? Not that I want to p-p-put the moves on my little s-s-sister."

Kayda bit her bottom lip. Did that mean he wanted to "put the moves" on *her*? His slow appraisal lingered on her lower half, where the hem of her dress hit her knees. Was he checking her out now? What on *earth* was happening today?

"There's b-b-blood on your d-d-dress," Henri said, snapping Kayda out of her fog of delighted confusion.

When she looked down, she saw the hem of her dress was indeed splattered with blood. As was one of her knees. "Oh, dammit. This is a new dress, too!"

"You don't need money for another dress. You'll get it dirty, like all the others," her father's voice echoed in her head.

"I should probably—"

"There's a b-b-booth down there run by a w-w-witch who makes the best potions," Henri said, cutting off yet another excuse to flee. "She's got a s-s-stain-removal one my m-m-mom swears by. I can walk you over there. If you want, I mean." He visibly swallowed. "It's a really p-pretty dress, by the way. I mean, you l-l-look pretty in it."

She cocked her head. "You still want to hang out today? I mean, after all that?"

His forehead bunched. "You act like I've never s-s-seen you k-k-kick a guy in the balls b-b-before. Reynard is a ... real jackass."

Kayda couldn't fight the smile, mostly because Henri rarely cursed. It was like a kid testing the word out for the first time on the playground to sound tough around his buddies.

"So ... you want to check out the b-b-booth?"

Her father's voice chastised her. *"Men don't like women who are stronger than them."*

Kayda ignored him and smiled at Henri. "I'd love to."

Chapter 7
KAYDA

Still on high from her afternoon with Henri, Kayda let herself into her apartment. She wasn't humming to herself and clicking her heels or anything dramatic like that, but she definitely couldn't wipe the smile off her face.

The state of her apartment, however, did.

Pulse pounding in her ears, her wide eyes took in the utter destruction. Books had been pulled off shelves and lay piled on the floor. The couch cushions had been yanked off and slashed, the stuffing spilling out like fluffy entrails. Kitchen cabinets stood open, their contents shattered on the tile. Her chest rose and fell, rose and fell. She hadn't taken more than two steps inside, her hand lingering on the doorknob.

Adjusting the mental dials on her hearing, she closed her eyes and went hunting through the familiar rooms of her home for anyone who might be lying in wait. She turned down the sound of her roaring torrent of a heartbeat. If anyone so much as gently cleared their throat from inside a closet, adjusted their position under her bed, or shifted from one foot to the other behind a door, she'd hear it. She blew out a slow breath, slackened her limbs, and heard the faint flutter of her bedroom curtains.

In three seconds, she'd opened her eyes, flung her door closed behind her, and strode across her living room. The door slammed into place, rattling the windows just as she reached the threshold of her bedroom. She studied the window, which stood open, the curtains swaying in the gentle warm breeze. That window had been closed and locked when she'd left. Banging it shut and flipping the lock into place, she took in the tatters of her bedroom.

Her comforter and pillows were strewn on the floor—those as slashed as the couch cushions. The drawers on both nightstands stood open, the contents on the floor and on the bare, gutted mattress that was propped up against the headboard at an awkward angle. The TV on top of the rifled-through dresser had a giant spiderwebbing crack in the middle. A bedside lamp lay smashed in front of the attached bathroom. She headed there next, sidestepping the debris. Toiletries weren't just on the floor, but things like toothpaste and shampoo had been squirted on the cabinets and counters, and rubbed into her bath mats. The mirror had been smeared with soap or cream in such a thick layer that she couldn't see her reflection, and words had been written in the muck.

WHERE IS HARLOW FLETCHER?

Kayda blew out a long breath, unsure if fear or anger was the ruling emotion right now. Figuring it was best to *not* touch anything in case she decided to report this to the police, she backed out of the bathroom and returned to the living room. The TV in there was smashed, too. This one, however, had one of her smaller dumbbells sticking out of it. The rest of the free weights that had been stacked on a rack in the corner were either on the ground or sliced clean down the middle. The cuts through the metal were clean, which probably ruled out humans being responsible for this. It had been someone with magic or magic-enhanced weapons. A witch or sorcerer, most likely. Cuts that clean could have been made by the razor-sharp claws of a shifter, too.

The worst of it, though, was her severed gaming console. Only weeks old, and now it was cut clean in two. The controllers were a pile of plastic and buttons—as if crushed by a rock.

The thing that was pissing her off the most was that the majority of the vandalism was petty—more than likely, whoever had done this hadn't come looking for anything specific. They'd wanted to send a message. They knew where Kayda lived, they could find her at any time, and they didn't give a shit about what kind of trauma they put her through to get what they wanted.

It had to be the Collective.

Kayda saw red at the thought of werecats prowling her apartment.

If it *had* been them, calling the cops was out. The police force, when all was said and done, was in the Collective's pocket. If some well-meaning officer tried to investigate the break-in, it was very possible they'd be coerced into dropping it if the Collective requested—demanded—it.

She needed help.

Unfortunately, only one person came to mind.

She stalked toward the kitchen, crunching over broken plates, bowls, and glass cups to reach her junk drawer where she'd left Felix's business card. That asshat better have a solution for this. He had one degree of separation from the Collective.

They wouldn't force her out of her home—wouldn't make

her into a fugitive like they'd done to Harlow. Kayda hadn't even *done* anything and knew even less.

She yanked the drawer all the way open, finding Felix's card inside, along with a few loose batteries and rubber bands. Her fingers were a breath from the card when she snatched her hand back.

That card had been faceup when she'd put it inside. Sure, it might have gotten flipped over while the vandals had been giving all her worldly possessions the rough treatment, but what if whoever it was had seen—and recognized—Felix's name? What if they were monitoring his calls? As much as Kayda wanted to punch him in his very punchable face, deep down she believed he'd come to see her under genuine concern for Harlow. He was bending as many rules as he could without getting caught. But he might have been compromised since then. It might not be wise to call.

Kayda knew that if the Collective swooped in here right this second to cart her off to a precinct to get loaded full of truth serum, she would truthfully tell them that all she knew was that Harlow was headed for Kensey. To do what? Hells if Kayda knew. Her anger at Harlow for keeping her in the dark lowered minutely. They couldn't pull a truth out of Kayda's head that she didn't have.

Maybe strolling down to the Collective headquarters to volunteer herself to a mental scouring would be the quickest way to get off their radar. Because Kayda refused to feel like a prisoner in her own damn home—but she didn't want to be ambushed in her sleep either.

Think, she told herself.

They knew where she lived and that she had a connection to Harlow. They could have snatched her off the street for any infraction—perceived or otherwise—solely for knowing Harlow now that she was officially a criminal thanks to the bounty they'd placed on her. But they'd left Kayda alone until now.

They had come after her in a way that completely violated her sense of security, yet hadn't threatened her person.

They wanted her scared because scared people made mistakes.

She blew out another calming breath.

Once she let her mind run freely instead of giving in to her anger, the answer was clear: they were desperate. They wanted Kayda to lead them to Harlow because they were running out of ideas. Thank the Goddess that the note Harlow had sent Kayda was in Jo's hands now, and that it hadn't been here when the place was ransacked.

Instead of calling Felix, because for all she knew, her apartment was bugged now, she grabbed his card out of the drawer and sent him a text.

Kayda: *Are you near a public telepost station?*

The reply came in a minute later. *No. But I can be.*

Kayda: *Text me the number when you get there.*

Felix: *Give me ten.*

That was one of the good things about Felix Turner: he knew when shit was real and didn't ask too many questions. It was one of the many reasons why he and Harlow had fit together so well—they navigated life much the same way. Which also meant they were constantly butting heads.

Since her purse's strap was still draped across her body and her apartment keys hung from the door, she marched back out without touching anything else. She'd take pictures of it later. Going through the proper channels would probably mean any paperwork associated with her filed report would "mysteriously" disappear. Maybe she could hire a private investigator. With one final disgusted look at her wreck of a home, she closed the door.

Like old-fashioned mundane phone booths, a handful of public telepost boxes dotted the city. Most stood outside highly populated areas to help discourage vandalism, but the glass walls of the one-to-two-person freestanding stations were always so splattered with blue and black ink from the attempted theft of the telepost pens that it almost looked like the boxes had been wallpapered from the inside. Which was just as well, because the looks Kayda got from strangers as she crammed her too-large body into the too-small booth implied they believed she was up to no good. The ten-minute walk from her apartment had been quick once she turned on the draken jets, and she hadn't even felt warm in the summer heat. Smashed into this box, though? Her chest tightened little by little, sweat beading on her upper lip.

Pressing a fist to her mouth, Kayda coughed. Now that she was fully closed inside, the permeating stench of urine was hard to ignore. Drunks were known to wander into the boxes late at night, confusing them with public toilets. Kayda felt terrible for the city employees tasked with keeping these things clean. Well, clean-*ish*.

She had enough space to move around, but not by much, and her head was cocked at a weird angle because the booth was shorter than she was. She resisted the urge to rub the top of her head, constantly being tickled by her short hairs brushing against the ceiling of the booth. Her phone beeped.

Removing the phone from her purse, she found a message from Felix with the number to the telepost box he was stuffed inside in some other part of the city.

Grabbing one of the few remaining pieces of telepost paper, she wrote a note to Felix.

Apartment was broken into. I think it was the cats. They want info on Low. Friends of yours?

A perk of the public boxes was that they took cash. Kayda fed a couple of bills into the payment box, whose screen flickered periodically. Hopefully the damn thing was functional, otherwise she'd have to consider a telepost office, where her transaction was more likely to be tracked. There, she could only pay with her telepost card, which was connected to her bank account. Digital paper trail. Now she wished she had a fake account like Harlow did. Paranoia had its uses.

Kayda double-checked the box number Felix had sent, then stuffed her note, sent with five-minute destruction, into the intake tube. After the door on the tube closed, the paper flapped lightly, then disappeared altogether.

Now she waited.

Within a couple of minutes, a note had appeared in the outgoing tube. Kayda slid up the plastic door and grabbed the note.

Felix: *Shit. You OK? Not friends of mine. File a report with Hansen—human cop. Act normal for a few days. I'll try to figure out what's going on. Have somewhere you can go?*

She didn't. There were a few acquaintances she could call, but no one she'd want to burden with this.

Someone pounded a fist on the door behind her. A muffled voice said, "You gonna be in there all day, lady?"

She shoved the door open and the guy jumped back to avoid getting a glass door to the face. "I'll take as long as I need."

The guy—a twenty-something human, she guessed—held his hands up as if he were under arrest. "S-s-sorry, ma'am!" Then he took off running.

Rolling her eyes, she closed herself inside the booth. The guy's stutter pulled up an image of Henri in her mind, but it was definitely too much to ask *him* if she could crash on his couch.

She'd go see Jo and ask about wards and locking charms. That way, at least Kayda would have a few seconds warning before someone broke in.

Kayda: *I'll be fine. They just wanted to scare me. I'll contact Hansen then lie low. Thanks.*

Felix: *Call me if things get worse. I'll try to get you a more secure phone. Be in touch soon.*

Kayda felt lighter as she stepped out of the telepost booth. She'd gotten some control back out of the situation, which settled her nerves. She didn't necessarily love that part of her sense of well-being was tied to Felix Turner, but she couldn't afford to be picky.

Next, she visited Jo and purchased a locking talisman for her door, locking charms for her windows, and three alarm-spell-infused crystals she'd need to activate and then attach to windowsills or doorjambs. Jo included a very detailed pamphlet to go with each, and assured Kayda they were all "foolproof," but Kayda was apprehensive. She'd never dabbled much in magic, even magic that was below a Level 3, which humans could handle. She'd been able to protect herself for so long that these warring feelings of mild fear and vulnerability had unsettled her even more than the break-in had.

Within two hours, she was back home, the mess had been photographed so she could show them to Officer Hansen, and she had installed the magic defenses to the best of her ability. Jo had said there'd be a faint buzzing from the crystals after the spell was properly activated, and they'd all done so. Foolproof, indeed.

After cleaning up her bathroom enough to take a shower, and getting her bedroom suitable for sleeping in, she checked all the windows to assure their locks were flipped closed. With her hand on the pull-cord of her living room blinds, intending to drop them, she caught movement across the street. Not the usual movement of someone walking across their living room or doing dishes at the kitchen sink—but the movement of shadows *among* the shadows.

Kayda opened the window, sensing the faint buzz of the newly activated crystal, but not setting it off, as the magic in it was tied specifically to her. Only she could come and go without tripping the alarm. She slipped out onto her balcony, her bare feet on the mesh metal platform. Squinting, she adjusted the dials of her vision, as she did with her hearing. Her sight became even sharper in the dark.

She waited, scouring the roof. She eyed the pair of protruding chimney stacks; the spindly arms of three antennas; the handful of domes housing spinning air vents.

A sleek black shape materialized out of the shadows of a chimney, as if the dark bricks had turned liquid and melted to the ground. A pair of whitish orbs appeared next. They disappeared for a breath, then were back. Blinking eyes. The longer Kayda stared, the more the shape solidified. It sat on its haunches and lifted a paw to give it a few licks before placing it back on the floor of the roof.

Kayda scowled. A werecat was keeping an eye on her apartment.

She flipped the cat the bird, climbed back through the window, and locked it behind her. With a satisfying clack, she dropped her blinds into place. She would not be intimidated.

She rechecked the wards.

Chapter 8
HARLOW

It took three days for a "WE BUY HOUSES" sign to appear on a wooden power pole on the corner of Bassett Way and Olive Lane. The pole was partially obscured by the leaves of a lush oak tree and stood next to a Thai restaurant. On the window was an elaborately painted ceramic bowl filled to the brim with a red-broth soup, a piece of shrimp clasped between a pair of chopsticks suspended above it. I'd had that soup the day before, and it was all I could think about as Caspian and I walked the five blocks to the restaurant from our motel. My appetite vanished the instant I spotted the sign, shocked it had finally materialized overnight. We'd planned to check the other three locations next, like we had the last two days. But here it was. I came to an abrupt stop in the middle of the sidewalk as if I'd locked eyes with a predator in the bushes.

Caspian stopped beside me. "Do you want to make the call, or should I?"

We'd gotten the password from Fiona yesterday.

"Can you do it?" I asked, eyeing the sign warily. "Use your authoritative voice. Mine will be too wobbly and will blow our cover."

"You said my authoritative voice is 'as stale as old toast.'"

"Yes, exactly. No one will think you're up to anything fishy."

Caspian huffed a laugh.

I followed him down the sidewalk so we were in front of a low brick wall that surrounded the patio of a restaurant that appeared to be closed today. As Caspian took out his cell, I hoisted myself onto the wall, my feet dangling a couple of inches above the ground. I did my best to look casual. No one else was out on the sidewalk, as the lone open business on this stretch of the street was the Thai restaurant. Farther up the road from where I sat were all middle-class family homes. Most everyone was at work at this hour. It was a wonder the Thai place stayed open, with such an obscure location, but even as I heard the faint ring of Caspian's outbound call, a customer walked out with a plastic takeout bag, and another one strolled in from the small parking lot.

The sudden slight stiffening of Caspian's back told me someone had answered the call on the other end. "Jakarta," Caspian said crisply. Then he glanced up at me and started making quick motions in the air with one hand. For a brief moment, I feared he was casting a spell because he'd seen some quickly approaching danger. But he only needed me to write something down.

I quickly tipped onto my hip, pulled my phone out of my back pocket, and opened the notes app. Caspian, in his slow, methodical way, repeated the address back to whomever answered the phone. I quickly typed it out.

"Tomorrow evening, seven p.m.," he said. "Noted. I look forward to it."

My heart was beating too hard by the time Caspian had ended the call and glanced up at me. "What are the odds those trolls are going to be able to sense your magic and rip off your arms?"

"That's a two-part question. The first is unknown, but the second is very likely." He offered me a flash of a smile. "Do you want more of that soup before we go shopping, or after?"

He believed it was very likely that a troll could actually rip a limb from his torso. Wonderful. Then I registered the rest of what he said and hopped off the wall. "Shopping for what?"

"It's a black-tie event," he said. "You need a dress and I need a tux."

I got lost in the image of Caspian in a tuxedo, unsure if it would fit him perfectly, or be perfectly incongruous. The image of a barrel-chested troll appeared behind him and popped his head off his shoulders. I shook away the very bloody sight. "I definitely need food first." Thinking of the bright red broth of the delicious soup, I said, "But maybe I'll get the coconut ginger one this time."

The following afternoon, I stood in front of the rectangular mirror positioned on the back of the motel room door and cocked a head at my reflection. This dress was entirely too fancy for my tastes, but Caspian was adamant that I needed to be in a "little black dress" or something akin to a ball gown if I didn't want to stand out like a sore thumb tonight. I turned to the side, wrinkling my nose at how the dress flared out dramatically once it hit my hips. It wasn't the wide skirt that bothered me so much as the giant black bow that rested against the small of my back. It somehow didn't look gaudy, though it should have.

My high-heeled shoes glittered under the fluorescent lights, the black fabric dusted with tiny rhinestones. Delicate black bows decorated either ankle.

I flinched, startled when the door to the motel room opened. The door slowly eased closed behind Caspian, then at the last second, slammed into place with a thunk that made my eye twitch—again. No matter what either of us did, the door closed at its own speed. I'd been awakened last night on three separate occasions by other doors along the corridor thunking closed so loudly that the windows and walls shook.

Caspian stood in the small entryway, looking dapper in his tux. We were completely overdressed for this run-down motel, but we figured it was best to stay off the radar in this town when we didn't know who—or what—would be descending on the area for the auction. His outfit was made slightly less dapper by the stack of towels over his arm, and his fist closed around a trio of small bottles.

"Raiding the maid's cart again?" I asked.

Caspian could afford to buy $500 bottles of cologne and then use them for batting practice if he wanted, and it wouldn't put a dent in his bank account. Hell, he could have exotic flowers flown in from remote areas of the globe and have their oils extracted to put into his bath. And yet, he'd become obsessed with the scent of Ocean Sunrise Bath Wash that came in travel-sized bottles from this tiny motel.

"Rachel caught me pilfering the bottles," Caspian said, gazing down at his loot. "I'm on a first-name basis with the maid because this new life of ours has turned me into a petty criminal. I had to sweet-talk her into keeping quiet."

"Was hush money involved?"

"There's a fifty-dollar bill in her pocket."

I laughed.

After depositing the soap and towels in the bathroom, Caspian came back out to give me one of his appraising head-to-toe sweeps. When his gaze finally settled on mine, he nodded once. "You look presentable."

"*Presentable?*" I asked, hands on hips. "That's all I get? I would have said you look very dashing, but I'll amend that now to 'All right, I guess.'"

A ghost of a smile graced his face. "Ah. The dramatics have begun. Is this because of the bows?"

I turned abruptly and shook my backside, then glared at him. "This thing is the size of a small bus, Caspian. I'm never letting you be in charge of my wardrobe again."

He walked past my giant bow, unperturbed. "When I took you with me to the last place, all you did was blanch at the price tags. You made the staff nervous. They probably thought we were planning to steal something."

I rolled my eyes, scrutinizing my reflection again, rather than admitting he'd been right. He'd purchased the dress and tux this morning. I'd picked up breakfast from Marley's Diner a few blocks from the motel, and when I got back, I'd found the dress in an elegant blue box on my bed. The price tag had made me sweat more than the brisk walk.

"I might also be a little frazzled because the pocket mirror has gone off like three times in the last hour," I said.

His reflection behind me froze. "Anything particularly alarming?"

"I don't think so. I'd developed a visceral reaction to the sound of the thing anyway and now it's worse," I said. "That oo code came up again, too. Still no idea what it means."

"We have to keep operating under the belief that our movements aren't being tracked. If we jump every time we get spooked, we'll drive ourselves mad."

I nodded, knowing he was right. Again. I just needed to hear it.

Staring at my reflection, I ran my hands down the sides of the dress in an attempt to dry my damp palms and calm my nerves. In addition to the whole "orc mob boss" thing, this auction would be the first time since we'd left Luma that we'd potentially be around a large group of fae. People who might recognize one of us, regardless of the glamoured accessories we both planned to wear. People who might sense my sword skimming the ceiling, keeping a watchful blade on the proceedings.

I glanced toward the bed, where my duffel bag lay. The sword was inside it. It had gotten sick of my complaints about the bows, too, and had settled itself inside shortly before Caspian's return from wandering outside, pulling innocent maids into his schemes while I got ready.

Caspian wouldn't readily admit it, but I knew this outing made him nervous too. I didn't know if he was keeping a brave face for my benefit or his own.

Behind me, I watched as he grabbed the hard-shelled black case of accessories Welsh had given us and made his way to the vanity table near the mirror where I stood.

He flipped open the latch and lifted the lid, revealing several small items in felt-lined partitions. Plucking that tray out, he revealed the neat rows of white pouches below it. The pouches contained glamoured tufts of hair that became seamless wigs once removed from the bag.

One after the other, all while keeping a straight face, Caspian tried on wigs. Short wigs, long wigs, puffy wigs, bright-colored wigs. By the time he had donned a feathered platinum wig that belonged on a pop star from the '80s and not a thirty-something sorcerer whose favorite color was beige, I couldn't stop laughing.

When I finally got myself under control and wiped my eyes, the sword was floating nearby, humming softly in irritation. Caspian smiled—one of the genuine ones that lit up his face and shaved off five years. "Thanks, Cas."

Caspian stiffened. The nickname had just slipped out.

"Any time ... Har."

I wrinkled my nose. "Absolutely not."

Caspian laughed, then rooted through the pile of hair pouches littering the vanity table. "I know you don't trust my fashion sense anymore, but I suggest this one."

It was one he hadn't tried on yet. I took the pouch from him and peered inside, the lock of hair resting in the bottom a light brown. Pulling the small piece free, a long, curly wig materialized. The curls were wider and looser than my tight, natural corkscrews.

"I like you best with curls." With Caspian's flat tone, it was hard to tell if this was a statement of fact or a compliment.

With the practiced flick of my wrist, I got the wig on top of my head and marveled at how it *became* my hair. I'd worn several of these glamoured wigs at this point, but the magic never failed to amaze me. The soft ringlets fell around my bare shoulders, and the color looked good against my dark skin.

I sighed. "Fine. Your taste isn't always horrible."

Chuckling, Caspian selected his accessories from the felt tray. A clip-on nose ring gave him a wider, flatter nose. A pair of contacts gave him light blue, almost gray, eyes, instead of his usual hazel. For his third choice, he went with a black wig that made him look a bit emo, but I kept the comment to myself. He reminded me of a lead singer in a grunge rock band, which, when paired with the tux, gave him the air of a rich troublemaker ready to spend cash. He'd fit in just fine.

In addition to the new hair, I gave myself green eyes instead of brown, and put on a pair of earrings that somehow gave me sharper cheekbones.

"Ready, cutlass?" Caspian asked the sword, who'd been observing our transformation.

It inverted itself and tapped once on the vanity table.

While Caspian worked his way through a camouflage spell for the sword—his hands and arms gracefully dancing through the air as if he were conducting a symphony—I fetched my newly purchased black clutch from the nightstand. I checked that I had my phone, Dad's pocket mirror, lip gloss, and some cash. As I slung it over my body, Caspian lowered his arms. My sword disappeared from view. Every time the spell was put on it, a pang seized my chest. I knew it wasn't *actually* gone, but the spell was a damn good one, making the sword utterly vanish from sight.

"I have one more accessory for you that you might like," Caspian said, but instead of returning to the box of glamoured items, he went to his suitcase.

He produced a rectangular black case from a side pocket. If he'd casually dropped a couple thousand dollars on a diamond necklace to help round out my ensemble, I would refuse it. I was nervous enough as it was. I didn't want to also spend all evening fretting about possibly losing a piece of jewelry that cost more than a month's rent. When he stopped before me and flipped open the lid of the case, it was a talisman that lay there. A familiar one—one I'd forgotten about entirely. The pendant was crescent-shaped—about the size of a quarter—and hung from a gold chain.

"Do you remember the night we met?" he asked.

From anyone else, that would have sounded romantic. "Kind of hard to forget getting dragged around by a feral vampire."

That ghost of a smile was back. "I went through your bag that night, trying to find out more information about you since Welsh wasn't answering my calls. This was in the bottom of your bag and it had gotten rather mangled—much like yourself. The spell on it was a bit glitchy. I repaired it for you." He turned the pendant over so I could see the intricately etched runes. "I improved the spell work as well. I believe that was damaged even before the altercation with the vampire."

I was temporarily speechless. "Thank you."

"Is it an important piece to you, or one you found while charm collecting?"

"The latter. I took it the same day I took the sword. Jo said it's imbued with a calming spell."

Caspian nodded. "It's a Level 2 spell, so it won't make you so calm you fall asleep, but it will take the edge off. It might make you sleepy if you wear it for too long, but it'll be fine to wear for the evening. Would you like to put it on?"

Nodding, I turned and lifted my hair.

Caspian draped the thin gold chain around my neck and clasped it in the back. The crescent rested below my collarbone. A moment after the runes touched my skin, some of the tension leached out of me, as if the alcohol in a recently consumed glass of wine had hit my bloodstream.

I dropped my hair and turned around.

Caspian contemplated my outfit again, nodding once. "Shall we?"

Blowing out a breath, I followed him and the very faint shimmer of the sword out the motel room door and into the warm summer evening.

Chapter 9
HARLOW

The auction was held in an old airplane hangar. The location had to be remote, I guessed, to not tip anyone off that anything illegal was afoot. Caspian wagered that Domino owned the land the hangar sat on, which also meant the cops wouldn't have any reason to check out the sudden congregation of people on private property. Just a black-tie party hosted by an orc mob boss—nothing to see here, folks.

Caspian had rented a sleek black SUV, as we didn't want to run the risk of his car getting tied back to us on the off chance things went sideways tonight.

It was 6:45 now, and the SUV crawled to a stop behind a stretch limo. A line of cars crept through the open chain-link fence lining the small airfield. It took several minutes before Caspian could inch the SUV through the gate and into the makeshift asphalt parking lot near the hangar. At least twenty vehicles were already parked by the time Caspian glided into a spot.

Before I got out, I glanced into the dark back seat where the sword lay—at least I thought it was back there. "Don't let anyone see you."

The faintest flash of red lit up the back seat, then faded just as quickly. Its angry color.

"I'm not insulting your intelligence," I hissed. "I don't want anything to happen to you, is all."

"Nor I, cutlass," Caspian said. "This Domino character surely has materials at his disposal that could be used to incapacitate you even more effectively than I did."

Another brief flash of red, like a dying ember, followed by a soft hum—meaning the sword was appeased for now. As I let myself out of the passenger side, I held the door open a while longer so the sword could drift out. It vibrated gently as it went by to let me know it was out of the car. After closing the door and fluffing up the hideous bow affixed above my ass, I made my way to where Caspian stood behind the SUV.

"You'll look less conspicuous if you take a breath every once in a while," Caspian said.

I exhaled deeply and shook out my arms.

A couple—humans, I guessed—walked by. The woman angled a dazzling smile my way. "I always get the jitters before one of these, too. I hear there's a treasure chest from the sunken pirate ship on the docket tonight! Good luck!"

My brows hiked toward my hairline. "You too!"

"That sounds promising," Caspian said, his bent elbow held out to me. "Ready?"

I wasn't, but I linked my arm through his anyway. Walking in heels was not one of my strong suits, so I kept Caspian's arm in a death grip as we walked across the slightly uneven asphalt. Ahead, the interior of the hangar shone like a beacon, the wide door lifted to half-mast.

A wide slab of concrete sat outside the door, a fabric awning erected over it. The edges of the awning were lined with elegant strings of white lights, which reflected off the smooth concrete like glittering stars. A pair of wide-set men stood outside the awning, their arms tucked behind their backs. I held tighter to Caspian, not because of my precarious balance, but because even from a distance, these two creeped me right the hell out.

Even though a wide range of fae called Luma home, I'd only seen one full-grown troll in my life: a lunch lady at my high school. She was the stereotypical crabby lunch lady from TV shows—but on steroids. Her skin had been a sickly yellow, her beady black eyes sunken into her wide, craggy face, and she'd been bald with a few long black hairs on her head that wafted periodically by a seemingly phantom wind. Her pointed ears angled outward instead of straight up like an elf's. She'd been a good six and a half feet, and nearly as wide as she was tall. "Cantankerous" didn't begin to cover her personality. She'd been suspended for a week after she'd clocked a coworker in the nose with the flat side of a lunch tray for accidentally dropping a dollop of mashed potatoes on her shoe.

It said a lot about my high school that they let her back after that. It was hard to get any sane person to work around teenage fae who had the horror of dealing with malfunctioning magic right alongside their malfunctioning hormones.

These two *looked* human but were most definitely trolls. My sixth sense told me unnecessarily to keep my distance. They didn't speak to anyone as the crowd passed between them, as if they were simply massive, decorative statues. Statues in expensive suits. There were no visible weapons on them, but they didn't necessarily need them. Those meaty fists of theirs were weapon enough.

As we reached the pair, I glanced up, searching the air for any sign of the sword. No shimmers gave away its location; I presumed it had made its way inside through an upper window, like we'd discussed. The farther it kept from everyone, the better.

My sixth sense pinged once more and I swiveled my head,

only to find one of the trolls leering down at me. I came up short, huddling closer to Caspian. Normally when it came to fight or flight, I was all flight. But this guy oozed so much menace and coiled magic that my lizard brain short-circuited.

He was fair-skinned, bald, and had a set of features that were pleasant enough, but largely forgettable. He looked like a retired pro wrestler who had picked up a security job he found deeply degrading.

I expected him to turn us away, or to sense the glamour magic in our accessories, or to discern Caspian was a sorcerer.

Instead of telling us to scram, he said, "Hi, gorgeous." His voice was a deep rumble. It wasn't a smooth, rich voice. It was reminiscent of an expansive cave—cold, foreboding, and echoing with the promise of lurking shadows armed with teeth and claws. Chills raced up my spine.

Caspian elbowed me gently in the side when all I did was gape at the troll.

"Uhh ... hi." I cleared my throat and attempted what I prayed was an eyelash flutter and not a facial tic. "Nice to, uh, meet you." I would not curtsy, I would not curtsy.

After an agonizingly slow elevator scan, he let out a soft moan. "I do like the tiny ones. We don't get enough of your kind here."

Tiny?

"Come find me later, yeah?" He took a not-so-subtle gander down my dress. His vantage point was high enough that he wouldn't have much problem with it. I resisted the urge to cover my chest with my hand. "The things I could show you, little one ..." He groaned softly again.

Caspian started to say something, but a sharp look from the troll cut him off.

"You don't need a puny man like him, dove," the troll said.

"I'll show you the night of your life and you won't even remember his name."

With that, he resumed his statuesque stance, dismissing us both.

Stomach roiling, I yanked Caspian forward. I gave a violent shiver. "Of course when I actually get hit on, it's by a man straight out of my nightmares."

"I may have wet myself."

A snorting laugh slipped out. "Good to know I'm on my own if he makes good on his ... threat?"

"Our other companion would probably be of more use. If the human boulder tries to ravish you, I'll fetch reinforcements. There will be carnage."

I shivered violently again. The notion of "being ravished" by the troll was too horrifying for words, so I changed the subject. "Now, Mr. Auction Runner. What should we do first?"

"Champagne, then we mingle."

I wrinkled my nose. With enough alcohol, I could mingle my bow-festooned butt off. I'd even be able to flirt gratuitously with anyone necessary. But too much alcohol would make me sloppy and would result in either blowing our cover or confusing the sword into thinking I required rescuing.

As much as sober mingling with rich, stuffy humans, and even richer, terrifying fae, sounded like a disaster waiting to happen, I was looking forward to seeing Caspian in action in an environment he was comfortable in. I rolled my shoulders back and willed my face to soften.

Though the hangar door was at half-mast, even the eight-foot-tall trolls behind us could stroll into the building without stooping. Just inside the door was a table lined with auction paddles. Caspian perused the remaining numbers and then selected a paddle with "89" on it.

With me attached to his arm, he angled us back toward the

room. We stood there for a few beats, taking it in. A wall that didn't reach the ceiling stretched horizontally across the wide-open space about two-thirds into the room. The wall served as a backdrop for the stage, on which stood a podium for the auctioneer. Perhaps the remaining third of the space was used as a residence when the front half wasn't hosting events.

Dozens of rows of black-velvet-padded chairs were lined up in front of the stage, a wide aisle bisecting the rows down the middle. Along either side of the room were more casual seating arrangements—black leather couches, love seats, and high-backed chairs ringing elegant tall tables. Waiters and waitresses in pressed black pants, crisp white shirts, and red bow ties wove through the crowd languidly, offering hors d'oeuvres and flutes of champagne. A few had trays covered in shot glasses of a sparkly pink liquid that Caspian warned me not to drink under any circumstances. Little did he know, I was already quite aware of the effects of elfin wine. That stuff was ruinous.

Consuming elfin wine was essentially what had gotten me into all this—my butterfly effect. Had I not been drunk on elfin wine that fateful night at the secret club, I might not have offended Norbert Haskins. Had I been in that sweaty fool's good graces, he might have let me into his basement—literally, not a euphemism—to have a gander at his collection of charmed goods. It was my unsatiated curiosity about his haul that had led me to break into his warehouse and steal his dragon sword.

One could argue, of course, that my current predicament of being a fugitive was my own fault for my kleptomaniac proclivities, but I'd much rather blame the wine, thanks.

"Is there any chance someone here would recognize you?" I asked, forgetting momentarily that the man on my arm looked like the cleaned-up lead singer of a grunge band, not a bland, wealthy sorcerer.

"I changed my appearance at every auction, so not even the

frequent attendees of my events knew what I looked like," Caspian said, guiding us toward the right side of the room. "It was originally Welsh's idea since we weren't sure how hard the Collective was going to try to thwart my efforts. I discovered that the mystery of who I was kept attendance high."

"Did you ever walk through the crowd to hear what people said about you?"

"Of course," he said. "Wouldn't you?"

I swiped a cracker with a fancy dollop of what I hoped was cream cheese off a passing tray. "Probably."

We'd only taken a few more steps when Caspian let out a tiny, choked noise of surprise. Before I could ask, he said, "We need to get closer to the wall. Away from the walkway."

I popped the mystery-cheese-covered cracker in my mouth, unlinked my arm with his, and I did as he said, weaving around tables and chatting patrons. I smiled at anyone who happened to glance my way as I pretended to seek out an open table.

I briefly glanced back at him. "What's wrong?"

"Instead of someone recognizing me, I have recognized someone moving up the center aisle," Caspian said.

Instinctively, I turned my head in that direction, as if the person in question would have an arrow above their head.

After moving around a few more clusters of mostly human-looking people, I found an empty two-seater couch. I figured if we sat, we'd be hidden by surrounding patrons. Since Caspian didn't look like Caspian, I wasn't sure what had him so jumpy.

Grabbing my elbow, he pulled me away from the sofa before I could fully sit down. I stumbled on my too-tall heels after him. We moved past a few more tables, as well as a very tall pair of women—one whom I was fairly certain had a spiked tail swishing under the edge of her maxi dress, and the other who had a pair of black horns poking out of her hairline by her temples.

What on earth are they?

Before I could ask Caspian that, he spun me around, took several steps forward, and pressed me against the wall. I was so stunned, I couldn't come up with anything to say.

He cocked his head, his face angling dangerously close to mine. My brows shot together as I stared up at him. I wanted to swipe that emo hair out of his false brown eyes to get a sense of what had gotten into him all of a sudden. He leaned in, pressing his cheek to mine. He whispered, "There's a Collective sorcerer here."

I stiffened. "One of ours?"

"Yes," he said, keeping his mouth close to my ear. "He was one of my professors at the academy. I saw him walking with a woman with a headset on and a clipboard in hand. It looked like he was giving her instructions."

My mind spun. "What, like he works here?"

"That's what it looked like." He glanced across the seating area. From my spot against the wall, my view was limited—plus I didn't know what I was looking for. "He's the one in the black suit."

I considered head-butting him. More than half the folks in here were wearing black suits!

"Amaranth-hued tie."

"What the hell color is amaranth?"

"Oh, don't be so pedestrian. It's in the red family."

"Then say *red*," I said, glaring at the side of his head. "Who insults someone by calling them pedestrian? And you say Welsh is a snob."

When he glanced back at me, he was grinning. "You're much easier to offend than he is. And when you're offended, you're distracted. When you're distracted, you're less likely to be flustered and call attention to yourself."

I placed two fingers on my crescent-shaped talisman as if

that would inject more of the calming magic into my system. The fact that I felt mildly panicked about a Collective sorcerer finding us here, despite the talisman's help, told me I was more anxious about everything than I'd wanted to admit.

Caspian glanced away. He must have noticed that Amaranth Tie had moved farther away from our current location, because he leaned back. I remained crowded against the wall, but at least our chests weren't practically smashed together anymore.

"All right," I said, slipping my arms behind me and propping my hands at the small of my back, palms against the wall. "What's cooking in that scary brain of yours?"

He propped one hand on the wall by my head and shoved the other in a pocket. Just a guy having an intimate conversation with his date. He kept his voice low.

"Trolls aren't predisposed to have heightened magical ... anything," he said. "They don't have any heightened senses either, other than sight. The thing that's been bothering me about Fiona's story is that the trolls fanned out into the crowd and singled out werecats in their human form."

It took a moment to figure out what he was saying. "Someone *else* sensed the cats and then sent the trolls after them?"

"That, or a spell was put in place to locate them." He jerked his chin toward the wall behind me. "If they've had this location selected for a while, a sorcerer with enough time could put runes all over this place. Usually locator spells are specific—you have a person you want to find, and then use a locator spell to find them. But if someone wanted to find a certain *type* of person, rune arrays could be tailored to ferret out that type of magic."

"Like shifter magic."

He nodded. "Auction starts, doors are sealed, the resident sorcerer activates the runes—"

"And it puts targets on their foreheads."

"It's just a theory."

"The cats here probably wouldn't have recognized the sorcerer either, since he's one of Luma's," I said.

"Most people wouldn't. Not many sorcerers go through the academy and then choose not to join a Collective. Not only was he one of my professors, but he's also a scholar on Rystel's Theorem. He postulated that when the inverse—"

I covered his mouth with my hand. "Don't you dare."

He smiled under my palm.

Dropping my hand, I said, "If your theory is right, are *you* in danger?"

"I don't think so. A locator spell specific to sorcerers would result in false-negative readings, as sorcery is taught, not innate. A human with no natural magical signature can be a sorcerer. If he ran the locator spell on humans in general, half the attendants would be labeled as targets, and even then there would be no way to discern which were sorcerers and which weren't."

I had to hope there weren't any hidden runes targeting sentient swords. "What do you think he's doing here?"

Caspian shook his head, his stringy black hair obscuring one eye. "All I have are guesses, and they could all be wrong."

Within a minute, the lights dimmed, brightening a moment later. I cast a wary glance upward, as if a prediction of how the evening would go would be written on the peaked ceiling. The lights brightened and dimmed twice more. Caspian took a step back and angled his head to the side.

"Let's grab seats on the aisle." He took my hand and pulled me after him.

I scanned the crowd moving en masse toward the velvet-padded seats, searching for Amaranth Tie. I found him near the front of the stage, talking in hushed tones to two people who bobbed their heads to whatever he said. Their severe expressions implied Amaranth Tie wasn't a barrel of fun. As soon as he stopped talking, the pair swiftly walked away from him up the center aisle. The guy definitely held authority here, but whose side was he on—the Collective's or the orc mob boss's?

Both were terrible choices, as far as I was concerned.

We settled into seats close to the aisle on the right side of the room. I'd only need to climb over the lap of one patron if I needed to get out of here in a hurry. A rattling clang from behind me told me the hangar door had been closed, though, which would make escape harder. I was fairly confident the sword could cut us out of here like a demented can opener.

I attempted to investigate the space above me while just moving my eyes, searching for the sword's glimmer, but didn't see anything out of the ordinary.

As an emcee stepped onto the stage to great fanfare, Amaranth Tie walked between the stage and the front row of seats. He didn't duck into the center aisle like I expected, but kept moving along the front of the room, and then rounded the bank of seats Caspian and I were in. Caspian fussed with his hair a bit, which looked like a natural enough gesture for his emo persona, but I knew he was keeping his face averted in case the sorcerer could see through the glamours with the aid of eye contact. I had expected Caspian to be playing it cool, having complete faith in Welsh's "exceptional" talent at glamours. I wasn't sure if it was unsettling or refreshing to learn there were things in this world that could rattle Caspian Blackthorn.

I suddenly wondered if there had been more to Caspian not becoming a Collective sorcerer. I couldn't imagine walking out on the profession was a common occurrence.

I did what I could to appear interested in whatever the emcee prattled on about on stage. I laughed when the crowd did, but a couple of seconds late. Pressing a finger against the talisman, I willed it to make me serene and unassuming.

Amaranth Tie didn't so much as glance down our aisle as he breezed past us. I felt Caspian relax a moment later.

The lights winked out completely then, throwing the room into total darkness. Then, like giant fireflies blinking into existence, the air above the seats filled with orbs of light. The orbs were bright enough to illuminate the majority of the stage, and I could make out Caspian's borrowed features. His ridiculous hair hid half his face. Homesickness seized me at the sight of the fae light—its glow a familiar blue.

A collective gasp sounded from the crowd as a dragon made of flame winged across the stage from behind the pulled-open curtains. The orange, red, and yellow body was so vibrant in the gloom, I had to squint while my eyes adjusted. The dragon sparked and popped as it swooped low to the ground, then sharply angled up toward the ceiling, soaring with effortless grace. I spotted a woman step into the wings on the other side of the stage, out of sight of most of the audience. She thrust her arms up, weaving her fingers in the air, and suddenly there was a second dragon, this one made of water.

The two dragons swooped about each other, hisses of steam erupting from the brief contact made by tails and wings. After an impressive show of agility, the elemental controlling the water dragon stopped her frantic hand movements. The dragon stopped, too. With a few elegant swipes of her hands, the dragon floated backward, hanging suspended on the water witch's side of the stage. The fire dragon had done the same on the other. The crowd held its breath while the two elemental dragons stared each other down, wings beating in slow, powerful strokes to mimic keeping their bodies aloft.

The water elemental suddenly pushed her palms forward,

propelling the dragon across the stage. The fire dragon left a thin trail of smoke behind it as it rocketed toward its opponent.

My sixth sense pinged, and while everyone leaned forward, eager to see who would win the battle, I looked over my right shoulder. I had to squint again, phantom memories of the fire dragon burned onto my retinas. Amaranth Tie had made a pit stop in the casual seating area, but he wasn't lounging. He stood between two couches with his palms pressed flat against the wall.

Chairs creaked as patrons braced themselves for impact. In the same breath that the dragons collided on stage—if the sudden burst of light and violent hiss of steam were any clue—a pulse of magic shot out of Amaranth Tie's hands. In the split second that his power poured out of his palms and skittered across the wall, nearly a dozen intricately designed rune circles were revealed in vibrant blue-green. If I hadn't been watching, I would have missed it. Hell, if I'd blinked a moment earlier, I would have missed it.

Amaranth Tie dropped his arms to his sides and spun, his laser focus honed straight on me. I sucked in a breath, too scared to look away. Partly because I feared I'd find a literal target on Caspian—the sorcerer's magic singling him out.

Another crash of magic and hiss of steam erupted behind me, and I flinched. In the brief breath of time that my eyes had closed, Amaranth Tie had started to move again, but instead of heading my way, he continued toward the back of the room. I'd already been caught staring, so I craned my neck to keep an eye on him. The bespectacled old man beside me wasn't remotely pleased with how squirmy I was, but I didn't care.

I half-popped out of my chair long enough to confirm Amaranth Tie had stopped at the back of the room to converse with one of the troll behemoths who had been manning the entrance earlier. The behemoth nodded but didn't move from his spot at the back of the room. The sorcerer strolled along the back of the hangar, then made his way to the seating area opposite. I thought he might activate hidden runes on that wall, too, but I lost sight of him when he sat down.

Brow furrowed, I settled in my seat, which earned a grumpy, "*Finally,*" from the old guy next to me. Had the runes told the sorcerer that the crowd was threat-free? Or at least shifter-free? Whatever his magic security system had told him, he hadn't pegged me as a problem. Just a nosy human. Fine by me.

The event progressed as many auctions in Luma had—the flashier ones Caspian had frowned upon: a few items were paraded on stage by beautiful, scantily clad people; auction paddles popped into the air like startled gophers; and after every fourth item or so, there was a performance of magic or acrobatics, and sometimes both. By the third performance of the night, I was restless. I had no idea where the sword was, and I feared it was restless too. An edgy sentient sword wasn't good for anyone.

There had been any number of interesting items on display tonight, but none of them were unique enough that I hadn't seen them in Luma. My thoughts strayed to the attendees rather than the items. I wasn't sure who made up the crowd here. Anyone who had spent as much time in a hub as Caspian or me wouldn't be oohing and ahhing with the frequency of this group. Were they exiles from the hubs? Criminal types who weren't welcome behind the veil? I grimaced at that, as it sort of described me. Were there humans in the crowd who had found out that the things that go bump in the night were real, yet their only contact with such things were auctions like this one?

I craned my neck to glance across the room. It was a wasted effort, just as it had been the other half a dozen times I'd done it: I couldn't see Amaranth Tie from here.

"And for our final item of the evening—the item you've all

been waiting for—we have a sealed treasure chest," the emcee boomed into the microphone.

I perked up and my wide eyes met Caspian's. The woman in the parking lot had had correct intel after all. When the group collectively leaned forward this time, I did too.

A pair of oiled-up men with washboard abs sauntered onto the stage, each with a handle of the pitch-black treasure chest in his hands. Sauntered was a bit generous; even with their muscular physiques, it was clear they struggled with the weight.

They placed the treasure chest in front of the auctioneer's podium and a pair of the glowing faelight orbs moved closer. Soft blue light cascaded over the curved lid of the chest and the metal bands that stretched over it like suspenders. A chunky black lock like something out of medieval times hung from the latch.

I clamped my hands together in my lap to quiet their twitching. I'd never wanted to use my lockpicks so badly in my life. What on earth could be in that thing? I shuddered at the idea of it being full of sentient weapons. If the sword came shooting out of the darkness to break its compatriots out of their treasure-chest prison, I was getting Caspian and me the hell out of here.

"This chest," the emcee said dramatically, "has never been opened. It was recovered from the *Element of Surprise*, a pirate vessel that was found off the coast of this very state a year ago. The ship's history is shrouded in mystery. It is said the ship was not capsized by a great storm, but by sea beasts marooned here a century ago from the fae realm. Very few items from that shipwreck have made their way into the hands of the public, so we're pleased to offer this incredibly rare item to you now. I must warn you that we have attempted to sell this chest a few times already."

Oh no, was it haunted or something?

"There is a reserve," the auctioneer said. "If bids do not

meet the minimum threshold, we won't be able to let it go. Are we ready?"

The crowd cheered.

"I'm sorry, I couldn't hear you. Are we ready?"

Even I crowed in excitement.

"That's more like it! Who will discover what secrets lay beneath her lid?"

The anticipation was going to eat me alive.

If I screamed up at the ceiling to the sword that the murder ban was lifted, how soon could he impale the emcee? Could Caspian magic us out of here with the chest without the troll guards at the door smashing us beneath their boots?

Curiosity didn't just kill the cat. It made a lady a touch ruthless.

"Bidding starts at two thousand dollars!"

Caspian's paddle shot into the air.

He was outbid a second later. Paddles were lifted with such frequency, I was amazed the fast-talking auctioneer could keep up.

Within minutes, the auction had turned into a bidding war between Caspian, a woman in the back, and a short man in front whom I guessed was a glamoured goblin. That, or a very wealthy mustachioed toddler with a vaguely green tint to his skin.

When the bids climbed into the low five figures, I started sweating bullets. I knew Caspian was rich, but was he rich enough that he could drop that much cash for a mystery box, or were pride and adrenaline pushing him beyond his limits? The brief glimpses I caught of his profile implied he was calm, but he'd probably also look calm in the middle of a twister.

"My, this wind is moving a bit quickly," he would say, as a startled cow flew past.

I cackled to myself. The auction had shredded what was left of my sanity.

The old man next to me muttered something about the good old days when women knew their place was in the home. Perhaps I could lift the murder ban for him instead.

Heads whipped right and left as bids were volleyed between Caspian and the woman in the back.

"Can I get twelve-fifty?" the auctioneer asked, having left the stage to stand in the middle of the aisle of chairs. One of the glowing orbs hung above his head like a spotlight.

Caspian raised his paddle.

Heads swiveled toward the back.

"Twelve seventy-five for the lovely lady in the back?"

It took a few long seconds, but the woman's paddle went up.

"Thirteen for the gentleman with the ambitious hairdo?"

Caspian's paddle lifted. Chairs creaked as the crowd shifted.

"Thirteen twenty-five?"

Her hesitation lasted longer this time.

"Thirteen twenty-five and the mysteries known only by the sea and time could be yours. The riches inside might pale in comparison to a measly thirteen twenty-five."

Even with the implied "thousand" missing from the total, my stomach churned. Nearly a year's worth of rent for a single chest that very well could hold nothing but the husks of dead moths.

The orb closest to Caspian's rival lowered, poised above her head. The placement of the light caused odd shadows to dance across her face. Her brow was scrunched. A woman beside her leaned in to whisper something into her ear—whether encouragement to keep going or to quit, I couldn't be sure.

Sighing, the woman raised her free hand and made a cutting motion across her neck, shaking her head. She was out.

She was out!

The auctioneer spun on his heel to address the crowd. "Last bid of thirteen thousand still stands. Is anyone going to challenge him?" He turned to the left, then to the right. "For thirteen thousand, going once ..."

I bit down on my bottom lip.

"Going twice ..."

Grabbing hold of Caspian, I squeezed his forearm. Was thirteen high enough to meet the reserve? If it wasn't, could Caspian put in a private offer?

"Sold!" the auctioneer bellowed. "Congratulations, Paddle 89! You've won the prize of the evening!"

Caspian let out a breath of what I hoped was relief and not, "Oh holy shit, what have I done?"

The crowd erupted in applause.

Turning to me, Caspian arched his brows, which disappeared from view behind his floppy hair. "Don't say I never buy you anything."

I laughed. "Let's go get our mystery box."

Chapter 10
KAYDA

Working extra hours at the casino proved to be good for Kayda's mental health. There was always some drunken idiot to contend with, or a crying patron to gently escort out after they lost their month's earnings in a few hours, or a fight to break up. The busy atmosphere let her forget about the werecat perched on the neighboring building's roof at night, and how tired she was thanks to her overly sensitive hearing waking her up every time she sensed anything moving outside.

She'd filed a break-in report with Felix's contact, Officer Hansen, yesterday. He'd been very sympathetic and had been impressed she'd had the foresight to take pictures of the mess. Kayda had little faith anything would come of it. It certainly hadn't made her feel more secure.

Especially when, today, someone had trailed her on her way to work. Every time she'd turned around, or discreetly checked the reflections in the windows of the buildings she walked beside, she couldn't spot her pursuer. Which meant it was a professional—probably another cat. She prayed Felix was smart and skilled enough not to approach her with his promised new cell phone when there were potentially so many someones who might see it happen. What kind of trouble could he get in if the guard cats informed the Collective that one of their bounty hunters had gone rogue and was undermining the Collective's agenda?

Currently, Kayda stood in her assigned spot near the ATMs at the back of the casino, making sure no one running low on luck tried to pickpocket a hopeful newcomer's recently dispensed cash. This corner rarely got much activity, so all she had to do was look menacing.

Half an hour into her very monotonous two-hour-long post, she noticed a lanky gray-haired man strolling down the wide blue stretch of carpet that, if one followed it, would take one around the outside perimeter of the playing area. Perhaps she was paranoid now, but her gut told her he was headed *for* her, not that he was casually perusing available slot machines until one struck his fancy. What if this was Deever, Felix's "nosy-ass partner"? Taking her menacing expression up a notch, she turned her back on the ATMs and stared the man down.

His casual stroll didn't falter. This didn't bode well. The guy didn't move like a shifter, nor was he built like one. But he *did* move like a man blessed with magic—a kind of swaggering confidence that even the most movie-star-attractive human men couldn't pull off. This was a witch or a sorcerer—and Kayda wasn't sure which was worse right now.

She quickly cataloged as many details as she could about him: mid-forties, pale skin, bright blue eyes. He wore a crisp white button-up tucked into pressed gray slacks. One hand was buried in a pants pocket, with the other by his shoulder, his suit jacket dangling from a finger and draped over his back. His salt-and-pepper hair was cut short and carefully gelled into place, and his beard was neat and trimmed.

He stopped before her. "Hello, Miss Verdan," he said in a

tone as polished as his cuff links. "May I speak with you privately?"

His head came to Kayda's chin. She considered head-butting him and calling for backup. Henri was on the casino floor tonight. He'd come help her if she told him this guy was giving her the creeps.

There was no reason for a physical assault yet, though, other than she didn't trust anyone with shoes that shiny solely on principle—and because he knew her last name. It wasn't necessarily hard to find, but he'd done his research in order to track her down. The fact that he was doing so in a public place made her less sure this guy was connected to the Collective, but maybe that was what they wanted her to think.

Goddess. Was this how Harlow lived her life every day? This shit was exhausting.

"I wish you no ill will," the man said. "I would like to speak about Fletch."

Kayda cocked her head. That was the name Harlow's clients used for her.

The man must have sensed a change in her expression because he inclined his head toward some spot behind her. A few paces away was a short hallway that led to one of the maintenance supply rooms. Without a word, he slipped past her and ducked into it.

She could walk away. She could tell her boss she didn't feel well and hole up in a bathroom for a while.

Sensing eyes on her, she glanced up. Henri stood directly across from her on the opposite end of a long, blue-lined pathway that led to another set of ATMs. His form was recognizable to her in an instant even from this distance, but he was too far away to properly read his facial expression. He cocked his head in question. She shrugged in response.

Seeing him buoyed her confidence. With a slight wave, she

turned on her heel and followed the mysterious man who somehow knew her name. The hallway wasn't more than six feet long, but it banked to the left, providing a small, recessed alcove with the supply room at the end. Anyone walking by or looking into the hallway wouldn't see them.

Her phone trilled in her back pocket. Stopping in front of the mysterious man, she pulled out her phone, where a message from Henri stared up at her.

OK?

Not sure yet.

Kayda glanced behind her, and then up, where a black dome sat in the corner of the ceiling. It was a camera that most casino staff knew didn't work. She scrutinized the well-dressed man. Was he a frequent patron of the casino, a former employee, or was their current location the result of more research?

Curiosity piqued, she pocketed her phone, crossed her arms, and glared down her nose at him. "What's this all about?"

He dropped the suit jacket to the floor, and along with it went his air of moneyed sophistication. "Hoo! I'm sweating right through this fancy shirt. I was so nervous. I've been practicing that swagger all day. Do you think they bought it?" He craned his head to look behind her as if anyone were nearby to see them.

Kayda had no idea which "they" he meant.

"Kayda! Kayda, it's me. Grayson."

It took her mouth a few long seconds to catch up to her brain. "*Grayson?*"

He perked up. "Yeah, man. Uh, lady. Sorry. I, uhh ... you *are* a big one, aren't you?" He poked her bicep and she resisted the urge to bat his hand away like a pesky fly. "Could you, uhh, maybe take the scary down a peg? These aren't my pants and I don't want to have to foot the bill for dry cleaning if I soil them.

Well, they somehow are my pants, I guess. They came with the getup."

She had no clue what he was talking about. But she did as he asked, shaking out her arms and taking a step back. Grayson visibly settled into his usual slouchy posture—though it looked strange when employed by this shiny version of himself. "What are you doing here, Grayson?"

"Have you heard from Fletch?" he asked. "She contacted me a month ago about that sword. You know ... *that* sword. I wanted to buy it, obviously, but then I think it tried to kill me?"

Kayda's brows shot up, remembering how the sword had sliced up her table and hacked her faucet clean in two. "Did you insult it?"

Grayson held his hands up in innocence, as if this were an interrogation. "I would never. Fletch was trying to hold the thing back, and she told me to use my element on her. After I blasted the two of them across the park, I made a run for it. I haven't heard from her since. I'm a little pissed off about it, actually. But I've also been worried sick that the sword hurt her."

"She's okay. Mostly *because* of the sword—though she wouldn't have been in trouble if she hadn't taken it in the first place."

Now that Grayson knew Harlow hadn't been skewered alive, his brows smashed together and his lips pursed. If this were anyone other than an elemental witch, Kayda would have told him to get over it. She didn't know if he was mad that Harlow hadn't been back in contact or if it was because he'd wanted the sword for himself—maybe both. Either way, he was taking this personally, and given the literal steam that was beginning to waft from below the collar of his shirt, Kayda needed him to cool it or *she* needed to get the hell out of the hallway before he flooded it.

Taking a gamble, she said, "She would have happily sold the

sword to you if it hadn't chosen her. It follows her like a very stabby puppy."

Wrong thing to say. His eyes began to glow a faint blue.

Hands up, she said, "She ditched me too!"

The glow dimmed.

Taking a cautious step forward, Kayda whispered, "I didn't know what was going on with her either. I *just* found out she left Luma—and I'm her best friend. Her ex, who she hates, knows more than I do. She kept her most important people in the dark to protect us."

Kayda knew Harlow liked the guy a lot, but mostly because he was an off-the-beaten-path kind of person. What she didn't know was if Grayson had made it onto the small list of people Harlow considered part of her found family. Kayda figured it was better to have him believe the potential lie than have him turn his anger on her. Apparently water elementals, if they were dedicated to their craft enough, could use their magic in such precise ways that they could use the water inside a person's body to drown them internally. Kayda didn't want to find out the hard way that Grayson had excelled in his studies.

"Really?" Grayson relaxed almost instantly. "How much does she hate her ex?"

"She kept a picture of him on her dartboard," Kayda lied.

Grayson sniffed and ran a hand under his nose. "She's like a niece to me. I was really hurt when she left without a word."

"Right there with you." Now that the initial threat had passed, she asked something she should have asked earlier. "Why does your face look wrong? Why do you sound like that?"

There probably was a more tactful way to ask, but Grayson didn't look offended.

"Glamour tonic. Wild, right?"

Kayda had never seen a glamour so thoroughly change a person. Well, perhaps she had and didn't know it. Her brain would explode if she thought about that for too long. Glamours were usually a cosmetic thing that wore off over time. Changing eye and hair color were the most common.

"Where'd you get it?" she asked.

"Zander Welsh," he said. "I went to him to find out if he'd helped Fletch skip town or something. He's the one who sent me to you. Sold me this wicked cool tonic. It's good he doesn't mass-produce stuff like this and sell it to criminal types, eh? You'd never be able to trust your eyes."

Kayda's lip curled. "I've been trying not to think about that."

Grayson's lopsided grin looked very out of place on his false dapper appearance again. The grin stayed in place too long, his cheeks twitching slightly with the effort. He blinked rapidly several times. "Do ... do you know how long I've been here?"

Kayda cocked her head. "Uhh ... ten minutes maybe?"

"Welsh said if anyone in this city knew what happened to Fletch, it'd be you," Grayson said, a bit goofy again, as if he hadn't remembered asking his previous question.

This was a very confusing conversation. Grayson was acting ... odd, but on top of that, what he was saying didn't fully make sense. She knew Welsh had played a role—possibly a large one—in keeping Harlow shielded during her time as a fugitive. If anyone in this city knew what happened to Harlow, it was Welsh himself. Why would he lie to Grayson about that?

"He hates humans. A lot," Grayson said. "Went on some long rant about how people like him and me were Ameliorates—humans on a higher plane of existence or some shit. The guy is a pompous asshole. But he said he heard you and Fletch were close, so you'd know more than he would because he'd never 'sully himself' by even being in the same room with Fletch even if she was Luma's most notorious human right now, making her more interesting than most."

Lies upon lies, Kayda thought. "Sorry. All I know is that she's out of Luma and safe for now."

Grayson nodded absently, fussing with one of his cuff links. He looked like a little boy who'd just found out he was an orphan. Kayda knew Grayson saw Harlow as a path to his own history. He'd been holding the promise of a sizable finder's fee over her head for years, saying that he'd reward her handsomely if she uncovered something that brought him closer to his pirate ancestors. Maybe he was worried that his chance of finding answers had left with Harlow.

"I can let you know if I find out anything." She wasn't sure why she felt a compulsion to comfort him. Maybe because he looked so damn sad.

"I'd appreciate it," he said, livening up a bit. "That makes the trip worth it, even if I don't remember the trip. I have to admit, I'm surprised I'm here."

How was he more confused by this conversation than she was?

He lowered his voice. "Between you and me, I think Welsh might have put a spell on me. I went into his office looking for any information about Fletch, and the next thing I know, I'm walking out disguised and with an intense desire to come see you. Memory's all scrambled up."

Then, all at once, his glamour was gone. He shot up two inches, his hair went from neat and trimmed to long and pulled back in a low ponytail, and his tailored suit turned into a pair of jeans and an oversized T-shirt. It didn't look like the abrupt transformation hurt, but it was clearly disorienting.

His gaze flitted left and right. "What's that sound?" he asked in a tight little voice. "Oooh no. Oh no, oh no."

She couldn't imagine Grayson's hearing was better than her own, but she dialed up the sensitivity and listened. Nothing out of the ordinary reached her ears: the constant trilling bells, cheery chimes, and simulated clink of coins from the slot machines; the tap, tap, tap of people slapping their hands against the touch screens, as if that would increase their chances of winning; the uproar of cheers from the playing tables. Probably craps—those players were always the rowdiest.

"This is a ... casino?" A bead of sweat dripped down his cheek. "Uh-oh. It's all coming back. I-I shouldn't be here." His chest rose and fell too quickly. "How am I going to get out? They can't find me."

Kayda managed a nervous chuckle, not sure how she felt about being in a secluded alcove with an elemental witch who was starting to lose it. "What, are you blacklisted or something?"

Grayson stilled, then nodded slowly as something else dawned on him. "Aw, shit. I remember now. Welsh mentioned that some of his glamours have magic-blockers. They, uhh ... suppress magical signatures. The tonic must have done something to my memory too because I would *not* have chosen to come here." He peeked around Kayda, but presumably saw nothing but the empty hallway. "I used to have a real bad gambling problem. I got mad about losing once and turned a blackjack table into a miniature pool. Then I froze it, lifted the ice, and smashed it into a wall, taking every chip with it. Since all the chips got mixed up—and it's not like there are names on them—there was no way to prove who had what on the table. I pissed off a lot of people—high-roller people. And I might have thrown chunks of ice at the guards as I fled the scene. I also knocked out the dealer."

Kayda blanched. "Did it kill him?"

"Nah. Just concussed."

She groaned, closing her eyes. "Not blacklisted then. Banned for life, with possible lingering criminal charges."

"More than possible ..."

"K-K-Kayda?" Henri somehow stood behind her, assessing the odd scene. "Everything good h-here?"

Before she could reply, a piercing alarm tore through the casino. Kayda flinched. A voice boomed over the loudspeaker. "Grayson Ipram, you have violated your banishment from casino grounds. Werecat guards have been dispatched to this location. You are to turn yourself over immediately to avoid further prosecution. Hiding is futile."

"Aw, *shit*," Grayson moaned, hands pressed to either side of his head.

"Kayda ... what's g-going on? Who is this?"

Grayson clasped his hands on Kayda's elbows. Her shoulders bunched up by her ears. "You gotta help me! If I get a truth serum injection, it's all over for me. I can't get exiled to Antarctica!" He swallowed hard, then tapped the side of his head. "There's stuff in here about Harlow, too. Nothing in here would help her case."

Slot machines clanged. Patrons hollered in triumph. Hundreds of feet padded on carpet. Dice clacked against the sides of felt tables. Cards shuffled. Grayson panted.

A face swam into view. Hands shook her—hard.

"*Kayda*," Henri said, tone surprisingly firm. The cacophony went down a level. "S-snap out of it."

Kayda heaved out a breath, then dialed down her hearing another notch. Henri let her go. Giving her head a shake, she said, "I'm going to kill Welsh."

"Who's Welsh?" Henri asked, the poor guy even more confused than he had been a second ago.

"If you can get me out of here in one piece, I'll deliver you to his doorstep," Grayson said. "And I'll even pay you to punch his lights out."

Kayda liked that idea. With another deeply exhaled breath,

she rounded on Henri. "I don't want you to get caught up in this. I'm fine."

Henri crossed his arms. "T-try again."

Kayda growled. It was not a ladylike sound. Henri was unfazed by that, too. Turning to Grayson, she said, "We'll have a better chance of getting you out through the back than the front. From this hallway, it's a straight shot to the middle of the casino, then if we turn left at the wall that rings the buffet, we'll be at the back entrance. There are four doors. I'm guessing cats will be stationed near there if they aren't there already. We'll be on the second floor of the parking garage. If I can get you out of the casino itself, can you turn on your magic to flush away any cats who might be waiting for us?"

Grayson nodded. "Sure can."

"We're going to play the sick patron card," Kayda said. "I can run faster than you, so I'm carrying your ass out. Gather up your magic while we move so you're ready to hit them once we get outside."

Luckily, Grayson had no qualms about a woman hefting him off the ground like he was an oversized infant. Before Kayda could plead with Henri to distance himself, he dashed away.

"C-clear out!" Henri yelled from the mouth of the hallway. "We got a m-medical emergency!"

"Guess that's our cue," Kayda murmured.

Grayson let his head flop back and went dead weight.

Kayda cast a look down the short hallway. Ahead, a few rubberneckers peered around Henri to see what all the fuss was about. Neon lights flashed, bells dinged, and somewhere in the distance, Kayda could just make out the rhythmic pounding of cat paws.

She broke into a run.

Chapter 11
KAYDA

Kayda barreled out of the hallway with Grayson in her arms. Henri was shouting at people to move out of the way, so Kayda took that as permission to steamroll anyone who didn't heed his warning. She shot past Henri and bolted down the blue walkway. Heads swiveled in her direction, glassy eyes focused on her instead of the too-bright screens of slot machines. She startled one woman so badly, she dropped her cocktail, a spray of small ice cubes scattering across the carpet and onto her shoes. The woman had a few choice words for Kayda, but Kayda couldn't be bothered with that now. She had to get the hells out of here.

She couldn't make out Henri's voice anymore, but the cats had made it onto the casino floor. The thunderous padding of their paws had slowed once they'd come in through the front door. Maybe they were being debriefed by casino staff. Maybe they currently had all their muzzles angled into the air, trying to sniff out the elemental witch.

Just a few more steps and she'd reach the intersection of walkways. Turning right would take her farther into the casino. Left led to the parking garage.

"You gotta be ready in the next fifteen seconds," Kayda whispered to Grayson.

Kayda dialed up the sensitivity on her hearing, trying to drown out the sound of her own pounding feet and her pulse in her ears. The cats milled by the entrance of the casino where most of the elevators were located. Once they had a direction to go in, though, they'd be able to eat up the distance between them and Kayda in a matter of seconds.

She banked around the corner. The four sets of dark glass doors loomed ahead. The slot machines were more spaced out here. The front entrance of the buffet was on this side of the casino, too, and a pair of families stood outside. A gaggle of children—both human and goblin—chased each other.

A faraway voice sounded in her head, her senses stretched to the limit in a place so riotous with noise. *"They ran that way!"*

The rumble of thudding paws sounded a moment later. And a moment after that, a goblin child tottered into her path, then tripped. Kayda leaped over the wailing toddler, but landed wrong and rolled her ankle. Though she kept hold of Grayson, they tumbled sideways into a ticket redemption kiosk. Kayda hit the side of it hip-first, denting the metal, and spilled Grayson to the floor. He hit a bank of chairs on the way down, taking two with him. Kayda narrowly missed landing on top of the elemental. She was back on her feet in an instant.

The glass doors crashed open. The two families outside the restaurant let out shrieks of surprise. The rest of the children joined in on the wailing pouring out of the goblin toddler.

Kayda poked her head out of the narrow aisle of slot machines she and Grayson had fallen into, quickly yanking it back. Four cats: one in human form, two pumas, and a snow leopard. "Shit."

She figured the families would eventually point fingers in

Kayda's and Grayson's direction. They'd assume they were up to something fishy, what with all the running.

Rounding on Grayson, who was a tangle of limbs and chair legs, she bodily yanked him to his feet by the front of his shirt. His eyes were glazed. Had he whacked his head? Still holding onto his shirt, she pulled him toward her.

"Change of plan," she hissed, the sharpness of her tone startling some clarity back into his eyes. "They're at the back doors now, too. We're going to have to head into the heart of the casino and figure out a way around them. Maybe if we stay ahead of them, they won't be able to catch us. I need you to stay in front of me and do whatever I tell you. Hopefully they can't scent you."

Grayson visibly swallowed, but wisely stayed quiet and nodded.

Kayda turned him, then shoved. "Go."

He vaulted over a fallen chair and took off running. She barreled after him.

Cartoon leprechauns, bug-eyed fish, and charging buffalo beckoned at them from the screens of the slot machines as they ran past. They squeezed through the narrow walkway made between chairs lining machines on either side of them. Grayson was slender enough that he could make it through unimpeded as long as he kept his arms tucked close to his body. Kayda hip-checked nearly every chair she passed, jostling players left and right, but was moving too fast to apologize even if she'd wanted to.

"Right!" Kayda shouted.

Grayson turned on a dime and headed down a slightly wider pathway.

They darted past a set of bathrooms and a few banks of video blackjack tables, the dealer a computerized faun woman who waved endlessly at passersby until someone was brave enough to try their luck with the fifty-dollar minimum bet. In a few feet, they'd reach a set of doors that led to the outside. She craned her neck, spotting a pair of coworkers standing guard there. Coworkers who might have been draken like her, so there was an assumed unspoken loyalty—but not with those two. Those two jackholes wouldn't hesitate to rat her out to the were-cats for abetting the escape of a blacklisted criminal solely to see what would happen.

"Right at the dancing donkey machine and head for the lounge!" Kayda called out.

The animated donkey brayed aggressively at Grayson as he ran by, but the elemental didn't break stride. Kayda strained to fine-tune her hearing, trying to sense which cats were headed their way and from which direction.

They pelted toward the C-shaped bar ahead that sat outside a lounge in the middle of the casino. An open doorway sat on either side of the circular lounge; it was a straight shot through and would help them cover more ground. Plus, there were no cameras in the lounge—it was too dimly lit and a thick haze of smoke constantly skimmed the ceiling. She wished she could tell if the cats were running along the outer walkway near the restaurant or if they'd fanned out through the building. Her gut told her it was the latter. The cats would probably catch her and Grayson faster if they'd scattered to every corner of the casino floor, but she told herself that could work in her favor. She could contend with one or two werecats if she had to. A pack of them? Not so much.

"Through the lounge!"

Grayson complied without question, his long ponytail flapping behind him like a banner as he ran.

The lounge was surrounded by frosted glass, decorated by intricately etched playing cards. Snatches of color revealed themselves in the small, clear windows created by the inch-tall spades and diamonds. As they ran inside, music assaulted her already taxed sense of hearing to the point of developing a raging headache at the base of her skull. A small dance floor off to the right was packed with gyrating revelers. Horns and wings and arms flailed in time to the beat of a pop song with a thumping bass Kayda could feel in her chest like a heartbeat. Shouts of alarm sprung up as she and Grayson knocked aside anyone in their way. Grayson tripped and went sprawling toward the floor, but Kayda snatched him by the back of the shirt and got his feet back under him, all without slowing.

They'd almost made it to the opposite open doorway when an ear-splitting roar boomed behind them. Grayson glanced back, the whites of his eyes like glowing embers in the dimly lit lounge—the first time his composure had broken. With his attention diverted, he hadn't seen the trio of men walking into the lounge and careened into them before Kayda could get out a warning. They went down in a heap of limbs and violent cursing.

Kayda came up short in the doorway, arms pinwheeling before she rocked back on her heels. Paws pounded across the glossy wood floor behind her. She whirled around. A snow leopard galloped toward her, mouth agape and canines gleaming. Gaze darting wildly, she shoved a faun out of her chair, grabbed hold of the chair's metal back, and swung with all her might. The faun she'd pushed hit the ground just as the chair connected with the snow leopard's head. The shock of the hit reverberated up Kayda's arms. The cat yowled and was flung sideways, crashing into a table of humans who'd thankfully fled before the cat collided with it. Glass mugs of beer toppled off the table and rained down on the cat.

The chair's metal legs had bent at sharp angles from the impact. Kayda tossed the mangled chair aside.

The cat shook its massive head and stumbled to its paws. It

gave a great shake, like a dog, sending a spray of spilled beer off its fur.

Kayda didn't wait for the cat to get its marbles rearranged. She bolted for the doorway again, where Grayson was on his feet now, thanks to one of the men he'd knocked over. He had Grayson by the collar and was gearing up to clock him in the face. The man was exceedingly drunk if his beet-red face was any indication.

The cat hissed behind her.

Time to go.

In three long strides, she'd made it out of the lounge, had sunk a fist into the drunkard's stomach, and had hefted Grayson over her shoulder like a sack of flour. Then they were off.

"Gonna need you to come up with something to get us out of here, witch!" Kayda shouted, struggling under the strain of Grayson's weight. He was facing backward, so at least he could tell her when the snow leopard made it out of the lounge.

Kayda had one arm wrapped around the back of Grayson's legs, and the other was outstretched like a running back ready to mow down opposing team members. Wisely, everyone stayed out of her way. Unfortunately, the parting of the crowd would likely tip off any nearby cats to her location. This was the main reason she hadn't wanted to go out the front—too many people. It was hard to stay inconspicuous when you were seven feet tall and had a grown man on your shoulder.

"I got an idea!" Grayson said. "Aw, fuck. Here comes the cat."

"Better do it now, witch!"

"Don't rush me!"

"Want me to drop your ass?"

"I'm doing the best I can!"

Kayda sped between two poker tables, grabbed a deck of

cards right out of a dealer's hand, and then tossed them over her head. They rained down like confetti. "Do better!"

Shouts of confusion rang out behind her from the players whose game was interrupted.

Grayson groused to himself about how disagreeable she was. She goaded him more. She'd tried damn hard to keep the temperamental witch calm before, but she needed him at the height of his power now.

Something popped above her and she glanced up briefly as she ran. She looked back down in time to narrowly avoid slamming into a freestanding kiosk of hot dogs. The pop sounded again but she didn't look up. The crowd was thick in this section of the casino. People slowly milled about. These were the fresh-faced ones. Patrons new to the casino. Others who were dazzled by the bright lights and cacophony of bells and chimes. And others still who gaped up at the dangling statues of dragons, their glass bodies jade green, scarlet red, and cobalt blue.

Pop, pop, pop!

Screams erupted behind them. People shouted in confusion. Kayda glanced back as a set of overhead sprinklers came to life. Water sprayed more forcefully than it would have otherwise, Kayda mused, had a ticked-off elemental witch not been magically manipulating the water mains in the ceiling. Screens of the slot machines flickered and died. A few electric sparks flashed to her left. A sprinkler head shot out of the ceiling and to the floor, a torrent of water following.

Pandemonium descended.

"Good job, witch!" Kayda called out, water running down her face.

She dropped Grayson back onto his feet. When the chaotic swell of people streamed for the exit, they slipped into the throng and were carried out with the current.

Once they'd made it off casino grounds unscathed and had

traveled several blocks without being followed, they slowed to a walk, strolling side by side. Adrenaline was ebbing, and her shoulder ached from where she'd had Grayson perched there. The other shoulder was soaked through. She wanted nothing more than to take a hot shower and sleep for a week—mostly because she was certain she no longer had a job after ... *that*. She was going to have to rest up primarily to gain the mental fortitude needed for job hunting.

She was going to kill Welsh.

"Still want to punch Zander Welsh's lights out?" Grayson asked, wringing water out of his ponytail. "Because I'm still willing to pay top dollar for it."

Her exhaustion fled at the sound of his name.

Grayson must have seen the murderous look in her eye because he chuckled. "Follow me."

Chapter 12
HARLOW

In order for Caspian and me to claim our treasure chest prize, Caspian first had to fill out some paperwork. Which was sort of hilarious to me, but we would comply with whatever rules the orc mob boss had in place.

When a few of the showrunners started rounding up winners to escort them to the back, I'd attached myself to Caspian's arm like a barnacle.

We were stopped at the door.

A woman with a sour expression and freaky eyes said, "Winners only."

"My, uh, girlfriend will be no bother," Caspian said.

His tone was so unconvincing that Freaky Eyes cocked a brow at him. Her eyes reminded me of Bonnie's—the young half-faun we'd helped rescue recently. They were goat eyes, with a vertical split down the middle. I guessed she wore glamoured contacts, but even those couldn't hide the fact that her eyes very much didn't belong in a face that human. I couldn't look at her very long.

"Winners only, 89. If you don't abide by the rules, you forfeit the prize."

Her weight shifted slightly from foot to foot. Her stance was as wrong as her eyes. I couldn't tell if she was bowlegged or if her knees didn't bend at an angle that made sense. I guessed her legs had been glamoured, too, to hide hooves. I had to assume her glamour was on the verge of wearing off, or it hadn't been that good to begin with. Perhaps Caspian *hadn't* been exaggerating when discussing Welsh's "exceptional" glamourer skill set.

While Freaky Eyes was small in stature, Domino wouldn't assign someone here who couldn't hold her own. Would getting kicked by a faun hurt as bad as getting kicked by a horse?

"It's okay, pookie," I said, solely to see the way the color drained from Caspian's face. "Hurry back. I'm dying to see what's in the box. When we open it, can we play the same game we played last time? You know, the strip—"

"See you in a bit!" Caspian said, peeling my hand from his arm and marching past Freaky Eyes.

She laughed.

"Can I wait in here for him?"

"Sure," she said, shooting a thumb behind her toward the casual seating area Amaranth Tie had been in during the auction. There was no sign of him now. What if the back area was lined with runes that performed magical mojo on the prize winners?

I plopped down on one of the sofas, the giant bow on my ass poking into my spine. A few of the waitstaff continued to offer refreshments, though the pickings were slim. I waved off an offer of elfin wine but grabbed a sandwich. Unfortunately, one nibble told me it was a cucumber sandwich. I hated cucumber.

A few other patrons lounged in the area too, but they kept to themselves. One of the very tall women I'd noticed earlier—the one with the tail—was in deep conversation with a hipster guy. The guy's eyeline was level with her lightly scaled cleavage, which he seemed to find far more interesting than whatever she was imparting to him, her hands in motion as she spoke. Her companion had won an item earlier in the evening, so presumably she was in the bowels of the hangar with Caspian.

My focus was locked on the triangle-shaped end of her tail that poked out from the hem of her maxi dress. The tail swished between her heels like the long, forked tongue of a snake scenting the air. Would it be rude to ask her what she was? Could she be a demon? *Were* there demons? It was hard to think of demons as anything other than evil beings from the underworld who ate babies or whatever—not posh ladies who attended black-tie auctions.

I had just taken another disappointing bite of my cucumber sandwich when the cushion beside me dipped. My gaze landed on a very wide chest and slowly tracked up to a face belonging to the man Caspian had dubbed the "human boulder."

Aw, hell.

He had an arm propped up on the back of the two-seater sofa, his cheek resting on his fist. "Hey, gorgeous."

How had this oaf snuck up on me?

I swallowed, the cucumber feeling too sharp on the way down. My tongue snaked out to swipe away a crumb on my bottom lip.

The troll's beady eyes tracked it intently. "Where's your little friend?"

"He won something at the auction," I said. "He won it *for* me. He's very considerate like that." I reached up and pressed a finger to the crescent-shaped talisman resting against the flat of my chest. Another jolt of calming magic poured into me, slackening my limbs.

His attention finally left my mouth and returned to my eyes. "You two serious?"

"Would it matter to you either way?"

Oh dear. Why had that come out so ... seductive? I glanced

down at the talisman. Jo and Caspian had said that if the pendant touched skin for too long, it could make a person so calm that it would put them to sleep. I didn't feel drowsy so much as mildly drunk. Had Caspian's magical fixes changed the spellwork?

The troll grinned. "Not really."

I'd almost forgotten I'd asked him anything.

His voice was so deep, I swear the leather couch vibrated softly every time he spoke. My instincts screamed at me to run away, that this was a predator in every sense. But when rabbits ran, beasts gave chase. My body, however, wanted nothing more than to sink into this couch. I wished I was in my pajamas in front of the TV, watching something trashy.

"You from around here?" the troll asked.

It registered belatedly that he'd taken one of my curls in his sausage fingers and was gently twirling it.

Run! my mind said while my body grew more sluggish.

I couldn't outrun him, but the sword could. I tipped my head back, searching the ceiling. I saw no telltale shimmer of it up there, but it had to be close. If given the choice between keeping tabs on me or Caspian, the sword would choose me, wouldn't it?

The rumble of the troll's laugh vibrated the couch. "Did you take a few too many sips of the pretty pink drink?"

I *was* a bit drunk, just not in the way he assumed. So I shrugged absently. That made the troll chuckle, too. If the sword went on a murder spree in here, there was no telling what consequences that could hold for Caspian—trapped as he was with a mob boss. I couldn't let the sword get us or itself into trouble. I would solve this issue myself without alerting the sword. I could do this.

The troll scooted closer to me, only an inch, but it was

enough that the heat of his massive body radiated against my arm. My sixth sense pinged out of control.

Woozily, I reached up toward my neck. I had to get the damn talisman off. It felt like lead weights were tied to my wrists, but I got my sluggish fingers to the back of my neck. They prodded clumsily for the clasp. My curls fell in a sheet on either side of my head as I leaned forward, making the pendant swing away from my skin. A burst of clarity slammed into my mind like a freight train, but then the pendant swung back, bumping against my chest. My thoughts went all woozy and soft. A headache bloomed behind my eyes. I couldn't imagine what this looked like to the troll.

"Dammit," I muttered, more frustrated with my lack of motor skills than anything else.

"Here, love, let me help you," the troll said, and before I could protest, the troll's warm hands were on mine. I fought a shudder.

"I think I almost had ... but then it slipped ..." I rambled, trying to find the clasp again, but my hands fell to my lap uselessly, suddenly too heavy to hold up.

He chuckled, removing his hands from the delicate chain. He turned me so my back faced him. Gathering my hair in one hand, he draped it over my shoulder then ran the back of his fingers along my spine. He murmured something about how soft my skin was, but I couldn't fully process what he said.

Get out of here! my mind screamed while the talisman continued to seep calming magic into my body. His touch wasn't comforting. The warmth of his hand didn't feel good. My survival instincts were at such war with the calming effects of the talisman that I feared I'd pass out before I could get the damn pendant off me.

Determined to remove the traitorous talisman, I got my hands up to my neck, fumbling for the clasp. I found it!

Triumph! Good work, Harlow!

"Dammit, I think it's caught ... ow, my hair," I whined, words slurred.

The troll seemed to remember that he was supposed to be helping and not attempting to seduce me, and his hands met mine. He lacked dexterity and I cringed when a few strands of hair were yanked out of my skull.

"Ow! I need necklace off ... not hair off."

The troll's hands stilled.

I slowly pulled a hand away from my neck to stare dumbfounded at the tuft of light brown hair in my palm. I'd mistakenly instructed my wig to remove itself.

The shock of it gave me a burst of coherence and I quickly reached up to unhook the talisman. The chain slipped off my neck, and the necklace landed in my lap. My head cleared instantly. My sixth sense was practically a five-alarm fire bell, making me light-headed from the sheer volume of it. In one fluid motion, I snatched up the pendant, shoved it and the glamoured hair in a pocket—the dress's single redeeming quality—and sprang to my feet.

The troll grabbed me by the arm and dragged me after him to a spot in front of the stage and away from the patrons waiting for their companions. He crowded me against the stage, the lip of it pressing into the middle of my back. I folded my arms across my chest, my shoulders rounded. My usual first line of defense when cornered—literally or figuratively—was to get snarky and repel the offender by being as prickly as possible. That wouldn't work with this guy. One slam of his fist on top of my head could break my skull open like an overripe melon. Ticking him off would hasten that along and I wanted my brain *inside* my cranium, thank you very much.

"What are you?" he asked.

I craned my neck to look up at him, surprised by the question.

"A witch?" he asked before I could reply. He lifted a hand and I instinctively shied away. His flattened palm was held out toward me—a silent request. I didn't know which thing he wanted. Guessing it was the wig, I pulled the tuft of brown hair out of my pocket. My fingers had brushed against the talisman and shot me a little gift of calm, which was appreciated as it currently felt like my heart was going to explode. The pendant was only great in small doses.

Sending a silent apology to Welsh, I dropped the magicked hair into the troll's palm. He squeezed it between finger and thumb, turning his head this way and that as he examined it. He shifted his focus to me over his fingertips. "I've never seen a glamoured item of this complexity with magic that lasts this long."

I wanted to point out that his own glamour was pretty damn impressive to make him look this "normal" when I knew what trolls looked like in their natural state.

"Potions are all that works for me, and even those have to be topped off every few hours. Most glamours on items last minutes, unless it's something small like contacts." He reexamined the tuft of hair. "Potions are so expensive. A third of my income goes to that. With an item like this, I could pay once for something that lasts."

Maybe if I let him ramble about his particular woes as a beast trying to live a normal life in a mundane-dominated world, he'd leave me alone to work through this crisis by himself.

"Who trained you?" he asked, tone suddenly sharp.

"No one. I'm a full-blooded human, not a witch. I'm just friends with one."

He inclined his head toward the entrance of the hallway being guarded by Freaky Eyes. "That little guy?"

"He's not a witch either."

Which was true. Witches and sorcerers were two wholly different things.

"Is being glamoured here a crime?" I asked, growing irritated with how badly this guy scared me merely by existing. "If so, you'd be just as guilty."

I mentally chastised myself.

He closed his fist around the tuft of hair. His beady black eyes bored holes into mine. "If you're human, as you claim, why would you need glamours? A mundane wig would have been much cheaper." He fingered one of my natural corkscrew curls. "Why would you want to hide your natural assets? Are you hiding from someone, little human? Or were you scared someone here would recognize you?"

The giant oaf was too astute. I knew I could call on the sword, but would the troll or the sword be faster?

"Where'd you say you were from again?" he asked.

"I *didn't* say."

"Are your eyes usually brown?"

I didn't know where he was going with this, but I didn't like it.

Without breaking eye contact, he withdrew a cell phone from his pocket, which looked like a kid's toy in his giant hand. He tapped the screen a couple of times, then pressed the device to his ear. "Hey, Sweeney. You still at the hangar? Something ... interesting came up and I've got a hunch you can identify it."

I had a bad feeling that Sweeney was Amaranth Tie and that the "it" he needed to identify was me.

Chapter 13
HARLOW

The troll didn't exactly drag me toward the hallway being manned by Freaky Eyes, but he wasn't all that gentle about it either.

"Uh-oh. Get yourself into trouble, did you?" Freaky Eyes asked, sounding delighted by my predicament.

"I'm supposed to bring her back to see Sweeney," the troll said.

If I wasn't so distressed about what was going to happen when I was tossed in front of Sweeney, I might have been amused that this giant beast of a man didn't barrel past the much smaller Freaky Eyes, but waited for permission.

She studied me from head to foot, her brows creased. Clearly she couldn't see why a lowly human like myself would need to be escorted to the back like a naughty schoolgirl, but she eventually shrugged and stepped aside.

The troll grabbed me by my upper arm and yanked me forward, then shoved me in front of him. "Straight ahead."

The hallway was stark white with nothing decorating the walls. A few cone-shaped fluorescent lights hung from the ceiling—a ceiling not connected to the wall to my right. My curiosity about what was in the last third of the hangar was finally going to be satiated, but I wasn't excited about it. I silently begged Caspian to be okay.

While I was eyeing the ceiling, I saw it: the shimmer of the sword. I heaved out a relieved breath. I was glad to see it—as it increased my chances of not dying by quite a bit—but it also dawned on me that if the sword had been captured somehow, I wouldn't have known. Resisting the urge to call out, "Hi, friend!" I regarded the stretch of hallway before me. I thought the troll might have been suspicious about my fixation with the rafters, but I needn't have worried.

"I'm disappointed things turned out this way," he rumbled behind me. "But, as much as I would have preferred to watch you walking down *my* hallway, the view is still exquisite."

I rolled my eyes so hard I sprained a muscle.

We soon passed a closed door to my right. Voices emanated from behind it and I fought the urge to call Caspian's name, to pound my fists on the door, to try the doorknob and burst in on the gathering. If I hadn't had the sword sailing along above me, I might have. All I had to do was give the word, and the sword would take the troll out. The giant creep was a walking tank, but the sword had dragon magic and the element of surprise on its side. I couldn't risk Caspian's safety. Not yet, anyway.

Another surge of relief eased my nerves at the realization that the sword could keep an eye on Caspian from up there too. All hail modern architectural design.

The troll didn't say anything more until we reached the end of the long hallway. There was a metal door to the left and another short hallway to the right, which ran along the back of the freestanding room Caspian was in.

"To the right, little one," the troll said.

I silently did as I was told.

"It's unlocked," he said, his voice unnervingly close to my ear. He moved too fast for a man that large.

I pushed the door open to reveal a small, tidy office. Behind the desk, with a pair of reading glasses perched on his nose while he pored over a stack of papers, was Amaranth Tie. Or rather, Sweeney, the Collective sorcerer from Luma. I wasn't sure if it was stranger for him to be here in this hangar, or me.

Sweeney glanced up. His gaze lingered on me for a moment before it slid up and behind me. "And what have you brought me, Cody?"

Cody? Cody was the name of a precocious ten-year-old boy. Or a puppy. I decided Cody's new name was Bruiser.

"You and the boss were talking about a bounty on a human girl from Luma, yeah? Black girl, curly hair, brown eyes. Traveling with a sorcerer and dragon sword?" Bruiser asked.

I clenched my teeth.

"Well, this one glamoured her hair and eyes," Bruiser said. "Thought it was weird for a human to alter her appearance just to attend an auction. Says she's friends with a witch. Her little friend won the bid on the treasure chest—the top item tonight. What kind of human is friends with witches and would know how to get into an auction like this unless she had a connection to one of the hubs? Since you're from Luma too, I figured you might recognize her."

"And you were hoping for at least part of the bounty for turning her in," Sweeney said, though his attention was focused squarely on me.

"Twenty-five g's is a lot of dough," Bruiser said without a shred of guilt.

Currently, I was mostly pissed at myself for assuming the bigger the beast, the dumber he was. Sure, the brute was well informed solely for the sake of financial gain, but he was no dummy.

"Thank you for bringing this to my attention, Cody," Sweeney said. "Do me a favor and keep an eye on the door? I have a few things I need to discuss with our new friend here."

I felt Cody hesitate behind me, probably annoyed that he was being dismissed and that he might get cheated out of the reward money.

"Sure thing, boss," Bruiser said, then let himself out of the room.

A tingle of magic fluttered in the air the moment the door closed. Had Sweeney cast a sound-proofing spell? I looked up. The walls didn't reach the ceiling in this room either, but they were well over twelve feet high, by my estimation.

I waited for Sweeney to reveal if he was friend or foe. He might have been working undercover for the Collective, trying to thwart Domino's operation from the inside. Items with magic levels this high were sketchy in the hands of humans in the hubs —they absolutely shouldn't be in the mundane population. In this case, I would be all for the Collective doing what it could to protect humans from themselves.

Sweeney stared at me for a long beat. "You *are* Harlow Fetcher, aren't you? I saw you watching me instead of the performance on stage. It was a bit odd, but I didn't think much of it. Now I'm starting to think Cody might be right."

"Going to turn me in, then?" I asked, tucking my arms behind my back and resting my hands on the ridiculous bow, if only to hide how they trembled. I would have slipped a hand into a pocket to grab hold of the calming talisman if I trusted it not to lull me into drunkenness.

"That depends," Sweeney said. "Did you get sent here on someone's behalf or are you here of your own volition?"

"Who would send me? The Collective wants me in custody."

He nodded sagely.

He sprang to his feet. "Then your disappearance won't come back to haunt me." He flung something at me.

Instinctively, I hit the ground. The moment my bare knees hit the cement floor, something thunked into the door behind me. Metal clanged against metal. Sweeney gave a short cry of alarm.

I braced myself for Bruiser to come charging into the room at the sound of a commotion, but I heard nothing from out in the hallway. Which probably meant I'd been right about the sound-canceling spell on the room. It wasn't a matter of Sweeney wanting to shield Bruiser from overhearing a conversation about how Sweeney was a spy—it was to keep Bruiser from learning that Sweeney planned to kill me instead of helping Bruiser get paid.

Cautiously, I rose into a squat so I could peer over the top of Sweeney's desk. Sweeney was pinned to the wall, the sword at his throat.

"Thanks, sword," I said, standing to full height. I wobbled on my heels but managed to stay upright.

The sword hummed.

Surveying the floor and Sweeney's desk, I spotted a few pieces of metal with wickedly sharp tips. Whatever Sweeney had thrown at me, the sword had sliced them in two before they'd had a chance to hit me.

Remembering the sound I'd heard, I faced the door. It had a goddamn *throwing star* embedded in the metal. Inching forward, I got as close as I could without touching it. Magic crackled off its spikes. I was grateful my instincts didn't fall into the freeze category, because if I'd tensed up, that star would have hit something vital even if the sword had been quick enough to destroy the other two. If the metal hadn't killed me, the spell it was imbued with most certainly would have. I shuddered. That had been too close.

I glared at our captive. "Really, Sweeney? A throwing star?"

Sweeney didn't reply. The sword's curved edge kissed his Adam's apple—so close that when he swallowed nervously, a small cut appeared on his lightly tanned skin. The cut beaded with blood. I strolled to Sweeney's side of the desk and skimmed the papers littering it. Nothing immediately stuck out to me as particularly nefarious, so I hopped onto his desk, my heels dangling above the floor.

"Since you're a sorcerer, I'm going to need you to fold your hands over your stomach and interlace your fingers," I said.

Sweeney didn't immediately move. Without me needing to say anything, the sword's blade went a pretty shade of pink. I guessed having a hot, razor-sharp sword to your throat was decidedly unpleasant, because suddenly Sweeney complied. The blade cooled.

"Good job, Sweens," I said. "Now, sword, if you even *think* you sense him using those hands of his to cast a spell, you have my permission to slice the offending finger off."

The sword glowed blue.

"Ooh! Blue is its happy color," I said.

Sweeney pursed his lips.

"Sword, you can ease up a smidge on his neck, though, so he doesn't get his throat sliced open when he's answering my questions."

The sword obliged.

"What do you want?" Sweeney ground out.

"I figure you're smuggling confiscated charmed weapons out of Luma and giving them to Domino to sell in his auctions. You, presumably, get a cut of the sale price," I said. "What I want to know is why you're doing it. Isn't it incredibly dangerous for this stuff to be outside the hubs?"

"There are restrictions on what I can say. The Collective

has a hierarchy system. I'm lower on the totem pole, so I don't know everything."

"Like security clearance levels, or restrictions from a Soul NDA?"

"Both."

Great. "Why are you doing it?"

"Mostly for the money," Sweeney said. "But also because life outside the hubs is getting more dangerous. The fae outside need protection."

"Protection from what?"

"The vampire population is growing," Sweeney said. "Ferals are popping up all over the place. They're ferocious. Guns are widely available outside the hubs, but they're rarely enough. I saw someone empty an entire magazine into a feral and it didn't even slow down."

"Oh, I know about ferals," I said. "Even charmed weapons might not be enough depending on the magic level."

Sweeney nodded. "Let's say I got into some trouble with Domino and I'm paying down my debt by bringing him items from Luma."

"Sneaking them out of the Collective's vaults?" I asked, brows raised.

"Something like that." Sweeney paused, his expression pinched. Urgently, he said, "I'm not exactly in the best situation, Harlow. If I skimp on Domino, his people will find me, even if I'm in Luma. If the Collective finds out I've been stealing charmed weapons *and* getting them out of the city? The Antarctic hub is almost a sure bet. Probably for life. Or until hard labor kills me."

"Well, it seems we're in a similar situation, aren't we?" I asked. "I don't want the Collective to know I'm here either. So why don't you let me out of here, I'll grab my friend and our auction win, and then you and I can pretend I was never here."

Sweeney squeezed his folded hands together so hard his knuckles turned white. He was clearly trying to decide if this arrangement was in his best interest, or if he could screw me over to help himself. Was he honestly contemplating betraying me while he had a murder sword to his throat?

"Option B," I said, "is that I lift the sword's murder ban and he decapitates you. It did that to a hybrid a few weeks ago. It's swift and painless. If I ask nicely, it'll go molten when it does it so it instantly cauterizes the wound. Then you won't get too much blood on that nice shirt."

Sweeney swallowed nervously again. "All right. Okay. I just need to think of what to tell Cody."

"I have an idea," I said, and walked into the corner of the room by the door and hunkered down. "Drop the spell on the door and call him in here. Sword? When the door opens, do the same thing you did to Leon at the Ghost Lily."

Sweeney looked decidedly confused, but the sword hummed.

"Now," I said.

The ward on the door fizzled, then dropped. There had been a constant buzzy feeling to the air that I knew had been there solely because now I felt its absence.

"Cody! Cody, help!" Sweeney shouted.

The door slammed open, swinging toward me. I reached out, palms up, to stop the door from crashing into me. I gaped at the throwing star embedded in it. That thing still buzzed, the metal a faint green. So much magic was pouring off it, I was almost positive it had to be a Level 5 spell. I'd have been dead on the spot if it hit me.

As Cody came crashing into the room, the sword sped away from Sweeney, blade first. Cody, it turned out, was a freeze kind of guy. His eyes damn near bugged out of his head as the sword flew at his face. The sword flipped itself at the last second and its hilt collided with his head. Those wide eyes rolled back in his skull and he hit the ground with a thud. Lights out.

I had just slipped out of my hiding place when Sweeney screamed bloody murder. It stunned me so badly that all I could do was watch as the sorcerer's hands whipped into a frenzy and then shot downward. Sweeney was propelled into the air by way of a wind spell. He grinned down at me as he soared straight up and out of sight. In the blast, papers shot off Sweeney's desk and scattered to the floor.

Shouts of confusion, a short-lived hush, and then the pounding footsteps from the room erupted next door. Fucking Sweeney!

"Let's go, sword!" I said, pulling off my heels.

I leaped over Bruiser's unconscious body and hustled into the short hallway. The sword zipped past me and rounded the corner. I followed it, the cement cold on my bare feet.

Freaky Eyes stood vigil at the mouth of the hallway—the marker at the end of my straight shot to freedom. But I didn't know what was happening with Caspian.

"Sword! I'll make a run for the exit. You get Caspian."

The sword, which had been flying straight ahead of me, doubled back to float alongside as I pelted down the hallway. I had to get past the door that led into the room Caspian was in.

"Please," I panted. "I can take … the lady at the end … of the hall. All I have to do is … get out."

Which was a lie. Even if I got past Freaky Eyes, Cody's troll companion was probably nearby. Not to mention the possibility of other trolls loitering out front. I didn't want to deal with my limbs being ripped off, but I couldn't leave Caspian behind either.

The sword was still hesitating when the door in the hallway swung open a few feet in front of me and I skittered to a halt, my chest heaving. The sword shot straight up into the air and out of view. My first panicked thought was that it had abandoned me, but I knew it would have a better perspective from above us. Plus, if whoever came out of that room had a fistful of alloy powder, I'd much prefer it if the sword was out of reach.

A massive beast of a man shoved his way out of the door. He'd had to stoop to clear the doorway, and had done so shoulder first. He frantically looked left and right, then his eyes settled on me. I cautiously took a step back. The nine-foot-tall towering man had to be Domino. Domino wasn't a troll, I reminded myself. This was an orc. He presumably usually glamoured himself when interacting with crowds, but his glamour had faded. He sported green skin, veins pulsed like thick rivulets in his neck and biceps, and a pair of small tusks angled upward over his top lip. The white T-shirt and jeans he wore strained against his muscled body, and his giant green feet were bare. I noted that his big toe was twice the size of my thumb. Weird thing to notice, but I was scared shitless and I fixated on weird details when my brain was on the verge of giving up the ghost out of sheer terror.

The orc fully stepped into the hallway, turning to face me and blocking the view I'd had of Freaky Eyes and my exit. He smiled down at me. I took another step back.

Oh shit. Oh, *holy* shit.

Where was Caspian? Was he okay? Was he bleeding out on the floor in there?

"I've heard some very interesting things about you from my sorcerer, Harlow Fletcher," the orc said, his voice so booming, I felt the vibration of it in the soles of my feet. "Let's have a chat, hmm?"

My eyelid twitched.

The smile slipped off the orc's face. "Let's put it this way. The only chance you have to walk out of here with your friend is if you convince me not to kill you." He held his massive hands out to either side of him. "I'm a fair orc. We can settle on something beneficial to us both. Or you can insult me by ignoring my generous offer of conversation, and I'll destroy your corpse so thoroughly that they won't even be able to identify you by your dental records." The smile was back.

"Con—conversation sounds great," I managed.

"Smart girl." He stepped aside so he could dramatically gesture toward the room. "Ladies first."

On shaky legs, I walked through the door.

Chapter 14
KAYDA

After a telepad ride and a long walk, Grayson stopped outside of a burger place. Kayda looked from the grease-stained door of Al's Burgers, to Grayson, and back to the door.

"What, are you hungry?" she asked.

Grayson grinned. "Yes, but this is also where we can find ... you know who." He dramatically whispered the last three words.

The last time Kayda had interacted with the jackwagon otherwise known as Zander Welsh was four years ago, when Harlow had been at the height of her obsession over locating her mother. Kayda had gone to Welsh, as he was *the* guy—according to Harlow, anyway—to go to when one had questions about missing people. But since he hated humans on principle, he refused to talk to Harlow directly. Information about Camila Fletcher was passed on using Kayda as an intermediary.

Yet, after Harlow had coughed up several months' worth of savings, Welsh had told Kayda that he'd never met nor seen Camila in his life. He was a slimy swindler and now he'd very likely semi-indirectly gotten Kayda fired. The logical part of her knew Welsh would know more about Harlow's current whereabouts than even Felix would, but the more dominant part of her said the only thing she needed to accomplish during this visit was breaking Welsh's face.

Grayson pushed the dingy door open and stepped inside. Grumbling to herself, she followed after him, ducking to clear the doorway. The smell of grease and cooking meat hit Kayda like a slap. The place was warm—humid, almost. She wasn't sure if that was from the dozens of sizzling hamburger patties, the rows of frying bacon, the vats of boiling oil that baskets of fries and onion rings were being dropped into, or the crush of bodies that filled every counter stool and booth. Several more stood clustered in a back corner as they waited for their takeout orders.

The uproarious conversation taking place between four men at a booth by the door stopped when one of the men noticed Kayda. He nudged his seatmate with his elbow. The other pair turned in their seats to see what had shut up their pals. When they made brief eye contact with her, they twisted back in their seat. It was then that she realized they were *all* humans—from the customers to the staff. And not magic-touched humans like Grayson, either. Just plain humans.

Kayda couldn't sense magic in a person, but she could sense other things about them—like the sound of their heartbeat ratcheting up around fae or the magic-touched. Even if a human tried to keep up a brave face when confronted by a being more powerful than them, their instinctual biological reactions couldn't be controlled. As Kayda slowly moved through the small diner after Grayson, despite the bustle of the place, she could hear the sharp intake of breath as she passed, the cautious shuffling of feet away from her as they noticed her looking their way, the nervous swallowing. For a man who notoriously hated humans so much, why was Welsh *here*?

Grayson stopped in front of the rightmost corner of the

counter and drummed his fingers on the small sliver of available worn wood not taken up by a cash register. A woman stood behind the boxy machine, a phone wedged between her ear and shoulder. She eyed Grayson and Kayda as she scribbled an order on the notepad she held. After hanging up, she tore off the order and waved it at the cook who managed to take the slip with one hand while flipping burgers with the other.

The woman strolled back over and slapped a hand on the counter. "Back so soon, witch?" she asked Grayson, though it was Kayda who got the appraising once-over. The woman was more curious than fearful—unfazed, really. Was that because their clientele was usually more diverse than it was currently, or because she was used to non-human types coming through to meet with Welsh?

Grayson cleared his throat. "Is Mr. Brown in?"

Kayda fought to keep the confusion off her face.

"He's in his office. Go on back," she said, then lifted a flap in the counter, swinging it upward on a hinge Kayda hadn't seen.

Grayson led the way past the counter and into the kitchen where a trio of chefs busily prepped ingredients. None of them looked up as she and Grayson walked through. When Grayson reached the mouth of a narrow hallway, he stopped briefly. A dingy break room was straight ahead, and an even dingier bathroom was to the right. This part of the restaurant was somehow more sweltering than the front, crammed as it was with bodies and flames. Kayda didn't mind the heat, but in a place this small and cramped, it felt like the sweaty walls were closing in on her.

Grayson cocked his head. "You all right? You look ... green."

Kayda wasn't sure if he meant that literally in her case. "Fine. Where's this *Mr. Brown?*"

Shrugging, Grayson went left down the hallway. Damp-smelling air blasted the side of her face as she passed the AC unit embedded in the wall. Her arms almost brushed the greasy walls as she walked, and she hunched into herself as she followed Grayson to the closed door at the end of the short hallway.

Before Grayson could knock, the door swung open, revealing a plain man wearing various shades of tan. This wasn't the Welsh she remembered, but the witch was an expert at glamour magic. If her priority wasn't breaking all his bones, she might have been impressed by him. Mr. Brown stepped aside and gestured them into his office with a sweep of a hand.

The tension in Kayda's upper back loosened minutely once they were in Mr. Brown's cooler, less stuffy office. The ceiling felt higher. She turned toward Mr. Brown, who stood near the door with his arms hung loosely by his sides.

He spoke before she could get a word out. "My sources told me the werecats planned on publicly arresting you at the casino soon," Mr. Brown said in a tone as dull as his wardrobe. "Soon as in less than forty-eight hours."

Kayda's mouth snapped shut.

"When Grayson came to me asking about Harlow, I figured I could kill three birds with one stone."

"Which three birds were those?" she asked.

Ticking them off on his fingers, he said, "Testing out this particular tonic on a willing participant, getting you out of your casino job before the Collective did it for you, and finding out if you'd be willing to risk your own hide for someone else."

Grayson jutted his chin at Welsh. "Hey, dude, did you block my memories? There's no way I'd volunteer to go into a casino. Especially not *that* one."

"Sort of," Mr. Brown said, tucking his arms behind his back. "The tonic is laced with very potent magic, but it's also short-lived. I believe the magic temporarily overpowered your own, and since an elemental's magic is so heavily tied to their emotions—which is in turn tied to their memories—it seems it short-circuited your whole system."

Grayson blinked several times, his mouth slightly agape. "Did you *know* that would happen?"

"I did not," Mr. Brown said. "You're rather distractible, though. One minute you're talking about Harlow, then the next you're blathering on about that woman from work you're obsessed with and—"

Grayson laughed nervously and rubbed the back of his neck. "I wouldn't say obsessed ..."

"You said you wished you could wear the skin of one of her friends for a day to find out how Loraine feels about you," Mr. Brown continued, undeterred by the blush that had overtaken Grayson's face, "and then somehow we were back on the topic of Harlow. You bought the tonic, I gently suggested you could find out more about Harlow from her best friend, and then off you went."

Kayda narrowed her eyes at Mr. Brown. At least ten steps between A and B had been left out of that explanation. But she no longer cared if Grayson had ended up at her job thanks to magic, manipulation, or *magical* manipulation.

Mr. Brown swiveled toward Kayda and her brows rose as his bland appearance sloughed off. Suddenly a very attractive guy in his late twenties or early thirties stood before her. This wasn't the Welsh persona she'd dealt with four years ago either, but it was closer than Mr. Brown had been.

"Since the werecats are quite interested in you now," Welsh said, his voice a pleasant rumble, "I'll catch you up to speed. Both of you. Harlow wanted you kept out of this because you're her close friends and she's got an annoying habit of caring about people. Neither one of you is safe now, so I'm no longer honoring her wishes."

Kayda wasn't sure how to feel about any of this.

Grayson rubbed the back of his neck once more. "Can I change my mind?"

Welsh pursed his lips. "You were practically begging for information this morning and now you're backing down because things have gotten a little hairy? I didn't peg you as a coward, Ipram."

Grayson grunted.

"Maybe you shouldn't antagonize the elemental," Kayda said. "Unless you don't mind a tsunami in your office."

Welsh eyed Grayson, who did look a touch furious. In her limited interactions with elementals, they'd been all big personalities and even bigger egos. Grayson had the aura of a person coursing with magic, but he covered it up with his casual personality and attire. He'd resided in Kayda's mind as the eccentric, unassuming client of Harlow's who looked like a hippie stuck in the wrong decade. But Kayda had seen him enraged now, with powerful magic at his beck and call, and she wouldn't underestimate him again.

"All right, all right, Ipram. Calm down," Welsh said, waving a hand dismissively. "Don't be so touchy."

Kayda wasn't sure that would work any better to quiet Grayson's irritation.

In a slightly strained voice, Grayson asked, "What I meant was ... if you tell us everything, couldn't the Collective pull all kinds of information out of our heads and use it against Harlow if we're caught?"

Welsh shrugged. "Don't get caught."

The guy didn't look the same—well, ever—but the abrasive, unfriendly personality was all too familiar. She had options that didn't include dealing with him. She could walk out of here and not look back. She could wait for Felix to get that magicked cell phone for her. She could walk into a precinct and volunteer to get dosed with truth serum. The Collective would know Kayda didn't have any useful information, and then they'd send her on her merry way to get to work on her résumé.

She said as much to Welsh. If he was going to be abrasive and unfriendly, then she would be, too. "Tell me why it's better being in the back of this hole-in-the-wall restaurant with you instead of clearing the air with the Collective."

Welsh chuckled. "You honestly think they'd just scour your brain and then leave you alone forever? When they don't find information about where Harlow is, they'll go deeper to find information they can use against you both. You two are like sisters, right? They'll find details of your friendships, little truths that only you two would know, and then weaponize it. They'll search for Felix and find that you two have been in contact, and that Felix has some idea of where she is, and then they'll haul *him* in. They'll shred his mind until they have what they need to move on to the next person and the next. It's possible that if you volunteer yourself, they won't even let you back out. They could toss you in a cell for aiding and abetting a criminal. They could keep you locked up until they track down Harlow, and then use you as leverage to get her to come back to Luma. Who knows what they'd do to either one of you then? Exile. A sentence in the Antarctic hub. Permanent disposal."

Kayda swallowed.

Grayson let out a low whistle. "*Shit.*" He drew the word out to two syllables.

"And what happens after *you* tell us everything?" Kayda asked.

"Then you two can help me figure out why the Collective is losing their shit over Harlow and that sword," Welsh said. "This is bigger than a dangerous sentient sword. If we can't figure out what it is, there's little chance that Harlow *or* Caspian can return."

Kayda laughed incredulously. "What, you want this ragtag

group to topple the government just so our friends can come home?"

Welsh shrugged. "Yeah. Don't you?"

Rubbing his hands together, Grayson said, "I'm in."

Shoulders slumped, Kayda asked, "Can we at least get a couple of burgers first?"

"Excellent idea," Welsh said. "Make yourself comfortable."

Seeing as the two chairs in the room were made of a flimsy plastic that would crumble beneath her, she opted to stand. Grayson had no problem flopping into one, his long legs stretched out. He folded his hands on his stomach, looking perfectly content.

Strolling for the door, Welsh's appearance morphed from the attractive twenty-something back to the humdrum Mr. Brown.

"One important question," he said flatly, glancing at them over his shoulder. "Want fries with that?"

Chapter 15
KAYDA

A small mound of wadded-up burger wrappers and empty paper french fry trays littered Welsh's coffee table. The dinginess of the restaurant belied the delicious quality of the food. She'd eaten three burgers and would have happily eaten another. Grayson had eaten one, while Welsh had scarfed down five, as well as a bowl of onion rings. The witch had the average physique of a twenty-something human man, not one who could put away that much food in a single sitting. She figured glamourers like him—especially one who used his magic so often—burned a lot of calories.

Kayda had paced while she ate, listening to Welsh's tale about what her best friend had been through during the last month. Felix hadn't been lying when he'd said Harlow had gotten in over her head this time. But now Kayda was asking the same questions Welsh had earlier: if this was solely a case of a human getting her hands on an illegal weapon, why had the Collective gone to these lengths to frame her for the murder of the caracal shifter? Humans got themselves into trouble with magic all the time in Luma, yet Harlow's case had been treated differently. The murderous sentient sword was a definite problem, but even Welsh had said that Caspian Blackthorn had found a way to subdue it with alloy powder. It seemed unlikely that the Collective wouldn't have the same, if not exceedingly better, resources as the rogue sorcerer. They could have incapacitated the sword and Harlow a while ago—so why had they become so engrossed with the murder cover-up instead of getting her off the street, if they truly believed she was such a danger to the city?

All of that was tied, however loosely, with Bliss and fae trafficking. The Collective either knew vampires were complicit in both trades and were ignoring it, or they had a hand in it themselves. The nutty Vampire Hunters of America weren't all that nutty and had been doing what they could to keep the feral vampires out since they could slip through Luma's veil. That last part was one Kayda wished she hadn't known. Seeing Jimmy Nance get pulled through the veil back when she and Harlow had been in high school was bad enough. It had been a very unfortunate thing that had happened to a reckless boy who'd reached into danger on a dare. The idea that those monsters could enter the city willingly was sure to have her hearing dialed to the max when she walked home at night.

Kayda mulled all this over as she paced, polishing off the rest of her fries. She thought of the map tacked to Jo's wall with a dot on it that had been heading north on a highway. She came up short and turned toward Welsh, who sat in one of the plastic chairs beside Grayson. "They're headed for Kensey because they think the sword is connected to that pirate ship, aren't they?"

Grayson perked up out of his greasy-food coma.

"Yes," Welsh said. "My guess is that the sword's history will loop back into whatever is happening under the surface here."

Yesterday, that would have seemed even less likely than

vampires being connected to Bliss, but Kayda didn't question it now. Her head spun with the flood of information.

Welsh snatched a napkin off the table and while he wiped the grease from his fingers, he swung his attention to Grayson. "As for you, do you know for certain that you have pirates in your family tree, or do you just 'feel it in your bones' or some bullshit?"

Color rose up Grayson's neck. "I've done my research. I have documentation."

"Great. Gather that up so I can look at it," Welsh said. "There might be something in there that will help Harlow and Caspian on their hunt."

"And what am I supposed to do?" Kayda asked. "Can I even go back to my apartment?"

"Not without being sure someone isn't following you," Welsh said. "Your superior hearing will serve you well up to a point, but the werecats are highly trained. If they don't want you to know they're tailing you, you won't until they pounce."

Kayda wasn't sure who to be mad at—Harlow, Grayson, Welsh, the Collective, herself, or all of the above.

"How do you feel about getting some training from the Vampire Hunters of America?" Welsh asked.

The suggestion blindsided her. "Training for what, exactly?"

"Pest control," Welsh said. "Seems like you need a place to put your pent-up aggression, and they're always looking for more recruits. Especially after what went down last month."

Welsh had told her that during their rescue mission, the hunters had been tricked into descending into the basement of a vampire nest—which then exploded, killing several hunters.

"The pay isn't terrible. They'd give you a place to stay. They're sort of run like a hostel: you can pay for your room and board by helping with chores. It's not an ideal situation, but it's better than being subjected to the Collective's interrogation methods."

He was somehow looking out for her and completely ruining her life at the same time.

She rubbed at a spot on her temple. This was all ... a lot. She needed time to think.

"Here." Welsh ambled to his desk. Pulling open a drawer, he shuffled through papers until he found a small notepad. Scribbling something on it, he tore it off the pad and then held it out to her.

Kayda cautiously took it. He'd written both a phone and a telepad number.

"You can reach me at either of those," Welsh said. "I check each of them a couple of times a day. I know this is a lot to take in right now. You just met me, and when you got here, you wanted to cave my face in with your fist."

"Still do."

A ghost of a smile. "Fair enough. And while this is all overwhelming, I don't recommend you stroll out of here without a solid plan. The Collective is desperate. Scaring you into coughing up Harlow's location didn't work the way they'd planned. They may hang back and wait for you to fuck up, but someone undoubtedly saw you and Ipram working together to get out of the casino. If the Collective doesn't know about Ipram's connection to Harlow, they're looking into it now. You may have a day or two until they make a move to track you down. It might be hours."

"Aren't you worried about us being here, then?" Kayda asked.

"Eh," Welsh said, shrugging. "If they stormed the restaurant, I've got fail-safes in place. Not to mention I can transmute myself into a rodent and run out of here between their boots before they'd even know I was in here."

Grayson whistled. "I thought glamourers could only turn themselves into other people, and that turning into an animal was the stuff of curses and shifters."

"Transmutation is one of the darker sides of witchcraft and it's not encouraged. Mostly because there's a risk of getting stuck as an animal. That or something in the transmutation going wrong and the witch getting trapped halfway between both forms. It's a very messy, unpleasant death." Welsh folded the last onion ring in half, used it to swipe up a dollop of ketchup, and shoved the whole ring in his mouth.

Kayda's headache hadn't gotten any better. "You think someone could be outside right now waiting for us to come out?"

Welsh shrugged. "There's no way to know. I can get you both outfitted with glamours to get you out of here, but there's a time limit on them. Get where you need to go as fast as you can and then hunker down. I can let Marisol from VHoA know I might have someone interested in joining her team. If you decide you're interested, I'll get you two in contact. If not, that's fine, too. You know how to reach me now. If you call the number and it's disconnected, then either the phone or I were compromised."

As Welsh went back to his desk to fetch a hard-topped black box from a locked bottom drawer, Kayda resumed pacing. The walls were closing in on her. The room was too small, the ceiling too low, the walls too close together.

Welsh had the bedside manner of a doctor used to imparting terrible news on a regular basis: to-the-point, emotionless facts with such an air of nonchalance that the true weight of the shocking things he'd said hadn't impacted her the way they usually would. She suspected once she was no longer in this stifling tiny box of a room and everything he'd told her set in, she'd snap. Maybe she had enough time before the Collective found her to go to the ax-throwing bar and take out her anxiety on a few innocent tree cores.

Welsh said, "After my time with Harlow, I started experimenting with more elaborate glamour tonics. Humans need tonics instead of spells, as their magic-free systems can't latch onto the spell for long. The tonics get into their bloodstream and can get a better foothold. A strong enough shock to the system will knock it loose for anyone, though. So avoid telepads when you're glamoured. Tonics are time-consuming to make, so I've gotten out of practice of making ones with more flair than the usual 'every guy' variety."

"Like Mr. Brown?" Kayda asked.

Welsh nodded. "Exactly. Mousy women and drab men of a certain age are nearly invisible. It doesn't take much for me to add a little variation to the template tonic so I'm not sending out clones. I'm not sure if the variations are even needed. When I'm Mr. Brown, it's rare to even get a nod of acknowledgment from strangers."

Kayda had to admit that if there were a lineup of similarly boring-looking men, she might not immediately be able to pinpoint him.

"Anyway, I've got enough to give you each two. The ones I have here are of human women—a redhead and a brunette. Who wants which?"

"Redhead!" Grayson said, then coughed to cover up his excitement.

Welsh explained how the tonics worked, that each would last for twelve hours, and reiterated that a shock to the system—like a fist fight—would dissolve or severely weaken the glamour. They each stowed their extra tonic in a pocket, then Kayda and Grayson uncapped their vials, clinked their bases together in a toast, and knocked them back.

Kayda shuddered as the tonic slid down her throat. It wasn't the taste so much—which was admittedly foul—but the texture. It was like swallowing a shot of vegetable oil.

At first, nothing happened. She glanced down at herself, wondering if the transformation would take place all at once, or in pieces. Suddenly, Grayson went from a six-foot man with long brown hair to a plump schoolmarm of a woman with a messy red bun atop her head.

"Am I a vixen?" Grayson asked, then immediately frowned. "Goddess! Why do I sound like my Aunt Myrtle?"

Kayda's vantage point suddenly lowered. Now instead of towering over Welsh by at least a foot, she was a foot shorter than him. Average human woman height, she guessed.

She felt ... vulnerable being this small. She'd always been curious if she'd like being the same size as Harlow—as the other mundanes in Luma, and the majority of Earth's population beyond the veils. But Kayda knew instantly that as much as her size could be a nuisance, she didn't like this new body one bit.

"Anyone can be a vixen," Kayda said in a voice that was very young and girlish. "Your appearance, however, suggests you teach the alphabet to kindergartners when you aren't knitting sweaters for your cat."

Grayson rounded on Welsh and jabbed a finger at him. "You didn't specify!"

Welsh shrugged, not hiding his grin. "You didn't ask." He nodded in satisfaction. "I haven't used this batch yet. I like it. The more variety I have on hand, the better."

Grayson, decidedly grumpy even after grabbing hold of his ample bosom with both hands, told them he had a place to go for the night and that he would check in once he gathered his pirate ancestor documentation. He tottered out the door, which he slammed behind him.

"Do *you* have somewhere to go?" Welsh asked.

Kayda found it very disturbing that she had to look up at him. "Yeah, I have a friend I can stay with."

That was a flat-out lie, but she needed to get out of this stuffy office. The fresh air would help her think. Then she could decide for herself if Welsh's doom-and-gloom outlook on her options made sense, or if they were the ravings of a recluse with bad people skills and a penchant for conspiracy theories.

Her gut told her it was the former even if her heart wanted it to be the latter.

"Good. Well, contact me if you need anything. I don't mind assisting you. I grew to only mildly hate Harlow."

"That's saying something coming from you," Kayda said in her false, sing-songy voice. Her mind's voice remained her own, at least.

"Well, you've got a solid half a day before you need another dose. I'll make you some more tonight now that I know this batch is effective."

Nodding, Kayda thanked him, then left the same way Grayson had. She refrained from slamming the door.

As she made her way down the hallway, through the kitchen, and out into the bustling restaurant, Kayda marveled at how extensive Welsh's skills were. Witches spent years learning how to master *one* glamour potion, and Welsh made them as if they were a dime a dozen. She'd never heard of glamoured items as complicated and long-lasting as Welsh's. He could make a killing selling his tonics if he wanted. She imagined how dangerous the werecats could be if they could turn into anyone they wanted. How criminals of all stripes could get away with countless misdeeds with Welsh on their payroll. And yet, from what Kayda knew of him, he used his gifts to help down-on-their-luck fae get out of Luma and/or develop new identities if they needed to start over.

Those who knew of him knew him as someone who hated

humans as a rule, and yet he'd gone out of his way to help Harlow. She didn't think he'd done that solely because of his close friendship with Caspian. Welsh considered Harlow a friend, too, regardless of whether he'd admit it.

Kayda pushed her way out of the sweltering restaurant and into the much cooler evening, the tightness in her upper body easing. Meandering down the sidewalk, one question kept repeating in her head: now what?

Chapter 16
HARLOW

I crept into the room, half expecting to find the walls coated in Caspian's blood. It was a wide space, one side dotted with couches, oversized pillows on the floor, and a couple of papasan chairs. Trays of snacks were heaped on end tables and a round coffee table stood on a white fur rug. Not a speck of blood anywhere. It was cozy, almost.

On the other side of the room—which shared a wall with Sweeney's office—were metal racks lined with charmed items. Weapons and shields hung from any wall space not covered by racks. In front of the racks were two long tables pressed end to end and covered in smaller trinkets. The treasure chest we'd won was on the floor just beyond the tables, and Caspian—still looking like a grunge rocker—stood behind it. My knees almost gave out in sheer relief. I vowed not to look up in search of the sword. I couldn't give it away.

Caspian might have been alive, but his situation was as precarious as mine. Sweeney was poised a foot away, hands out with his fingers cocked at odd angles. He had a spell primed and ready to go—all he needed was the authorization from his boss to unleash it. Caspian looked the picture of calm, but even from this distance, I saw how the crease between his brows had smoothed out when he saw me.

"*Hi*," I mouthed.

He offered me a small, pained smile in response.

There didn't seem to be any other auction winners in the room. Domino had saved Caspian for last, as he'd purchased the big-ticket item of the evening. Had it been true that they hadn't been able to sell the treasure chest before tonight because the bids hadn't hit the reserve? Or did Domino cart the chest to each auction location as a lure, promising its mysterious contents to one lucky buyer, and then once he received his money, "destroyed" their corpse so the chest stayed in his possession to entice the next batch of buyers? Given his weapon wall, Domino was a collector of the rare and dangerous. So why had he never opened it? Or had *that* been the lie? It seemed impossible that he'd be uninterested in what riches lay beneath its metal-banded lid.

I inched farther into the room, turning when I was halfway between the seating area and the wall of charmed goods, Caspian at my back. I was by no means shielding him from Domino and his very large goons, especially not with Sweeney behind me as well, but it was the only act of defiance I could muster up.

Domino strode over, stopping a few feet away with his arms folded over his massive chest. The veins in his neck pulsed in time with his heartbeat. I had no idea if that was normal for an orc, or if this guy was barely keeping his murderous urges in check.

As much as I wanted to ask what he wanted to have a conversation about, I didn't speak. He probably liked seeing me squirm, which I was doing with relish internally. But I wouldn't crack on the outside. I might have been a tiny, magic-less human, but I still had my dignity, dammit.

It was Domino who broke the silence first, and I mentally cheered. "So, *Fletch*, my sorcerer here says you're quite infamous in Luma. Is that true?"

"Yes," I said, but my voice trembled. I cleared my throat. "Yes. They said I killed four shifters."

One of his minions whistled, impressed.

"With the aid of a dragon sword, correct?" Domino asked.

Was it better to lie? Eh, probably not. Sweeney had already seen the sword. I needed the sword's help, but I feared Domino had something on hand that could subdue it. The guilt would be unbearable if I lost the sword to this behemoth.

A shimmer in my peripheral vision decided for me. An intake of breath told me Caspian had seen it, too. I mentally cursed the sword. Life would be so much easier if we could talk telepathically. Though it was possible that the sword wasn't an eloquent thinker, and that it maintained an endless mantra of *Me want murder, me want murder!*

Domino and his pack of five troll guards watched in fascination as the shimmer coalesced into ... me. An invisible wind whipped my curls about my face, a sliver of stomach and knee showed through slices in my shirt and jeans, and I held a sword aloft.

Sighing, I gestured to myself. "The sword didn't need my help to kill them. It just borrowed my form to do it."

Domino was temporarily dumbfounded, which was good, because it meant he didn't have a stockpile of sentient weapons of his own. The existence of this one was beyond anything he'd seen before. My sword was still unique. Phew.

"Can you ... control it?" he asked.

I tottered my hand back and forth in the air. "I can make suggestions, but the sword does what it wants. Right?" I asked, eyeing my apocalyptic self.

The sword dropped straight down and tapped its hilt once on the cement floor. My image dissolved.

"That means yes."

"Tell it to do something," Domino said.

"Uhh ... sword, do a flip."

In the inverted position, it flew toward me and stopped a couple of inches from my nose. The blade glowed red and vibrated, as if saying, *"I'm not a dog who will do tricks on command."*

"You have a serious ego problem," I whisper-hissed at it. "Remember the whole 'destroying my corpse' thing? I thought you liked me being *not* dead. A few flips doesn't seem like too much to ask for in the face of potential annihilation."

It glowed brighter. I squinted. The sword shot away from me, performing a series of flips in demonstration of how obedient it was.

Domino smiled wide as he gazed at the sword. "Excellent. I'll take it."

The sword halted in midair, then angled its blade in the general direction of Domino's heart.

The orc would not be deterred. "Leave it here and you and your friend may leave."

The blade went cherry red in an instant, and it vibrated so quickly, the air around it pulsed. A troll behind the orc visibly swallowed. Another took an involuntary step back. The sword harpooned toward the seating area, slicing a papasan chair clean in half. Stuffing spilled out of the severed cushion. The base fell open like the halves of a pistachio shell. The sword turned on a dime and hurtled toward one of the goons.

The troll let out a high-pitched scream and bolted for the door. The sword whipped around the troll. The troll finally had the good sense to stop moving. Half his pants hit the floor; the sword had sliced the troll's slacks into thigh-high shorts.

The sword glided back to the same spot it had been in less than a minute ago—blade re-aimed at Domino's heart, the blade cherry red. I wanted to admonish the sword for once again letting anger power it instead of self-preservation, but it wasn't as if it would have listened to me anyway.

Domino might have been greedy, but he was no idiot; he held his hands up, seeing the threat for what it was. "Call it off," he said, eyes narrowed.

"Stand down, sword."

Immediately, it flipped itself into the inverted position and floated back by my side. By the time it had reached me, the blade was the color of cool steel.

"The sword imprinted on me. It's not for sale," I said, grateful my voice didn't shake that time.

Domino chuckled. "Not as timid when you have it by your side, I see. Would it give itself up to protect you, I wonder? Does it feel the same loyalty to your friend as it does to you?"

Before I could think of a reply, the sword beelined for the tables to my right. The sword sheared through four legs of the tables lined with charmed items. The cuts were made at a steep angle, and a moment after it returned to my side, the tables toppled, sending small weapons, talismans, and jewelry to the ground in a raucous crash.

An eyelid twitched. A ruby-colored pendant on the end of a chain slid across the cement floor toward me. I felt the flicker of its magic and stepped back, not wanting it to touch even one bare toe.

"Not only did a dragon sword choose you, but you can sense magic as well, little human?" Domino asked. "You are a curiosity, aren't you? No wonder the Collective wants you back."

"Is that the plan then? Shipping me back so you can claim the reward money? Cody was sure hell-bent on it."

A few of the trolls laughed, though I wasn't sure which part they'd found funny.

Domino waved a dismissive hand. "What would I need with a measly twenty-five thousand when I can make twice that in an evening such as this? I'm sure you're quite keen on eventually returning to your prison city—presumably *not* as a fugitive—but many fae *choose* not to live in hubs. I tried it. Wasn't for me."

"They kicked you out, didn't they?"

Domino's lip curled, angling one of his tusks closer to a wide nostril. "They said I didn't play nice with others."

Shocker.

"For those of us who want to live on the outside, we need protection," Domino said. "That's the service I provide. Security for fae and the humans who are aware of faekind."

Sweeney had said the same.

I sized up Domino, from giant foot to giant head. "I would think fae and humans would need protection from *you*."

"Oh, many do. But haven't you wondered why the Collective is gathering up all these supposedly illegal weapons? If you believe they're doing it to keep the streets of hubs like Luma safe, you're a fool," Domino said. "They're preparing for something. Signs of it are already evident on the outside."

I'd seen the feral vampires in action—seen how vicious they could be—but surely Domino and his goons could hold their own against them. Unless the problem was even worse than Marisol and her group at the Luma chapter of the Vampire Hunters of America knew.

"How bad is the vamp problem out here?" I asked.

Domino's posture straightened slightly at the question, seemingly pleased that I already knew what threat he spoke of. "There's a small draken enclave about half an hour from here. Remote location. One of my contacts lived in that community. About a week ago, he went off the radar. Didn't answer my calls or texts. His wife contacted me yesterday—said she'd just gotten back from a girls' trip. The entire enclave had been slaughtered. The veil circling their community was still up, though. The draken were torn apart as if they'd been nothing more than prey animals. We've been hearing for a while that the all-protecting, tried-and-true veil magic isn't keeping the fuckers out anymore. Not even the Collective's trained cats could do that much destruction without losing any of their own. But a pack of ferals could."

I swallowed, thinking of Kayda, of Luma's veils that were already failing at keeping the ferals out.

"Weapons like that sword can be taken apart and used to make others," Domino said, jabbing a finger in the sword's direction. "Fighting the ferals would be a hell of a lot easier if weapons could be sent into the battle on their own. A feral can't tear out an opponent's throat if it doesn't have one."

It was a bad day when an orc mob boss was making sense.

The sword's blade blazed red in protest. Of which part? I wasn't sure. Maybe all of it.

"How did you come in possession of it?" Domino asked.

I told him the story of how I'd pilfered it from Haskins's basement, and the theory that it had come from the now infamous sunken pirate ship.

Domino's eyes went wide and he tapped the end of one of his curled tusks. "The sword was part of a weapons *shipment?*"

"Yes. We don't know how many of the weapons ended up in Luma, but the rest of the shipment was destined for Nevada."

"So there *are* others ..." Domino mused. "Is that why you're interested in the treasure chest? To find other blades such as this?"

Eh, close enough. "Yes."

"It was fortuitous you wound up at one of my auctions, then."

I chewed on my bottom lip, waiting for the other shoe to drop. He'd been rather agreeable so far, other than the corpse destruction threats, anyway.

"I will allow you, your friend, and that exquisite sword to leave here on one condition," Domino said.

Here we go ...

"If you find another sentient weapon, you turn it over to me. I can appreciate that this one has selected you as its own, as it will likely aid you in finding others. Your resources led you here, after all."

I couldn't say I liked the idea of this guy having a sentient weapon to do his bidding. The idea of him breaking down a weapon like the sword to use it as parts for others made me queasy. I knew it wouldn't be like killing an animal or person, but the sword *was* alive. There was something akin to a soul residing behind its blade, I was sure of it.

"Sweeney," Domino said, apparently allowing me to mull over his offer a while longer. "Let the boy go. Come here."

Caspian sidled up to me a few seconds later, while Sweeney kept walking until he reached the orc. I glanced over at Caspian. "You okay?"

His gaze roved my face. "Yeah. You?"

I nodded, silently asking him if he believed we were going to survive this encounter. He offered me a small shrug in reply.

Sweeney wrung his hands. "How can I be of service, my lord?"

Good grief. *My lord?* How much trouble had Sweeney gotten himself into?

"I need you to perform a binding spell on them both," Domino said, eyeing me over the top of Sweeney's head.

Caspian stiffened next to me, cursing under his breath.

"What?" I whispered.

"A binding spell," Domino said, answering before Caspian

could, "is an oath you make to me. By donating your blood to Sweeney here, you're permitting him to use that blood in what will essentially work as a tracking device. I will be able to tap into that spell whenever I want to pinpoint your exact location. If I find out you've discovered one of these weapons and decided not to bring it to me, I will know. Once I know, I will use that spell to locate you. And then I'll hunt you down."

I swallowed.

Caspian leaned toward my ear. "Remember how Rory found you at the factory? Welsh used a tracking spell using the blood you'd given him for the glamours he made for you. Welsh was able to find your location in a matter of hours. A spell like this made by a Collective sorcerer would be even stronger."

I hated the idea of the orc having access to my movements, but I wasn't sure we had much choice.

"Like I said: I'm a fair orc. As long as you keep up your end of the bargain, your organs stay in your body," Domino said cheerfully. "What do you say?"

I looked at Caspian, brows hiked in question. After a beat, he nodded once.

Oof. We were going to make a deal with a mob boss. Fantastic.

"We agree."

The orc clapped his hands once—a sharp, booming sound. "Excellent. Sweeney, get to work."

Ten minutes later, Sweeney had what he needed and retreated to his office to complete the necessary spellwork. I had a feeling it was less the mixing of ingredients with a mortar and pestle like Welsh had done, and more like drawing intricate runes with our blood. I didn't want the details, honestly.

Caspian and I waited on a couch for a half hour, the sword hovering in front of us and jabbing itself menacingly at any of the trolls who tried to get closer for a better look. Domino spent the time making several phone calls in a back corner. I didn't want details of that either.

Caspian and I didn't speak. I'd run out of words. We sat with our sides flush though, his warmth keeping me steady—though my leg bounced.

Suddenly, Caspian and I winced, lifting our right arms. Well, Caspian winced, and I bit down on my tongue to stifle a scream. It felt like a branding iron had been pressed to the inside of my right wrist. I grabbed hold of my own arm, squeezing my thumb against my forearm as if that would stave off the pain. The throb faded to nothing a few seconds later, leaving behind a trio of runes in what looked like dark ink across my skin. An identical tattoo stained Caspian's wrist.

Domino took that as his cue to saunter over, his phone stowed away. He stood on the other side of the coffee table in front of us, covered in an untouched tray of fruit and sweating cheeses. The chairs next to him looked like something out of a child's dollhouse when compared to his massive size. My brain had tried to make me forget that the man was the size of a small house.

"It was lovely to meet you both," he said pleasantly. "We're mostly squared away here. We just have one more thing to take care of."

What else could this beast possibly want?

Domino rounded on Caspian, smiling broadly. Fluorescent light winked off his shiny tusks. "You still owe me thirteen thousand dollars. Will that be cash or credit?"

Chapter 17
KAYDA

Kayda stepped out of Al's Burgers as if she were venturing into a foreign nation. It would probably take her twelve hours to get used to this new body, and then she'd be back in her old one.

Her back pocket buzzed and she nearly jumped out of her skin.

"Move it or lose it," someone barked and she jumped to the side, bumping into a brick wall.

She swallowed hard as a draken man stalked past her. He wore a sharp business suit and an even sharper expression. He growled as he passed, then resumed his phone conversation about a merger or something else equally "businessy" sounding. First time in her life anyone looked at her like that. Even her father had maintained a mild level of fear.

More alarming than the interaction, though, was that she hadn't heard him coming. Even now, as she tried to adjust the dials on her hearing to better hear the business draken's conversation—she couldn't. The glamour, as it had with Grayson, had negated her innate abilities. This kept getting worse.

Though she supposed if anyone had come looking for a draken with superior speed, hearing, and strength, they would never suspect that this cowering human could be one and the same.

Her phone vibrated in her pocket again. She flinched less that time, but not by much. Pulling her phone out, she saw the screen was filled with text notifications—all from the same person. Henri. Shit. He'd helped provide cover for her and Grayson, and then she'd taken off on him.

Her thumb hovered over one of the texts, hesitant to swipe it open and reply. She'd gotten him into too much trouble already. She pushed a button on the side of the phone to turn off the screen and then shoved it back into her pocket.

Marching down the sidewalk, she tried to figure out where she could go. Could she pretend to be her own neighbor who was popping in to check on "Kayda's" plants, because "Kayda" had left on a trip? *Oh, to where? The Honolulu hub for some much-needed time on the beach. When will she be back? In a month, if not longer ...*

She was starting to crack. Going batshit was Harlow's bag, not hers.

Kayda grasped a fistful of her shirt above her heart. Goddess! What if the human glamour also came with human emotions and a complete lost grasp on sanity?

Her phone rang in her pocket this time and she shrieked.

A woman bustling past with bags of groceries was so startled by the sound that she dropped one of them. "The hells is wrong with you!"

Apples, oranges, and a head of lettuce tumbled out of the bag. A bright green apple rolled across the sidewalk, over the curb, and bounced into the street.

Kayda whispered an apology and speed-walked down the sidewalk. She yanked her ringing phone out of her pocket and considered throwing it into oncoming traffic. She needed to take her growing panic and dismay out on someone, but since she was as puny and defenseless as a hamster, her phone was the only viable target.

Henri's smiling, bespectacled face filled her screen. Her stomach gave a happy lurch at the sight. Then she furiously shook her phone. "*Not now, Henri!*" she hissed at his face, hitting the "end" button.

Before she could stow it inside her pocket, he called *again*. The worst part was, she couldn't answer it and tell him to leave her alone, not when she sounded like a giggly mouse. She hit "end."

Someone forcibly grabbed her by the elbow and hauled her into a narrow alley that ran between two apartment buildings. His frame was so wide, his shoulders nearly brushed the walls. She shrunk away from him, all her usual bravado having fled the scene with her natural form. Kayda hated feeling like this. *Hated* it.

"Who are you? Why do you have Kayda's phone? Are you following me?"

Was *she* following *him*? Just her luck to catch the attention of a total nutter this fast. Then she froze. She knew that voice. Her gaze traveled up into Henri's face.

"Goddess. How did you find me?" she groaned, though it sounded mildly chipper in this silly new voice. "Wait. You asked if I followed you? Why would I follow *you* here?"

He narrowed his eyes. "Who. Are. You?"

This series of volleyed questions was giving her a headache.

She could lie. Henri might have been a bouncer and was currently more hostile than she'd ever seen him, but she knew he wouldn't lay a hand on her. He could, however, be very persistent.

Sighing, she said, "It's me. Kayda."

Settling further into his intimidating pose, he jutted his chin at her. "Prove it."

"Your little sister's name is Liberty, but she prefers Libby. Your locker is number twenty-three. You have a peanut butter and banana sandwich every day for lunch even though I've told you a million times that it's criminal—not only because it's gross, but because it's boring."

Henri's mouth dropped open. "Kayda? That's really you?" The anger fled in an instant. He poked a large finger into her cheek.

"Hey!" she squeaked, swatting his hand away.

"This must have cost a fortune! It's so ... complete. Have you seen it? Your new face, I mean?"

She glanced down at herself. She wore the same clothes she'd been in before, just smaller. Grayson's glamour had come with a floral dress. She had no idea how in the hells *that* worked. "No. Is it bad?"

"Not ... bad. You look eighteen. A very *innocent* eighteen." Henri chuckled. "Did you purposefully choose something that was the exact opposite of you?"

She hadn't, but Welsh probably had. Feeling a touch offended, she propped her fists on her hips. "You don't think I'm innocent?"

Henri beamed. "This is amazing. You must hate this."

Throwing her head back, she moaned pitifully. "This is the worst thing that's ever happened to me."

"What about that time the drunk faun cornered you at your post and read you his love poems?"

Kayda grunted. "Yeah, that was pretty bad."

"Or the time that witch got mad that she'd lost her month's rent at blackjack and then put a hex on the dealer and he projectile vomited over the side of the table just as you walked by?"

She put a fist to her mouth, her stomach churning at the memory.

"Or the time—"

"All right, all right!"

Still grinning, he pushed his glasses up his nose. "Wanna start at the beginning and tell me how you got from point A to B?"

Craning her neck, she tried to look past Henri's hulking body in a futile attempt to determine if anyone might overhear them. If Henri had managed to follow her here, who knew who else might have.

Her brow creased. She'd never been to Henri's place before, but she could have sworn he lived close to the casino. "Why did you ask if I followed you?"

"Oh. I live a few blocks from here. Moved recently." He offered a quick, tight smile that was far more strained than it had been earlier. "I've been calling you and texting you since I started walking home from the telepad station. The last few times, every time I sent a text, I'd hear it ping from up the street. So I followed the sound."

As he talked, she examined the sides of the two buildings and the sliver of sky beyond their roofs. She half-expected to see the glowing eyes of a werecat watching her from up there.

"Come back to my place."

Kayda's attention snapped back to his face. "What?"

"You're too nervous to talk about it out here," Henri said. "My place is warded—both against intruders and eavesdroppers."

Kayda cocked a brow in question.

Rubbing the back of his neck, Henri said, "I had a stalker. We went out a couple of times, but it wasn't working, so I broke things off. She started following me around and kept saying I was her fated mate. Which, you know, isn't even a thing. Not for draken, anyway. I kept telling her I wasn't interested. She broke into my old apartment—the one by the casino—and was threatening to hurt herself if I didn't take her back. Had to call the cops. It was a whole thing. She's getting help now, but I never felt comfortable in that place again, so I moved."

"And warded it to kingdom come just in case?"

Even in the low light of the alley, Kayda could tell he'd gone a little blue in the cheeks while telling her that. Hopefully he wasn't embarrassed. But now she'd feel terrible if she sent him packing without an explanation.

Sagging, she said, "Lead the way."

Taking a couple of steps back, he asked, "What should I call you when you look like this?"

She followed him as he tapped a finger to his bottom lip. "Kay?"

"Nope. Too close to the real thing." He inspected her face, and while it wasn't her actual face, she flushed under his focused attention. "Aww! You're almost pink now. What's that cutesy old animated show ... Strawberry Shortcake! 'Shortcake' fits your size, too."

He was enjoying this entirely too much.

"When I'm back to normal, you know I'll be forced to kill you, right?"

Chuckling, he said, "I've got it. I'll call you Angel because you look like a precious little cherub."

Yep, she'd have to murder him. There was no other option.

After successfully backing out of the alley and onto the sidewalk, he gestured for her to continue walking in the same direction she'd been aimlessly wandering before he'd found her. "Right this way, Angel."

She did her best to suppress a smile as she fell into step beside him.

Henri was seated on his couch, watching Kayda as she paced between his TV and coffee table. She hadn't stopped talking for the last ten minutes, which was decidedly out of character for her—especially in front of Henri—but once she started, she couldn't seem to stop. She'd glanced over at him twice to get a sense of his reaction to her increasingly wild tale—first when she mentioned that her apartment had been broken into, and second when she described braining the snow leopard with a chair. He'd looked dismayed both times, so she kept her eyes rooted to the floor instead.

When she finally concluded her saga, she was exhausted. Partly because these tiny human legs felt like they weighed a million pounds. It was like wearing a suit of armor—in water. It wasn't as if gravity worked differently on her natural form, but perhaps her abilities had been reacting against gravity all this time without her being aware of it. Or she was damn tired, and unloading it all on sympathetic ears had settled her.

Goddess, she missed Harlow.

"When I said point A to point B, I should have said Z," Henri finally said. "So first things first, we need to get your things out of your apartment. You up for that?"

She hesitated. Having personal items was all well and good, but then what?

"You're staying here until we get something else figured out," he said, seemingly reading her mind. She started to protest, but he cut her off. "If you don't stay here, where would you go? You already said you don't want to pull anyone else into this to keep them from getting into trouble with the werecats, too— which, in Harlow's defense ..."

"You're not making a very good case for me *not* stabbing you when I have my strength back."

"It's impossible to take you seriously when you're that cute. And I mean like stuffed-bear cute. When you're you, you're also c-cute. But in a d-d-different way."

It dawned on her then that this was the first time his stutter had made an appearance since he'd yanked her into the alley.

He coughed. "Anyway ... it'll take a while before anyone in casino management figures out it was you who helped Grayson escape. It'll take the werecats time to piece together the connection between you, Harlow, and Grayson, too. I got a text from Boris that said he and Julianne saw you running out of the casino carrying some guy like a baby, and since they hate the cats like it's their job, they redirected them to a side entrance saying they saw you go that way. It's possible Grayson's water trick also obscured the cameras in the front, and if they watch the footage, they might not be able to see it was you."

Kayda didn't want to rely on speculation, but it made her feel a little better nonetheless.

"So ... do you have a better place to stay?" Henri asked. "Remember, I warded this place to keep people out. I know what it's like to have your place broken into. It's a violation and it sucks."

She sighed.

"Thought so. After we get some of your stuff, you can have my room. Don't argue. I'll take the couch," he said, holding up a hand to quiet yet another one of her attempted protests.

"Thanks, Henri."

"Not a problem."

The trip to Kayda's apartment was uneventful other than the fact that she learned Henri owned a three-wheeled motorcycle—complete with a sidecar that was apparently for Libby because their mom wouldn't let Libby on the bike otherwise. The cycle ran on fae essence and was as quiet as a mouse. Kayda wanted to ride it when she was back to herself, so she could truly appreciate it. In her tiny human form, she clung to Henri's middle like a barnacle, convinced she was going to be flung off the back.

Henri checked out the interior of her apartment for any signs of a further disturbance. To Kayda's useless human ears, all she could make out was the too-loud rumble of her ice maker. Once he'd declared the place was werecat-free and had closed all her curtains, Kayda filled two bags with her clothes. She stuffed her largest duffel bag to the gills, knowing Henri would volunteer to carry it downstairs for her.

The duffel was stuffed into the sidecar, held in place by the seatbelt. Henri's mom would be happy to know the sidecar appeared perfectly safe for passengers.

While Kayda showered in a bathroom that smelled so much like Henri it made her head spin, Henri had busied himself with getting his bedroom ready for her. He'd stripped off the sheets and replaced them with new ones. He cleaned all his dirty laundry off the floor; she'd stumbled over a wadded-up pair of jeans on her way into the bathroom. He'd even lit a candle on the bedside table. Kayda figured he wasn't being romantic so much as doing what he could to alleviate the slightly musky scent of bachelor pad. Kayda had sort of liked the musk, if she was honest.

Standing on his bath mat with a towel wrapped around herself, she stared in wonder at the dirty clothes heaped on the floor that she'd shucked off before her shower. They'd been small when she'd removed them, yet now they appeared to be her normal size. Bizarre. She dressed in a fresh pair of sweats and a T-shirt that were wildly too big on her at the moment.

She hoisted up her pant legs and padded out into the living room where she found Henri on the couch with a controller in his hands, giant headphones over his ears, and his tongue caught between his teeth.

He glanced over for a brief minute and laughed. "You look like you're wearing your mom's clothes!" he shouted.

She walked over and yanked the headphone plug out of his controller. The room filled with the death cries of Henri's enemies.

He nudged one of the cups off his ear. "Sorry! I just—"

"Did the expansion release already?" she asked, staring at his TV screen.

"It leaked early, yeah. Well, not early for us, cause the mundane world got it two weeks ago, but someone pulled some strings," Henri said, smashing his fingers on the buttons with practiced efficiency.

"The werecats severed my console when they broke in," Kayda said, tracking Henri's avatar as it loped across the familiar landscape.

"Monsters," Henri said, disgusted.

"It was the 5 ..."

"Daaaamn. I'm sorry, Kay."

She stood transfixed for another twenty minutes before he cleared the level he was on.

He saved his progress and muted the game.

"You can keep playing," she said.

Placing the controller on the coffee table, he patted the couch cushion beside him. She sat with her feet hanging off the edge.

Kayda stared at her weird, tiny human toes. "Are you sure this is all okay?"

When he didn't immediately answer, she hazarded a glance his way. He had an arm slung over on the back of the couch, watching her intently. "Yes, this is all okay. Want a kind of pathetic overshare?"

She scooted back on the cushion and folded her legs. "Obviously."

"I'm glad I get to be on one of your adventures. I've always been j-j-jealous of you and Harlow."

Kayda hiked a brow as she idly fussed with the wads of fabric bunched up on an ankle.

"I never told you this," he said, pushing his glasses up his nose unnecessarily, "but a year before I m-m-met you, my great, great g-g-grandpa Sid contacted Harlow."

"Really? What for?"

"He was almost ninety-eight then, and his memory was fading. He was selling his house and wanted to sell several of his bigger items—like antique furniture—to help him afford a draken retirement home. He wanted to go. That place is apparently full of randy old folks who like to party," he said, laughing. "We all tried to help him sell stuff, but he was stubborn and took on a lot by himself. He got caught up in some scam with a real estate guy who, we found out later, took advantage of seniors and talked them into all kinds of nonsense."

Kayda shook her head. She'd had to deal with a few sketchy people herself when her grandma was sick, and then again after she'd passed.

"Anyway, this scumbag convinced Sid to essentially donate most of Great Great Grandma Telly's prized jewelry. There was a bracelet in particular that she'd loved. It had come with Telly's grandma from the fae realm when she got stuck here during the Glitch. It was supposedly made by a master dragon jeweler. It wasn't priceless so much as a beloved family heirloom.

"It took him a while to figure out that he'd been cheated, and was so upset—saying he didn't deserve to look Telly in the face when he saw her in the afterlife—that I honestly thought the heartbreak would kill him. We tried talking the slimeball into at least giving the bracelet back, but Sid had legally signed it away. That was when I mentioned Fletch to him. I hadn't really known who she was then. I told him there was a charm collector in Luma who was known for finding magical items and getting them back to the rightful owner. I didn't even know how to find her. Sid contacted her on the sly—determined to get that bracelet back himself no matter what it took."

This was all coming back to Kayda now. It was a job Harlow had gotten Kayda's help with. Harlow had landed a job as a waitress for some fancy dinner party, allowing her to gain access to the ins and outs of the estate. When Harlow figured out where the bracelet was, she'd waited until the night of the dinner party to hatch her plan. The first part had been to pinch a few charmed items from the house and stash them in a box in a strategic spot outside. Kayda, meanwhile, waited in the bushes for her cue.

Harlow snuck away from the festivities long enough to call in an anonymous tip to the werecats, including where to find a box of contraband. While the werecats stormed the house— armed with proof that the sleazy Realtor inside was dealing in illegal goods—Kayda had darted for the shed at the back of the elaborate garden. Harlow kept the Realtor's guard dog Buster occupied with scraps of meat she'd pocketed during the course of the evening, while Kayda broke the lock on the shed with her bare hands. Based on Harlow's description of the bracelet, Kayda had found the item in question, and then they'd stolen into the night before the cats, or the Realtor had figured out what happened. She and Harlow had split the finder's fee, dressed to the nines, and treated themselves to a very expensive celebratory dinner in uptown for a job well done.

It wasn't until now that Kayda learned the bracelet had belonged to Henri's family.

"I eventually figured out that the Harlow you talked about

all the time, and the Fletch who got Gigi Telly's bracelet back, were the same person," Henri said. "Before that, you were just this very c-c-cool woman I worked with who was doing all these exciting things, and I envied the adventures you w-w-went on. If helping you now—other than the fact that you're m-m-my friend —is a way to thank you for giving Gigi Sid some of his s-s-soul back before he died, then I'm happy to do it. Consider it a f-favor to Harlow, too."

Kayda didn't know what to say.

As if her crush on the guy wasn't completely out of control already ...

"So what's the next part of our adventure?" Henri asked, hopeful.

"Well, according to Welsh, I'm supposed to join the Vampire Hunters of America," Kayda said, deadpan. "He said I should get training on 'pest control' because the ferals are becoming a problem and the Collective doesn't seem to care. I'm not ready to become a full-on member just because Welsh tells me I should. That guy kind of scares me, frankly. And, I don't know, it's like finding out there's a Bigfoot Society that slays Sasquatch on the regular and no one knows about it because they do such a good job. I can accept a lot of things, but I can't wrap my head around this feral stuff."

"For what it's worth, there's definitely a Bigfoot Society. My uncle is a chapter head."

Kayda laughed, unsure if he was joking or not, and deep down longing that he wasn't. She refused to ask any clarifying questions.

"Let's go to a meeting and check 'em out," Henri said. "They're usually downtown most days passing out those flyers. Then you can judge for yourself if you want to get involved with them after you go to a recruitment meeting. If you don't, we'll figure out something else."

Kayda stared at him.

He flushed navy. "W-w-what?"

She didn't know how to say this without offending him. She'd never been able to be completely blunt with Henri, always fearful that she'd send him scampering away. But there was a strange kind of anonymity right now, sitting in front of him as herself while wearing a mask she couldn't remove. "Just wondering if you'll be like this in the morning when the glamour wears off. Less terrified of me, I mean."

In a low tone, with his eyes diverted, he said, "You don't have any idea how intimidating you are."

Her father used to say the same thing. That if she kept being so intimidating, she'd never get married off so he wouldn't have to deal with her anymore. That if she was less *her*, life would be easier. Perhaps Henri had felt the same way as him all this time.

They'd had a good time on Sunday though, hadn't they? Had she completely misread that?

Henri muttered to himself under his breath. She didn't need her heightened draken hearing to catch what he said. "*Just say it, Henri.*" Sighing heavily, he looked up at her. "You're out of my league. I know that. I'm kind of nerdy and I talk too much when I'm nervous. I've h-h-had a stutter since I was a k-k-kid but I went to speech therapy to better c-c-control it. It's nearly gone most of the time, but it only really gets bad with y-y-you because you make me so n-n-nervous." The poor guy was the color of a blueberry. "And I can say all this now because you look like a human doll. Honestly, Kayda, it's so horrifying."

A laugh burst out—some combination of delighted and surprised.

He smiled briefly. "Harlow intimidates me too. She's like a miniature version of you. The two of you together ..." He shook his head. "Talking to even one of you is rough, but two of you at the same time? Forget it. So now Harlow's not here and you look like ... that. So, in short, I don't know how I'll be in the morning either. But at least you know how I feel now." He heaved out another dramatic breath as if he'd just run a marathon. "Goddess, I feel like I've been drinking. W-w-why can't I shut up? Is it h-h-hot in here? I feel hot."

Henri popped off the couch and wandered into the kitchen. Kayda twisted in her seat. He guzzled three large glasses of water in quick succession. She wanted to launch over the couch and shove her tongue down his throat, but she couldn't do that as a "human doll." Henri would have nightmares for the rest of his days.

A glamour could be knocked loose with great force if absolutely necessary. Could she run into a wall repeatedly and get rid of this glamour before she gave herself a concussion?

When Henri went for a fourth glass, she decided to give him some space. Besides, she was very bad at actually articulating feelings with men. If he had said all of this to the real her, she probably would have panicked and thrown herself out his window to get away from this squirmy feeling in her gut. In the past, all she'd need to say to a man was, "You're sexy. Take off your pants." Which had always worked for her and had gotten her exactly what she wanted.

But she didn't want that with Henri. Okay, she did, but she wanted more than that.

What was she supposed to do now that he'd said everything she'd ever wanted him to say? When she was her, she was too big, too aggressive, too ... much. Maybe she wouldn't be "like this" in the morning either. Only time would tell, she supposed.

Climbing off the couch, she walked toward the bedroom. She forced herself to turn in the doorway, though, not wanting to leave him hanging. Henri watched her with a pained expression. "For what it's worth, you're not out of my league. I thought I was out of yours."

Henri lit up with a smile so wide, it caused a funny little twinge in her chest.

As she closed the bedroom door, wearing a smile of her own, she decided this glamour wasn't the worst thing that had ever happened to her after all.

Chapter 18

KAYDA

Kayda awoke with a start from a nightmare. She'd dreamt that the glamour potion had worn off while she slept, but all her parts had been put back out of sync, like a Picasso painting. She stared up at the unfamiliar ceiling while she patted her body. Her *familiar* body. She grabbed hold of the comforter and lifted it to double-check. She wiggled her toes and had never been so happy to see them.

Then she remembered her conversation with Henri last night and pulled the comforter over her head. *Please don't let today be awkward.*

As giddy as she was to hear that he'd been harboring a crush all this time too, she knew her Henri-specific insecurities would flood back if he was a nervous wreck around her.

She couldn't let any of this get in the way of her attempting to get her life back in order. Today was a day for investigating the Vampire Hunters of America, not lamenting about her love life.

She climbed out of bed and used the bathroom, then stared at the remaining vial of glamour potion on the counter beside her toothbrush. Henri was one of the few people in the city she trusted fully, but he was in a better headspace when she wasn't ... her. She took off her pajamas and changed into her standard fare of black on black, then chugged down the potion before she could convince herself otherwise.

Within a minute, her sweet-faced persona was back. Kayda curled a lip at her, but even that looked cute on this face. "Hi, Angel," she muttered at herself.

Would the Vampire Hunters of America believe this cherub was truly interested in slaying vamps, or would Kayda need to pick up dark makeup at a corner store and turn this doll into a goth?

Back in the bedroom, Kayda found her pants from the night before and pulled out the note Welsh had given her. Henri's apartment wasn't far from Al's Burgers. The hole-in-the-wall restaurant served as one of Welsh's offices, but the guy didn't sleep there, did he? There hadn't been a couch in the room, and the break room had been the size of a shoebox. She supposed he could glamour himself into a gnome and sleep on a chair like a cat, but Kayda figured that was an excessive waste of magical energy.

A faint, consistent series of rumbles filtered in from the living room, and Kayda figured it was Henri's snores. Maybe he's stayed up late playing the new expansion. Jealousy burned hot in her belly. When this was all over, she'd find a way to make the werecats reimburse her for the cost of her destroyed console.

If she was going to do recon on the vamp hunters, she'd need more of the glamour tonic. Possibly *two* sets of tonic. Tapping the folded note on her palm, she eyed her cell phone lying on the nightstand. Was it stupid to have that on her here? Those could be tracked, couldn't they? She willed herself to believe Henri was right—that if evidence of her helping Grayson escape existed, it had been obscured or outright ruined by Grayson's water magic. There were no cameras in the circular lounge where she'd attacked the cat, at least.

She'd call Welsh, but from one of the public boxes. Picking up her phone, she saw she'd received a text message overnight.

Jo: *The dot is in Washington. It's been in this location for two days. It's a few miles out from Kensey.*

Maybe Harlow and Caspian were biding their time before heading into the hub. For what reason, Kayda couldn't guess. She typed out a thanks, then looked up the closest public box before stowing the cell back on the nightstand. Padding to the door in her shrunken black combat boots, she pressed an ear to the door. Definitely snores. She couldn't blame him; it was barely after six in the morning. As she eased the bedroom door open, she prayed to the Goddess that Henri was a heavy sleeper. If he woke up while she was gone, maybe he'd forgive her if she returned with breakfast.

Kayda had just unlocked and opened the front door when a whoosh of magic outlined the jamb in vibrant red.

Shit! She'd forgotten about his wards.

She quickly shut the door and pressed her back to the wood. Henri snorted and shot bolt upright.

"Ung wha?" Henri asked eloquently, rubbing a hand down his face.

Kayda wrung her hands. "Sorry."

He grabbed his glasses off the coffee table and finally got them on his face after two tries. Giving her a quick appraisal, he asked, "You trying to sneak out on me?"

She explained her plan. "I wanted to find out if it was even possible before I asked you. It's probably expensive. And you might not even want to do it."

"I told you last night that I wanted more adventure. The real stuff, not video game adventures. If my first one as your sidekick means I end up as a creepy doll boy, I'll do it," Henri said. "Going in disguised is a good idea. I'm sure the vampire hunters have members other than humans on their crews, but it does seem like the majority are human. We'll stick out less if we're glamoured."

Kayda nodded.

"I'll deactivate the ward, you go make your call, and when you get back, I'll have breakfast ready," Henri said. "Don't get excited, though. I basically only know how to make toast."

She laughed.

Henri padded over to the door and pressed his thumb against the wall by the doorjamb. The spot below his thumb glowed a vibrant red. The outline of the door itself glowed bright too, then with a hiss of magic, the lines went dark. She saw the echo of the rectangular glow when she blinked.

"Be back soon," she said, slipping into the deserted hallway.

The nearest public telephone booth was a few blocks away from Henri's apartment and she speed-walked on her little legs to get there. The booth felt much less claustrophobic than the last telepost box had been. This one smelled just as ripe with old urine, though. You win some, you lose some.

She consulted the note, then dialed Welsh's number. The old-fashioned phone was unsettlingly sticky. She opted not to press the receiver directly to her ear, in case it fused to her skin. If Welsh was as paranoid as Harlow, he might not answer. Then again, he likely had unfamiliar numbers calling him on a regular basis.

"Who is this?" came a gruff voice. He'd answered it so quickly, she hadn't heard it ring.

"Kayda," she squeaked, then sighed.

"Oh, hi. You're up early. Any issue with the glamour? It should have worn off by now."

"It did. I took the second one," she said. "I'll need a few more of the tonics if you've got them. I'm not going to join the hunters without checking them out first. Can I pay you to get a set of human male tonics for a friend of mine?"

"The big one with the glasses?"

Kayda stared at the "MARCY WAZ HERE" graffiti etched into the glass wall of the booth. Had Welsh been spying on her as the werecats had been? "Yeah, him."

Welsh didn't reply right away. "I can get you another batch of yours and a batch for him by this afternoon. I'll be back at Al's around 4 p.m. Most VHoA meetings happen in the evening. Mind if I join you two?"

She did mind, but she figured if she didn't give him a "Sure!" in response, he would have shown up anyway. Then she'd have to deal with the unpleasant reality of not knowing which person in attendance was him. "Fine by me. See you at four."

After breakfast, Henri drove them to Downtown Luma on his cycle. Her ass had gone numb after the half-hour ride and she considered taking a telepad back even if she went into a tube as Angel and came out as Kayda.

Downtown Luma had stringent vehicle restrictions, so Henri had to park his bike in a high-rise parking structure near Luma Central Station, and then they hoofed it into the heart of downtown's bustle.

As Henri predicted, the VHoA group—as Welsh called them—were in their usual place on one of the corners of the massive five-way intersection across from the station. VHoA's rival group wasn't currently posted up across the street, but they'd set up their lounge chairs, laptop, and speakers soon enough, blasting their anti-vamp hunter propaganda.

The only other group nearby was a gaggle of folks in flowing brown robes. They referred to themselves as the Moon Children, descendants of nymphs. Or was it dryads? They were out here most months, trying to recruit people to what Harlow was convinced was a sex cult. Kayda wasn't so sure. They didn't do the greatest job of recruiting—they mostly writhed, doing interpretive dance to music only they could hear. One of the members currently wore a deer head replete with wide antlers; they were celebrating the upcoming Buck Moon. There was a full moon every month, and each one had a "special" name, so Kayda wasn't sure what all the fuss was about.

She turned her back on the Moon Children and assessed the VHoA contingent. They were smaller in number than usual, Kayda thought. She expected the group leader to be shouting into his megaphone about the viciousness of vampires, citing the attack that had happened outside Luma last month. According to Welsh, they'd lost seventy-five percent of their team to an explosion set by the vampires. Kayda supposed shouting about it wouldn't help their cause. It would further prove that vampires were a danger to anyone *outside* the hub, while inside they were protected. Currently, no one person seemed to be in charge. The eight of them had pamphlets in hand and were asking passersby if they were interested in learning more. No one was.

Everyone in the group, regardless of age, wore all black and had a band of red paint circling their necks.

Kayda marched toward them instead of giving them a wide berth. She did her best to plaster a look of deep curiosity on her cherubic face.

She stopped before a floppy-haired boy of sixteen or seventeen. He started when he realized she was staring right at him and he blushed so furiously, the color in his cheeks almost matched the paint ringing his neck. A couple of other boys noticed and crowded in on either side of Kayda's young victim.

"Hi. When's your next meeting?" Kayda asked.

The boy started to answer, then his gaze flicked to something over her shoulder—*high* above her shoulder. His friends' mouths dropped open. She tipped her head back at Henri who had sidled up behind her. Smiling at him upside down, she said, "Uncle Jeffrey! Back up. You're going to scare them!"

Henri coughed awkwardly. "Sorry, uh, my little dove ... child."

Note to self: Henri is terrible at improv.

One of the boys snickered. "He calls you 'dove child'?"

Kayda shrugged. "Draken aren't really good at human stuff, but my uncle is *really* clueless. He hasn't lived here long." She glanced back at Henri who stood a few feet away now, hands in his pockets while he whistled idly up at the sky, trying to look nonchalant. Leaning in conspiratorially toward the trio of boys, who mirrored her, she added, "He was rescued from a cult. He knows almost nothing about modern life."

The boys glanced around her to get another look at Henri.

"Oh my!" Henri said behind her in a tone so unnatural, she flushed in sympathy embarrassment. "What on earth is this contraption, my little dove child?"

Kayda schooled her expression into one of neutrality before she turned around. Henri had his hands on the round lip of a metal trash can and was peering into it as if it were a well. "Uncle. We've talked about this. That's a trash can."

Henri leaned back, nodding sagely. "We did not have trash cans on the cult farm. We only had the firepit. If I wanted a toy, I had to collect items from the pit and make it myself before they incinerated it all during the monthly burning. I do not miss the commune, but I do miss Mr. Tuna Can Man."

Kayda turned back to the boys. "See? He's a mess. He means no harm."

The boys relaxed in light of Uncle Jeffrey's plight, but not by much.

"I promise I'll leave him at home if I come to the meeting," Kayda said when the boys remained quiet. "Is there one soon?"

"What is your interest in VHoA?" the first boy asked. His tone wasn't accusatory or even suspicious, merely curious.

"A friend and I were attacked by a feral vampire who got through the veil," Kayda said. "We both got away, thankfully. Our parents don't believe us. We know what we saw, but they think we're trying to get attention. They're sending her away to some private school hub in Kansas to help fix her. Only my uncle believes me ..."

They all turned to look at Henri again, who was once again peering into the trash can as if it held the answers of the universe. Okay, maybe he wasn't *that* bad at improv. He was just rusty.

"I want to learn how to protect myself and the city, you know? Learn more about what these things are." Kayda felt bad about talking to these kids under false pretenses, but she'd meant that last part.

She hadn't heard it from Harlow herself that the veil was threatened and that ferals were slipping through, but Kayda's gut told her that Welsh, regardless of his questionable methods, hadn't lied to her about anything. She didn't want to accept this as a possibility yet. If she denied it, then she was safe—from this threat, at least. Kayda needed information to soothe her fears. Once she had information, she could formulate plans of attack. Right now, she wasn't on sure footing anywhere, when sure footing had always been her thing. She was the levelheaded, confident one—the person people came to when they needed logical advice. She didn't feel like any of those words described her now.

The first boy produced a folded piece of paper from his back pocket and handed it to her. "Next meeting is tonight. Call that number before you head out and you'll get instructions on where to go. Tell them Liam vouched for you."

"Cool," she said, taking it and putting it in her pocket. "It was nice meeting you. I'm Angel."

The other two boys introduced themselves as Ollie and Ben.

She took a few steps back. "See you boys tonight. Thanks for the help, Liam."

As she joined Henri and pulled her clueless "uncle" away from the mysteries of the trash receptacle, she caught Ollie and Ben playfully shoving Liam around—probably teasing him about catching the attention of a girl.

"Want to grab something to eat?" she asked Henri as they made their way down one of the crowded streets.

"Sounds good," he said. "This new world is so confusing to me, my little dove child. You may have to teach me how to use utensils."

She laughed, hooking her much smaller arm over his elbow. "Don't worry, Uncle. I'll take good care of you."

By six thirty, Kayda had four more tonics, and Henri had three of his own. Welsh had charged them for Henri's—at an apparent discount—because Welsh had said his "generosity only went so far." Given what he charged for them, Kayda didn't think generosity had been involved.

By six forty-five, they were back in Henri's apartment. The VHoA meeting was being held in the Industrial District on the western side of the city. It would take an hour to get over there on Henri's cycle. The meeting started at nine.

By seven fifty, Kayda had taken a shower and downed her tonic, restarting the twelve-hour clock. Henri, however, still sat in the same spot she'd left him in when she'd slipped into the bathroom. He stared at the glass vial as if it contained cyanide pills.

Kayda was dying to know what Henri's glamour was. All Welsh had said was that it would complement Kayda's well. Maybe he would be a cherubic doll child as well and they could skip down the streets cackling, scaring the crap out of everyone they met. She stood on the other side of his coffee table and crossed her arms. "What's wrong? The tonics were too expensive, weren't they? We could ask creepy-ass Welsh to give you a refund."

Henri finally looked up. His elbows were propped on his knees and his eyes were wide. "Does it hurt? The glamour, I mean?"

She stifled a laugh. "That's what you're worried about? Nope, doesn't hurt. It tastes foul, but you've eaten the pizza surprise in the canteen at the casino, and that's definitely worse."

"The surprise is that it isn't pizza," Henri said, as was customary whenever the horrendous mysterious dish was mentioned. "Here I was all excited about adventures and now I'm chickening out."

"It's all right," she said. "You'll get better with practice."

He picked up the vial. "I've never eaten or drunk anything above a Level 2." He started to say something else, then hesitated. "Actually, no. That's a lie. In high school a couple of friends and I bought winterberries and I ate three of them on a dare."

She muffled a gasp.

"Kayda, I was so high I didn't sleep for four nights."

She pressed her lips together. The poor guy looked so horrified by the memories that laughing now would make him feel worse. "What's the weirdest thing you hallucinated?"

"A talking goat. But it had my mom's face. Any time I almost fell asleep, the mother-goat would kick my door in and bleat so loudly I'd scream myself back awake. When I finally did fall asleep, I woke up naked in the rosebushes out back. I had thorns ... everywhere."

She did laugh then. She couldn't help it. Henri, flushing the color of a midnight sky, smiled softly.

"I promise you it isn't like that at all," she said. "You don't even feel it happening."

Nodding, he popped the lid off with his thumb and knocked back the milky, pale blue liquid. Holding the empty vial tightly in his fist, he stared at her with unblinking eyes.

Five seconds passed, then ten, then—Henri went from a six-foot-three draken to a five-seven human man who had giant Puss n' Boots eyes. They were almost too big for his face. Nope, definitely too big for his face. Kayda frowned unintentionally, her instincts warring between wanting to care for this doe-eyed boy at all costs and wanting to shove it down the garbage disposal because clearly it was borne from something unholy.

"It's bad, isn't it?" Henri asked. "Oh. Wow. I sound like I swallowed helium."

Kayda grimaced. The helium voice tipped things even further into the unsettling category. "It could be ... worse?"

Henri got up and swayed on his new smaller feet. She watched, amused, as he attempted to get used to his shorter height and different gait. "Magic is bizarre. How does this even work?"

Kayda had no idea.

Henri stumble-walked into the bathroom while Kayda waited, bracing herself.

He unleashed a muted cry and came stumbling back out. "Kayda! I'm even more disturbing than you are!"

"Yeah, it's not great," she said. "But those VHoA folks are even weirder. We'll be fine. Your new name is Damon, by the way. Because it's close to 'demon.' As soon as someone trusts something with eyes that innocent, they'll find their insides on the outside."

"I can't even argue with you."

Kayda sauntered to the door. "See, isn't adventuring fun?"

When he didn't answer her, she glanced over her shoulder—and froze. Henri had his head cocked, his bug eyes bulging. Clasping his hands under his chin, he said, "Please, Mama. May I have another nibble of the flesh pie?"

Yeah. This was going to be a problem. She pointed at him. "Knock that shit off."

He shuffled toward her, dragging his foot behind him as if his ankle had been snapped. "Please, Mama ..."

Kayda yanked open the door and practically ran down the hallway. Henri's high-pitched laugh followed her out.

Chapter 19
HARLOW

I stared at the treasure chest sitting on the floor in front of my bed. It had taken all three of us to get the damn thing into the rented SUV, across the parking lot of the motel, and into our room. When the door slammed home of its own accord behind us, I flinched so badly I almost dropped my side of the chest. Which would have been especially bad for the sword, as it was underneath the treasure chest, pushing from below to help alleviate the strain in our arms.

Caspian stood beside me now, his hand to his chin as if he were studying an esoteric painting in a museum. "That lock is rather substantial, and it doesn't appear to have been tampered with much. Do you think it's possible Domino has no idea what's in the chest?"

I idly rubbed at the marks on my inner wrist. They didn't hurt or itch, but the phantom heat of them searing into my flesh lingered. "Yes, but he also put in a fail-safe. If we open it and ten sentient weapons fly out, we have to hand them over."

"True," Caspian said slowly. "I would have said that perhaps the chest is warded or locked by magic, but Domino has

197

a Collective sorcerer in his pocket. If *Albert Sweeney* couldn't manage to open it, I'm not sure I could either."

"I'm sensing some hostility. Did he give you an A-minus on a test once and you've never forgiven him?"

Caspian's lip curled. "Something like that."

There was a story there, but we could get into that later.

I elbowed him. "You're honestly saying that the great and mysterious Caspian Blackthorn can't figure a way to unlock something that measly?"

That got a brief smile out of him. "It's also possible that the lock has been spelled to open with a specific key—meaning it will repel all magic and blunt force. Or perhaps it has a series of complicated tumblers that have a perfectly mundane solution."

Tumblers! I could deal with tumblers. I rooted in my clutch for my lockpicks. In a world full of magical beings when you were a boring human, you acquired unique skills to prove your usefulness. Picking locks was one of mine.

I crouched in front of the chest and gently took the hefty lock in one hand. It had to weigh at least a pound and looked like something off a medieval prison door. It screamed simple more than complicated, but I wouldn't judge it too soon. I slipped one of the picks in, heard a click, and then slipped in a second one. With one eye squinted, and my tongue trapped between my teeth, I gave the second pick a jiggle while holding the first in place. I shifted the second one a fraction to the left, heard another click, and then ... "Oh shit."

The buzz of the magic vibrated up the picks, into my fingers, and spiderwebbed across my palms. I was hurled backward by the force of a cyclone. A foot clipped the corner of the vanity table, but my body kept going. My backside slammed into the full-length mirror on the wall. I heard the crash of shattering glass and had enough sense left to throw my arms over my head to protect myself from the inevitable collision with the ground when gravity joined the party.

I hit the ground hard, knocking the breath from my lungs. I didn't hit my head though ... so yay? The stupid bow on my ass helped cushion my tailbone when I hit the mirror, so it could have been worse. I groaned and rolled onto my back. Hopefully I wasn't flashing my goodies at Caspian. Oil spots danced in my vision. My stomach roiled.

Caspian's face swam into view. "Goddess, Harlow! Are you okay?"

"I think the chest is spelled," I groaned.

He huffed a laugh. "You're going to give me a heart attack, you know that?"

I whimpered.

"Grab my hand," he said, helping me sit up.

My vision went hazy for a moment but cleared quickly when a sharp pain lanced up my forearm. I lifted it, finding several protruding shards of glass. A few more slivers poked out of my knee. "Ow. Ow, ow, ow!"

Caspian blanched. He left my side to pull open various drawers and closet doors until he found an ancient first aid kit. As he plucked glass out of my limbs and dotted the cuts with stinging antiseptic, I glared at the treasure chest.

"We *have* to get this thing open now. I don't care how long it takes." I swallowed hard as my stomach gave a heave when Caspian pulled a large chunk of glass out of my forearm. "My curiosity will kill me before the magic in that lock does."

"I have a handful of runes I can try, but they'll—"

"Take time. Yeah, yeah, I know. Ow!"

"Stop squirming. You're like a toddler."

"Rude," I said, then stopped squirming.

"We also might need more supplies than what I have with me. Graphite powder would work the best, but it's messy. Chalk would do," he said, opening a giant Band-Aid and fastening it to my arm right above my elbow. The fabric of the bandage darkened with blood before our eyes. "And maybe some gauze."

"Do I need stitches? I've always wanted stitches."

Caspian stared deeply into my eyes. "You're very strange."

"Aw! Thanks. Kayda always said that to me."

He sighed dramatically. "C'mon. Let's make a store run before the blood loss makes you even stranger. Though, is that possible?"

Tap-tap, the sword said.

"Both of you are rude."

Freshly showered and bandaged up, I sat in the middle of my bed putting my hair in twist-out curls while I watched Caspian. He had changed into a pair of sweatpants and a T-shirt when we got back. We'd returned the rental and taken a cab back to the motel. If the cabbie was alarmed by the number of shopping bags we piled into the back with us, he didn't show it.

Caspian's hair was mussed from the many times he'd run his hands through it as he tried to figure out the best way to get the chest open without blowing up himself or this motel room in the process.

Every time I thought I heard a sound outside, I froze. With the tracking runes on our wrists, Domino and his troll goons could know where we were at any moment. What if, when Caspian got close to getting the chest open, Sweeney or Domino sensed it and showed up to snatch away whatever loot we'd found inside?

Caspian assured me that it wasn't like the runes were a window into what we were doing. Domino couldn't spy on us through the runes, or even listen in on our conversations.

Rumors spread in magical circles, though, even outside the hubs. If there was even a hint that we'd uncovered yet another sentient sword, Domino would be after us.

I dozed off at some point, curled up on top of the comforter in a ball. The sword lay nearby, as if it had dozed off too. I woke with a crick in my neck and a stab of pain in my tailbone when I stretched. My heartbeat thrummed in time with the pulse emanating from the largest cut on my forearm. We'd purchased a few over-the-counter painkillers at the store, but I hadn't taken any yet. I definitely needed them now.

The numbers on the bedside alarm clock read 4:30 a.m. The light in the narrow hallway was on, and Caspian had migrated that way over the course of the evening. Several of his tomes were spread out across the threadbare carpet, as well as balled-up scraps of yellow paper that he'd torn off a legal pad and thrown aside. We'd purchased a few poster boards at the store, and he'd scribbled runes all over one of them. It looked more like the start of spells than anything concrete, if only because it was so messy.

I padded over to him, and he flinched when my bare feet stepped into his line of vision.

His gaze traveled up my feet, to my bandaged knee, my even more bandaged arm, and finally to my face. His eyes were bloodshot. "How are you feeling?"

"Worse than you look right now, but not by much," I said.

He chuckled and sat back, resting against the closed door of the closet. "I haven't found the right combination of runes yet. I've tested the lock with a few basic spells to determine if the spell that attacked you was a spell against tampering or a spell that rejects anything other than a specific key. I haven't been able to determine which it is yet." He reached forward to pick up a scribbled-on piece of paper. He stared at it as he continued. "If it's the first, even unlocking spells will trigger the anti-tampering spell. If it's the second, a spell still may work, as the key may be a spell rather than a physical unlocking mechanism. I think if I use a distilan rune for my next diagnostic test instead of a variation of a frenrick rune, then I might—"

"Cas," I said, and he looked up. "You need to sleep. I have the utmost faith that you'll figure this out. But, speaking from experience, if you happen to trigger the anti-tampering spell and get your ass thrown across the room, you'll recover faster if you aren't already exhausted."

He frowned. "I suppose you're right."

"Go take a shower."

I knew he was tired because he didn't argue. While he was in the bathroom, I went through our newly purchased supplies. By the time he came back out, drying his hair with a towel, I had eaten an entire sleeve of tiny powdered doughnuts. I'd also taken two painkillers.

I glanced down at my pajama top to find it splattered with white powder. When I swiped my tongue along my bottom lip, I found that covered in powder as well. I squinted at him, daring him to comment.

He smiled to himself, shook his head, and retreated to the bathroom.

The sword had settled into its favorite duffel bag by the time I climbed into bed. I hissed as my bandaged forearm protested about all the jostling. Caspian turned off the light in the hall, plunging the room into darkness. I listened as he settled into his bed, to the loud clang of a door closing down the hall, and the distant rumble of cars on the highway.

Several minutes ticked by in the dark and I knew Caspian wasn't asleep yet. He didn't snore, but I'd gotten used to the rhythm of his breathing when he slept.

"Do you think I'll ever be safe in Luma again?" I asked.

"You're a sorcerer. You might have gone rogue on the Collective, but they'd let you back in. I don't know about me, though."

It took Caspian a few beats to reply. "I don't know if it'll be safe for either of us for a while, honestly. And after our chat with our new friend Domino, I'm not so sure how safe it is beyond the veils either."

"Not safe from Domino or the impending vampire horde?"

I'd meant it as a joke, but Caspian's tone was very somber as he said, "Both."

I was awake long after his breathing finally settled into that familiar cadence.

It took two full days for Caspian to finally say, "I think I figured it out!"

Which was a good thing, too, because I was half out of my mind with boredom. Again. Road trips were supposed to be chock-full of excitement and new experiences. Road-tripping with a bookish sorcerer was a lesson in patience. I had begun to question whether I had any.

The only other interactions with living beings other than Caspian were people who delivered food to the room, the diner owner a few blocks away, and Rachel the maid who delivered towels in the morning. I'd tried to engage her in conversation yesterday, but I'd scared her off. After being peppered with questions from me—which I'd asked solely because I needed to hear words that had nothing to do with runes—she'd hurriedly said she had to finish working and shoved her cart away. There were some odd patrons in this motel, and she'd probably already had her fill for the day. When I went into the bathroom afterward to deposit the fresh towels on the counter, I'd blanched at my wild-haired reflection. No wonder she'd run off. I was one of the kooky motel residents now! Ugh.

The sword and I had improved the game we'd first played while holed up in the old factory in the Necropolis. The sword wasn't a sore loser so much as a sword that needed clear ground rules. We also had purchased a few small balls from the toy section of the store we'd raided two days ago, and the sword was much less likely to incinerate those than it had balls of paper.

The ball we'd been using beaned me in the side of the head when I whirled at Caspian's declaration, temporarily forgetting that the sword and I'd been in the middle of a game.

"Ouch, sword!"

Its blade was the cheeriest shade of blue—the equivalent of its laughter. I turned my back on it, but it happily took up its usual spot by my shoulder. The blue in my periphery didn't fade for a long while. Jerk.

"What'd you figure out?" I asked, bouncing lightly on my toes. "Wait, I don't need details. Are you ready to test it?"

A few stains decorated the front of Caspian's gray shirt, and a hint of stubble graced his jaw. He'd been growing steadily scruffier over the last two days, and while I was delighted to see him less polished, I wasn't sure if I should be concerned.

He gave his neck a scratch. "It's ready for testing."

"Let's give it a go then."

He gathered up an armload of papers and shuffled across the room toward where the treasure chest sat at the foot of my bed. I wrinkled my nose as he passed. He'd also gotten a bit ... ripe. He'd refused to take another shower and had hardly eaten anything, even when I had an extra-large pizza delivered to the room last night. Despite telling him that I didn't need details, he rattled them off in a constant stream of nonsense I wasn't even pretending to understand. There was a nervous energy to him, which might have been due to the five cups of coffee he'd had today, but I had a feeling he was anxious. Anxious about the spell not working and him needing to go back to square one. Anxious about the magic hiding in the lock deciding to toss him about like a rag doll, too. Anxious about what might be in the box and whether it would send Domino to our doorstep.

"Can you grab the poster board by the closet?" he asked, pointing toward the hallway while he consulted the papers now scattered across the vanity table.

I did as he asked. He'd taped two pieces together, making a roughly four-foot-by-three-foot rectangle. The white backs faced me, their scribbled-on sides lying against the closet. I grabbed the board and flipped it over, my mouth dropping open at the intricately drawn rune circle. I couldn't count how many individual runes were here. The complexity of the design reminded me all over again that this was not a discipline for me. Each rune had a wide range of uses and meanings. Runes could then be grouped for other uses, like words forming a sentence. Groups of runes could then be combined in a seemingly endless number of ways. A tiny change in a rune phrase, a rune word, or a rune letter could drastically alter the spell.

I walked back toward Caspian with the board. The guy might be a mess now, and be in serious need of soap, but I was glad to have that brilliant brain of his on my and the sword's side. "Thank you," I blurted.

Caspian, bleary-eyed, looked up from his notes. "For what? We haven't even tried it yet. I do think I could get one more use out of it if the destril rune fails, as I could redraw the tail end of the—"

"Thank you for trying," I interrupted.

The sword tapped once on the vanity table in agreement, then hummed and glowed blue for good measure.

Heat flushed Caspian's cheeks and he rubbed the back of his neck. Coughing awkwardly, he said, "Happy to help."

"What do you need me to do?"

Caspian gave instructions on where to place the drawn rune circle, and when to help him put the chest on top of it. "Now I need you to stand back in case I messed up somewhere and I spontaneously combust."

I laughed, but Caspian did not. "Oh. Shit. You weren't joking." I hastened into the hallway littered with papers and books. I didn't really think Caspian would combust. As disheveled as he was, he wouldn't risk our lives, nor the lives of the innocent people in the motel. The mere fact he was joking about it said he was completely fried, so I would humor him.

"You're going to have to buy this motel to avoid all the charges for incidentals," I said, peering out the door of the bathroom. I could only see half of Caspian's profile from here. The sword joined me in the doorway. "Especially if you spray every surface with blood and guts."

"I can't very well buy a motel if I'm reduced to a pile of meat."

"It's cute you don't think I know all your login details and that I can't forge your signature by now."

He guffawed. A full-on belly laugh of a sound that was as loud as it was unexpected. I shot a startled look at the sword, which vibrated in response. It didn't know what to do with this development either. Caspian and I were due for a serious talk after he got some sleep.

"Okay," he said, taking a deep, post-laughter breath. "Here goes nothing."

Once Caspian got going on the spell, his hands and arms flailing about as if he conducted a symphony, I edged out of the bathroom doorway. A sorcerer in his element was like watching an artist at work, flinging paint on a canvas only he could see. With his wild hair flapping about, he was more mad scientist than artist, but there was something beautiful in how free he looked while casting.

I was less enamored with the spectacle when the chest jumped. I honestly couldn't tell if the chest itself moved, or if something inside it had woken up and was now trying to get out. Frowning, I took a step back toward the bathroom. Now I was picturing the lid flinging open and possessed meat cleavers pouring out like a swarm of murderous bees. The sword sensed my unease and moved in front of me. Ready to fend off said murderous bees, I supposed.

A great blast of blue light erupted in front of Caspian and I curled inward, anticipating the crash of his body against a wall. The mirror I'd broken with my ass was nothing but a tattered frame now, the glass swept up and dumped into the bathroom trash can. I heard a *thunk*, but it sounded metallic, not made of flesh.

"Cas?" I called tentatively, the sword blocking my view.

"Still alive," he said, his voice labored. "I ... think ... it worked."

I sidestepped the sword and fully crept back into the hallway. The bulky curve of the lock hung open from the clasp, like a mountain climber hanging from a ledge. Caspian rested his backside against the vanity table, his hands gripping the lip on either side of him. Sweat beaded his brow and dampened his armpits, but he was upright, in one piece, and breathing—albeit heavily.

He glanced over at the sound of my approach and smiled tiredly. "Back at the hangar, while I was stuck with Sweeney and you were negotiating with Domino, Sweeney called me a dropout. Said I had no chance of deconstructing the spell because I'd given up on the academy after all the exhaustive work they'd put into me. Like I was their disappointing prized pony. He said when it mattered, I turned coward and then debased myself even further by going rogue."

I'd been curious about the details of Caspian's decision not to become part of a collective, but him being a "dropout" hadn't been among my theories. Caspian didn't strike me as a quitter. "Wanna talk about it?" I asked.

"I do not."

There was more going on here than a random professor being a royal asshole. I'd badger him endlessly about it later. He probably knew that. For now, we had to see what was in the chest.

"Can I take the lock off?" I asked.

Caspian nodded. "Do the honors. I'm not sure I could move even if I wanted to."

Blowing out a slow breath, I squatted before the chest. My hands shook, the memory of getting flung across the room still strong in my mind and my tailbone. I grabbed the lock and maneuvered the curved end out of the clasp. No zaps of magic. So far, so good. I lay the lock on the ground, then placed my hands on either side of the lid's base and heaved upward. The lid and I both groaned with the effort, so the sword flew over to wedge its blade in the space made between the top of the chest's body and the bottom of the lid. It used itself as a lever to help me get the lid all the way open.

The lid fell back to rest against the foot of the bed. I stared at the contents of the chest, my head cocked. I half expected it to be heaped with shiny gold coins. Instead, it was full of small, unlabeled wooden boxes that appeared to be nailed shut. The treasure chest was stuffed with them from what I could see. Crude jewelry boxes?

"What's in it?" Caspian asked, sounding more worn out than he had a minute ago.

I glanced over my shoulder. "You look exhausted. Maybe you should take a long hot shower, hmm?"

"Later," he mumbled. "What'd my thirteen grand buy us?"

I scrutinized the chest. There was enough give between the boxes that I could shove my fingers between two of them and pry a box out with some finagling. The one I got out first was about nine inches by four by four. I gave it a shake by my ear. It was filled with a lot of small items that slipped and slid over each other. I didn't think it was anything metallic, like coins. Which might knock "pirate booty" off the list of potential things the chest held.

"Sword, can you help me pry the lid off this too?" I asked, holding the box out at arm's length.

Like it had done with the lid of the chest, the sword wedged its tip between the two pieces of wood and used force to pry it upward. It took a while to finally get the box open, and I spent most of the time convinced the sword was going to slip and skewer me through the neck.

Once I was finally able to fully pull the top piece of wood free, the anticipation was killing me. All I knew was that if this was full of old plastic beads because the owner had been a maker of gaudy costume jewelry, I would be livid.

"*Oh*," I breathed, staring at the sea of iridescent items shimmering under the motel's muted lights.

Caspian said what I didn't have the words for. The anticipation had been eating him alive too, and he'd moved to kneel on my other side. "Dragon scales."

I held the box firmly in one hand and then gently skated my fingertips over the top layer of scales. They were cool and slippery to the touch, almost like wet river rocks. "I could make an absolute fortune selling these on the black market."

A bright flare of red flashed in my peripheral vision.

"I didn't say I *would* sell them," I told the sword, but I only had eyes for the scales. "I just mean this box alone could make Domino very, very rich. It's further proof that he had no idea what was in this thing."

I glanced into the treasure chest. If all the nailed-shut boxes inside were roughly the same height, there could be dozens upon dozens of other boxes. Give or take. I failed geometry. I gave the scales another gentle shake, watching them slide over each other. They were roughly the size of guitar picks. How many were in this one box? One hundred? My brain couldn't process this.

"We have to open the others," Caspian said. "When the Collective hired me to make weapons, not even *they* had this many dragon scales. The number of charmed items I could make with these ..."

The blade blazed red again.

"Simmer down, cutlass," Caspian said. "I'm not saying I would do it, either."

I started pulling the boxes out of the chest, while Caspian went foraging for another tool we could use to get the boxes open faster. He scampered out to his car in the lot and came back with a pair of flat-head screwdrivers he kept in a toolbox in the trunk. Of course he'd have a toolbox. It was a very practical thing to have. Which made his current state even more upsetting. The sooner we got the boxes open and had cataloged everything, the sooner I could get him to go to bed. I wondered if it was unethical to drop a couple of my melatonin pills into a glass of water and force him to drink it.

The first two layers of boxes were all the same size. I laid them out on the carpet so Caspian and the sword could start prying them open. The sword figured out that it could open one on its own if it nudged a box across the floor until it was against a wall to keep it in place while it wedged the lid free.

The next layer had larger, thicker boxes—these with twelve-inch, square lids, and a depth of about five inches. The contents of these didn't rattle and slither as I shook them lightly by my ear.

The following layer wasn't a layer of boxes at all, but two leather-bound journals. They were as wide as the two flatter boxes that had been above them and lay side by side. Nothing adorned their covers. I gently pulled one out, finding the leather soft, supple, and flexible. A few loose, yellowed pages slipped free and fluttered out to rest inside the chest. I stared at the fallen pages, clutching the journal to my chest like a life raft. The page was covered in what I instantly recognized as runes.

"Cas ..."

He abandoned the war he was having with one of the boxes to peer inside. "Oh my," he said, gently taking the pages out and quietly studying them. "These are the more archaic form of runes. Harder to master, but more powerful. A dead language, almost—like Latin. How the sorcerers at the academy would love to see these ..."

"Like Sweeney?" I asked, mostly to gauge his reaction.

His nostrils flared. "Like Sweeney. If you want to give me those—"

"I'll set them aside for you to look at ... *tomorrow*. If you're a good little boy and sleep for at least ten hours, you can have them."

Caspian grumbled, then returned to the box he'd started to open on the vanity table.

The next box in the chest was almost the same width and length as the chest itself. It took some work to get it out because there wasn't much clearance around the sides to get my fingers comfortably between it and the side of the chest. It was also heavier than all the others. When I finally got it out, I semi-tossed it onto the bed, as my arms were too strained to get it to the floor without dropping it. The contents clanked, like metal. Like maybe it was full of hundreds of pieces of silverware.

Caspian and the sword both abruptly stopped what they were doing. We remained frozen for five solid seconds, perhaps all waiting for this box in particular to react to the rough treatment. Then we descended on it—Caspian and I with screwdrivers, and the sword with its blade working the top of the box off.

The nails shrieked free as we finally got the lid removed. When I visually confirmed that an army of sentient weapons *didn't* lay in the box, I wasn't sure if I was relieved or disappointed. What did rest in the box were chunks of metal. Flat pieces, rough hunks, large and small metal balls, metallic cylinders, hollow square tubes, and pouches of white powder Caspian said contained borax. The last box was even heavier, this one crammed with tools: ball-peen hammers, small sledgehammers, metal tongs, chisels, wire brushes, and rulers.

"Ball bearings ... Damascus steel ... wrought iron ... these are blade-making materials," Caspian said. "I've opened boxes of dragon scales, one full of various beaks, chunks of ivory. I think whoever owned this box was a bladesmith."

"And a sorcerer," I said, gesturing to the journals I left stacked on my nightstand.

"Most assuredly. The items I'd received from the Collective when they hired me already had their magical properties extracted and pulled to the fore so they were ready for use." Caspian ran a finger over a few of the dragon scales in a nearby box. "The magic in these is dormant."

Interesting.

I asked, "Could the owner of this box be someone who made a weapon like the sword?"

"It's a definite possibility," Caspian said. "You must let me read the journals."

I stood tall and pointed toward the bathroom. "Shower. Sleep. Eat. *Then* you can read the journals."

Caspian stood straighter too but listed to the side. I grabbed his arm to keep him upright. His eyes glazed over.

"All right. That's it," I said, forcibly angling him toward the bathroom. He offered very little resistance as I guided him across the room. We crunched over the discarded papers he'd left in the hallway, and I gently pushed him into the bathroom. When he turned to face me, my arms were crossed and my shoulder rested against the doorjamb, blocking his exit.

"Turn the water on," I said.

"So bossy."

"I trust you're able to take your clothes off yourself?"

He offered me what I suspected was supposed to be a flirtatious wink, but came off like he'd lost control of the muscles on one side of his face. Which was interrupted by a deep yawn that turned into a full-body effort. His eyes were watery when they met mine. "If you hear a thud from in here, assume I've fainted, and please come save me from drowning."

"Will do." After he managed to turn the water on, I closed the door. I rummaged in his suitcase and found a fresh pair of clothes for him. I opened the bathroom door long enough to toss the clothes on the bathroom counter.

The sword and I then got the rest of the boxes open. In the smaller ones, the most notable finds were chimera tail tips, a gray powder that had an unsettling heft to it, a box of hundreds of tiny teeth the size of rice—which had to be pixie in origin—as well as dozens of perfectly intact pixie wings, and a box of hair that smelled of unwashed dog. In one of the larger boxes were dozens of beautifully preserved feathers—white, pink, blue, purple, and red. Some were no longer than my pinky, while others were as long as my arm. I had no idea what kind of creatures they'd come from. Another large box held six severed unicorn horns.

I couldn't get over how much money could be made from these items. I could buy a private island and retire at the ripe age of twenty-eight. These charmed goods weren't gold coins, but in a place like Luma? They might as well have been.

The terms of our agreement with Domino meant we didn't have to divulge what we'd found, as what we found weren't sentient weapons. He might be *more* pissed if he found out what he'd given up, though. With the right combination of bladesmith and sorcerer—or both in one person—Domino could have dozens of charmed weapons made. And if the spells in those journals detailed the runes that ran along the fuller of my sword's blade? Well, who knew how many weapons could be granted sentience, too.

I wished we had a secure place to store this stuff. Anyone tuned into the black market—whether they were in the hubs, the Collective, or in Domino's entourage—would want this haul. People got robbed and killed for a lot less.

I'd moved all the boxes onto the vanity table, arranged by type, by the time Caspian emerged from the bathroom with a billow of steam flooding out in his wake. He looked better, but that might have been from the healthy pink tint of his skin brought on by the hot water, instead of the ghostly pale of exhaustion from earlier.

I pointed at his bed. "Ask me no questions. We will discuss this in the morning."

Without a word, Caspian staggered to his bed and flopped onto it. I swear he'd passed out before his body hit the mattress. He was on top of the comforter, and one bare foot hung off the side, but he looked comfortable enough, so I let him be.

Once showered and dressed in pajamas, I turned off all the lights except for the one by my bed. Caspian, for the first time since this road trip started, was snoring like a buzz saw. I wondered how many times he'd worked himself to the point of exhaustion in that big house of his. Or how many times he'd been like this at the academy studying for what had to be grueling exams.

I pulled the top journal off the stack on the nightstand and laid it over my crossed legs. I eased open the cover and found a name on the front page.

THE WORK OF MARGARET FENGAST

Margaret Fengast. Our potential lady sorcerer/bladesmith. I was relieved that the vast majority of the journal, from a quick skim of the pages, was in English. Even though the ship, where the treasure chest had come from, had been found off the coast of the United States, it hadn't meant the ship—or any of its passengers—had been from here. It would have been just my luck for our first big clue about the sword's origins to be in Swahili or something.

With Caspian's snores resounding in the background, I settled against the headboard and started to read.

Chapter 20
KAYDA

Before leaving for the Vampire Hunters of America recruitment meeting, Kayda called the number on the folded piece of paper Liam had given her so she could get the details on where to go. The meeting, she found out, was to take place in an office park. The security guard on duty was a secret, honorary member of VHoA, and would let them into one of the buildings. Since he knew the security of the place inside and out, he had given VHoA detailed instructions on where to park and how to approach the office in question to avoid cameras.

Being a member of VHoA wasn't illegal, but it wasn't well received. The secrecy made Kayda leerier of joining them. If they were truly fighting the good fight, how could they be so reviled that they had to sneak around in the dark to avoid harassment?

Perched behind Henri on the cycle, Kayda felt far less secure now that he was in his new, smaller form, but they managed to get to their destination in one piece. They parked in the designated area and then crept alongside a freestanding metal bungalow, into a copse of trees that hugged the side of the office building, and around the back where the weeds were overgrown and the light bulbs had burned out. Kayda had to grab hold of the back of Henri's shirt so she wouldn't lose him in the dark. The lack of night vision with this glamour was the pits.

Henri groped until he found the third door. He knocked four times quickly, then twice slowly. They waited.

Just when Kayda was going to suggest he knock again, the door opened. It swung outward and Henri jumped out of the way to avoid getting clocked in the face. The hallway beyond was dimly lit, but Kayda could make out Liam's young face.

Liam craned his neck to peer around Henri. "Hey, Angel. Nice you could make it. Who's your ... friend?"

Kayda wasn't sure if the hesitation was due to how off-putting Henri's appearance was, or because Liam himself desired to be Angel's "friend." "This is Damon. He's my ... twin."

Liam stared at them a beat longer, then nodded and stepped aside. "Come on back. We're starting soon."

The door snicked shut quietly behind her, making the hallway even darker. Kayda had never been scared of the dark before; she'd always been able to see in it. No need to fear the shadows lurking in the darkness when the shadows were visible. But with these human eyes, she felt half-blind. *That* was what disconcerted her.

Liam led them down a couple of short hallways before stopping at one labeled "Conference Room." It had windows that looked out into the hall, but the blinds were drawn closed. With a dramatic flourish, he pushed the door open. Kayda squinted as bright light spilled out.

A long table ate up most of the space in the room, ringed with black desk chairs. Nothing adorned the gray walls other than a giant whiteboard up front. A flat-screen TV was perched in a corner, its screen dark.

Of the sixteen chairs in the room, half were filled. A brown-skinned young woman stood at the front of the room in front of the whiteboard, her attention focused on her phone. One thumb quickly danced across the screen.

"Grab a seat anywhere," the woman said with disinterest, waving her hand vaguely toward the table, all without taking her eyes off her phone.

Kayda and Henri slipped into a pair of chairs near the door. She knew Welsh was meeting them there, but she had no idea what form he'd arrive in. For all Kayda knew, he was the bored woman at the front.

Liam was apparently in charge of escorting people to the meeting place, because after Kayda and Henri were situated, he slipped back out. A trio of twenty-something men was across from Kayda, all of them sitting quietly. The two boys who had been with Liam earlier today were near the end of the table, clearly trying to work up the nerve to say something to the pair of younger girls—probably no older than eighteen—who sat talking in hushed tones with their heads together.

A minute later, Liam let someone else into the room. It was Welsh in the form she'd seen him use most often. He was dressed casually enough but wore a knee-length trench coat despite the cloying summer heat.

The woman in front looked up when Welsh came in, and a bright smile lit her face. She stuffed her phone in her back pocket and strolled over. "Welsh! What are you doing here?"

"Hey, Marisol," he said. "A couple of friends asked me to join them." He motioned to Kayda and Henri.

There was no mistaking Marisol's gasp of alarm when she noticed Henri, who grumbled something under his breath. Welsh grinned, clearly pleased with his terrifying handiwork.

The woman's name clicked then. This must have been one of the women who had been part of the VHoA team that had gone outside Luma to get the fae girls back from the clutches of vampires. Marisol had lost many of her crew that night. Kayda imagined the grief made it hard enough to get through the day, but then Marisol had to turn around and try to recruit more people to join an organization where getting killed was a real possibility. Kayda didn't envy her.

"They're close friends of Fletch's," Welsh said.

Marisol somehow lit up further. She shook Henri's hand, then came over to greet Kayda. "It's so nice to meet you. Have you heard from Fletch?"

"She's okay as far as I know," Kayda said. "I heard about what happened out in Fresno. I'm sorry."

Marisol sighed and nodded. "Thanks. The cause is worth it. I firmly believe that. But the cost can sometimes be higher than I want to pay."

Kayda didn't know how to reply to that. This "cause" was such an abstract concept for her. VHoA had been known as Luma's resident nutcases for as long as Kayda could remember. It was hard to discard years of one belief to exchange it for the total opposite.

"On that note," Marisol said with a laugh. "Let's get started, shall we?"

Welsh took the open seat beside Kayda, leaving that ridiculous trench coat on, and Liam took the spot beside Welsh.

The meeting was a crash course on the vampire problem in Luma. On the whiteboard, Marisol covered nearly every inch of it with details about the three types of vampires: pure vampires who lived in places like Tercla and fed exclusively on human blood, hybrid vampires who dabbled frequently in the consumption of fae blood, which altered them physiologically and mentally—not for the better—and ferals, who were the vampires who had fully given in to their fae-blood addiction and were now bloodthirsty animals. It was because they were closer to animals that they could slip through the veils.

"It's not a pleasant experience for them," Marisol said, "but it doesn't hurt enough to completely stop them. We see the most activity in the Necropolis. There have been a few sightings uptown recently, too."

Kayda started at that. Uptown was in the middle of the city, where most of the wealthiest citizens of Luma lived. To get to uptown, a feral would have to travel through at least one neighborhood. If ferals mostly got in through the Necropolis to the south, it would mean they'd traveled through downtown, too. Downtown was so packed with people at all hours that it seemed unlikely that they could get through there without being noticed.

Which would mean the logical path of travel from the Necropolis would be northwest into the Industrial District, and then cut east into uptown. But why? According to Marisol, the ferals were crafty in the way a raccoon or fox was crafty, but not calculating the way a human would be. How would a feral even know how to navigate the city?

It registered a moment later that she'd asked that last part out loud.

"Good question ... uh ..." Marisol said, raising her eyebrows.

"Angel," Kayda offered.

Welsh snickered softly to himself.

"Good question, Angel," Marisol said. "Hybrids, as far as we can tell, can control the ferals, using them like attack dogs and scouts. The unsettling thing with that, though, is that hybrids can't breach the veils themselves. So where are the hybrids getting the information that they're then relaying to the ferals?"

"Someone on the inside ..." Kayda said.

"Exactly." Marisol tapped her own nose. "Our mission a month ago proved there's someone here in Luma who has been in contact with the vampires on the outside. We don't know who or why they're aiding the vamps."

Kayda was still mulling over the implications of this when Henri nudged her in the side. She snapped out of her musings, realizing the meeting was coming to a close. She had no idea how long she'd been zoned out.

"If you're interested in joining us," Marisol was saying, "I have a sign-up form in front here. We do have a rigorous vetting process, but if you're selected to join us, you'll receive training on how to combat the ferals. We're most in need of patrol guards to help us at night in the Necropolis. We also have spots open on our research teams, as well as chapter liaison positions where you'd be in communication with other chapters in the state, as well as across the country. Our organization is completely donor-funded, and thankfully we have enough money in the coffers right now to offer a few paid positions. As I've said many times tonight, it's not an easy job, nor is it for the faint of heart. But if what I've told you tonight speaks to something deep within you, please consider joining us. Thank you."

There was a smattering of applause. The pair of girls in the back left without signing up, as well as one of the stoic men across from Kayda. The rest stayed.

She knew Welsh believed joining the organization was in Kayda's best interest, given how closely the Collective was surveilling her home and job. Kayda liked Marisol. She was confident, and though her potential recruits hadn't been wildly enthusiastic about the cause, it was clear this was a passion for Marisol, which Kayda respected. She just didn't know if this suited her.

The door to the room banged open. Kayda was half-convinced it was going to be a pack of werecats here to break up the meeting. The person who stood panting in the doorway was a man in a security guard outfit. Oh, hells. Had someone who worked at the office park shown up because they forgot their briefcase or something? They'd all have to pile out the back door like a gaggle of underaged kids fleeing a party at the shout of "Cops!"

"Jerry," Marisol said, abandoning the young man she'd been speaking to. She took Jerry by the shoulders. "What's wrong?"

His pale skin had gone even paler, the whites of his eyes prominent. A bead of sweat rolled down his temple. "Feral!"

"What? Here?" Marisol asked.

Jerry swallowed hard. "I saw it running through the parking lot. It jumped on top of one of the bungalows. Heard its claws tearing into the metal."

"Liam, Ollie, Ben, come with me. Welsh, I'd be happy for the help if you can spare it. Everyone else, Jerry can get you out of here while we distract it."

The trio of young men sprang out of their seats and tore out of the room after Marisol, who had fled without a backward glance.

"Come on. We gotta get out of here!" Jerry looked four seconds from leaving everyone behind, screaming the whole way home.

The remaining potential recruits lurched to their feet. Kayda went to do the same, but Welsh shot out an arm across her middle to stop her.

After the last of them had fled the room, Jerry waved his hand frantically. "You heard Marisol! Move it."

Welsh fluidly got to his feet. "You go ahead. I'll take care of these two."

Jerry didn't need to be told twice. "It's your funeral, man!" And he was gone.

"I'm sorry about this," Welsh said.

Kayda's draken abilities might be gone, but her instincts weren't. She scrambled out of her chair. Somehow she knew he wasn't apologizing for anything that had happened; he was apologizing in advance. Slowly, she asked, "Sorry for what?"

He'd pulled something from the inner pocket of his coat and threw it. All she could note about it before it hit the ground was that it was small and made of glass. It exploded on impact, filling Kayda's lungs with a noxious yellow gas. Her eyes watered, her chest was racked with coughs, and her vision flickered. She distantly heard Henri hacking up a lung. Her muddled brain idly wondered if Welsh had shown up only to kill her. Maybe he was friends with the vampires.

A blink later, the gas was gone. Kayda had collapsed to one knee. Henri's heartbeat was pounding out of control. Welsh's, however, was calm and steady. The *creeeak* of a slowly spinning office chair grated on her nerves.

Her head snapped up. Her hearing was back to normal. Whatever in the hells Welsh had thrown at them had dissolved their glamours—and had done so quickly.

"I've fought these things before," Welsh said when Kayda's watery gaze met his. "They're rarely alone—at least not recently. Those boys with Marisol are getting trained, but they're green. You two have muscle on your side."

Kayda gave her head a good shake and unleashed a final cough to dispel her lungs of whatever foul concoction Welsh had thrown at them. She pushed herself to her feet, then helped Henri.

He pushed his glasses up his nose. The whites of his eyes were streaked with angry red lines.

"You can probably still catch up to Jerry," she said, her voice raspy. She coughed.

Henri shook his head, then tipped it toward a nearby chair. "Think it'll be as effective against a feral as it was against a snow leopard?"

She managed a shaky laugh.

"You two can flirt later," Welsh said. "Follow me."

Kayda noted as he ran by that he now had a dagger in his

hand that sparked with lightning. Maybe his coat was a magical one full of pockets of infinite sizes. The buzz she felt from the dagger made her teeth vibrate in her skull. Goddess, what was in that thing, a Level 4 spell?

She ran after him, Henri on her heels.

On the way out, Kayda scoured the area for weapons. She was strong, sure, but a feral sounded like a grizzly bear on acid, and she wasn't going to be able to fight one of those off with her bare hands. She heard Henri's footsteps veer off course and she glanced back as he returned to the hallway with an industrial flashlight in hand. Maybe he'd found it in Jerry's abandoned security room.

Upon reaching the exit, Kayda spotted a fire extinguisher attached to the wall. She yanked it free and hustled out the door after Welsh. The parking lot at the front of the building was deserted thanks to Jerry's instructions meant to keep them away from the watchful eyes of the security cameras. So much for that. She cast a sweeping glance at the eaves and found one of the sleek black devices, its lens marked by a semicircle of red dots. Kayda considered waving at it.

With great precision, Welsh chucked his dagger at the camera, hitting it dead center. Kayda shrunk back. The crackle of electricity that came off it, in addition to a riotous flash of blue sparks, was so intense, she shielded her eyes with her forearm. The power in the building short-circuited, and what little light had been inside went dark. That was one way to get rid of the camera feed.

"Can you get that for me?" Welsh said, pointing to the ruined camera. "It takes them a minute or so to recharge, so you won't get blasted into next week."

Kayda got up on her tiptoes and plucked the dagger free. Bits of black plastic and glass pieces plinked to the sidewalk. Kayda handed it over.

Then she heard it: snarling. Henri had heard it first and took off like a shot past her. She didn't know if Henri was determined to prove himself to her or if she'd created a reckless monster by bringing him into this mess. Groaning, she followed.

Henri led them in the opposite direction of where they'd parked. The parking lot was huge, supplying spots for three separate blocks of offices. Henri hurtled past all of them, leaping over cement-lined hedges in a single bound. She followed suit, but she could hear the change in footfalls behind her, telling her that Welsh wove around those. He never lost pace with them, though, which was impressive since Henri had kicked his speed into high gear.

They rounded a standalone bungalow and came up short when they spotted Marisol, the three trainees, and not one but *three* ferals squaring off. Kayda had no idea where their weapons had come from, but Marisol wielded a spear surging with red power, and the boys all had what looked like oversized batons. Maybe it was the kind of thing vampire-hunters-in-training carried in their cars. Marisol and Ollie were back-to-back, while Ben and Liam were paired up not far away. Each pair had a feral circling them, while the third sat perched on top of a work van with LUMA CITY CONSTRUCTION printed on the side.

The ferals were even worse than Kayda had imagined. They moved in an almost insect-like way, scuttling and crawling on all fours instead of upright. Their bones must have broken and healed in odd ways thanks to whatever the fae blood had done to warp them. Their shoulder blades seemed spaced too far apart. With her heightened hearing, she could make out the soft chittering sound they made, as if their teeth clacked against each other constantly. That sound alone made chills race up her spine.

The feral atop the van spotted Kayda, Henri, and Welsh. It

cocked its head to the side and chittered. One of the others glanced up as well, mimicking the motion and noise. Perhaps that was one of the ways they communicated.

She heard the sound of the feral bending its limbs, preparing to launch off the truck, mere moments before it happened. "Incoming!" she said, getting a better hold on the fire extinguisher. Henri got into a wider stance, brandishing the flashlight like a baseball bat. Welsh's dagger had recharged, and he held the hilt tightly in one fist, the blue lightning rippling along the surface of the short blade.

The feral leaped off the truck, hit the ground on all fours, then sprang into the air again, leaping over the others circling each other in the lot. It galloped toward Kayda, Henri, and Welsh at an unnerving speed, necrotic black claws scraping against the asphalt. The sound was like nails on a chalkboard.

Kayda was going to die in this parking lot. She was sure of it.

The feral reached them in seconds, targeting Kayda first. She didn't know if it had singled her out as the biggest threat, or the weakest, but if she could help keep Welsh and Henri alive longer, she could deal with that. The feral leaped for her, and she braced herself. A streak of blue whizzed past her head and slammed into the trunk of the feral. Sparks radiated out of the blade like a supercharged Taser. It knocked the feral off course and it crashed into a bush. The damn thing was back up in a second, though, leaves caught in its stringy blond hair.

It wasn't nearly as fast now, weakened by the lightning spell. The fact that it was still moving said a lot about what Kayda was up against and she didn't like her odds. They charged for each other, it swiping with its claws and Kayda swinging with the fire extinguisher or lashing out with her feet. This thing was scrappy. It lunged for her and Kayda raised the fire extinguisher in time to stop its claws from slashing across her face. The claws got wedged in the middle of the canister. White foam exploded out of the gash, spraying the feral from head to toe. With it disoriented, Henri dashed forward and brought the flashlight down on its skull. Its cranium crunched under the impact and it went down. Kayda slammed what was left of the fire extinguisher into its skull too. It lay sprawled on the ground, and even over their ragged breaths, Kayda heard when it took its final gasp. The other ferals heard it, too, because across the parking lot, they threw their heads back and unleashed tormented cries at the heavens. Goose bumps rose on Kayda's arms.

The temporary distraction allowed Marisol to get a solid jab of her red-magic-coated spear into her feral's throat. It chittered twice, then it was lights out. As Marisol yanked her spear free, the last feral decided it was outnumbered here and sprinted for the far edge of the parking lot, and then along the edge of it, back the way Kayda had come.

"Oh, no you don't," she said, tossing the ruined fire extinguisher aside. She took off after the creature.

She heard Henri and Welsh giving chase, as well as at least two of the humans, but she couldn't slow down. If she followed the feral, maybe she could see where it had gotten in. Maybe there was a breach in the veil up here that no one else knew about.

The feral galloped across the parking lot with such speed that its necrotic claws kicked up chunks of asphalt as it ran. It glanced back, lamplight winking off its bald, oddly shiny head. Its eyes were black pits, but Kayda sensed the panic in them—a scared animal in survival mode. It kicked up the speed.

Kayda did, too.

Welsh and Henri were still behind her, but they grew more distant as Kayda and the feral maintained their breakneck pace.

They left the parking lot and raced down sidewalks, deserted streets, and into a small, forested area. Kayda had never been in this part of the Industrial District, but she recognized the sight far out on the horizon. It was the same shimmery magic she'd grown accustomed to seeing in the Necropolis in high school, when she and Harlow went to parties out near the rail yards. The same shimmery glow Jimmy Nance had stuck his hand through, only to be yanked away by a vampire waiting on the other side.

This feral could have reached the veil much sooner if it had run due east. It had run for its life in sheer panic, yes, but that panic was leading it in a very specific direction. Kayda suspected it was heading for the same spot it had used to get it into the city.

They were on a stretch of road now that, according to the periodic signs, ended at a designated exit. Sorcerers were the lone type of fae who could alter the runes on the obelisks that ringed Luma and kept the veil intact. During the day, a sorcerer —if not several—was assigned to designated exit points to lift sections of the veil to allow authorized people and vehicles in or out. This was a service road. Goods coming and going in trucks and semis from Luma destined for other hubs would pass through here. Designated exits were some of the strongest sections of the veil because the rune magic was refreshed so often. This would be the worst place for a feral to try to get out. It would be like having an open window in the Necropolis and deciding to go headfirst through a triple-reinforced metal door here.

The shimmering veil magic was so close now—maybe a few hundred feet—that Kayda could see it glittering, like the ripples in a pond. She'd been so mesmerized by the veil that she almost missed when the feral altered its course, running not on the road that led straight to the exit, but through a cluster of trees that lined the road. Kayda crashed through the crunchy leaf litter. Dead pine boughs, sticks, and other forest debris snapped under her heavy boots. If this damn thing decided to scale one of these trees, Kayda was screwed. Her energy was finally starting to ebb, and she wasn't sure she'd have the strength to follow the monster if it tried something sneaky to get away.

Her hearing picked up something in the near distance, barely audible over the racket she and the feral made. It wasn't Henri or Welsh; she'd lost them both a while back. She adjusted her dials and strained to make out the new sound without losing track of the feral who had veered inward again, continuing to run alongside the veil instead of through it.

If Kayda didn't know any better, she would say it was the sound of an animal in its death throes. It was a good-sized one, whatever it was. The panicked panting and moans of agony grew louder as the feral kept up its pace.

Lungs burning, thighs screaming, Kayda kept pushing, refusing to lose this thing now. The feral was just ahead of her. Twenty feet, ten feet, five.

Kayda reached out to grab it, her fingertips grazing its tattered clothing, but it suddenly dove to the left, disappearing through the shimmery magic. She skittered to a stop, her chest heaving. The magic rippling off the veil made her skin itch. Being close to the veil was always unsettling—that image of Jimmy being yanked out of existence burned into her mind.

With her hands on her knees, she took in great gulps of air as she stared at the spot where the feral had vanished. There was a strange patch of darkness there—a sliver of a scene that didn't quite fit. And in front of that mismatched scene of dark forest that wasn't quite this forest, lay a coyote. Blood matted its fur, its eyes wild with agony. Kayda knew there was nothing she could do for it other than to be there when it passed.

Its chest rose and fell in two quick pants, then stilled. There was an absence in her head now that her frantic chase and the final breaths of the coyote were no longer there.

The moment the coyote's chest stopped moving, the veil

shimmered above it. She couldn't explain it, but it was as if a curtain made of water and starlight swished closed. The slice of not-right-forest was gone, too. The veil settled back into place then, the magic leveling out.

As everything quieted, Kayda studied the coyote. She took a step closer, her brows pulling together. What she first thought were streaks of blood along the coyote's front leg were runes painted on its beige fur.

Kayda straightened, a sick realization settling over her. Animals could pass through the veil without it affecting them—which was why the ferals had become a problem. This poor coyote had been used to keep the veil open. When the animal died, this section of the veil snapped closed, as the veil no longer recognized the unthreatening life force of the creature.

She took a few steps back, suddenly feeling like a bug trapped under one-way glass. Was someone or something on the other side of the veil watching her now?

She knew in her gut that the ferals hadn't found a way in—someone had *let* them in.

Chapter 21

KAYDA

Kayda didn't know how long she'd stood there staring at the dead coyote, numb all over. The animal lay half in Luma and half outside it, so with the veil once more intact, she could only see the canine's head, front legs, and half its chest, as if its body had been severed right down the middle. What the hells was happening in her city?

Eventually, she heard Henri and Welsh making their approach. She figured Henri would be able to track her for miles solely by the sound of her ragged breathing. A sense of comfort washed over her at the sound of them, though, and it snapped her out of her fog.

The fear that someone or something could be on the other side of the veil reignited. She stared at the runes on the coyote's leg and pulled out her phone. Stooping beside the poor animal, she got as many pictures as she could. The veil provided a little light, but not much. Hopefully the flash on her phone illuminated the runes rather than washing them out. If nothing else, the flashes would help Henri find her easier. Maybe Welsh would know what the runes meant.

"Sorry, my friend," Kayda whispered to the coyote, placing a hand on its chest. "You didn't deserve this."

She stood when the men got closer, waving an arm to guide them over. Perhaps she wanted them to see the coyote carcass to prove this had really happened—that everything VHoA had been spewing, that Marisol's cause, was all valid and real and terrifying.

"Kayda! Kayda, are you okay?" Henri called out.

"Yeah! You have to see this!"

They broke into a run.

"W-W-What is it?" Henri asked as he stopped in front of her, then his eyes widened. "What h-h-happened to it?"

"There are runes on its foreleg." Welsh moved past Kayda, grabbed the coyote, and gave it a pull. He groaned with the effort. The canine couldn't have weighed more than forty pounds. "A little ... help ... here? I think it's snagged on something."

Kayda was about to tell them that she'd taken pictures—and would rather not haul an animal carcass back to Welsh's car— when he gave a yelp and lurched forward. Henri grabbed him by the collar of his trench coat before he could pitch headfirst through the veil.

What might have been a grunt sounded from the other side. The coyote slid farther away from them.

"Nu-uh," Kayda said, picturing her feral vampire nemesis trying to make off with the body for a midnight snack. Kayda fisted up a large chunk of blood-matted fur and yanked it forward.

She and Welsh stumbled backward a few inches, bringing more of the coyote into view, as well as a hand. Pale skin, mostly blemish- and wrinkle-free. Not a feral's hand. Kayda let go of the coyote to grab the hand instead, but the second her palm wrapped around the disembodied wrist, a blast of magic shot out. Welsh and Henri, who still had hold of his coat, were whipped off their feet and flung past Kayda's head as if they were mere pieces of debris. Kayda had been flung off her feet too, but she held fast to the disembodied hand laying claim to the coyote. Kayda's body flapped like a banner in a windstorm.

The hand she clung to had to belong to a witch—maybe a wind elemental. The hand rose from the coyote, and Kayda imagined the person on the other side of the shimmery veil standing. Kayda rose four inches off the ground. If she let go, the torrent pouring out of the maybe-witch would send her careening backward on a current. It was the smartest option. But if she did that, she'd have no idea who was on the other side of the veil. The pull of her body against the person's arm had to be substantial. Their muscles would fail faster than Kayda's would. She just had to hold on.

A muted cry erupted on the other side, barely audible between the wall of the veil and hurricane winds. Kayda felt the impending threat before it hit her—literally. Another pulse of power that seemed to shoot from the person's fingers slammed into Kayda with such force, it ripped her hands free from the wrist she'd been clutching like a lifeline. She fleetingly grabbed the still-outstretched hand for purchase, seizing a few fingers for a breath of a second before the cyclone of air took her and hurled her into a tree. She didn't need heightened senses to detect that something in her side shattered. A sharp spasm tore a scream from her already aching lungs.

She blacked out.

When Kayda's eyes opened, she found herself staring up at a dark canopy of leaves. A rock or sharp stick dug into the back of her thigh. A bead of sweat or possibly blood tracked from her hairline, down her cheek, and onto her neck. It felt like an elephant sat on her chest every time she breathed. That probably wasn't good. Pain radiated from her right side. Slowly reaching for it with probing fingers, she hissed when she applied the gentlest of pressure to the spot.

Welsh's most-familiar face swam into view. It was streaked with dirt and one of his eyes was a bit puffy. "You've broken a rib, possibly several. Can you sit up? Henri went to get his cycle."

The idea of getting jostled on that damn cycle made Kayda groan preemptively. The vibration alone would probably make her pass out again.

"I can offer you a little help, but I've got a broken arm to match your ribs. Henri landed on it."

Gingerly, Kayda rolled partially onto her uninjured side and used her elbow to lever herself into a sitting position. Every move resulted in a convulsion, which caused a sharp intake of breath, which made her chest feel like it was going to collapse on itself. She was near the tree that had broken her fall—and her ribs—so she ungracefully shuffle-scooted on her ass until her back was against the bark. Welsh cradled his left arm by the elbow, and his face had taken on a glossy sheen. She rested her skull against the tree and tried to take slow calming breaths without causing herself more agony.

An ambulance was a call away, but they'd ask questions at the hospital. Questions could get her into trouble. Not to mention that the Collective could have alerted places like hospitals to contact them if she strolled—or was rolled—through their doors. A person was decidedly vulnerable in a hospital. A vulnerable Kayda could be coerced into coughing up information about Harlow. Welsh's warnings of what could happen to Kayda if she ended up in the Collective's clutches flitted through her head.

She had to get up.

Welsh stepped in front of her. He cringed as he pressed his ruined arm against his stomach and held out his uninjured hand. "Use the tree more than me, if you can help it."

Swallowing hard, Kayda dug the heels of her boots into the ground, then grabbed hold of Welsh's offered hand. With great effort and copious cursing from them both, Kayda pushed and lurched herself to her feet. Welsh immediately took his hand back to use as a brace for his broken arm. Kayda pressed a flat palm against the tree to steady herself. Nausea roiled in her stomach and her head swam. With her luck, she'd vomit and then black out and faint face-first in her own sick right when Henri showed up.

"Coyote's gone," Welsh said, jutting his head toward the veil.

That wasn't a surprise. She just wished she knew who had been out there. Were elementals the ones inside Luma helping the vampires? Kayda couldn't imagine why. But she was so sick with pain, very little made sense.

"Oh, and you dropped this," Welsh said, carefully letting his broken arm go once more so he could fish something out of his pocket. He held out a gold band to her between finger and thumb.

It wasn't until she took it from him, and was staring at the plain band, that she said, "This isn't mine."

Welsh cocked his head. "It was in your hand when you landed. Well, it was until you passed out, then it rolled into the grass."

It clicked then, and she shot a look at the veil. "It must have been on the elemental's hand. It came off when I was thrown back."

His brows hiked toward his hairline. "That could be very useful in figuring out who that was."

And Kayda knew just the witch to ask for help. The rumble of Henri's cycle suddenly reached her ears, and she wondered if she might have smacked her head during her collision with the tree. She should have heard it a while ago. Perhaps the pain was blocking out everything else.

"Knowing what runes were on the coyote would have been helpful too," Welsh said.

Without a word, she pulled out her phone, relieved to find only a solitary crack in her screen. She'd once dropped her cell phone on carpet and the screen had splintered as if she'd taken a hammer to it. Tossed into a tree? Right as rain. She tapped in her password with shaky fingers and pulled up her camera app. Sagging in relief, she handed the device to Welsh. As the light from her phone washed over his pinched expression, she told him what had happened, as well as her theory about what the coyote had been used for.

When Welsh started clumsily tapping at the screen, she knew he was sending copies of the photos to himself.

The headlight of Henri's cycle appeared in Kayda's peripheral vision. He'd arrive in a minute or so.

A question that had been niggling at Kayda came out of her mouth before she could stop it. "Did you know this was going to happen tonight?"

Welsh's head snapped up, the light from her phone casting eerie shadows across his face. "What exactly are you accusing me of?"

"Why did you volunteer to come tonight?" She lightly shook her head. The questions weren't coming out quite right. "Why did you come with glamour-breaking potions in that weird-ass coat of yours?"

Welsh looked down. "Weird? I rather like this coat." A flare of pain must have seized him, because any attempts at levity disappeared. When he spoke, his voice was strained. "I've been to every meeting VHoA has held since Caspian and Harlow left. This is the first time a feral has made an appearance."

Kayda's brow pinched. "But Marisol seemed so surprised to see you."

Welsh shrugged his uninjured shoulder. "I don't attend as the same person, and she's not the only one who leads the meetings. I was thinking that if there are people in Luma who are aiding the vampires, a group like VHoA could be seen as a liability. The public at large doesn't believe vampires are a problem, but VHoA is a tight-knit community spread across the country. They're the biggest group—as small as they are—that potentially could thwart the vamp-sympathizers' plans. VHoA is who's keeping the feral problem under control. At least for now. Who better to attack than new VHoA recruits? I'm honestly surprised this was the first time a meeting has been ambushed, but this is also only the third one that's been held in the Indie. Usually they're downtown or at someone's house in the suburbs. This spot is remote enough that if an attack took place, there'd be few witnesses. Ferals also tend to take their kills with them so they can eat in peace. If this attack had been successful, this would have been a case of several missing persons, not murders. And we already know how much the Collective cares about missing humans. They don't even seem to care about missing fae girls."

Henri's cycle lurched toward them, crunching over leaf litter and expertly dodging trees.

Kayda turned back to Welsh. "So you keep showing up to help defend them in case someone tipped the ferals off that there would be easy pickings? Untrained vampire hunters plus a possible leader or two?"

Welsh nodded. "I don't feel personally responsible for what happened to Marisol's crew—as Harlow does—but it was a tragedy nevertheless. They helped us track down those girls.

Keeping an eye on Marisol and any new recruits now seems like the least I can do until we figure out something else."

We. She didn't think he meant her and himself. Kayda supposed Welsh felt as abandoned by Harlow, and in his case, also Caspian, as Kayda did.

Henri's cycle lurched to a stop in front of them, the headlight temporarily blinding Kayda. She hadn't considered until then that Henri also might have sustained injuries during the altercation with the elemental. As he lumbered off his cycle, she noted a black eye and a substantial goose egg of a bump above it. He limped as he made his way toward them. She prayed a killer headache was the worst of it.

"Normally I'd suggest the fae clinic in Montclaire," Welsh said, "but ... uh ... my place is closer. I've got healing tonics there that aren't as potent as what the clinic has, but I'm worried about how much of a hit Kayda took. If she's punctured an organ, we need that taken care of sooner rather than later."

Henri studied Kayda intently, as if he contemplated the probability of carrying her wherever they needed to go. "I'm honestly s-s-surprised you're standing. You hit that tree ..." He chewed on his lower lip. "You hit it s-s-so hard, Kayda."

She was truly touched that he was this concerned about her, but the pain was creeping back in, and the act of standing was starting to wind her. She pictured one of her lungs shredded like a ship's sail battered by turbulent winds. Which was fitting, given the situation.

"Enough yapping," Welsh said. "We're starting to lose her."

They piled onto the cycle—Welsh in the sidecar, much to his horror—and Henri headed to an address in uptown of all places.

Kayda wasn't sure if her abilities were still on the fritz, but she didn't immediately register that Welsh had changed his appearance. They pulled into an underground parking garage in a swanky apartment building and then slid into a designated spot Welsh directed him to. She'd glanced over to ask who in the hells "Mr. Bosworth Hemmingsley" was, since that was the name on the plaque on the wall, but when she saw Welsh's new persona, the question died on her tongue.

Sitting in the sidecar was a dapper gentleman of maybe sixty-five, with lightly tanned skin. Kayda couldn't tell if the hue was from genetics or a tanning bed. He had a robust head of hair, all of it gray, that was arranged in a sleek gelled-down style that swooped up effortlessly in the front. A veritable silver fox of the non-shifter variety. He wore a crisp gray suit, and an honest-to-Goddess ascot around his neck. It was a silken paisley pink number. His arm was clearly still broken, yet Welsh managed to climb out of the sidecar with the grace of an elegant, moneyed man. She wondered again who Welsh truly was—was he the twenty-something guy, this older gentleman, or someone else entirely?

"If you would follow me," Welsh said in a honey-smooth voice that was fit for voice-overs.

Kayda got off the cycle with much less grace than Welsh had, cursing like a sailor under her breath. Even in the parking garage, she felt self-conscious. She couldn't imagine how banged up she and Henri looked. The moment they stepped foot in the ritzy lobby of this place, they'd have the cops called on them for trespassing. Henri swayed unsteadily as he got off the cycle and Kayda had to grab him by the elbow to make sure he didn't pitch backward. His eyes rolled back in his head as if he might faint. If she tried to hold up his full weight with her side as ruined as it was, they'd both faint.

Henri visibly swallowed, lucidity returning. "I'm good."

A spiderweb of cracks fanned across one of his lenses. That couldn't have helped the headache. She would have hugged him for getting them here alive if the mere act of raising both arms wouldn't have felt like getting kicked in the chest by a horse.

Welsh stood in the middle of the parking garage waiting for them. Once they were shuffle-walking after him, Welsh continued his casual stroll toward the elevator. Before her eyes, a black cane with a silver top appeared in his hand. The cane's tip clicked on the cement every few seconds.

"What do we call you?" Kayda asked.

Welsh didn't answer until they reached the elevator. He was already inside, his cane held out to keep the door sensor triggered. Soft piano music piped in through invisible speakers in the shiny silver-and-chrome elevator. "Bosworth is acceptable whenever there are potential residents nearby," he crooned.

After Kayda and Henri piled in and leaned against the walls, Welsh hit the button for the fifteenth floor. The highest was twenty-five. The walls of the elevator weren't mirrored, but she got a gist of what her reflection looked like and it wasn't pretty.

They didn't utter a word on the smooth-as-butter ascent to the fifteenth floor. The ride to the apartment building had taken half an hour, and while the ride was mostly smooth, and Henri was both a quick and careful driver, the experience had been borderline excruciating. Now that she was relatively safe, and she was winding down, she wasn't sure how much longer she could stay on her feet. Her vision went dark and distorted on the edges, eating up her view of the shiny doors. She gave her head a shake, pushing out the encroaching black. She willed herself to stay conscious.

"Kayda!"

She started, finding Welsh and Henri now standing in an elegant hallway, while she remained slumped against a wall of the elevator. Lurching onto her feet, she lumbered after them. The walls of the hallway were two-toned—black on the bottom, and white on the top, bisected by a line of dark wood that matched the floor. Kayda studied her scuffed-up combat boots as they lightly squeaked on the polished wood. Every step she took hurt. Her muscles would have already ached by now from the full-broke run she maintained for several miles. She wanted a hot bath. Maybe she could convince Henri to sponge her down. She chuckled to herself.

"She's n-not doing well," she heard Henri say ahead of her, but it sounded like he was in a tunnel.

Her vision went black and crinkly on the edges.

A sharp shake of her shoulders jolted her out of it, and she found herself lying on a couch that she guessed was leather. Her feet hung off the end of the armrest, with her head in the middle of a cushion. It was so soft and she was so tired. She closed her eyes.

They flew open when something poked her in the side and she spasmed. She attempted to swat the hand away, but the effort zapped her of what energy she had. Closing and opening her eyes wide a few times to force her mind to clear, she found Henri crouched beside her. She lifted her head enough to catch sight of her side as he lifted a portion of her shirt. Her light brown skin was covered in a sickening swath of black, purple, and green. She lay back down.

Henri's eye had purpled further, but the goose egg on his head had gone down considerably. His eyes looked less blood-shot behind his ruined lenses.

"How are you?" she croaked.

Henri scrutinized her face for signs of something she couldn't guess at. He gently lowered the edge of her shirt. "Welsh gave me some healing tonic that I was sure w-w-was poison. It m-made my brain feel like it was going to ex-explode out of my head for twenty s-solid minutes."

"It's too bad you missed it," came another voice from behind the couch. Welsh was back to his twenty-something persona, his skin ghostly pale. His arm was in a sling. "He was writhing on the floor sobbing. It was quite the sight. He was flailing and kicking so much, he knocked over an end table and broke a very expensive vase."

Kayda wasn't sorry she missed it, but was surprised she hadn't heard it.

"Not like you weren't screaming into the crook of your arm after you took your dose," Henri said.

"We forced a healing tonic down your throat too," Welsh said, ignoring Henri's comment, "but I mixed a pretty heavy sleeping tonic in there as well, so you slept through your first wave of healing. I figured all the flailing would potentially make your injury worse."

"Trust me. Sleeping through it is ideal," Henri said.

"How long was I asleep?" Kayda asked, smacking her lips absently.

"I'll get you s-s-some water." Henri disappeared from view faster than her tired eyes could track. Hopefully the sluggish way every part of her was moving was a result of the last dregs of the sleeping tonic, and not something having gone very wrong internally.

"Three hours," Welsh said. "The tonic I gave you is powerful stuff. I paid a premium for a batch from the fae clinic last month after Harlow got her wrist smashed to bits by a werecat. Humans break so easily; I wanted to have a supply on hand."

A werecat had broken Harlow's wrist?

"Anyway," Welsh said. "For broken bones, you'll need at least three rounds of tonic. It's been reduced to a fracture by now, I'm guessing. Rest and food are your best bet tonight, and then I'll give you another dose in the morning."

Henri reappeared with a glass of water, and he helped her

sit up enough to guzzle it down. As she handed the glass back, she registered that her side still hurt like a sonofabitch, but not nearly as bad. The ache in her chest had lessened significantly, too. He took the glass back to the kitchen to refill it.

Feet on the ground, she sat up, a hand pressed to her side as she got comfortable. The full water glass sat on the coffee table, and Henri and Welsh stood side by side in front of her, twin expressions of mild concern furrowing their brows. It was very unsettling how she kept losing chunks of time; she hadn't even seen them move. "Thanks for letting us crash here," she said, wondering what he was going to charge them for this. "What's your going rate for house calls?"

"Is it a house call when it's my house?" Welsh asked.

Henri said, "I assumed that meant an even more exorbitant price. Or indentured service for the next ten years."

"Eh," Welsh said, waving his uninjured arm dismissively. "Only five years."

Henri chuckled.

"You helped keep Marisol and those boys alive," Welsh said. "We're square."

"How's your arm?" Kayda asked.

"About the same as your ribs," Welsh said. "We'll be considerably better after another dose or two. The tonic repairs tissues first and patches them up. If there's any tonic left in your system after that, depending on how much damage you sustained, it'll heal bones. We can stop by a clinic tomorrow too if it looks like the tonic won't be enough. And to make sure nothing healed ... incorrectly."

Kayda didn't want to know what "incorrectly" entailed in this situation. If she was going to bleed out in her sleep because her lungs fused with her spleen or something, she'd rather be left in the dark. Henri absently touched tentative fingers to his forehead, as if to check that an extra limb hadn't sprouted from the bump.

A sudden, all-consuming yawn overtook her, and she groaned as her chest and side both twinged. Her eyes watered.

"Okay, Sleeping Beauty," Welsh said. "Get some rest. Henri, come with me."

Kayda wanted to make some saucy comment about Henri joining her on the couch, or her joining him wherever he was going, but sleep was tugging on her hard now. She didn't even have the energy to glance over the back of the couch to see where they went. She got back into the same position she'd been in before, with her head on the cushion and her booted feet over the armrest, and fell deeply asleep.

Chapter 22
HARLOW

The first handful of pages of Margaret Fengast's journal were about a spell she'd been working on. Caspian would have said something like "rune array construction" rather than "spell" to be as accurate as possible, but "spell" suited me just fine. I was sure I would hear all about the boring details in the morning—or, better yet, afternoon—when he woke up and wrenched the journal from my hands.

The spell Margaret wrote about was to aid the ship in better navigating storms.

Runes have been branded into the hull of the ship, on the main mast, and stitched into the sails. Yet, as sturdy as this vessel is, we only narrowly avoided being capsized in the last storm. I know it is not my duty to maintain the integrity of the ship. There are others far more skilled than I who have been assigned that task. I don't pretend to know more than they do, but I do fear they are not equipped for the job.

There are three other sorcerers on board, all with extensive skills in manipulating the elements—be that water, earth, or wind. Two hail from Europe, and one from the Middle East. Though runes are a universal language, it is a language of magic, not communication. While their minds are brilliant, their reaction times are sluggish. Sorcery is a powerful discipline, but it is slow. We might be better able to combat these frequent, and dare I say, unnatural, storms if we had elementals on board aside from the captain.

Captain Ipram is as powerful a water elemental as I've ever met—

"Well I'll be damned," I whispered.

Grayson had been sure from the start that his many-great-grandfather had been associated with the ship found off the Washington coast. I didn't know if that had been a lucky guess, a hopeful one, or one based on knowledge he didn't want me to know he had. I had even less of a way to contact him than I did with Kayda. Maybe Welsh could help with that.

I returned to my reading.

Captain Ipram is as powerful a water elemental as I've ever met, but one who could speak to the wind would be able to free us more quickly from this unrelenting stretch of sea. I have told Ipram that I worry we have angered the gods, if not nature herself, with what we've done. He reminds me often that I was paid handsomely before we left, that my family is financially stable in my absence because of his generosity, but that generosity would be rescinded if I go back on my word. He tells me to keep my theories to myself so as to not cause hysteria among the crew. Sailors are a superstitious lot.

So I toil away in the wee hours by the light of my candles, doing the work I swore I would do—work I believe will come to haunt us, sooner or later. Even now, I can hear it. The rumble of something below the ship melding with the now-familiar groans from the ship itself.

Deep in my bones, in the part of me that has a soul connection to magic, I know the protective runes branded into the hull and the keel are unstable. We sustained too much damage during the last assault, and when repairs were done, and runes redrawn, something went wrong. Our protection against sky, sea, and beast will not last until we reach shore.

The captain will not listen to the "hysterics" of a woman half his age. The sorcerers cannot understand me, and the captain refuses to relay my warnings. I do not possess the schooling to fix the failing runes myself; I only know enough to know they will crumble.

I fear we will all go down with this ship.

I sat back and stared blankly at the dark TV screen. Since the ship had gone down, had Margaret been right? Had the protective runes on the ship failed, and then some monstrous water beast had capsized the ship for "what they'd done"? My gaze slid to the wooden boxes stacked on the vanity table. The box filled with feathers sat on a chair.

I'd always known that charmed weapons got their magic from parts of magical beasts. The dragons on Earth had been slain in large part by humans who had taken scales, claws, and blood, and used the latent magic within them to strengthen their weapons and armor. The stronger humans got, the easier it became for them to slay the ancients.

And yet ...

I quietly climbed off the bed and padded to the assorted boxes on the table. I was drawn, as usual, to the dragon scales. I ran gentle fingers over their soft, slippery surfaces. I was perhaps more in tune with magic than the average human, and there was only so much I could detect, but, just like before, I felt no tingles of magic when I touched these. Caspian had said that until certain spells were cast to draw the magic "to the fore," the magic in the items was dormant.

Back when beasts like dragons were on Earth, humans knew even less about magic than they did now. So how had mere humans been able to wipe the ancients out of existence on their own?

I supposed that answer was easy: they hadn't. They'd had help. Even if humans, armed solely with steel and determination, had managed to kill a dragon, they wouldn't have been able to do anything with the parts of said dragon without a magic wielder to pull that magic out. The Collective had always said that one of the reasons why it was so important to create the hubs was that even though humans didn't possess magic themselves, they were a resilient, ruthless, calculating, and abundant people who would find a way to come out on top if given the opportunity. The hubs were created not only to protect the fae from humans, but to allow the fae to live life as close to what they'd have had in their own realm without humans decimating everything they held dear. They'd used the death of the ancients as proof.

But had it been sorcerers who'd ultimately led to the ancients' extinction? They supplied humans with what they needed to be successful, then blamed them for the very thing they'd been set up to do.

Why would sorcerers have wanted the ancients gone? Would they have been competition—a threat to their power on Earth? I'd never questioned it before, but what place in society had sorcerers had in the fae world anyway? With their "slower" magic, perhaps sorcerers hadn't been as revered there as they were in the hubs. It would be hard to compete with dragons, especially if they were a dominant force. *The* dominant force?

Here on Earth, a magical wasteland, sorcerers would immediately be viewed as immensely powerful. Since it was a discipline that could be taught, sorcery could boom here, spreading fast and wide like a virus, as long as the sorcerers found enough people willing to go through the rigorous training. The ancients were a formidable foe, but they had been eliminated once humans were given the tools to do so—by fae who must have known a great deal about dragons and their weaknesses. Dragons, at least according to what I'd learned in school, were largely peaceful and only resorted to violence if provoked.

Behind me, the sword rested quietly in the duffel bag on the foot of my bed. Had the Collective been threatened by the sword's existence, or what the sword represented? A sword made by a sorcerer, crafted from parts of ancient beasts whom they'd helped destroy. How would the draken feel to know their ancestors—trapped on Earth through no fault of their own—had been driven to extinction here not by humans alone, but with the aid of fae?

The Collective might have wanted the sword and me locked up so we couldn't find out where it had come from. If my theory was right, the Collective would prefer no one know that the sorcerers' path to power had been paved on the backs of dead fae.

Mind spinning, I climbed back onto the bed and pulled the journal onto my lap. Margaret interspersed writings about her life on the ship among long-winded ramblings about runework. Caspian would probably find that all fascinating, but they made me sleepy. I was on the hunt for the personal stuff, for a detailed description of "what they'd done." I found a plethora of complaints about Captain Ipram. He might have been the great-whatever-grandfather of a friend, but it wasn't surprising that a pirate from the 1900s was unkind to one of the few women on board. He never got physical with her, from what I could tell, but he chided her about her gender at every opportunity. He didn't want her to be seen or heard, unless he specifically asked for something or if she had completed an assigned task.

Margaret didn't lay out the specifics of that task until almost two-thirds into her journal.

Before I ever got on this Godforsaken vessel, I'd heard rumors about humans who had gained the power of the ancients. Shields with chimera hide stretched over their surfaces, making them as strong as steel. Spear tips made of unicorn horn that were so strong, they could slice through metal like a hot knife through butter. Armor whose steel was mixed with the powder of an orc's tusk, creating unbreakable metal.

I didn't believe such a thing was possible. Perhaps I didn't wish to believe it. I'm a second-generation fae and I still find it impossible that these magic-less humans would have the strength or desire to commit such heinous acts. I told myself it had to be stories made up to scare fae children into keeping close to their own kind, to not get too familiar with the native population here, for we don't understand them.

But when Captain Ipram stepped into my dressmaker shop and showed me the schematics for the very weapons and armor from those tales, I was intrigued. I am ashamed of that intrigue now.

I had grown bored with my work. With a combination of alchemical concoctions and intricately designed rune arrays, I created fabrics impervious to rips, thread that held its stitching regardless of rough treatment, and pockets with depths so hidden, a lady could carry her favorite dagger without disrupting the elegant flow of her skirts. It just so happens that I made daggers on the sly as well.

Bladesmithing was not a respectable hobby for a young lady, so I got myself a dress shop, and when the doors were shuttered for the evening, I went to work in the hidden basement, sweating in my moisture-repellent dress made by my own hand as I heated steel and hammered it into weapons fit for a lady.

My indestructible dresses were renowned in my town, somehow catching the notice of the likes of Captain Ipram. I'd jumped at the chance to test my mettle and craft sails that could stand up to the harshest of weather for his ship.

But it wasn't until my payment was in the bank, the contract was signed, and I was sailing on the high seas that Ipram revealed he knew about my secret bladesmithing. He proposed the possibility of combining my skills to create magic-imbued blades. It wasn't until that moment that I truly questioned <u>where</u> we were going, and why. And by then, it was too late.

Captain Ipram had an astonishing theory, dear diary—a theory that led him on a months-long mission to collect a crew of fae and humans who could help him find what he sought. My father told me of Frederica Kensey, a sorceress who had been considered largely mad by the fae back in the home world. News had spread that Kensey had proposed to the Sorcerers Symposium that if one devoted oneself to the work, a sorcerer could be powerful enough to literally move mountains. To the Symposium, she revealed her research and demonstrated her "transporting" arrays. She would place a small pebble on an array, activate the magic, and, in the blink of an eye, the pebble would disappear from the first array and onto a second, inches away. As her experiments grew, so too did the size of the objects and the distance from which they traveled.

By the time she came to the Symposium, she was ready to show them her biggest experiment yet: transporting the small island on which she lived with her ailing husband. No one believed she could do it. As impressive as her transporting arrays were, how would one draw such a thing on an island, let alone an array in a second location in the middle of the sea? I do wonder if Kensey would have been lauded as a genius had she not been a woman. I do not know if women are so routinely belittled in the fae realm as they are on Earth, but I do hope they were doubtful because of the magnitude of the task, and not her sex.

They needn't have doubted her. Kensey had discovered how to craft small-scale arrays on a sheet of parchment before pulling the lines and shapes free, where they hung, glowing, in the air. A simple rune-casting for increasing the size of an object grew the glowing array to such a width that it floated directly above the island. This proved ideal, as drawing the array in the soil would have ruined the details by way of dips and valleys caused by flora, as well as any potential tampering from curious fauna.

For her first attempt, Kensey didn't anticipate moving the island a great distance. The act of even moving it a few inches was sure to exhaust her magic to the point of her being bedridden for weeks. She had been rumored to acknowledge that this experiment might be her last. But she soldiered on, longing to prove she could succeed.

Little did she, nor the five Symposium members who stood nearby to observe, know, but at the exact moment Kensey cast her completed array into the air, the Unplanned Exodus began. The island did indeed transport—just a much farther distance than anyone could have imagined: an entirely new world!

Kensey had some of her research with her on the island, but much of it had been turned over to the Symposium to study before her greatest feat. If they had deemed her worthy, Kensey would have joined the Symposium as an illustrious member. Though a great deal of her work was left behind in the fae realm, the other sorcerers transported with her were some of the most celebrated in their field, bringing decades of combined knowledge to this new land.

When I was a small child, Father read Kensey's papers to me—the ones written after she'd become trapped on Earth. In his soul, Father wished for me to follow in Kensey's footsteps. And I did so idolize her—this sorceress who changed the face of the discipline and single-handedly reached new heights, and then forged even more on Earth. The life-changing event could—and most assuredly did—break many a spirit, and send frightened fae into debilitating depressive episodes. But it did not stop Frederica Kensey's tenacious drive for knowledge and the expansion of sorcery.
Though we couldn't afford the academy, and I could not qualify for a scholarship, I studied on my own for years, learning all I could. So when Captain Ipram arrived with those schematics with Kensey's signature in the corners, my childhood ambition answered him with a resounding "Yes!" without consulting with my adult sensibilities.

At first, I was joyous. For we found her island, dear diary! We found her island and its fae inhabitants. I laid eyes on unicorns, chimera, griffins, and even a few dragons. Great beasts not from my father's storybooks, but from biology textbooks. Beasts he'd seen with his own eyes his whole life before the Unexpected Exodus sent him to Earth.

We had discovered these magnificent creatures who had found a sanctuary on this harsh, magic-devoid world. Magnificent creatures who were ambushed night after night by Ipram's band of pirates who were shielded by cloaking magic, and had been trained by a difficult life that had taught them a mercilessness borne out of necessity and desperation. Earth elementals wreaked havoc on the island inhabitants with sinkholes, cave-ins, wrapping vines with the vise-

grips of boa constrictors, and even commanding swarms of venomous insects to sting their victims until they fell unconscious. Ipram used his magic to snatch up any who tried to flee by sea. Humans outfitted with impenetrable armor and unbreakable steel took down hoofed creatures with spears and swords enhanced by the bones and horns of the animals' predecessors. Giant men with bloodlines shared with trolls, orcs, and ogres used their strength and speed to capture large mammals whose teeth and claws were no match against chimera-hide-plated shields and armor. Others flung nets over majestic birds, trapping them on the ground.
Rune arrays that had once been used to craft my indestructible dresses were now used to strengthen nets to keep phoenixes, bouranys, and neevah birds encased in fabric so strong that their talons, beaks, and even fire-magic couldn't penetrate it.

I lay in bed at night, listening to the dying screams and death throes of fae creatures being mutilated for their contributions. It's impossible to know if Kensey knew this is what it took to make the revolutionary weaponry in her schematics, or if they'd been the idle musings of a brilliant mind. I suspect it is the former. One is not supposed to meet their heroes, for reality always brings disappointment.

I shouldn't have been surprised, either, that the same charismatic captain who spoke of adventure and thrilling challenges is also a ruthless killer. He's a pirate, through and through. It was naive of me to expect anything less. The money he will make for delivering these pieces will make him a very wealthy man. He doesn't care how bloody his hands have to get to earn it.

Worst still, he let slip once that there were financial backers for this expedition. My gut tells me it was one of the many high-ranking sorcerers who have risen up the hierarchy on Earth after the Unexpected Exodus. Only a person with deep pockets and an insatiable yearning for power would seek out ruthless pirates to do their bidding. Like calls to like, as they say.

These are the thoughts that keep me awake now, days and weeks after the creatures' cries for aid have died along with their bodies.

Now it is a matter of time whether it will be the guilt of my choices that will kill me, or the thing circling us in the sea.

I begin to long for the latter.

I wasn't sure when I'd started crying. It was almost as if I could see and hear those poor creatures, calling for help that wasn't coming. I felt even worse now about potentially sharing any of this with Grayson. His ancestor was a pirate all right, but a raging jackhole on more levels than I could count.

I read through the passage again, registering on the second read that Kensey the sorceress must have been who the Washington hub had been named after. Was it also possible that her "transporting" rune arrays had led to the invention of the telepad and telepost system? Her name had been lost to history, it seemed, because I didn't remember it coming up in school.

There had to be museums in Kensey that had exhibits devoted to the genius sorcerer who brought so much knowledge with her from her homeland. Too bad Caspian and I couldn't guarantee we could cross their veil without setting off any potential alarms.

A phone chimed, startling me out of my musings. Caspian groaned in his sleep. He curled into the fetal position but didn't wake. The phone chimed a second time. He would wake, though, if the phone wouldn't pipe down. It was Caspian's phone, not mine. It being single chimes meant they were text messages, so it could be Welsh checking up on us. When the phone chimed for the third time, I got concerned. He'd call if it were an emergency, right?

Caspian whimpered softly, then resumed snoring.

What if Welsh was drunk texting Caspian because he was lonely? There was no way a guy that grouchy had many friends.

I eased off the bed and toward Caspian's suitcase. Normally he kept everything folded neatly inside, with his clothing arranged by color. He may have even alphabetized his sock section. My suitcase, on the other hand, always looked like a localized bomb had gone off in it, even if we were only staying in a place overnight. His bag currently resembled mine, partly because I'd ransacked it earlier while searching for pajamas for him, and partly because he was coming apart at the seams. I rifled around the contents, and checked the side pockets and front zippered area. No phone.

A fourth chime, this time from behind me. I got up and quickly tiptoed to the vanity table, finally finding his phone underneath the box of feathers on the chair. I had every intention of turning the phone to silent, but froze when I saw it was a series of pictures from Welsh.

Caspian had given me the passcode to his phone a few days ago, and I typed it in, then swiped open Welsh's text thread. I'd been granted access to Caspian's phone when mine had died and he'd refused to turn off the classical station he had blasting —again. So I'd tried to drown it out while playing the one game Caspian had on his phone: Word Jumbles for All Ages. A check-in text had come in from Welsh while I played, and I'd changed his contact name to amuse myself. I was even more amused that Caspian hadn't changed it back yet.

Zeef Wellington: *Had a run-in with a feral in the Indie. Kayda chased it down. It got away, but she figured out someone from inside has been using animal sacrifices to hold the veil open* *to let the damned things in. Pictures attached. Do the runes mean anything to you?*

There were four pictures attached of a dead coyote lying in the grass. Oddly, it looked like the poor thing had been cut right down the middle. The cut was too clean though, and there was no blood or torn fur there, so based on Welsh's text, I assumed the other half of the coyote was outside the limits of the veil. Veil magic couldn't be photographed, so the background of the picture was mostly a wall of black. The foreleg of the coyote was lined with runes, inked in what I guessed was blood. I tried not to look at the poor animal's vacant eyes. I already felt heartsick about what I'd read in Margaret's journal. Seeing this wasn't helping.

The following three photos were of the coyote from different angles. The last one had the most clarity. Caspian would have a lot to study tomorrow.

Before I could convince myself not to, I typed out a reply.

Me: *Cas is asleep, but I'll make sure he looks at these in the morning. Is Kayda okay? What is she doing chasing ferals! Are you corrupting my best friend?*

I hit send and waited. Then waited some more. There wasn't even a series of dots indicating he was typing a reply.

Me: *A quick "No one is dead!" reply would be great.*

Another five minutes with no reply.

What if Welsh was downplaying the situation and Kayda was bleeding out from a feral attack and he didn't want me to know? I'd drive my ass back to Luma right this instant if I found out Kayda was in real trouble—and Welsh knew that.

I called him.

The call went straight to voicemail.

Shit.

After plugging Caspian's phone in, and leaving it to charge on the vanity table, I got my phone out of my backpack and called the lone programmed number.

I slipped into the bathroom and closed the door. Sitting on the closed toilet lid, I chewed on a thumbnail. Four rings, five, six. Voicemail.

"Hey, Felix. It's me," I said, keeping my voice low, but feeling like it was echoing loudly off the bathroom walls. "Can you check on Kayda when you get a chance? Sounds like she's gotten into some trouble. I just want to know what's going on. I ... uhh ... hope you're okay, too."

I disconnected the call and stared blankly into space for a while, waiting for a returned call from Felix that never came. The pocket mirror had gone off a couple of times this evening while I was reading. Evenings were often prime bounty-hunting time, so he was probably rounding up bad guys at the behest of my sworn enemy. That, or he was sleeping like a sensible person.

I eventually gave up on hearing from anyone and slunk back out of the bathroom. Caspian was on his side now, hands tucked under his pillow, and looking like an innocent little boy. The sight made my heart ache a bit.

Sleep came in fits and starts. When morning sunlight started to pour in through a gap in the curtains, I knew I hadn't slept much at all. My eyes burned. I checked both phones. No calls or texts had come in from Felix or Welsh during the night.

I hoped Kayda was safe, and that nothing I'd done in my effort to keep her shielded from my messes had resulted in the exact opposite.

Chapter 23
KAYDA

When Kayda next awoke, it was because she desperately needed to pee. Grunting, she got into a sitting position and gave her body the appropriate time to spasm in discomfort in a great number of places, and then slowly got to her feet. She'd been so out of it when she arrived, she hadn't taken in the details of the apartment. She'd been exceedingly curious about who Welsh truly was—what better way to learn more than to see where he lived?

He could, of course, have dozens of places all over Luma, with a persona to go with each. He certainly charged his customers enough to afford residences all over the city.

She remembered Henri's and Welsh's voices disappearing to her right last night, so she figured a bathroom would be in that direction if the bedrooms were. She crept as quietly as she could along the dark wood floors, not wanting to wake anyone up. The curtains on the windows in the living room where she'd slept were drawn closed, so she had no idea if it was night or day. All the lights inside were off save for a dim one in the kitchen some-where behind her.

A dining area sat in a recessed nook to her right. The

rectangular table had a white marble top, and four plain black chairs ringed it. A black-and-white photograph of a snow-capped mountain hung on the wall above it in a thick black frame.

She passed under an arched open doorway that led into a hallway lined with a plushy beige carpet. A pair of closed doors stood to either side of her. The short hallway opened into an oval-shaped space that had one door in the middle of the crisp white wall. She figured that was the master bedroom, and that Welsh was in it. She was tempted to try the door, but what if she found him hanging from his feet like a bat? The assumption was the guy was a human witch, but he could be anything. Her bladder issued a reminder. Her curiosity would have to wait.

She backtracked to the short hallway and played a very mature game of "grab the scale, not the tail." At the end of the nursery rhyme, her pointed finger landed on the door to the right. Biting her bottom lip, she eased the door open.

Bathroom. She was mildly disappointed. As she stepped forward, she glanced over her shoulder to eye what she guessed was Henri's room, and whacked her forehead on the top of the doorjamb.

"Shit," she hissed, oil spots swimming in her vision. She managed to use the facilities without further injury.

She nearly screamed, though, when she stepped back out to find Welsh standing in the hallway. Clearly her senses weren't fully back in tip-top shape.

"Sorry," Welsh said, but his faint smile said he wasn't. His arm was still in a sling. "My meds wore off. I'm ready for my next dose. You?"

Kayda lifted the side of her shirt to peer at her side. It was awash in black and purple, with an oozing outline of green. She wasn't sure if that was ancestral-scale green or not. "Ready."

She followed Welsh through the living room, past the couch

she'd been sleeping on, and by the small foyer she didn't remember walking through last night. They stopped in Welsh's large open-style kitchen. Most of what she'd seen of the apartment was minimalist in decor—everything was expensive but sleek and simple, like something out of an interior design catalog. Nothing personal. The kitchen, though, was well-loved.

Copper pots and pans hung from hooks above a wood-topped center island. The C-shaped marble counter was lined with high-end appliances, a full knife block with their stainless-steel grips poked toward the ceiling, and a wooden cylinder filled with wooden spoons fanned out like a bouquet. The hefty wooden cutting board on the island bore faint stains from previous meals and countless tiny nicks from knives. Welsh pulled open one of the shiny steel doors of the fridge and revealed shelves brimming with plastic containers of leftovers—or ingredients for his spells, she supposed.

He pulled three containers out of the fridge and dumped them into two pans, which he placed on the two front electric burners. A large cast-iron skillet sat on one of the rear ones. The ease at which he did it all spoke to how comfortable he was in this space—even more so because he only had full use of one arm.

She slowly lowered herself onto one of the stools that sat on the short end of the island. By the time the food had been warmed up, Henri was awake too. He sat on the other stool, his knee resting against hers.

Welsh plated out a heavenly smelling chicken dish with rice, a colorful selection of vegetables, and a sauce drizzled over the top. Kayda was so hungry she could have eaten anything, but the food was so good, she devoured it in seconds.

Chuckling, Welsh watched as Kayda nearly licked her plate clean, while Henri did. "Glad you like it."

Henri glanced over at Welsh from his vertically held plate.

The tips of his ears went navy. He coughed awkwardly and placed the plate on the island. "Did you make that sauce yourself?"

"Yeah," Welsh said. "I dabble."

"D-Dabble!" Henri said, incredulous. "Forget all this other s-stuff you do. You'd make a k-k-killing opening a restaurant. A killing, m-man."

Welsh wrinkled his nose and polished off the last of his food.

Kayda casually swiped a finger through the last small glob of remaining sauce and stuck her finger in her mouth.

Henri shot a thumb at her. "See?"

"I have to consume a lot of calories because glamour magic burns through a lot of them. When I was a teenager, going out to eat all the time wasn't financially possible, so I had to learn to cook for myself. I got bored with the basics pretty quick, so I leveled up as much as I could. It's for me, though. I don't want to turn something I love into a job. That would take all the joy out of it."

"It's a c-crime, you know. Keeping this from the w-world," Henri said. "Is there more?"

"Yeah, top shelf. The red lid has chicken, the blue has the vegetables, and black has the sauce. Help yourself," Welsh said. "Kayda and I need to dose ourselves. The food in our stomachs will help."

Kayda assumed, if the experience was as miserable as Henri implied, that recently consumed food would end up on Welsh's floor—which would also be a crime—but she kept the comment to herself.

Welsh grabbed two vials out of the fridge and then left Henri to it in the kitchen. Kayda listened intently to Welsh's warnings as she held the chilled vial in her hand. Inside was a pearly white liquid shot through with undulating streaks of silver.

The pain was indeed terrible—as was the taste. Kayda eventually ended up on the couch, flat on her back with the edges of a couch cushion grasped tightly in either hand. It felt like a hot poker had been jammed into her side and it took everything in her power to not writhe, as that made it significantly worse. Henri appeared by her side.

He sat on the floor, holding one of her hands. He told her to squeeze when it got bad. Clearly, he regretted that immediately, but he stuck with her. "I'm a terrible friend. I prioritized food over you. Don't tell Welsh, but I drank a lot of the sauce straight out of the container. It's even good cold!"

Kayda laughed, then bit back a scream. Tears streamed out of her eyes and into her hairline. Henri switched to uttering soothing words instead of funny ones. The pain was blinding. She couldn't concentrate on what he said for long, but the timbre of his voice was like a life raft to hold onto. When his words finally gained clarity, she knew there was a light at the end of the tunnel. The magic had worked itself out of her system or was simply fading now that it had done its job. Either way, she was able to unclench her jaw and loosen her grip on both Henri's hand and the side of the couch cushion. Sweat coated her entire body, but as the last remnants of the tonic faded, she could already tell her side was better. The ache in her chest was almost entirely gone.

As miraculous as these healing tonics were, she wasn't sure if she'd opt to go through this again. It was faster, sure, but Goddess above, it was excruciating.

An hour later, after one more incredible meal unearthed from leftover containers in Welsh's fridge, a shower, and a downed glamour tonic for Kayda and Henri, they left Welsh's apartment. They left the cycle in the parking garage this time, and Mr. Bosworth Hemmingsley, Angel, and Damon strolled out of the pristine lobby of the Sarq and onto the streets of uptown.

"After this outing, I'll need to pick up a new phone. This is sooner than I usually change numbers, but after our incident last night, mine has been reduced to a pile of plastic and glass. Ironically it happened while in that terrible sidecar of Henri's, and not when Henri's gargantuan backside turned my bones to powder. The phone must have bounced out of my pocket while I changed forms, and it got crushed under my heel," Welsh said as he strolled ahead of them. "You'll need to update your records to remain in contact with me."

He'd said all that with complete nonchalance. The last few days had felt like utter insanity to Kayda. Even her periodic mishaps while on jobs with Harlow had never been this intense. And yet Welsh didn't seem fazed. He lived a very strange life.

As they walked, Kayda getting a kick out of how many double takes Henri got, she fingered the ring in her pocket. The ring that had been on the hand of the wind elemental who had ruined all their bodies. Jo could hopefully locate him. If Kayda had her way, they'd find out he lived in Luma. Then Kayda would personally drop by to let him know exactly how she felt about his little stunt. She planned to let her fists do the talking.

A few employees wandered Jo's Apothecary helping customers, and Erik was in his usual spot behind the counter, but Jo was nowhere to be seen. Kayda assumed she was holed up in her back office working on custom orders, or bespelling inventory, or whatever it was she did. Kayda had warned Welsh that Erik, Jo's assistant, was an uptight jerk, so revealing their true identities to him would result in problems. She needn't have worried, though, because when Mr. Bosworth Hemmingsley inquired about Jo's whereabouts, Erik was all smiles. Like many people, Erik was easily swayed by a polite, well-dressed man in a business suit. Even if said businessman was flanked by two big-eyed doll people.

"Josephine is currently in her study, but I would be most pleased to check if she has time to converse with you," Erik said in a tone befitting a butler. With a slight bow, he added, "I will return posthaste."

Kayda rolled her eyes so hard she gave herself a headache.

Jo emerged from her "study" a minute later, a slight crease between her dark brows. When she stopped before them and gazed at Kayda longer than the others, she wondered if the astute witch could see through glamours somehow. When Jo finally spoke, though, she addressed Welsh. "What can I help you with, Mr. Billingsley, was it?"

"Hemmingsley, ma'am. But you may call me Bosworth," Welsh intoned with great poise and class. "We have an item that we believe you might be able to help us with. You did this recently for a ... mutual friend."

Jo's gaze slid back to Kayda. "Do get those shoulders away from your ears, dear."

Kayda rolled her neck.

"Better," she said. "Follow me, then."

No matter Kayda's size, Jo's office felt claustrophobic. Kayda did well to keep her shoulders down, though. Once inside the more open space where Jo kept her desk, Kayda caught sight of the map on the wall. The dot that represented Harlow remained in Washington, though not in Kensey.

"She's been at the same spot for a few days," Jo said. "It moves a mile or two from that location every once in a while, but otherwise stays put."

What are you up to, Harlow?

"So what's this item you brought me?" Jo asked.

Kayda turned her back on the map and faced the group crammed into the tight space. She pulled the ring out of her pocket.

Jo took it between two fingers and held it up to the light, turning it this way and that, and peered along the inside edge of the band, presumably searching for anything engraved there. As she did so, Kayda told her about the run-in with the wind elemental, the feral vampire that got away, and the coyote used to keep the veil open. Kayda didn't know Jo as well as Harlow did, but trust didn't come easy for Harlow, so if she trusted Jo, that was good enough for Kayda.

After Kayda's recounting, Jo silently moved to her desk and pulled out another map—this one only of Luma. Jo went through the same motions as she had when conducting a locator spell on the note Harlow had sent via bird courier. They all huddled near Jo, quietly listening to the lullaby-like cadence of the spell.

As before, when the final words left her lips, nothing happened for a few long seconds. Then a dot materialized on the map.

"There," Jo said, pointing a dark manicured finger toward a spot in the northeast part of the city, in the Warehouse District. It wasn't far from Kayda's now-abandoned apartment in Ardmore.

"Can we take this map with us?" Welsh asked. "I'm not as skilled as you are with locator magic, ma'am, but I should be able to keep it going now that you've started it."

Jo turned to him, arms crossed. "Stop with this 'ma'am' business. Name's Jo."

"I apologize, Jo," Welsh said, bowing slightly.

"I won't ask you to reveal who you are, but I must ask if this is the result of tonic or glamour magic," Jo said, motioning to the trio. "I can't see through the glamours, but there's a fuzziness to the magic around those two that isn't there with yours. Yet, the magic coming off you is ... off-putting."

"It's a magic that changes the natural state of a person," Welsh said, "so it would make sense that it's unsettling to a nature witch as accomplished as yourself."

Jo smiled faintly. "Does the charm come with the glamour or the person beneath it?"

"The glamour," Henri and Kayda said in unison, then grinned at each other. They both grimaced at the sight, which caused even more grimacing.

"Either way, I can say I've never met a witch with a command of glamour magic as extensive as this," Jo said. "I am impressed, even as my own magic recoils."

"I'm impressed you can detect it at all. That says as much about your skill as it does mine," Welsh said.

Jo idly fussed with a lock of hair that had slipped loose from her long, jet-black braid. Oh hells, she was enamored with Mr. Bosworth Hemmingsley!

Kayda imagined an endless trail of ex-lovers left in Welsh's wake, with them never able to find him again because no one knew his true face. She wondered if anyone really knew him. Caspian, maybe. "Can we take the map with us?" she asked again, hoping to snap Jo out of it.

With a little shake of her head, she smiled at Kayda. "Yes, of course."

"What do we owe you?" Welsh asked, slipping a hand into his back pocket.

Jo waved him off. "Tell Fletch she owes me free charmed goods for at least a month when she gets back. I assume this is all tied up in whatever mess that girl has gotten herself into now. I'm here to help if you need anything else."

Kayda took the map from the desk and stared down at the

black dot, which moved a fraction of an inch to the left, then went stationary. "Thanks, Jo."

"Anytime."

They filed back down the cramped hallway, Welsh leading the way. Kayda folded the map and stuck it in her back pocket. The lock clicked open for Welsh before he reached the door, and he pushed it open to reveal the brighter, livelier store.

Erik scuttled over when they'd made it halfway across the shop. "Mr. Bellingsworth! I trust you found what you needed. I wanted to extend my aid to you. Lady Josephine is often so busy, but as her assistant, I hereby offer my service to you for any matters that she cannot fit on her already-full plate. It would be my honor to work with a man as distinguished as yourself." He bowed deeply.

Welsh hadn't divulged anything about his "work." Erik was operating based on the assumption that an impeccably tailored suit equaled distinction.

"No, thank you," Welsh said simply, brushing past him.

Kayda didn't miss Erik's crestfallen look as she followed Welsh out the door. The three of them stood on the sidewalk, the sounds of downtown a constant cacophony of voices—talking, shouting, laughing. A man dressed as a colorful clown stood on the other side of the sidewalk, creating magically animated balloon animals. The scent of baking bread wafted past her.

Welsh pulled back the cuff of his suit jacket to check his watch. "I have an appointment in an hour. Where would you like me to drop you off? We can touch base later."

Kayda turned to Henri. "Do you work today?"

"Called in sick, what with the head trauma. I'm up for whatever."

"Including surveillance?" Kayda asked.

Henri nodded. "Especially surveillance."

"I find you two nauseating," Welsh said, then walked away.

Somehow, the insult put a bounce in Kayda's step as she and Henri followed Welsh back to the Sarq.

Twenty minutes later, they were back in the parking garage. Henri climbed onto his cycle and Kayda slid on behind him. Instead of waving them off, Welsh rested a forearm on a handlebar, eyeing them in turn. In his more familiar gruff voice, he said, "Try not to do anything stupid, yeah? Healing tonics aren't cheap and if you wrap yourself around another tree, I'll have to charge you to patch you back up. I'll text you from my new burner once I get it so you have the number. Call if you find anything."

"As you please, my liege," Henri said in his best nightmare voice and reversed out of the parking spot.

There was a faint hint of a smile as Welsh watched them go.

Kayda and Henri stopped in Ardmore to pick up lunch. The good thing about doing surveillance with a magicked map meant they didn't have to physically keep eyes on the guy; they just had to be ready to follow him at a moment's notice if his dot suddenly sprang into motion. There was a park in the Warehouse District not far from where the dot was now, so they planned to have a picnic in said park while they waited for the dot to do something interesting.

The park was in one of the fancier parts of the district, surrounded on three sides by high-rise apartment buildings with towering gates to help keep out the riffraff. The park was open to the public, though, so Kayda happily paid no mind to the stink eye she and Henri got from the well-dressed fae women who were clustered nearby, pointedly ignoring their children swarming the play area.

After plowing through their sandwiches, Kayda and

Henri lay on their backs in the grass and stared up at the few wispy clouds scudding across the bright blue sky. The warm sun beat down on her skin, relaxing her. Though her side felt wildly better than it had last night, the walk from Welsh's apartment to Jo's shop and back again had worn her out. Now, full and warm and lying beside Henri, she fell asleep.

She'd been having another racy dream about Henri when someone gently nudged her awake. Henri, she thought, imagining waking beside him in bed. Letting out a contented sigh, she snuggled closer to him and drowsily opened her eyes. He gazed down at her, his head propped on his fist.

Kayda screamed bloody murder.

She rolled away from him and got to her feet so fast she experienced vertigo. Henri's bug eyes were even larger now. Kayda shuddered. "Your face is horrible!"

Henri gasped. "Sorry! I forgot!"

"How could you forget!"

"Ahem!" someone said, coughing loudly.

Who said "ahem" in real life?

Kayda found five mothers and eight children of various races all gawping at them from the play area a few hundred feet away. Maybe they suspected Henri was trying to suck Kayda's soul out of her face.

"Don't you ... children? ... have a better place to be?" one of the mothers asked.

Henri dropped onto all fours and cocked his head sharply toward one side. "Don't you have somewhere better to be?" He scuttled forward a few feet and the mothers collectively gasped. "For tonight is the eve of the rising! You do not want to be here when night falls unless you want your children to join me. Once they have a taste, they will be mine forever."

Scuttle, scuttle.

The play area cleared quickly. Kayda cackled, despite how fast her heart raced.

Henri stood to his full height and beamed at her, clearly delighted with himself.

"You're demented," she said.

He bowed.

"Did you wake me for a reason other than causing heart failure?" she asked, a hand to her chest.

"Oh!" He rushed to the spot where she'd been sleeping, pulling out the map from underneath a half-full bottle of water. "The dot moved!"

Kayda joined him and peered at the map. The dot had moved from its original location to a spot a few inches away on the map. It remained stationary for nearly a full minute—then disappeared entirely. "What the?"

"There," Henri said, pointing. "Now it's in the Necropolis."

"Damn telepads," Kayda said.

There wasn't much in the Necropolis that the average person would be interested in, other than a smattering of rougher bars and restaurants that lined the border between the district and the ones above it. When the dot in question stayed put for a couple of minutes in a location that sat between the Necropolis and Montclaire, they gathered up their trash and took off for the parking lot where Henri had left his cycle.

As he drove, Kayda kept one arm around Henri's middle and used her free hand to hold the map between their bodies, his back serving as a windshield so she could keep an eye on the dot in case it darted somewhere else.

By the time they arrived, it was just after seven in the evening. The dot was still in place. In a neighborhood such as this, there were two establishments the mystery guy could be in on Yelena Avenue, unless he was in one of the abandoned buildings behind the chain-link fence across the street.

They stood in the middle of the parking lot that both buildings shared, first staring at the Golden Muskrat to the left, and then Fry on the Wall to the right—a bar and a restaurant respectively. The Fry on the Wall boasted "Best chicken-fried steak!" from a tattered white banner above the door. A pair of cars sat outside.

The windows of the Golden Muskrat were dark, not because the lights were out, but because they'd been coated in streaky black paint to keep people from peering in. That half of the lot was packed. A neon yellow outline of a muskrat in a hoop skirt gyrated from a window, casting jerky bursts of light across the hoods of cars.

The front door opened and out poured a burst of noise, as well as a very drunk man who immediately vomited into a pot of dying daisies by the door. He stumbled down the sidewalk toward the Fry on the Wall, but seconds after stepping inside, he was kicked back out, given his shout of "I have rights!" aimed at the door, his fist in the air. He slumped onto the curb outside the door. Less than a minute later, he flopped onto his side, snoring loudly.

This did not bode well, given the hour. If there was a wind elemental in there who tended to get plastered before the sun fully went down, questioning said elemental would probably result in even worse injuries than she'd already sustained.

Kayda looked at Henri and sighed. "Given our luck, he's probably in the Golden Muskrat, isn't he?"

Wordlessly, Henri marched toward the door.

There was no one checking for IDs, so they strolled inside. A long bar stretched across the left side of the room, and every stool was taken. A small dance floor took up the back corner; the right side of the room was lined with booth seats; and a random assortment of tables filled the space in the middle. The two bartenders were fast at work.

Kayda had no idea how to find the owner of the ring now that they were here. Most of the booth seats were taken, but the ones in the middle weren't. Empty glasses and plates covered in half-eaten food were left on the surfaces of several, but Kayda wasn't sure if that was a sign the waitstaff was backed up, or that the owners were on the dance floor and would come back to finish later. The frenzy of shouts and laughter she'd heard when the drunk had stumbled out had been from the dance floor. There was a very lively group dance to "The Wobble," and an intoxicated pair of faun ladies were scream-cackling and holding each other up, the clomping of their hooves like an off-kilter drumbeat. Kayda angled herself behind Henri and pulled the map back out, hoping that the dot would be moving minutely left to right to indicate he was on the dance floor. No such luck. So he was either at the bar, in one of the booths, or enjoying chicken-fried steak next door.

She was about to ask Henri what they should do next when a pair at the bar hopped off their stools and headed for the exit. Kayda grabbed Henri's arm and pulled him toward the vacated seats. She felt like a toddler crawling onto the barstool but managed it without incident. When the man beside Henri glanced over at him, he jumped and sloshed his drink onto his own pants. He was human, Kayda guessed, but built like a tank, his bulging arms covered in tattoos. He looked like the type to get in someone's face about making him spill a drink, but even he was so creeped out by Henri that he slid off the seat and guided his female companion toward an unoccupied table in the middle of the room.

"Does that make you feel bad?" Kayda whispered.

Henri angled his giant, sorrowful eyes at her. "I've never felt so liberated in my life."

Kayda snorted a laugh.

The female bartender hadn't seen them sit down, busy as

she was mixing a drink for a patron. She sauntered over now and assessed the pair. She blinked a few times in rapid succession but didn't recoil. Bartenders had seen far worse, Kayda imagined. "What can I get you two?"

Kayda leaned her crossed arms on the sticky bar top and leaned forward. The bartender mirrored her, her brows raised. "We're looking for someone. Do you know if there are any elementals here tonight?"

The bartender's friendly expression shuttered. "Why do you ask?"

"We have something he lost."

She eyed Kayda a few seconds longer. "We don't have any policies specific to magic type, but elementals only cause trouble here. We can tell from a mile away if we've got one in and send them packing after a couple of drinks. It's not discrimination so much as business security. If you're looking for an elemental, you're in the wrong place. They know not to come here."

"Thanks," Kayda said, trying not to sound disappointed. Either they'd all been wrong about the elemental thing, or the person they were trying to find was in Fry on the Wall.

The bartender shrugged, then moved down the bar to help a newly arrived customer.

Kayda turned in her seat and studied the patrons. Since many fae appeared human at first glance, it was mostly impossible to tell what magic type one had simply by looking at them. During the wrestling match over the coyote carcass, a hand had been pulled through the veil. From what Kayda could remember, the hand hadn't had any discerning marks: pale skin with clean, blunt nails that appeared masculine. But she could be wrong about that, too. The person she scoured the bar for might not be an elemental or male.

One of the booths was occupied by four pale-skinned people—two female, two male—all of them quietly nursing their beers and silently eating their dinner. An obligatory family meal where everyone wanted to be somewhere else? The longer Kayda observed them, the less they seemed to share a close connection. She observed a few awkward attempts at conversation that died quickly. Eye contact was avoided. They all had that timeless fae thing going on, making it hard to determine age, but she guessed they were young. Late teens, early twenties, maybe. Was this an internet meetup of introverts that had gone off the rails immediately?

The door to the bar opened again, and in strolled a blond-haired woman who had the same general features as the younger group, but this one was more mature than the others. The sullen teenagers perked up at the arrival of the newcomer, who grabbed a chair from a neighboring table and positioned it at the end of the booth. The teenagers leaned in as one to listen to the woman, whose upright posture and hand gestures had commanded the teenagers' complete attention. Kayda cursed her disguise. If she'd been here as a draken, she could have manipulated the dials on her hearing to listen in on the conversation. It wasn't as if she expected one of them to say, "Oh, what did I do last night? I lost my ring after letting some ferals into the city. What about you?" but she might have gleaned some detail to let her know if she was spying on the wrong patrons.

"Any change on the map?" Henri whispered to her. He'd also turned in his seat to observe the customers; he'd been absorbed by the activity on the dance floor, though. The dance was now "The Electric Slide," and the drunken fauns were howling with laughter because they were too drunk to dance in the same direction as everyone else. There would be a fist fight soon if the fauns stomped on one more toe with their hooves.

Kayda took the map out of her back pocket, half expecting the dot to be clear across town. But it was in the same spot it had been in before. A few seconds later, it shuffled to the right.

Kayda's head snapped up. The group of five were getting to their feet and heading for the door. One of those four teenagers had to be the owner of the ring in her pocket.

She leaned toward Henri and cupped a hand over her mouth. "When those five people make it out of the bar, we'll follow them out."

"What, the elves?" Henri asked, his helium voice even more grating when so close to her ear.

She peered at him. "How do you know they're elves?"

"Saw the pointed ears on one of them when we walked in," Henri said. "She was scratching the side of her head and an ear poked out from her hair. The guy next to her elbowed her and she covered it up."

"Interesting."

"The door just closed behind them," Henri said.

They hopped off their stools and scampered out the door.

The wispy clouds Kayda had fallen asleep staring at earlier were inked orange and pink now, the sky a navy blue that reminded Kayda of Henri. The elves piled into two cars, then drove out of the lot. Kayda checked the map, confirming that the dot went in the same direction as the departing vehicles.

"Uh ..." Henri said, glancing down at his watch. "Crap. I just realized something. Our glamours are going to wear off in about twenty minutes. You have any spares on you?"

Kayda sighed dramatically. She'd forgotten too. "I had one in my pocket when I hit the tree, but it smashed along with the rest of me. I forgot to ask Welsh for more."

"I'm out too. What do we do? Go back for more, or follow them as us?" Henri asked.

Kayda watched as the dot moved farther away, centimeter by centimeter. "Let's go."

Henri pumped a fist in the air.

Smiling to herself, she pulled out her phone and found a

text from Welsh's new number. He hadn't sent a message with anything so helpful as, *"Hello, Kayda. This is Zander Welsh's new phone number."* Instead, all it said was, *"New one."*

Deciding to send him a message as lacking in detail, she typed, *"Ring belongs to an elf."* Then she climbed onto the cycle behind Henri and held on tight as he sped down Yelena Avenue.

Chapter 24
HARLOW

Since I was sleep-deprived and punchy, as soon as morning had officially arrived—punctuated by the slamming of doors up and down the hall—I got up to shower, then walked two blocks down the road to get coffee. I'd donned a few of the glamoured accessories, and wore sunglasses, but no one paid me much mind.

When I returned with two large cups and a bag of pastries, Caspian was awake. He was propped up against the headboard and rubbed his eyes with the heels of his palms.

"How you feeling?" I asked as I handed him his coffee. He took it black, like a masochist.

I took mine loaded down with so much cream and sugar that it didn't taste like coffee anymore, like a normal person.

Caspian took a long sip and sighed. "Better. What's in the bag?"

I handed him an everything bagel and a single serving of chive-and-onion cream cheese. Masochist.

While we ate breakfast, I told him what I'd found in the journal, knowing that informing him of how many utterly boring passages there were about "rune arrays" would wake him up the rest of the way. When I had him frothing at the mouth, I hit him with the rest.

"Welsh texted last night about Kayda and him getting attacked by a feral. I called and texted, but he's not answering. Does he have any other numbers you can try? I checked with Felix and he hasn't returned my call either."

Caspian found his phone on the vanity and unplugged it. "I'll call him."

I chewed on my lip while I waited.

"Disconnected," Caspian said. "He probably just changed numbers again. I'm sure we'll hear from him soon. It's quite early."

Although I'd downed most of my coffee, I yawned loudly.

"Did you sleep at all?" Caspian asked.

"Not really."

"Get some rest and I'll wake you if I hear anything," he said.

I eyed him dubiously.

"I promise I'm fine. I can get carried away when I'm immersed in a project. You were right to force me to sleep," he said. "Now let me do the same for you." He pointed to my bed and smashed his brows together, attempting to look menacing. "Go to bed!"

I snorted. "Fine. The second you hear anything, wake me up."

"Uh-huh," he said absently, his gaze flicking toward the journals on my nightstand.

"You just want me to sleep so you can have uninterrupted reading time!"

"That will be a bonus, yes."

I wanted to issue more complaints, but a deep yawn interrupted me. Climbing onto my bed, I kicked off my tennis shoes, leaving them on the floor in between the two beds. "Don't get so caught up in reading that you don't check your phone."

"Yes, yes," he said, pulling the topmost journal off the stack. He shuddered in anticipation, as if he'd picked up a pornographic magazine. "Go to sleep," he said absently as he flipped open the cover.

I was asleep moments later.

"Ah! Felix, that tickles!" I heard myself say, punctuated by a very girly giggle, right before my eyes flew open. Caspian's face was inches away. I pressed my head further into the pillow, disoriented.

Memories of the dream slammed back into place. My cheeks heated.

"Was I talking in my sleep?" I asked.

Caspian stood, wincing slightly. "Talking. Laughing. Moaning ..."

"Be right back," I said. "I'm going to throw myself into the nearest river."

"Don't be embarrassed. It's quite natural. I'm happy your sleep was ... enjoyable."

"Oh my God," I said, sitting up. My face was so warm, I was starting to sweat. Needing something to do with my hands, I pulled the elastic out of the messy bun flopping on the side of my head. It had come loose in my sleep. I vowed to sleep in the shower stall tonight.

"I woke you because Welsh finally texted."

"Oh!" I rubbed an eye. "What time is it?"

Caspian scratched the side of his nose. "Eight. Uhh ... in the evening."

Great. I would be up until 5 a.m. now. I glanced at the alarm clock on the nightstand for confirmation that I'd slept the day away. Yawning and stretching, I went to use the restroom. I noted with some amusement that there were yet more bottles of Ocean Sunrise Body Wash on the counter. Caspian hadn't thought to wake me earlier, but he'd sweet-talked the maid into coughing up more soap. We'd have to leave her a massive cash tip when we finally left this place.

"You read both journals cover to cover, didn't you?" I asked when I came back out.

"One and a half," he said. "My phone chiming snapped me out of it."

He had the phone in his hand and I snatched it from him before he realized I'd moved. I typed in his password and got into his messages.

"Caspian Blackthorn, he sent his new number this afternoon!" The message that had come through a few minutes ago had been Welsh checking that Caspian hadn't met his demise while Welsh had been between phones.

"Margaret was a truly fascinating woman," Caspian said as if that were a proper excuse.

At least these messages were confirmation that Welsh was alive.

I dialed the new number and then put the call on speaker. Sitting cross-legged on my unmade bed—Caspian perched on the side—I placed the ringing phone on the comforter.

Welsh's familiar gruff voice answered after the second ring. "You good?"

"Are you?" I snapped. "You can't text about ferals, dead coyotes, and my best friend and then disappear on us, Welsh! I get needing to change your phone number often but you can't—"

"Hello to you too, Harlow," Welsh cut in. "I didn't change the number out of paranoia. Shortly after texting you the pictures, we got blasted by a wind elemental. I was distracted. My phone was ruined shortly afterward."

"Blasted?" Caspian said. "Didn't you say it was a feral attack?"

"First it was the ferals, then it was an elemental who took offense at Kayda trying to steal its animal sacrifice. Kayda just texted that it was an elf who let the ferals in, though—not an elemental."

I rubbed the spot between my eyebrows, where a headache was forming. I wasn't sure if this was nap fog or if Welsh wasn't making any sense. "An elf let ferals in? Why?"

I recalled the afternoon not that long ago when I'd helped a human guy get to a Visitors Center because some asshole elf had tricked him into crossing the veil and into Luma. That had seemed like nothing more than a typical elven prank. Letting feral vampires into the city was so much more than that.

"That I don't know," Welsh said. "You know as much as I do at this point."

"But you're all okay?"

"Kayda wound up with some broken ribs, but she's healing nicely. She spent the night at my place partly because she needed to get patched up immediately and partly because her apartment's obviously been compromised, what with the break-in."

"Broken ribs? A break-in? Who broke in?"

"Werecats. But I promise you she's fine," Welsh said with a gentleness I didn't know he possessed.

I couldn't believe she was fine until I heard it from her myself. Tears pricked the back of my eyes and my throat tightened.

Caspian grabbed hold of one of my shaking hands and squeezed.

Blowing out a shaky breath, I said, "Next time you see her, can she call me using your phone? Oh, any chance you've been in contact with Felix? He's been MIA, too."

Welsh snorted. "That's our fault. Ever since that broadcast with the fae girls, mindsets of the fae have started to change about the Collective. I've gotten more calls than usual with requests for help to get out of Luma, if not the entire hub system."

"How is that connected to bounty hunters?" I asked, though I had already suspected as much, given how often the pocket mirror had been going off since we'd left Luma.

"I'll give you an example. A father of three contacted me because bounty hunters arrested his wife. She'd been in the shower when werecats showed up for an unannounced raid on their house, supposedly tracking down leads about where you two might be hiding. Her kids were asleep. She didn't answer the door when they knocked, so they forced their way in. When her kids started screaming about intruders, she came running, a fire spell already thrown before she made it into her front room. The werecat in its path got out of the way in time, but the fireball burned off his whiskers on one side. For that offense alone, they gave her a ticket for unlawful use of a deadly weapon against an officer.

"She works days; her husband works nights. She couldn't afford to go to her court appointment, especially when she thought it was bullshit that she got ticketed in her own home because the werecats broke in and terrified her children. Bounty hunters picked her up three days ago. She was returned home tonight and is a shell of herself, he said. He doesn't know what they did to her, but he wants out of Luma. They can't afford to stay, either financially or mentally."

"What possible connection does this woman have to me or Harlow?" Caspian asked, his voice tight.

"Hells if I know. Maybe she was a client of Harlow's. Or had attended one of your auctions. Maybe it's an even looser connection," Welsh said. "There have been press conferences almost every day detailing the efforts they're implementing to find you. They're preoccupied with Harlow and the sword, though. Her reward amount keeps going up. If I didn't believe you were more useful as a fugitive, Harlow, I'd totally turn you in for the fifty g's."

Caspian chuckled. "You would not."

Normally I'd toss in a snarky comment, but I was fixated on this family Welsh told us about. A family who had been minding their own business and now their lives were turned upside down because we'd ticked off the Collective.

Because *I'd* ticked off the Collective.

In a small voice, I asked, "Is this my fault?" I stared at the sword lying in the duffel bag. If I had never taken it, it wouldn't have killed those shifters. The Collective wouldn't be after me, or Caspian, or Kayda ...

But those fae girls—Nyla and Bonnie and all the others—wouldn't have been found, either. They'd still have been in the clutches of Stan the hybrid vampire. And who knew how many other fae girls would have been trafficked out of the Ghost Lily, leaving behind more families and friends forever wondering if their girls would come home.

"Don't be so egocentric," Welsh said, but his tone remained kind. "Luma was careening for chaos already. You just hit the gas when it started going downhill."

That didn't make me feel better, but I knew what he meant.

"I'm meeting Kayda and Henri tonight," Welsh said. "I'll have her call you soon."

My brain misfired. "Wait. Kayda *and* Henri?"

"You good, Blackthorn?" Welsh asked, ignoring me.

"I'm good," Caspian said.

"How is Henri involved now?" I tried again.

"The journals of Margaret Fengast have provided me with a wealth of information," Caspian said. "She has extensive notes on the ancient rune language. She was a second-generation fae who was largely self-taught, which I find most admirable. It sounds like she has fascinating theories on the—"

"Gotta go! Glad you two aren't dead," Welsh interrupted.

I said, "Yes, but what about—"

"Bye!" Welsh had disconnected the call.

"I know that's your boy," I said, staring at the screen, "but he's infuriating."

Caspian chuckled.

I cocked my head. "You do that to him on purpose, don't you?"

"What, bore Zander Welsh intentionally solely to make him uncomfortable? Who me?"

I blinked at him several times. The sword rose out of the duffel bag enough to poke its blade out, like a rodent popping out of a hole. "Did you ... just use sarcasm?"

"Duh."

I clutched my invisible pearls. "Sword! What do we do! Caspian must have a fever."

"Are you hungry?" Caspian asked, smiling.

"Starved."

"Let's go grab something to eat and we can discuss Margaret's findings. I promise to keep the boring parts to a minimum."

"Want to come with us, sword?" I asked.

It flew out of the duffel bag so quickly, it was a wonder it hadn't ripped it.

Tap.

It glowed bright blue, paused for an appropriate length of time, then tapped again.

I laughed. "I didn't think swords could get cabin fever."

Tap. Tap. Tap. Tap!

"Okay, okay! You're coming too."

It spun around me in a dizzying circle.

Once we were dressed, ready to go, and standing in the hallway, though, Caspian didn't immediately open the door.

"What's wrong?"

"This will be the first time we've both left the room since we got the chest opened. I think I should put up a few wards," he said.

It wasn't a bad idea. We'd mostly been using the sword as our version of an attack dog. If someone happened to track us down and tried to ambush us while we slept, the sword would slash them to pieces before we opened our eyes.

Setting a trio of wards on both the windows and the door took Caspian twenty-five minutes. As we headed into the still-warm evening, I felt a light tickle of magic pass over me, like static electricity.

With the sword tucked away in the duffel bag strapped over my shoulder, we walked the few blocks to the diner down the street. I chattered away about my theory that sorcerers had aided humans in the extinction of the ancients on Earth. I got a funny look from a teenage boy who'd overheard part of the conversation, but he only asked what movie we'd been talking about. I made up a title on the fly that the boy would have a hell of a time trying to find online later.

Some of my pent-up anxiety dissipated as Caspian and I laughed about the interaction. He was no longer on the brink of mental collapse, which was nice. I'd eventually have to pry out the details about his animosity toward Albert Sweeney now that Caspian was rested. For now, though, he seemed stable. Welsh, Kayda, and apparently Henri were okay, too. I still didn't know if I'd ever be able to go home, but for the moment we were safe, and that was enough.

The diner offered the standard greasy American fare. We both ordered burgers and fries, and I even splurged for a milkshake. The sword lay in its duffel bag beside my thigh, while Caspian sat in the booth across from me. The place was more packed than I would have expected since it was in a small town and the hour was late. But it was also close to a highway exit and was open twenty-four hours, so I figured a lot of these diners were people stopping for a bite to eat on their way to somewhere more interesting. The din of voices was an odd comfort after being cooped up in that room with Caspian for days. It made me strangely homesick. I missed the frenetic energy of downtown. I missed my old apartment. I missed Kayda.

"Hey," Caspian said softly, and I glanced over at him instead of staring forlornly out the window. He hiked his brows in silent question.

I shrugged. "Wanna tell me about Margaret Fengast?"

His eyes lit up.

Before he could get started, though, a solid mass of a person appeared at the end of our table. I expected to find a waiter there, our plates of food in hand. Instead, I met beady eyes sunk into a familiar face.

"Hello, Harlow," he said, then nodded once to Caspian.

We donned glamour accessories every time we left the motel, but apparently my disguise wasn't distinctive enough. A little voice told me it probably wouldn't have mattered. Either he'd followed us here, or the magical trackers branded onto our wrists had given up our locations.

"Can't say I'm happy to see you, Cody," I said, resisting the urge to call him the name I preferred—Bruiser.

He grabbed a chair from a nearby table and plunked it in front of the booth. I was grateful he hadn't tried to smash in next to me, but he was honestly such a bulky guy, he might have gotten stuck. The sword twitched in the bag beside me, and I placed a gentle hand on the duffel to keep it in place.

"Don't try to make a run for it," Bruiser said. "I've got a friend stationed outside in case you try anything stupid. I'm just here to chat anyway. No need to cause a scene and ruin all these people's night, right?"

I was less comforted by the busy diner now. It would be much harder for Caspian to use his magic or for the sword to do its thing when there were this many innocent bystanders. If we were in a diner in Luma, I would be much more willing to risk it. But if Caspian, the sword, and I were trying to maintain a low profile, ending up on a mundane's viral social media feed wasn't the way to do it. Which Bruiser knew. I wanted to give him a quick kick in the shin.

"Chat about what, Cody?" Caspian asked, arms folded on the table.

The waitress showed up with our burgers and fries. Maybe I could dump the milkshake over Cody's bald head. "Did you want to order any food, sweetie?" the waitress asked, placing a hand on Cody's wide back.

"I'll have some of theirs, ma'am. Thank you."

"You bet," she said. "Holler if you need me."

Cody snatched a fry off my plate and popped it in his mouth. "Boss wants to know what's in the chest."

"Us telling him that wasn't part of the deal," I said.

"True." Cody grabbed another fry. "But you're not telling him. You're telling me."

"We haven't gotten the chest open yet," Caspian said.

Cody tsked. "Oh, now that's not true. I'm disappointed you'd lie to me. I've only just arrived to enjoy a nice meal with you and you're already lying."

I sat back, arms crossed. "Why do you think we're lying?"

Cody's hand dropped out of view below the table, materializing a few seconds later with a cell phone. He typed and swiped at the screen, let out a satisfied, "Ah!" and then turned the screen toward us. "This is your room, isn't it?"

Caspian and I leaned forward simultaneously and peered at the phone. My pulse pounded in my temples. Was someone in the room right now? But Caspian would have known if someone triggered the wards. I shot him a look, my eyebrows hiked. He lightly shook his head, shrugging.

"There are more," Cody said, craning his neck so he could look at the screen too while keeping it facing us. With a thick finger, he swiped to the next picture. A close-up of the box of feathers on the chair. Another swipe. A hand pulling up the lid of the box full of dragon scales. "We've been keeping tabs on you since you left the hangar, as I'm sure you would have guessed."

We had not.

"And we started to notice some things," Cody said, pocketing his phone. "Like how the young housekeeper—that shy blond one—makes her rounds down your hallway every day between 9 and 11 a.m. She doesn't rake in a lot of dough making beds and bringing ungrateful guests extra towels, so when we offered her a stack of cash to take a couple of pictures of the inside of your room for us, she wasn't hard to convince."

I clenched my jaw.

"Dammit," Caspian said. "She came by this morning with more towels while you were asleep. I asked if she had more soap I could purchase, as I was getting ready to take a shower. She said she'd drop them off. When I got out, the extra bottles she'd brought by were on the vanity."

"She let herself in while I was sleeping?" I asked, unnerved.

"Apparently," he said, lips pursed. "I thought we'd developed a camaraderie."

"Aw, don't be so sad, chum," Cody said. "Everyone can be bought."

In Luma, I would have been suspicious of everyone. But outside the hubs, where next to no one knew about magic, I'd started to lose my constant paranoia. Shy, very human Rachel the housekeeper hadn't been on my radar as anyone to look out for.

The color leached from Caspian's face. He shot a death glare at Cody before eyeing me warily. "Something jostled the ward on the motel door."

"Ah, so you do have wards up," Cody said. "We figured you would. It's the first time you two have left together since buying the chest. Well, other than that same night when Harlow was bleeding all over the place. There was one hell of a protection spell on that lock. Zapped Sweeney's ass quite a few times.

"After three days, though, when you left together again, checking out the room was a gamble we were willing to take. Sweeney said you were good, Blackthorn. Between you and me? I think he's jealous you got it open so fast."

Caspian's expression remained blank.

"Anyway ... using Rachel was a less invasive way to get into the room to see if you found anything we'd want. Turns out you did. The amount the boss can get off those scales alone ..." He whistled appreciatively.

Three buzzes sounded from a pocket of the duffel bag.

"Oh, good. You have that with you, too," Cody said. "One of my boys heard it go off on one of your walks back from the coffee shop. Go ahead and check it."

How did Cody know about the mirrors? Did Domino have a bounty hunter on his payroll too?

Reluctantly, I unzipped a side pocket and took out the mirror. I read the message three times before my panicked mind registered what the words meant.

"What does it say?" Caspian asked.

Without looking up, I read, "Code 158. Fletcher and Black-thorn. Last known location 2576 Greal River, Washington. Armed and dangerous."

True to form, Caspian used the most accurate word for the situation. "Fuck."

"Fuck indeed," Cody said, snatching another fry. I pushed my whole plate of food over to him. He happily picked up the burger.

Caspian flinched. "First ward is down."

I glared at Cody, who now had a glob of ketchup on his chin. "Who ratted us out to the Collective? You? You're the only one who seemed to care about the bounty reward."

"It was kind of a group decision. Domino runs the show, but he runs it like a democracy, you know? Everyone gets a voice." Cody took a huge bite of the burger, chewed slowly, and swallowed. "Once we saw what was in the box, we figured the dough we'd get from selling that stuff plus the bounty reward for you three would be real nice financially for the whole crew. Maybe you could find another sword for Domino, but that could take months. Years, even. With this plan, we get the money a lot quicker. Maybe we could even figure out how to make one of those swords from all that stuff. Domino is fair, but he's not patient."

None of the pictures Rachel had taken had included the journals. Maybe she hadn't seen them. The covers were plain. No labels. I hoped Domino's goons currently breaking into the room wouldn't find those. Sweeney would be knowledgeable enough about runes to know what those schematics were. Domino was wealthy enough and well-connected enough that he'd eventually figure out how to make his own sentient weapons.

Caspian asked, "It was Sweeney who put in the call to

Luma, wasn't it?"

"Good guess! We figured with Sweeney's clout, the Collective would treat the tip as premium intel and send out its hunters and cats as soon as possible. The Collective thinks he's in Washington visiting a sick sister, so they wouldn't even question why he's out here." Cody laughed, revealing a mouthful of half-chewed food. "His sister moved to Vermont two years ago."

"Second ward is weakening," Caspian said, one eye twitching. "This is either a sorcerer or someone with a high tolerance for discomfort. The first one would have been strong enough to stun the average human for at least an hour."

"Domino only hires the best." Cody pointed a finger at Caspian's plate. "You gonna eat that?"

Caspian shoved his plate over as well. He'd had one hand below the table for a few minutes now. I envisioned his quick fingers etching out runes on the underside of the table. If I tried to scoot out of the booth past Cody, he'd probably crush my windpipe in one giant hand while using his free one to shove the rest of my burger in his stupid mouth.

One of my hands stayed on the sword, while the other clutched the pocket mirror. I honestly had no idea what to do. Cody's casual air was doing what he intended: for it to freak me out even more than if he was being aggressive. He knew he had the upper hand simply by cornering us in a crowded restaurant with his bulk blocking the exit.

I yelped when the fabric beneath my hand grew hot. I instinctively scooted away, which put me closer to Cody. The sword had burned through the duffel bag, turning it into a blackened pile of melted zippers and singed fabric. The plastic coating on the booth's back warped and bubbled.

Before I could get a word out, the sword glided off the bench seat and out of sight.

Cody continued rambling. "I give the bounty hunters half

an hour tops to descend on the motel. They'll hop in a telepad from Luma to Kensey, and then book it to that address. They'll run into a very helpful fellow in the parking lot that will guide them to this diner, and—"

Cody froze, his eyes wide. He forcibly shoved his chair back, the legs scraping along the tile floor. He clipped the foot of an unsuspecting waitress bustling by with a tray covered in drinks. She and the drinks went down. Sodas and ice spilled across the threadbare carpet.

Someone screamed.

Not because of the fallen waitress, but because of the giant man sitting in the middle of the walkway with a thirty-inch sword sticking out of his stomach.

"Fuck," Caspian eloquently offered once more.

"Dammit, sword!" I said. "You have got to consult with me first."

Cody had his hands on the hilt now, desperately trying to pull the sword from his gut. The sword allowed itself to be pulled free by a couple of inches, then slammed home again. Cody screamed.

The din of the restaurant was fading now. People were on their feet, trying to figure out what the commotion was.

Blood seeped into Cody's white shirt like ink in water, the circle of red growing ever wider. With his hands on the hilt, suddenly Cody's arms jerked sideways as the sword violently twisted itself in Cody's stomach.

Ohhh, shit. Oh shit. "Oh shit!"

He coughed, blood dribbling out of his mouth. A woman fainted.

I scrambled out of the booth, saliva flooding my mouth. I would not throw up. I would not pass out. I squeezed past Cody on my way to Caspian and stupidly glanced back at the troll. Ohhh, shit. So much blood.

Caspian, if he'd been working on a spell, had been shocked out of it now. He just ... stared at the dying troll. The dying troll whose pale, human skin was starting to turn a very sickly shade of troll-gray. His glamour was fading along with his life.

"Cas! We gotta go!" As I made a break for it, I grabbed a fistful of Caspian's shirt and yanked.

He stumbled after me.

"Hey! You can't leave!"

"Did they murder him ... with a sword?"

"I'm calling the cops!"

I let go of Caspian and booked it for the door. "Sword!"

We weaved around tables of patrons too stunned to move. We were almost at the door when a man bounded into my path. I skidded to a stop. A few others sprang to their feet too, surrounding me. "I don't think so," the first man said. "Sit your ass down until the cops show up."

"Look, I know this looks sketchy, but—" I tried.

"You killed a man in cold blood!" a woman snapped. "My son's a cop. I told him everything. You're both going away for a long time!" She waved her phone above her head.

Oh, hell, this was bad.

"Sit. Your. Ass. *Down*," the first man said again, pointing to his own vacated chair. "I don't want to, but I will use force if you don't cooperate."

"Harlow?" Caspian whispered behind me. "Duck."

I hit the ground without hesitation, hoping the sword wasn't hurtling across the diner to take down the Good Samaritan.

A blast of air rocketed over my head. The people surrounding us were thrown back in all directions by Caspian's air spell. A hand grabbed my elbow and hauled me up.

With the path clear, I bolted for the front door, slammed it open, and ran hard toward the direction of the motel. I knew

Caspian was behind me from the sound of his pounding footsteps. I didn't dare look back.

Leaning against a pole in the parking lot, smoking a cigarette and scrolling through his phone, was the other guard we'd seen outside the auction. He glanced up at the sound of us sprinting down the sidewalk. "Hey!" He tossed his cigarette onto the pavement and stalked toward us.

The sword flew past in my peripheral vision, lamplight winking off its blade. I tensed, anticipating the sound of metal slashing into flesh. The sword, however, flew toward the troll with such speed that it made the man come up short so quickly he lost his footing and slipped in an oil-slick puddle. He went down hard. The sword slammed its hilt into the man's head and his limbs flopped to a halt instantly.

"How ... are the wards ... holding up?" I panted.

We had four more blocks to go. Assuming the human cops didn't catch us fleeing the scene before we got there. I could already hear the faint sound of sirens in the distance.

"Second one is down," Caspian said. "The last one isn't ... going to last much longer."

"I'm very ... mad at you again, sword!" I yelled as I raced around the corner of a bank building. A man at the ATM whirled at the sound of pounding feet, no doubt fearing that he was about to be robbed.

We were being picked up on cameras all over the place right now, I was sure of it.

The sword sailed up next to me, glowing a faint red.

"I know you were protecting me ... but we've talked about how ... inconvenient it is when you ... murder people. Especially in public."

The sword glowed brighter.

When we finally reached the motel parking lot, my lungs were on fire and my heart raced so hard it hurt.

"Third ward just went down," Caspian said as a horrible rending sounded ahead.

Upon reaching the stretch of hallway that included our room, my stomach dropped. From two doors down, I could see that our door, which was too heavy to ever stay ajar, was half off its hinges. Blasted open or torn free, I wasn't sure. Caspian moved to stand in front of me, a protective hand held out to keep me from going first.

I had no idea where my diabolical sword had disappeared to now. Faint sounds of destruction came from our room. That was probably the burglar pawing through our stuff, and not the sword disemboweling another troll.

The door nearest us opened and a wide-eyed man poked his head out, blocking my view of our room. He recoiled when he found us standing so close, his eyes glassy and bloodshot. Either he'd been roused prematurely from a nap, or he was baked. "The fuck is going on out here? Do I call the cops?"

"We are the cops," Caspian said.

My heart almost gave out. I was too frazzled for acting!

The guy eyed Caspian dubiously. Thankfully this was a post-shower-and-sleep Caspian, and not mad-scientist Caspian. He looked pulled together enough, despite the pell-mell run to get over here.

In his authoritative voice, Caspian said, "We've been following a band of thieves who've been hitting motels along highways. Can you tell us if you saw anything unusual?"

"Other than that weird guy going all Dr. Strange on the door and practically smashing it in half?" the guy asked, flailing his arms to possibly mimic martial arts but looking more like he was swatting bees. "Nah."

"Can you explain what you mean by 'going all Dr. Strange'?" Caspian asked with complete sincerity.

"You know, like the superhero?" the guy asked.

"Oh, yes, of course. The one from the FC graphic manga novelettes," Caspian said.

"I will strangle you," I said without thinking.

The guy's eyes ping-ponged between us. "You two sure you're co—oh, holy shit, what the fuck is that?"

I didn't have to look to know the sword had returned—and that it was probably still coated in blood. "Perimeter clear?"

The sword inverted itself and dropped straight down to tap on the concrete once.

The guy at the door tracked the sword as it lifted from the ground and back up by my side. "I'm high as hell, my dudes. Is this shit real?"

"Part of it," Caspian said cryptically.

Something crashed down the hall, and before I could react, the sword harpooned away from me, blade first.

"Nope. I'm not doing this." The guy slammed his door.

"You're 100 percent going to have to buy this motel," I said, then quickly sidestepped Caspian's outreached arm and ran after my sword.

The door to the room was bent down the middle, like a smashed soda can. Had someone's foot done that? I craned my neck to peer through the open space. I could squeeze into the room if I pressed my back against the wall and slid in. Problem was, I wasn't sure I could get back out. If Domino was in there, I wasn't sure the sword would be able to fend him off.

Although Domino was in the business of selling protection to fae, he was more unscrupulous than I'd given him credit for. Did he plan to rob us of the chest's contents even after Caspian had paid him fairly for it? Here I was being naive again—taking the orc at his word. Sure there was no honor among thieves, but I'd worked with plenty of unscrupulous types in Luma and no one had ever pulled shit like this with me.

Domino had been exiled from hub life, though. If the

Collective deemed the guy too problematic, I shouldn't have been surprised. Or this pissed.

Apparently Caspian was pissed too because he once again instructed me to duck. I sidled sideways as another concussive blast shot from Caspian's outstretched hands and blasted the mangled door the rest of the way off its hinges.

I registered belatedly that if the boxes of the chest's contents hadn't been in disarray from the manhandling of whatever oaf had broken in, they surely were now. The cry of pain from inside the room made up for it.

Caspian darted into the room first, hands whipping about in front of him gearing up for another spell. He wouldn't be able to cast too many more before it depleted his energy, but there was a fury rippling off him that I wasn't sure I'd be able to quiet even if I wanted to.

Peeking under Caspian's flailing arms, I spotted our intruder pressed against the back wall, the sword near his throat. The smashed door lay half on my unmade bed. Sweeney glared at us.

He must have used his magic to deflect the flying door, but had been ambushed by the sword shortly afterward. The slice along his cheek was beaded with blood. It wasn't deep enough to wound him too badly, but it had to hurt.

Murderous leer fixed on Caspian, Sweeney said, "If you unleash that array in here, you're going to incinerate your spoils from the treasure chest along with all of us. But you were always impulsive, weren't you?"

I barked a laugh. Caspian? Impulsive?

Sweeney shot a glare my way. "Did he tell you he quit the academy during final exams? It was a slap in the face to everyone at the academy, but he also disgraced his family and left them in financial ruin."

My brows hiked up of their own accord. Caspian looked so

angry, I was unnerved by the perplexing notion that he might currently be more dangerous than the sword.

"You left out the part about why I quit," Caspian snapped.

Sweeney rolled his eyes. "Student deaths are rare but they're not unheard of." He focused on me. "Every student and their families know the risks when they enroll. If they survive physically and mentally, their family gets the tuition amount back double-fold, and the graduating student is guaranteed a position in any hub amongst any Collective of his choice. Your rogue friend here quit, leaving his parents in the lurch. All because a classmate died during his exam."

"He was my closest friend, you asshole," Caspian said through clenched teeth. "You pushed him to the point of exhaustion. He was twenty-five and his heart gave out. You could have failed him. Held him back a year. You saw him suffering and pushed him anyway and you killed him."

Sweeney's lip curled. "The risks are even higher for humans without a magical background. What happened to Marcus—"

"You don't get to say his name."

"What happened to your friend was a tragedy. There's no question about that," Sweeney said, then gave Caspian a head-to-toe scan. "You quitting to honor his memory was the worst tragedy of all. The raw power you possess, the dedication, the creativity you bring to the discipline, was all wasted. We could never fully break you of your impulsivity. Our theory was that you rightly perceived you weren't as ready as you thought, so you used his death as an excuse to avoid humiliation before the entire academy. You might be powerful, but you're a coward. You knew you couldn't handle the pressure, so you fled with your tail tucked between your legs."

The sword's blade burned red, and Sweeney's wide eyes flicked down to where it was poised, tip-first, at the side of his throat.

I took the momentary distraction as my cue to stand in front of Caspian. His hands were held out in front of him, fingers cocked at strange angles. A hovering, circular rune array glowed just beyond his fingertips. It looked like an ancient transparent coin, the edges of the circle made up of runes. It was poised and ready for Caspian to throw at Sweeney. Would a twitch of a finger throw fire at his former professor? Was there enough power locked into the array that it could burn the entire room to the ground?

"Cas," I said slowly, studying his face. "I can't believe I'm saying this to you, but I need you to think this through. If you go nuclear, you might destroy more than Sweeney. Think of Margaret's journals."

His gaze shifted down to me for a second, then back to Sweeney.

"Remember that journal full of yellowed, old-as-shit paper covered in really boring ancient rune crap that made you cream your pants?"

The corner of his mouth ticked up.

"You might feel good for a while after you roast Sweeney's ass, but if you fry those journals, you're going to be miserable for a lot longer," I said. "Unless you have an idyllic memory you forgot to tell me about it."

Caspian pursed his lips. With complete exasperation, he said, "Harlow. It's eidetic, not idyllic."

"I know," I said. "I can be annoying on purpose, too." Then I inclined my head toward his hands.

His fingers had fallen out of formation during the distraction. The rune array glowing between us flickered and went out as he lost concentration. He huffed a sigh, dropping his arms to his sides. Some of the raging fury in his expression had dimmed, too.

He grabbed my elbow and dragged me closer to the bathroom. "If we don't kill him, who knows what he'll tell the Collective about where we are."

I held my arm up, wrist facing him. "We have bigger problems out here than the Collective. You don't think Domino is going to be pissed as hell when he finds out Cody is dead? And that Sweeney failed at stealing the chest back? Not to mention, if we kill his sorcerer too, he's probably going to make us—well, you—pay whatever debt Sweeney owes him. Maybe that's money—maybe it's something else. I don't know about you, but I'd rather not owe that orc more than we already do. He can find us whenever he wants anyway. Best not to make him even madder."

"So you honestly propose we leave him here?"

"I didn't say I was above injuring him," I said. "I'm guessing we have ten to fifteen minutes to get the fuck out of here before either bounty hunters, werecats, or the human police find us. Whoever gets here first will find Sweeney. With any luck, it'll be people from Luma who will haul Sweeney back with them. Maybe we'll get lucky and the Collective will truth serum him and he'll reveal all his illegal activities. Hell, maybe the Collective will find some justification for taking Domino down for us. Either way, we need to leave. Now."

Caspian shot a look at Sweeney, then back at me. "Fine."

I nodded, then stepped out from behind Caspian. "Sword! You have permission to nonfatally maim him. No murder, you got that?"

The blade went cherry-hot.

"Don't argue with me!"

Caspian and I started frantically collecting our things. He grabbed clothes and stuffed them into suitcases. I grabbed whatever papers I could find, locating a few under Caspian's bed. I stuffed the two journals into my backpack that had gotten pinned under the door.

Sweeney screamed. I cringed but didn't dare look. I knew that if the sword—or Caspian—had murdered Sweeney, it would have haunted us. Well, Caspian and I would have been haunted. Currently, I wasn't sure listening to Sweeney being lightly maimed was going to be any better for me mentally.

The box of dragon scales had tipped over, spilling the slippery discs all over the vanity table. I scooped them back into the box. We haphazardly tossed the smaller boxes into the treasure chest that had somehow suffered minimal damage during the chaos. But seeing as it survived a hundred-year-old shipwreck ...

Something bellowed outside. I shot a wild look out the gaping doorway. It wasn't the bellow of a feral vampire, nor a werecat. It was a deep, rumbling sound. Like a cavernous echo that elicited images of dark caves.

I packed faster. "Troll incoming!"

I guessed it was Cody's guard buddy who had woken up from being knocked out cold in the parking lot by the sword. The thud of pounding feet sounded like localized earthquakes. Furious trolls were just as bad as furious elementals.

Sweeney laughed, sickly wet. "You'll die here."

The sword knocked him out then, and Sweeney slumped to the floor.

I strapped on my backpack. Caspian flung the thick strap of his duffel over his shoulder and grabbed the handle of my bag.

"Sword, can you help us with the trunk again?" I asked. "We gotta get to the car. It's not far."

Caspian grabbed hold of the handle on one side of the treasure chest and I took the other. We heaved up on the count of three and the sword slipped underneath it to help lift.

We shuffle-ran toward the door, turning the chest sideways so we could get down the hallway. We only had to get to the car. I would drive because the last thing we needed right now was sensible Caspian behind the wheel.

Sensible Caspian who almost murdered his old professor …

The bellow resounded again, this time so close and so loud I jumped, dropping my side of the trunk. I was mere inches from the threshold and it sounded like the troll had screamed directly into my ear. "Shit, sorry!"

I bent down to grab the handle. I froze when a shadow washed over me. Caspian cursed very colorfully.

Slowly, I looked up, up, up and found a troll heaving in the doorway. Gone was his glamour. His sickly gray skin was on full display. His head was bald save for a few straggly strands of black hair. The veins in his arms bulged. His yellow-clawed hands opened and closed into fists by his sides. Caspian had dropped his side of the chest, too, and was working his way through creating another rune array. The sword was trapped under the box, thumping and thrashing.

The troll let out a horrible growl and pulled his gray fist back to wallop me, but instead of hearing myself scream, it was the troll who yowled. My eyes sprang open and I stared in confusion at the shaft of an arrow protruding out of the troll's armpit. His arms were too bulky to easily reach it. He spun in a circle like a dog chasing his tail, trying to pull the arrow free.

Another one whizzed by from somewhere to the left, thunking into the troll's torso. It howled, turned toward his attacker, and gave chase, his heavy footfalls like thunder. Concrete splintered under his massive feet.

"I don't know who the hell is out there, but they bought us some time," I shouted. "One, two, three!"

We hoisted up the treasure chest, got out the door, and took off to the right, toward the parking lot. Sirens wailed in the distance. It wasn't long now.

We just had to get to the car.

My stomach sank like a stone when we reached Caspian's vehicle. Three of the tires were slashed. "Shit. Shit, shit, shit."

I twisted toward Caspian, keeping hold of the chest's handle. Tears welled in my eyes. "What do we do, Cas?"

Another roar, but this one belonged to a car's engine. I whipped the other way, watching as a black SUV barreled up beside us. A sense of defeat squeezed my throat. It was anyone's guess if this was a bounty hunter or a werecat.

The driver's-side door opened and the driver's head popped up over the roof. "Get in!"

My mouth dropped open. The face was so familiar in this unfamiliar place that my brain stopped working. I couldn't move. Shouts were echoing down hallways and getting closer. I could make out the flash of red and blue lights on the corner. My vision had tunneled out.

"Harlow!" the new arrival shouted. "Get in the car. Now! We have roughly ten seconds before we're caught."

Caspian's voice pulled me back to the surface, though it sounded as if he were underwater. "Is this wise? Who is she?"

The back of the SUV swung open.

I dashed forward holding my side of the treasure chest, Caspian scrambling to keep up. We hefted it into the back. Slammed the trunk closed. Pulled open the back passenger doors. Flung ourselves in. The SUV lurched forward before we'd gotten the doors all the way shut.

As the SUV took a wide turn, my shoulder bumped into the window. Poking out between the front passenger seat and the door were the feathered ends of arrows protruding from a quiver.

Caspian's warm hand landed on my arm and pulled me back to sit properly. I fastened my seat belt. He urgently repeated the question.

I swallowed hard and tore my gaze from her profile and toward his troubled expression. "That's my mother."

Chapter 25

KAYDA

Henri had the good sense to drive his cycle through an alley seconds before the glamour wore off and they shot into their natural forms. While the change didn't hurt, it was completely disorienting. Henri yelped and swerved, clipping a trash can and knocking it over. The sound startled a swarm of pixies into the air, who then buzzed about their heads like human-shaped overgrown hornets who screamed obscenities. Henri hit the accelerator to get away from them, and Kayda swatted wildly with her free hand while holding onto the map with the other.

Henri rocketed out of the alley and banked right, narrowly missing an oncoming car. The driver laying heavily on the horn made the remaining pixies scatter in an instant. Kayda rested her forehead on Henri's back, trying to catch her breath. She really hated pixies. The back of one of her upper arms ached and she figured one of the demonic little beasts had bitten her.

Kayda kept an eye on the map and called out directions to Henri, wishing there was a second dot on the map marking their location. She had to rely on her knowledge of the city's layout to get them to the right spot.

It took nearly twenty minutes to figure it out, but Kayda was almost positive the elves were heading for a small nature preserve in the farthest southwest corner of the Necropolis. Now that Kayda knew how real the threat of ferals was, being anywhere near the Necropolis's border felt even stupider than it had in high school. Crowding out her concerns was a single question: what connection did elves have to vampires?

The preserve, like many things in the Necropolis, had been a business idea that had gone belly-up before being overtaken by nature. In its first life, it had been a zoo meant to house the animals that had slipped through the portals during the Glitch. Many of the smaller animals that had made it through didn't come in groups, or even pairs. In school, Kayda had read about exotic birds, small mammals, and a few larger predators that had stumbled onto Earth. Species had been introduced and gone extinct in a matter of years because they'd had no other animals of their type to procreate with. A scant few crossbred with Earth natives, creating a handful of bird species that existed nowhere else in either world. A handful of unique insects thrived here, too. But most hadn't made it—much like the zoo.

Henri drove his cycle over the rutted road that led to the preserve, dodging potholes and small logs that occasionally obstructed the path, the single headlight cutting through the growing dark. Kayda's hearing picked up the faint scurrying of critters diving for cover at the sound of their approach. Squirrels scampered up trees to chitter from the branches. Small birds burst into flight. Ground mammals dove into holes and under bushes.

Kayda praised her map-reading skills when Henri rounded a bend and, beyond the ivy-choked welcome gate to the zoo that was now permanently stuck open, there were the elves' two cars. Henri eased to a stop in front of the gate, the cycle idling softly. Kayda supposed he wanted enough space between them and the elves in case they hadn't gotten out of their cars yet and he and Kayda needed to make a quick exit. But no lights lit up on the cars' exterior, nor did they flare to life in their cabins. Kayda's hearing didn't detect any movement from the parking lot, but she closed her eyes and dialed up her senses to conduct an additional sweep of the area. Other than the soft purr of the cycle, she could only make out the sounds of animals and insects in the vicinity. She relayed this to Henri.

"Yeah, that's what I got, t-t-too," he said. "I'll park the cycle on the side behind that tree. Then w-w-we can go in on f-f-foot."

As they inched back toward the gate after leaving the cycle behind, Kayda wished she'd worn different shoes. The combat boots were too clunky for this, but she did her best to step lightly.

Once they'd moved past the cars, along the broken concrete path that led to the run-down ticket counter, and through the stuck-open gate into the park itself, Kayda could pick out the faint sound of voices. She glanced over at Henri beside her, her brows arched. He nodded; he heard it, too.

They picked their way over a fallen tree that had smashed through the glass windows of the gift shop. Weeds sprung up between cracked pavers, and brambly bushes and vines snaked over walls, columns, and iron statues of manticores, unicorns, and other Earth-extinct beasts she'd forgotten the names of years ago. As they rounded the bend in the broken path, the distant voices grew a smidge louder.

The park stretched out beyond the end of the pathway. A giant tree, its base ringed with moss-covered bricks, stood in the middle, and from that wove half a dozen paths. A large signpost stood askew, arrows pointing in haphazard directions to long-lost attractions. The restrooms had been to the right and an animal-themed restaurant to the left. Most of the letters on the arrows directing patrons to the reptile house, bird sanctuary, and insect exploratorium had been lost to the elements.

"T-t-this way," Henri said, taking the fork to the right of the central tree.

Kayda trailed after him, eyes and ears combing the shadows for any lurking elves or feral vampires. The animals had either gone silent in here, or they didn't venture inside. Neither was a good omen.

The voices ahead slowly morphed from discordant notes to words with a steady cadence. They'd been talking at first, and now they were chanting—in unison. That wasn't a good omen, either.

Wordlessly, Henri and Kayda picked up the pace while doing their level best to be as quiet as possible. An elf's hearing was much better than a human's, but perhaps they'd miss Henri and Kayda's approach, what with their sinister ritualistic chanting in an abandoned zoo.

An area covered in tall grasses opened up to their right, where a large circle made of a thin stretch of metal sat on the ground. Six run-down boats were affixed to the circle by their wheels. Two sets of seats were in each boat, and a steering wheel sat at the helm. Kayda supposed this had been a play area for kids and was once filled with water. Suddenly, a creature with wide, unblinking eyes peered at her over the side of one of the boats, its paws clinging to the lip. A pair of smaller faces popped up next to it. Kayda eased out a relieved breath. Raccoons, not rabid vampires.

"I t-think they're in t-t-there," Henri said, redirecting Kayda from the worried-looking raccoon family.

Ahead loomed the giant glass-walled building that had once been the bird sanctuary. It reminded Kayda of a greenhouse. Several panes of glass were missing or were sporting holes—

vines poking through as if they'd punched their way out of prison and were slowly making their way to freedom.

The chanting came from inside. Now that she and Henri were closer, the sound echoed off the glass walls. The teenagers had been awkward and unsure while in the Golden Muskrat, but now their voices were steady and confident. Unfortunately, Kayda had no idea what they were saying. She assumed they chanted in Elfin, but she couldn't say for certain.

Kayda and Henri bent low behind a leafy hedge outside the entrance.

"Do y-you know anyone who sp-speaks that?" Henri whispered, jutting his head toward the door. "Would it be worth recording some of it and p-p-playing it for W-Welsh?"

Kayda shrugged helplessly. "He'd probably be able to get it to the right people for a translation if he doesn't know the language himself."

A soft light shone on the lenses of Henri's glasses as he nodded. The broken lens had been fixed. Perhaps that had happened while she'd been passed out on Welsh's couch.

"There's a pretty b-b-big hole in one of the windows over there," Henri said. "I can t-try to record s-s-some of it."

"Sounds good. There's not a lot of clearance between the bushes and the sides of the building, so it'll be better if we split up. I'll go around the other side and try to get a better view of what's going on. They'll see us for sure if we go in the front," Kayda said. "If things go south, bolt, and we'll meet back at the cycle."

Henri nodded, then hunch-walked away from her. She smiled softly after him. She'd underestimated the guy. She could tell he was anxious about being out here—but hells, so was she. Maybe she was just amazed that she hadn't scared him off yet.

Steeling herself, she went the opposite direction, keeping

herself low and close to the three-foot-tall ring of metal that circled the base of the building. Above that were hundreds of rectangular glass pieces that made up the walls and roof. The glass was thick, with a cloudy bluish temper. One couldn't glance into or out of them and get a clear picture, but if the elves were paying attention, they'd surely detect the shadow of her wide, seven-foot-tall frame.

She let the chanting be her guide, assuring her that the elves were deeply involved in whatever this was and that they'd be less likely to notice her because they were otherwise occupied. When she reached a rectangle of glass that sat above the metal base of the structure, she dropped to a squat. After a few seconds, she inched up to peer inside. A shelving unit stacked with cans and bottles blocked most of her view, but she could make out two of the elves standing in the middle of a cleared-off spot of cement flooring. The young girls had their hands in the air in a V, their eyes closed and faces tipped heavenward. A gentle white-blue light cascaded over them. It didn't seem late enough in the evening for moonlight to be filtering in through the broken roof, so perhaps it came from glowing orbs of faelight.

A giant insect swooped in front of Kayda's face. She violently swatted it away, lost her balance and fell on her ass. A rock poked into her butt cheek, and she bit back a yelp. Holding her breath, she listened for the chanting. When it was clear it hadn't slowed or faltered, she slowly exhaled. She got back into a crouch, ready to inch her way back to the missing pane. However, standing on the shelf beyond her spy hole was a damned pixie. Kayda's lip curled.

Like most pixies, this one wore clothes made of plant parts. She sported what looked like biker gear, except green and made of leaves. Her black hair was short and spiky, and a minuscule nose ring glittered from one nostril. She tapped one of her leaf shoes, a tiny dark eyebrow arched at Kayda.

When all the pixie did was stare at her, Kayda resisted the urge to put thumb to middle finger and flick the pest into the sanctuary. Instead, she whisper-hissed, "What do you want?"

"You made quite a mess of things back there," the pixie said.

Her voice was a quiet squeak, but Kayda could hear it if she dialed back the chanting and dialed up the pixie. Fearful that the elves would hear them, Kayda crouch-walked back several feet to huddle behind a tree. She could still hear the chanting from here. As predicted, the pixie followed.

"Made a mess of what?" Kayda hissed.

The pixie fluttered in front of Kayda's face. Her wings moved so quickly, like a hummingbird's, that they were nothing more than a blur. "There was a heated card game going when you came crashing through on that motorcycle of yours."

"It's not my fault you were playing in an alley, pixie," Kayda said.

"My name is Aster, not 'pixie,' draken."

"I don't care."

Aster let out an indignant squeak of annoyance. "So typical! Just because we're small doesn't mean we don't matter."

Kayda didn't have time for this. "Sorry, okay? Will you go away now?" She started to move past her, but the pixie zoomed into her line of sight again. "Ugh. What?"

"I was late to the card game tonight," Aster said. "I got there right when you and that other one came crashing through the alley."

"So?"

"So I saw you change," Aster said. "You were human-sized and then you both turned into drakens! Glamours like that must cost a fortune. Was it a spell? A tonic?"

Kayda cocked her head. Why in the hells would a pixie care about that? And then it clicked. "Oh, I get it. You want to experience a few hours of being bigger than a mouse."

The pixie flushed, her entire body going pink. "So what if I do? How much does it cost?"

"I don't know. I've got an in with a powerful witch," Kayda said.

Aster pursed her tiny lips. Kayda could almost see the gears working in the pixie's head. "I've seen them here before, you know. The elves, I mean. Not always the same young ones, but the older one is always leading them."

"Do you know what they're doing?" Kayda asked before she could stop herself.

A mischievous smile broke out across Aster's face, but she remained silent.

Kayda's shoulders drooped. "If I promise to get you in contact with my witch friend, will you tell me what you know?"

Aster nodded vigorously, then pointed a finger at Kayda. "If you go back on your word, the girls and I will ruin your life."

Remembering the havoc a band of pixies unleashed in her apartment building one summer, Kayda didn't doubt her. "I can't promise you that he'll agree to help you—or that he even can—but I can promise that he'll at least talk to you."

Aster smiled. "I'll take it. I can be very persuasive."

"Annoying," Kayda corrected.

Aster shrugged, unfazed. "So I don't know what they're saying, but we're all sure they're trying to open a portal."

Kayda blinked several times in rapid succession. "Excuse me, what?"

"Yeah. My brother and his *new wife* live in the preserve. A lot of pixies do. It's the closest thing we have to a sanctuary in Luma; it's a dangerous city for us." She shot a pointed look at

Kayda. When she realized the look had no effect whatsoever, she soldiered on. "Anyway. She said the elves have been coming in here for months now. Always that older lady elf with younger elves. They chant a lot, do their communing-with-nature thing, and then they leave. But one time last month, Iris and a few others followed them over here to watch. It only lasted for a few seconds, but the elves made this swirling vortex of energy appear. Iris said there was something in the vortex—like a scene from somewhere else."

"It happened just the one time?" Kayda asked.

"Pretty sure," Aster said. "Iris said when it happened, the whole preserve—like the plants and everything—shuddered. I know that sounds weird, but when your magic is tied so closely to nature, when something messes with nature, we can feel it. She said it was like every living thing in the preserve held its breath when the portal opened, then heaved a sigh of relief when it closed."

Kayda wondered if that was because the portal magic itself was wrong—throwing off the natural balance of things—or because of where the portal had been opened to. It was hard to believe that the fae realm was the sole plane of existence beyond Earth. Kayda admittedly knew next to nothing about portal magic, but in school, the prevailing message wasn't that opening a portal to worlds unknown was impossible, it was that it was highly unstable—which the Glitch had made abundantly clear. Were the elves trying to get back to their homeland?

Yet, if that was all this was, why had one of the elves in that sanctuary let ferals into the city?

Begrudgingly, Kayda said, "Thanks, Aster. I appreciate the information. How can I get in contact with you?"

Quick as a snake, Aster zipped toward Kayda. She instinctively swatted the air. "Ow!"

A moment later, Aster was back in the same place she'd been, but now had a strand of Kayda's short hair clasped in her tiny fist. "I'll find you. Have a nice night!"

And then she was gone.

Kayda rubbed the side of her head. She really, really hated pixies.

She froze. The chanting had stopped. Darting back to the broken window, Kayda crouched low and peered in. She couldn't see anyone now, and the light that had been shining on the upturned faces of the elfin girls had gone dark. Henri better have been staying out of sight.

Dialing up her hearing, Kayda slowed her breathing, which slowed the rapid pounding of her heart.

"Do not be disheartened," a woman said. "We grow closer every day. You all did splendidly. I wish for all of you to return to our next attempt. I'm very impressed with how your studies have progressed."

Happy murmurs filtered to Kayda's ears. Perhaps this ritual was also a test of ability.

The faint shuffle of footsteps told Kayda they were making their way out of the sanctuary. She hunkered lower, willing herself to blend in with the wall and the shadows. From this angle, she could make out the five shapes of the elves moving along the path that would eventually lead them out of the park.

When they were out of sight, she crept back to the front of the building. Henri joined her a few seconds later.

"I think I g-g-got a lot of it," he said, grinning.

She was glad he was enjoying the adventure so much. She figured he'd be less excited when she told him what the pixie had relayed to her. She was sure Welsh wouldn't be pleased by the development in the least, mostly because she assumed he hated pixies even more than she did.

As they slowly made their way back toward the parking lot,

Aster's words echoed in her head. "She said it was like every living thing in the preserve held its breath when the portal opened, then heaved a sigh of relief when it closed."

Kayda had no idea what was happening in Luma—and had even less of an idea about how to stop it.

Chapter 26
KAYDA

By the time Kayda and Henri had gotten back to his bike, it was full dark, and the elves were gone. She checked her phone and found a text from Welsh.

It had come in a few minutes before.

Welsh: *Still alive? Your glamours will have worn off by now.*

Kayda: *Yes. And got some interesting info from a pixie.*

Welsh: *Not possible. Pixies are never interesting. Need a place to crash?*

Glancing up at Henri, her eyes adjusted from the bright glow of her phone to the low light of her night vision. "Did you need to get home, or did you want to—"

"Y-yes to w-w-whatever the second op-ption is."

Smiling to herself, she typed a simple "*Yes*" to Welsh.

Her phone rang. The sound startled some night creature into scampering in the other direction. She answered it quickly. "Hi."

Welsh's gruff voice asked, "You know where Little Talonia is?"

"Sure. The draken neighborhood downtown."

"Meet me outside Mewro's in an hour. I gotta carb-load for this one."

Kayda had no idea what he was talking about.

"Oh, I talked to Harlow, too. She's very needy and whiny. You can call her from my phone when we meet up."

Kayda blinked several times. "Way to bury the lede!"

She couldn't ask any follow-up questions because he'd already hung up.

Kayda wondered if Harlow's desperation to talk to her meant her paranoia had started to ebb the longer she was away from Luma. Or if some big event had happened while on the road trip. Maybe she'd bumped uglies with the supervillain. Maybe she wanted to tell Kayda that she wasn't coming back. Harlow would harbor less apprehension about potential eaves-droppers if all the call entailed was telling Kayda goodbye forever.

Aster's tale about the portal rose in Kayda's mind unbidden. "Ever wonder what authentic tinka fish would taste like?" she blurted.

Henri had been about to throw a leg over his cycle but stopped now to cock his head at her. "Sometimes, I g-guess," he said. "What's up? You seem ... I d-d-don't know ... off."

"If you had a chance to go back—to the fae world, I mean— would you?" Kayda asked, ignoring his question.

He shrugged. "I've always been c-c-urious about w-what it's like there, but I can't go b-b-back to a place I've never been. If I could visit and then come back here, to my h-h-home, sure."

Kayda didn't know the answer to her own question. She hadn't given much thought to the fae realm. It was an ancient, lost place. A place she could only visit through books, or through stories told to her by her grandma, who had heard them from her grandma.

Opening portals from Earth wasn't going to happen. That's what she'd always been told. No point in the what-ifs if the what-ifs weren't an option. But that one conversation with Aster had suddenly opened up a literal world of possibilities for Kayda. She didn't think she'd abandon the life she had here on Earth, but she also didn't know if she'd pass up an opportunity to see the place she'd come from—a place where draken still had their ability to shift into dragons.

"K-Kayda?"

She snapped out of her thoughts. The crease between Henri's brows made something twinge in her chest. "I'm okay. Sorry. To Mewro's?"

He studied her a moment longer, then nodded. She climbed on behind him. Before long, the bike was back on solid, paved road, and Henri hit the gas. Kayda rested her chin on Henri's shoulder and closed her eyes, letting the cool wind buffet her face. She imagined she was flying.

When the fae were ripped from their world, and the reality had set in that the portals weren't going to open again, the fae had grown homesick. Like most marooned fae, the draken had missed the food of their homeland. Ophelia Mewro had always found solace in cooking, and when she wound up stuck in a new world, surrounded by draken as sullen as herself, she did what she did best. Earth didn't have the same animals, plants, and spices that the fae realm had, but Ophelia had been determined to get as close to authentic as she could. At first, Mewro's had merely been the kitchen in Ophelia's house, her door open to any draken who needed something to remind them of home. As her food gained popularity, and Little Talonia formed around her, she opened a restaurant. Any chef who joined her ranks had been trained to cook in the draken way, and the recipes were said to be kept under lock and key. It wasn't long before Mewro's became an institution in Little Talonia.

Kayda, when she first arrived in Luma as a teenager, had come to Mewro's with her grandma so often the staff had known them by name. As Kayda's grandma got sicker, Kayda had started making the trek to Mewro's a few times a week to get her grandma tinka fish bowls—a Mewro's specialty and Kayda's grandma's favorite.

Kayda hadn't been back since her grandma died years ago. There were too many memories tied up in the place. They crowded in on Kayda now.

Henri parked his cycle in a designated lot on the edge of Little Talonia, and they made the rest of the trek on foot. Kayda wasn't sure if Henri sensed how "off" she still was, lost in memories of her grandma, but he kept quiet as he strolled beside her, his hands in his pockets.

They trudged up a hill, passing draken-run shops and restaurants. A gaggle of draken kids went sprinting by so fast they were nearly a blur. Their giggles seemed to sweep past Kayda a breath later, as if even laughter couldn't keep up with the kids.

When Kayda and Henri crested the hill and turned right down the sidewalk, Kayda came up short. The sight of Mewro's sign—the name red against a bright yellow background, and the apostrophe shaped like a dragon's talon—knocked the breath from her lungs. The grief of missing her grandma hit her less often than it had when she first passed, but it occasionally snuck up on her and tried to take her out at the knees. Kayda had stood on this very corner staring up at this sign, her grandma's calloused hand in hers, so many times. The same four round red tables sat on the patio, ringed in wooden chairs with their faded yellow paint. The scent of frying fish, baking bread, and sautéed garlic washed over her, and her chest constricted.

A gentle hand touched her elbow and she flinched slightly, looking up at Henri. He'd been watching her with concern far too often. She was just going through it lately and the poor guy was forced to deal with her roller coaster of emotions. She wanted to get off the ride, but every time she got close, she plunged over another blind drop.

"My grandma and I used to come here all the time before she died," Kayda said, needing her voice to drown out the one in her head. The furrow to his brow loosened as understanding dawned. "I haven't been here in a long time, is all. The memory hit me harder than I expected."

"If it's t-t-too much when we go in, w-w-we can tell Welsh to m-meet us somewhere el-else." Henri chewed on his bottom lip for a few seconds, staring at her while he wrestled with something. "My cousin d-d-died unexpectedly about a y-year ago. Freak heart attack even th-though he was pretty young. I'd seen him the d-d-day before. We'd been hanging out at a park, talking and dr-drinking. There was n-nothing special about it, but now that afternoon is my l-l-last memory I have of him. It took me over a m-month before I could even look at the park without getting choked up. Took me another m-month after that to walk through it. I always took the long w-way around it." He shrugged. "Do w-w-whatever's comfortable."

To her absolute horror, her eyes welled up. Kayda Verdan did not cry. She hadn't done that since her grandma's passing either. Crying was for sad, life-changing events—and weepy humans—not for her. She sniffed.

From behind her came a sultry voice. "I made better time than I expected."

Startled out of her tears, Kayda turned to find a draken

woman in a sleek pants suit. Her light brown hair fell to her shoulders in a straight sheet, which complemented the faint red hue that made her brown skin reminiscent of a color one would find on a desert-dwelling lizard. Her makeup was done to perfection, sporting long black lashes, a natural rosy blush on her cheeks, and a bright red lipstick on her thin lips.

"W-W-Welsh?" Henri asked, then visibly swallowed.

Kayda's brows rose as she angled her wide-eyed expression Henri's way. "Hey! That adorable stutter is for me. I'm the one who makes you nervous, not ... him." Kayda flailed a dismissive hand at Welsh.

"He's ... she's ... this glamour is ..." Henri coughed.

Kayda sighed. "I can't even argue. Welsh, you're hot. I assume going draken is the reason you need to carb-load?"

Welsh nodded. In his silky purr of a voice, he said, "Maintaining a draken persona drains my magical stores very quickly if I don't consume an absurd amount of food. The wherian beef platter is basically a mountain of protein, though, so that'll give me a good boost. Ready to eat? I'm famished."

Without waiting for an answer, Welsh sashayed away from them. Even his ass was better than hers. Not fair.

"I didn't m-mean—"

Kayda put her hands on her hips.

"I-I-I think you're—"

She pointed a finger at him. "There is no saving this, Henri Beryl."

"No?" he asked, brow cocked.

"No."

He closed the distance between them, took her face in his hands, and kissed her. Kayda's knees went liquid. She grabbed hold of his waist partly as physical proof that this was actually happening, and to provide her shaky legs with some stability.

Henri broke the kiss much sooner than she would have

liked, but he still held her face. When her brain finally turned back on, her eyes fluttered open. Henri smiled down at her. "W-What were you s-s-saying about not being able to s-s-save this? The look on your f-f-face said I just did."

"Since when are you this bold?" she asked, hearing the unsteadiness in her voice. That made him smile wider.

"N-n-never should have told me you thought I was o-o-out of your league." The right lens of his glasses was smudged. "You won't be able to k-keep me away now. P-p-plus! So much adventure happens when I'm around y-y-ou. There's no going b-b-back."

Her stomach was doing a weird flipping thing that she very much liked and was very much freaked out by at the same time. Her father's admonitions were trying to push their way in. They tended to creep up like weeds when she was feeling particularly vulnerable.

"Any day now!" Welsh sing-songed from the porch of the restaurant.

"G-g-guess we should head in there," Henri said, fully letting her go now. As they headed for Welsh waiting across the street, Henri added, "I ap-pologize in advance if I ogle W-Welsh."

Welsh had a hip cocked, and his arms crossed, one of his red manicured nails tapping out a restless rhythm on the sleeve of his black pants suit.

"Honestly, same," Kayda said. "I gotta get me one of those suits."

"Y-y-yes," Henri said. "Yes, you d-do. I find authority terrifying and very h-h-hot."

Kayda laughed. "Good to know."

When she stepped inside Mewro's after Welsh, she wasn't surprised by the fact that the restaurant's interior hadn't changed an iota in the years since she'd been here. What did surprise her was the elderly draken woman behind the counter who saw Welsh, smiled wide, and bustled out to hug him. She was about six feet—a bit short for a draken, but age had stooped her posture. Wrinkles covered every inch of her. She wore a strikingly black wig that was plaited, the tip of the braid falling past her backside. Her eyes were a clear, vibrant blue and though there was a shakiness to her voice, it was confident and sure.

"Oh, Zander!" the elderly draken cooed. "It's been a while since you've been here. You're looking as lovely as ever."

The woman knew Welsh's first name? And recognized him as Welsh when he appeared as a vixen of a draken?

"How is your granddaughter?" Welsh purred.

"She's doing well, my sweet boy. That louse of an ex of hers was officially shipped off to the Antarctic hub a couple of weeks ago. She's coming home to us soon now that she's no longer in danger. I can never thank you enough for what you did for her—for the whole family."

Welsh patted the back of the woman's wrinkled hand. "No need to keep thanking me. It's my job, Adriana. And you paid me a lot to do it."

"We both know it's more than a job to you. But you can hide behind your grumpiness and masks if it makes you feel better." Adriana tapped Welsh on the nose with a finger. "I see right through to the heart of you."

Color actually rose up Welsh's cheeks, painting them a soft purple. This evening was full of all kinds of revelations.

"Can we have a powwow in the back booth?" Welsh asked. "These two are with me and we need a bit of privacy."

"Of course, of course," the woman said, then turned her wide smile toward Kayda and Henri, acknowledging them for the first time. "Why! Is that little Kayda Verdan?"

Kayda didn't recognize her, but she smiled. "Yes, ma'am."

The woman hustled over to hug her, too. "You might not remember me, as you were a young girl when you first started coming in with your Grandma Ruby. You were such a meek, shy thing then. Not long after you started coming around, I had to help one of my daughters over in Florida for a spell. I heard about your grandma's passing while I was gone. I was truly sorry to hear it. She was a gem—she was aptly named."

Kayda's chest constricted. "She really was."

"Oh, look at me carrying on! You go on back and get settled and I'll bring you some water," Adriana said. "Whatever you want, it's on the house."

"That is an unwise offer," Welsh said. "We will eat you out of house and home."

"Pah!" Adriana said, waving a wrinkled hand. "The Halycons are forever grateful to you. Accept the offer if you don't wish to insult me."

Welsh sighed. "Fine. But consider yourself warned."

Adriana, all smiles, shuffled back behind the counter to presumably fetch glasses of water. Kayda and Henri followed Welsh toward the back wall, where there was a section of three bright red booths. Above them, the wall was painted with beautifully rendered dragons flying among the clouds. A scarlet red dragon with curved horns atop its sleek head flew with a sunshine-yellow dragon with wicked black talons on the ends of its outstretched wings. They appeared to be racing each other, the yellow one in the lead.

Kayda slid into the booth beside Henri, her leg flush with his. Welsh sat opposite them, unbuttoning his suit jacket as he did. His cleavage was now on full display behind a tight white button-up shirt. Kayda heard Henri audibly swallow.

"Really?" she asked Henri, fighting a laugh.

"M-m-maybe I should w-w-wait outside," Henri said, pushing his glasses up his nose.

Welsh chuckled, then fastened another button on his shirt to hide the rest of his assets. "I've had a handful of clients here in Little Talonia, and found that draken do best interacting with other draken when it comes to sensitive matters. You lot have the strongest sense of community among all the fae in Luma, and the best way to make headway was to look like you. I may have modeled Dawn here after what I gathered was the ideal draken woman. I perhaps went overboard, though, as Dawn has rendered quite a few dumb on sight."

Kayda cocked her head, giving "Dawn" an assessing consideration. "She's like a Hollywood version of a draken. One of those way-too-beautiful types that the average woman can't compare to."

Welsh nodded thoughtfully at that. "Anyway. Tell me what you two found out."

Henri launched into describing the ritual, then played the video he took of it. The picture quality was terrible, as he hadn't had a great view into the sanctuary either, but the sound was great. Kayda was almost positive it was in Elfin.

"Do you understand it?" Kayda asked.

"Not a word," Welsh said. "Can you send that to me, Henri?"

Henri was caught up with that task when Adriana appeared with three glasses of water. Welsh waved off the menu Adriana started to hand them and ordered two platters of wherian beef, three tinka fish bowls, and an order of pork-filled bread rolls. Kayda's mouth watered at the promise of excellent food.

Once Adriana had departed again, Welsh asked Kayda about her "interesting" conversation with the pixie. Both men were eerily silent after she finished recounting what Aster had told her.

Welsh spoke first. "When the Collective first dubbed themselves our faithful leaders, they promised that they'd work tirelessly to get the portals back open. Or, at the very least, figure out why they glitched in the first place. Caspian said there's a specialty field academy students can go into devoted solely to studying portals.

"Some of the unrest among the fae is because they feel like the Collective has abandoned any attempt to get those portals open. I've had quite a few fae come to me with requests for new identities because they want out of the entire hub system. The Collective, they say, has grown too drunk on their own power on Earth and have lost sight of one of their early priorities. If these unhappy fae are going to be stuck here on Earth, they'd rather live life their way instead of the Collective's way. Which doesn't make a ton of sense, if you think about it. The fae outside are bound by the even stricter rules of the mundane population. But as long as they pay me, I don't really care what they do when they get out. What I wonder now, though, is if the Collective is oblivious to the elves attempting to open portals, or if this is yet another thing they're aware of and actively ignoring."

Henri said, "All this time, I thought only sorcerers h-had access to portal magic, and that th-the access came after years of st-study. It doesn't seem like elves are the t-type to enter the academy. And even if they are, h-h-how would a teenager or young adult have the knowledge n-necessary to perform the kind of magic needed to h-hold the veil open? I know elves don't age the same w-way we do or humans do, but it's not th-that different. The ones we saw all looked like they were barely out of high s-school."

Welsh said what Kayda had already been thinking.

"It would seem sorcerers aren't the only ones who can manipulate the veils," Welsh said. "The potency of that air spell was impressive for someone that young as well. It being an air elemental made sense—the power felt unchecked and raw. Teenage elementals can cause a lot of damage without proper training. Their wildly fluctuating hormones rarely gel with elemental magic. It would seem that the elves—at least the one we interacted with—have more innate nature magic than I was aware of. And now they've also figured out portal magic ..."

"Aster said the older elf has been coming to the sanctuary for months to have the teenagers try the ritual," Kayda said. "That speaks to a larger plan, doesn't it? I didn't get a sense of whether the incident with the feral was a reckless teenage decision, or if that was part of a grander plan, too."

They sat in silence again, each lost in their own thoughts. Kayda's stomach rumbled when she heard the sound of sizzling meat before Adriana and a younger male waiter came out with their food. Kayda resisted the urge to take great fistfuls of the meat and shovel it into her mouth without bothering with utensils.

Welsh consumed half of his small mountain of wherian beef before he spoke. "I'll get the video to someone who might be able to understand what's being chanted during the ritual. I've also sent the coyote pictures to Caspian. For tonight, all we can do is eat this delicious food, get some rest, and then tackle more in the morning. I've got a place in Little Talonia you can stay in tonight."

"And I can talk to Harlow?"

Welsh nodded. "And you can talk to Harlow. It's a tiny place, but you can have some privacy in the back bedroom to gush about Henri licking your tonsils or whatever you two need to discuss."

Henri did a spit take.

Welsh dabbed at his dress, now splattered with water. "Very classy, Henri."

As Henri apologized profusely, and Welsh pretended to be upset, Kayda wondered if being Zander Welsh was a lonely existence. He didn't belong in any one body, didn't reside in any one place. Yet he had connections all over the city. No one seemed to truly know him—as he only showed parts of who he was to certain people, never giving anyone the full picture. He didn't appear sad or lonely, though. He seemed perfectly content. A nomad in body and spirit.

She marveled at how at home he seemed to be no matter where—or who—he was, while she had had years of being in one place, as one person, and still felt like she was figuring it out.

Chapter 27

HARLOW

I stared at my mother's profile, unable to process what I was seeing. I was vaguely aware of Caspian's hand on mine, of the sword lying across my lap, but all I could do was stare.

She was fifty-seven now. She'd experimented with different hairstyles throughout my life. Braids, extensions, relaxed and straight, and natural and full, like how I wore mine. Right now, it was cut short. Her tight, corkscrew curls were jet-black, but I spotted a few hints of silver mixed in when the speeding SUV passed under a particularly bright streetlight.

Despite the summer heat, she wore a black leather jacket. Her figure, what little I'd seen of it, was trimmer than I remembered.

I was working up the nerve to blurt out something eloquent like, "Where in the fuck have you been?" when her cell rang from its perch on the dash.

The number came up as private. She hit accept.

"This is Robin," she said.

Robin, not Camila.

A male voice piped in through the speakers. "Robin! Thank Christ. Did you get her?"

My mother's gaze met and held mine in the rearview mirror. "Got her. There's a guy with her, too. And the sword."

The sword. She knew about it? How did she know about it? My brain was seconds from exploding.

"You got a tail?" the guy asked.

My mother checked her side mirrors. "Don't think so. There was quite a mess back at the motel for authorities to deal with. We got out of there before the cops showed up."

"There's also a dead troll in the middle of Marley's Diner," the guy said. "The cats who were sent for your kid are now doing what they can to clean that up and keep the mundanes occupied until they can get sorcerers or witches over there to make sure they forget. A couple of pictures of it are online already. Gonna take them a while to smooth that mess over, too."

My mother sighed wearily. "We'll be there in forty-five minutes."

"Roger that."

The call disconnected.

It was silent in the car for a long stretch, my mother breezing through yellow lights, taking tight turns, and weaving in and out of lanes with competency. I kept a hand on the hilt of the sword, not for protection but stability. It also hadn't stopped softly humming since this car ride started, and I needed it to know that skewering my mother wasn't what I wanted, even if the energy I gave off dipped periodically into the rage category.

"Are you two hungry?" my mother asked, as if she'd just picked us up after soccer practice.

"Does that guy know your actual name is Camila?" I snapped—the first question uttered to my long-lost mother after six years of wondering if she was dead.

She nodded. "Soren does, yes. Most of the people at the compound do. But I go by Robin these days because you never know who's listening. It would be best if you two used different names as well when you're not sure you're among people you can trust." Her gaze in the rearview shifted. "I assume you're the 'Blackthorn' who's been linked to Harlow?"

"Yes, ma'am," Caspian said.

She addressed me. "Is the sword the only item that triggered the 154 code violation?"

It took me a moment to piece it together. "You still have your pocket mirror."

"When 'Fletcher' popped up as a violator a month or so ago, I finished up the job I was on in Georgia, pulled up stakes, and came back to the West Coast in case the Fletcher was you."

"What if it had been some hardened criminal named Fletcher?" I asked.

She shrugged a shoulder. "Worth the risk if I was right."

I felt the rage mounting. It was such an intense, bubbling-in-my-core kind of anger that it didn't feel like mine. Someone hurt and unstable had hijacked my body. I glared out the window. Caspian's hand lingered on mine, and he rubbed a thumb back and forth across my knuckles. I snatched my hand away, burying them both under my folded arms.

Guilt overrode the anger and I glanced over at him, expecting him to be angry in return, or for him to be wearing such a wounded expression that I flipped from rage to tears. But he offered me a small smile, like he understood the torrent churning in my chest. Which was incredible, because I was experiencing it and didn't understand it.

After another ten minutes of tense silence, she turned on the radio, filling the car with the murmuring voices of a public radio station. Conversation was over for now. The Fletchers could be a quiet, brooding lot when emotions ran high. A screaming match was just as likely. I didn't know which one of us would break first.

We eventually ended up in an industrial area. Nondescript, rectangular buildings with metal siding were lined up in neat rows behind chain-link fences. Logos for construction companies and manufacturing graced the sides of trucks and vans. My mother drove through an alley where closed roll-up doors faced oil-spotted asphalt.

Pulling to a stop near one of them, she tapped on her phone's screen and scrolled through her contacts. She selected "Soren."

"Yo," he said by way of greeting.

"We're here," my mother said. "There any food left?"

"Should be a few slices of pizza. I'll nuke 'em." The call ended.

"Are you sure it's safe here?" I blurted.

My mother turned in her seat to peer back at me.

Something gave a rattling clang. A door that was big enough for two buses to pass through side by side trundled open. The space beyond wasn't as wide open as the hangar had been, but it wasn't that far off.

"Perfectly safe," she said in her Mom Voice that soothed some instinctive part of me.

I held up my right wrist. "We sort of made a deal with an orc mob boss and he can track our location any time he wants."

She pursed her lips. "I would think it would go without saying that one shouldn't make blood oaths to orcs."

"If I may," Caspian said. "He did threaten to pulverize our corpses to the point of being unidentifiable even through dental records."

"Ah. Well, I suppose it was an excellent choice then," she said. "Can I guess that part of why you were being ambushed by a troll was because of whatever is in that trunk in the back?"

I briefly told her about the auction and the chaos that had ensued afterward. "Domino seems like the kind of guy to hold a grudge. He might track us down here because he's pissed we got away. I don't want anyone here to get hurt because the oaf decides to seek revenge."

"I'll warn the others," she said. "The security here is top-notch. If the orc shows up, we'll get a warning a mile out. It'll give us enough time to split."

The matter apparently settled, she drove through the still-open door and over smooth cement. She turned right, where a small fleet of similar all-black SUVs were parked.

"On paper, this is a security company. Couple of the guys here like to chat up the construction workers during the day and plant the story that we get a lot of government contracts. Helps explain away all the black, camo, and tactical gear."

Tactical gear?

She climbed out.

Muttering to myself, I started to get out too, but Caspian gently grabbed me by the arm. My mother must have sensed we wanted some privacy, because she closed the door, moving away to meet up with a guy striding toward her. The cabin lights dimmed a minute later.

"How are you?" Caspian asked. "Honestly."

It took me a moment to reply. "I haven't seen her in six years." I paused, frowning. "Seeing her makes me think of my dad—he died the day she left. I didn't know if I'd ever see her again. And now she's ... here."

"Which part of that makes you the most angry?"

I chewed on the inside of my cheek, annoyed with myself for being unable to hide that—how mad I was. "That she's got a life outside Luma I know nothing about. That all these people probably know her better than I do. That I was stuck in Luma alone trying to survive, trying to find her, and she just ... left." I stared at him for a long beat. "What if she never tried to get back to me?"

"To know, you'll have to ask her," he said. "I think you owe it to yourself to know, even if it's an answer you don't want. If she truly abandoned you and never looked back, she doesn't deserve you. Give me the word and we're out of here. I'm rich, remember? We'll be fine."

I managed a small smile, slowly swiping my thumb along the scales of the sword's hilt. They warmed beneath my skin, and I liked to think the sword was trying to comfort me. "I'm also very annoyed that instead of saying the things I've been rehearsing in my head all these years, I immediately went into grouchy teenager mode."

"You were, what, twenty-two when she left? In Harlow maturity years, that's somewhere in the toddler range. So you being a teenager now makes sense."

I gasped, though an incredulous laugh slipped out first. "That's not nice!"

"Maybe not, but I got a laugh out of you, so I'll call it a success." He peered out the window, where my mother and the guy talked.

Beyond the pair of them, the middle of the room was outfitted with several long tables covered in computer equipment. People sat around the tables busily tapping away at keyboards. Others paced the room with cell phones pressed to their ears. Most everyone wore black or camo. Kayda would love the uniform.

"Does something about this place seem familiar to you?" I asked.

"I was thinking it looks a lot like Marisol's setup."

"Me too," I said. "My parents were private investigators before they got to Luma. They first met at an amateur vampire hunting group. They tracked down missing people mostly, but they kept getting caught up in cases involving fae. They had quite a few run-ins with vampires along the way. It actually wouldn't be that surprising if she ended up a member of VHoA."

Facing me again, he asked, "Are you ready to stop hiding in the car?"

"We could start thrashing in here to make the SUV rock. They'll think we were getting in a quickie."

Caspian pursed his lips. "You must not be feeling too badly if you're back to your crass ways."

"Oh, you know you like it." I patted the sword. "What about this? Just let it float around?"

Shrugging, Caspian said, "Your mother is already aware of the cutlass, and she trusts these people, so you have to decide if you do, too."

I only thought about it for a second. "I'm going to let you out, sword, but there's no murdering or maiming allowed here. Even if you see my mom and me arguing."

The sword hummed. Its quick acquiescence either said it was comfortable here, and therefore maiming wasn't necessary, or it was so antsy it would agree to anything.

We piled out.

While Caspian stuck by my side as we approached my mother and the animated guy with her, the sword took off to explore the warehouse. Quite a few people stared open-mouthed as the sword flitted about the ceiling or bobbed behind unsuspecting people working at their computers, quickly darting away once it was spotted.

"Hi there!" the animated guy said when we reached him. "You must be Little Robin. Nice to meet you. I'm Soren." He stuck out a hand.

I shook it. I guessed he was in his forties or so. He had an infectious smile, and while I didn't feel much like smiling, around him, it was harder to keep under wraps.

He was a big guy in every sense: size, volume, exuberance.

His presumably brown hair had been cut close to the scalp and dyed platinum blond. He wore black slacks and a black button-up like several others, except it was paired with a neon yellow tie covered in silhouettes of rubber ducks.

"So is this a chapter of VHoA?" I asked.

Soren chuckled. "Skipping small talk, eh? Like mother, like daughter. I can dig it. Yeah, this is the biggest VHoA chapter in Washington." He regarded me, arms crossed over his wide chest. "Are the rumors true, then? You and that sword helped take down a hybrid in Fresno?"

"Yeah. The sword decapitated him," I said.

Soren whistled, then wrapped his big hands around his own neck. "I don't need to be worried, do I?" His laugh was big, too.

"Eh, I think you're fine." I gestured across the warehouse to the sword who appeared to be playing keep-away with a little girl. I guessed she was about six. The sword, in the inverted position, hovered its hilt above her head. When she jumped for it, the sword shot upward. Her continued peals of laughter implied she was enjoying it. The blade's blue hue said it was, too.

"The ... uh ... explosion at the hybrid's nest ..." Soren said, sounding unsure for the first time. "We heard that the hybrid instructed one of his own to blow up the house after VHoA was inside."

I couldn't talk about that night without breaking down. I still heard the explosion, and Marisol's screams of confusion as it dawned on her that two-thirds of her crew had been inside.

Caspian answered for me, telling them about Stan talking to his second-in-command and giving him the supposed go-ahead to release the captured fae girls from the basement. In actuality, he'd given his second cryptic permission to blow the place up, knowing we'd kill him for it. Stan had pulled his suicidal stunt thinking we'd believe the kidnapped fae girls had died in the blast too. Sneaky hybrid vampire asshole.

"A friend of mine died in that explosion," Soren said, his expression pinched.

"I'm sorry," I said, and meant it. I'd gone over that night a million times, coming up with other courses of action I could have taken. Maybe there had been a way to keep everyone alive—well, except for the undead ones.

My mother hadn't said much since this conversation started, just scowled at some spot in space. Was she upset that I'd gotten involved in something so dangerous? My petulant teenage anger began to bubble up once more.

Before I could get out a snippy comment about her losing the right to be upset about anything I did or didn't do, she turned to me. "We heard about the attack because word spreads quick in this community when one of us disappears or gets killed. It was one of the worst losses VHoA has had in a while. The spin on the mundane news was that a gang fight broke out and people were killed in the pandemonium. The Collective swept in there fast and cleaned up a lot of it—everything from physical evidence to people's memories. Their tech team got a lot of the videos taken down within a couple of hours. The Collective is very good at making things go away." She sighed. "I'm not thrilled about the mess you're in, but I'm glad you're finally away from the Collective."

The anger was clawing its way up my stomach, into my chest.

If you're going to fight with your mother, Harlow, don't do it with an audience. Breathe. Don't—

"I have every intention of going back," I spat. "I didn't run away from Luma. I'm waiting until things cool down."

"I didn't run away either."

"Well, you sure as shit didn't try to come back."

I saw Caspian in the corner of my eye grab Soren by the elbow and yank him from us.

"Before you start accusing me of anything, you sure as shit better consider the source of your information," she snapped. "What bullshit did they tell you? That when my husband was murdered, the grief was too much so I abandoned my only child? Really, Harlow?" Her voice caught, and her bottom lip trembled when she said, "I royally fucked up somewhere if that's what you think. If you honestly believe that I'd give up on you."

My throat felt like it was caught in a vice. My eyes burned. "Then what happened?" I asked, unable to keep the wobble out of my voice either.

"They exiled me," she said on a great huff of air, like she'd been holding onto those three words for six years. "When you're exiled, they add you to the list of people forbidden from entering the city. They need your blood to add specific spell-work to that master tower of runes in the middle of Luma Proper. They had that on hand because of my job, and put a repulsion spell in the veil that was geared specifically for me. First line of defense is searing pain. If I kept pushing my way through, the veil magic would have killed me. If I somehow survived, the alarm bells going off in the tower would have resulted in the cats finding me eventually."

My brow knitted in confusion.

She forcefully unzipped her jacket, yanked her left arm free. Her tank top revealed scarred skin from shoulder to wrist. Patches of her dark skin were fused together with thick ropes of mangled tissue. A few sections had an unsettling sheen to them.

Tears slipped down my face.

"The pain was so bad I blacked out," she said, shoving her arm back into her jacket. "Luckily a friend knew what I was doing and found me. Got me patched up." She coughed to clear the catch in her own throat. "Do you remember Naomi West?"

I sucked in a breath at her name and wiped tears away with the backs of my hands. Felix had told me that Naomi had known my parents. He'd recently informed me that someone had planted Naomi in my life to get intel about my parents. Felix knew who had sent Naomi to spy on me, but because of the stupid Soul NDA, he couldn't tell me. It was information he'd learned from the Collective after signing the contract.

Something clicked then. Maybe it had been that "leading the witness" tone she used to employ when I was much younger, trying to get me to confess to some wrongdoing—like breaking a favorite lamp while sliding on the hardwood floor in my socks.

"You sent her," I said.

She nodded. "She was with us the night your dad ..." Letting out a shaky sigh, she said, "She was with us that night. We'd been doing a raid on a nightclub—a very similar situation to the one in Fresno. We had our suspicions that the Collective was trafficking fae teens out in exchange for something from the vamps. There was a popular rumor that a stipulation in the pact with Tercla was that Luma had to pay the vampires there in warm fae bodies to ensure they left Luma alone."

"Tercla is all pure vamps, though," I said. "They wouldn't want fae."

She smiled softly at that. "That's right. But that's not common knowledge. We found out that the Collective, as far as we can tell, isn't directly responsible for the fae disappearances, but they're not trying to stop it either. They've got bigger fish to fry."

"Which bigger fish is that?"

She tapped her temple. "Can't say."

Figures.

"We were convinced Bliss was coming from outside Luma. Your father and I were already in hot water with the Collective because we wouldn't stop investigating it. We even threatened to go public with what we'd discovered. Bliss is a major problem for humans—it kills too many of them. They kept telling us to drop it.

"We kept in contact with people we'd met during our private eye days in Sacramento. An old friend said that the kids of a contact had gone missing. A son and a daughter. The daughter, Naomi, somehow escaped capture. Our friend needed backup raiding the nest where they believed the boy was being held. Naomi volunteered to be our decoy. She had unique insight into the Bliss scene because she'd been dragged into it by a hybrid. That night, it was your father and me, Naomi, four Sacramento VHoA members, and two Luma bounty hunters we had a close friendship with. While leaving the Sacramento VHoA meeting spot, the whole party got ambushed by ferals. Your father was killed trying to protect me.

"I figured out that one of the bounty hunters was a plant from the Collective itself. Somehow a hybrid must have been tipped off about where we were and that we were getting close to figuring out their scheme, and sent in their ferals. Naomi and I were the only ones who made it out alive. I knew the area well, so I was able to get us to safety." She chewed on her bottom lip, staring into space. "I got a call from my bosses that night, telling me of my exile. They didn't know about Naomi though, because their inside man had died too and therefore couldn't report back about what happened. Naomi and I worked on a plan for a while to get her into Luma to find you. She reported back to me often. But someone found her. Threatened her. Threatened Felix, too, from what it sounded like."

"The Collective killed Naomi?" I asked, incredulous.

"I don't think so. I think whoever is in on the Bliss trade

inside Luma is who took her out," my mom said. "They figured out Naomi had been there that night and shut her up for good. After that, I ... it got harder to know how to get to you. If Naomi hadn't been in Luma at my request, she'd be alive. I went off the rails for a while. I'd lost your father, then you, then Naomi, then you again when I no longer had a lifeline to you."

"What about Felix and the Turners?" I asked. "They could have gotten a message to me."

"Jan Turner contacted me that same night," she said. "Jan suspected that the entire bounty-hunting team would be interrogated via truth serum about the side mission in Sacramento, since two Luma bounty hunters had died. She told me not to contact her anymore for everyone's sake. They destroyed their phones to get rid of whatever physical evidence they could. I know that last part because Felix and I ran into each other about six months ago on a job. I was on scene because a house party in San Diego had twenty dead humans in it, thanks to Bliss overdoses. A half-goblin girl from Luma who was visiting her human sister for winter break was the sole survivor and called it in to Luma police. A neighbor reported a noise complaint to the mundane police, and an officer on scene figured out what he was looking at and contacted me.

"Anyway, Felix said his parents retired shortly after the department-wide interrogation following your dad's death. Whether their retirement was a choice or forced, I don't know. I haven't talked to the Turners since. They were our closest friends."

I wanted to be pissed at Felix for not telling me he'd seen my mother.

"Don't be angry at that boy," my mom said. "He had been on a Collective-assigned mission. That puts anything that happened on that job under the Soul NDA. I can tell you he was very upset to know he couldn't tell you he'd seen me. Not that you two were on speaking terms then anyway ..."

"He left not that long after Naomi died. They got to him too. Threatened to kill me if he didn't back off his side investigations into why you and Dad were so obsessed with Bliss cases. Rumor going around the hunters was that you and Dad were distributors and a deal had gone bad with your dealer."

Mom barked a laugh. "Lying bastards." After a beat, she said, "You should thank Felix the next time you talk to him. When he figured out you were likely heading to Kensey, he got in touch with his contacts in Washington to ask them to find me and tell me about your intended destination. I was already in the area when the message with the motel address popped up on the bounty mirror."

Damn Felix. Always looking out for everyone else.

"Wait ..." I said, my mind stuck on the topic of bounty mirrors. "Back up a second. The night Dad ... those messages on the pocket mirror. It said someone named Ferguson was at large. It said Dad was killed in action and you'd gone AWOL."

"Like I said, consider the source of your information," she said. "They'd already informed me of my exile when those appeared on my mirror. And I wasn't even in Luma. It was all part of their cover story. They want Bliss to be a fringe human problem, nothing more. Your father and I kept threatening to expose it as the Collective's gross oversight—that fae teens were disappearing and humans were dying on their watch because they refused to treat Bliss like the epidemic it is. We didn't know how we'd get it past the Soul NDA to inform the press, but we were going to try."

"Did you know then that Bliss had vampire venom in it?" I asked.

"Nope. We'd known for a while there was some connection between it all—Bliss, vamps, missing fae teens. You and your friends provided the thread that tied it together. We just don't know how widespread it is across the hubs. The hybrids who do this all seem to have the same MO: fae teens out in exchange for Bliss getting smuggled in. Is there a highly connected drug cartel with a strict set of rules? Is it a coincidence they have similar setups because it's the most effective? Is there something even bigger going on? We don't know."

I recalled my conversation with Welsh, and even with Domino. The feral population was growing, and they were starting to breach the veils. Even if Luma was the biggest hub in the nation, it seemed unlikely that it was the only one being targeted. It felt like something larger was brewing, but I had no idea what that something was.

"I know you're angry with me," my mom said after a few beats of silence. "But don't say I didn't try for you, baby girl. I did the best I could. I beat myself up every day about how badly I failed."

It would probably be easier to stay mad at her. But it wasn't as if she hadn't been through hell and back, too. People could say a lot of things about my mother—but the one universal truth that couldn't be denied was how deeply she'd loved my father. She'd lost the love of her life that night—a piece of her soul.

I stared at her for a long moment longer then closed the distance and threw my arms around her. We squeezed each other so tight it hurt.

We started sobbing at the same time.

We grieved together for my father for the first time. And for Naomi. And the last six years taken from us by the Collective because they'd deemed her too much of a problem.

A whole hell of a lot was a mess right now, but I had my mom back. I'd figure out the rest.

Chapter 28
KAYDA

Kayda awoke in Welsh's guest bedroom. She'd tried to call Harlow last night from Welsh's phone and had gotten to finally speak to the infamous rogue sorcerer. He'd sounded perfectly normal, if not a bit stuffy. She'd been mildly disappointed.

"Hello, Kayda," he had said. "This is Caspian Blackthorn. I hope we're able to meet in person someday soon. I'm afraid Harlow is currently occupied with something ... rather important. Not that speaking to you isn't, mind you. She will be quite upset she missed you, but this is something she needs to take care of."

"And that would be?"

"It's not my place to share," he'd said. "But I'll tell her to call back as soon as she's able."

Harlow hadn't called. Talking to the rogue sorcerer had been a balm, though. It confirmed that all the things she'd been told about Harlow's latest set of adventures had been true. Which also meant it was true that she was alive and well.

Welsh's place in Little Talonia wasn't as spacious as his spot uptown. It was clean and comfortable, but he'd told Kayda that he didn't spend much time here himself. It was often used as a halfway house for his clients who needed a secure place to stay. Neighbors in the surrounding apartments knew who Welsh was, and what he did, and helped keep an eye out for any suspicious behavior, especially when young adults were staying here alone.

Henri had taken the couch this time. After sleeping on this bed that was so small Kayda's heels dangled off the end of it, she figured he'd gotten the better deal. She rolled onto her side, listening to the sound of Henri's steady breaths in the living room. The guest bedroom was sparsely furnished with only the bed and a small nightstand with a lamp on it. She'd placed the elf's ring on the table last night, and she picked it up now. She held the ring in front of her face, peering through the center and turning it this way and that. The sunlight beyond the closed blinds of the single window was bright enough to reveal nothing new about the ring. She slipped it onto her pinky for shits and giggles.

Magic singed her skin and she yanked the ring back off, sitting up. This wasn't a mundane, decorative ring; it was charmed.

Maybe this young elf wasn't nearly as powerful as Kayda had thought. She didn't know magical items the way that Harlow did, but Welsh might.

She flung off the comforter and crossed the short distance to the door. The doors to her room, Welsh's, and the bathroom all opened into the same small circular swatch of tiled hallway. Welsh's door was closed, so she walked straight ahead into the bathroom. By the time she emerged, Welsh's door was open and he and Henri were sitting on the couch. Welsh was back to his twenty-something self, tiny next to Henri's bulk. Henri rubbed the heel of his palm against an eye and yawned deeply.

Kayda bounced lightly on the balls of her feet.

Welsh squinted at her. "What's gotten into you this morning?"

"Put this on," Kayda said, pulling the ring out of her pocket and holding it out.

Though his brows pinched, he did so, pulling the ring free an instant later. "Well, shit. Magic-enhancing spell. Level 5, I'd say." He held the ring up to reexamine it, one eye squinted. "I can sense the magic in it now. Given how hard the elf hit us, I'm guessing it takes the spell a while to recharge. At least twenty-four hours."

Kayda had thought she'd felt a slight buzzing in her pocket while she was washing her hands, and now she knew she had. The ring was amped up for reuse.

She'd left the map on the small dining room table last night, and Henri got up now to grab it. "The dot's downtown. Not far from here, actually. What if we offer to give the ring back in exchange for information? It was probably really expensive."

Welsh "hmmed," considering it.

"Do you have an elf persona?" Kayda asked.

Welsh pursed his lips, seemingly insulted by the insinuation that the suggestion might be beyond his skill set. "Of course. And I have an idea. But it would mean you two would need to pose as my security detail."

"That was my job until you ambushed it," Kayda said.

Welsh shrugged. "I'll buy you some pork rolls on the way out if you stop complaining about it."

It was Kayda's turn to shrug. "Deal."

An hour and a half later, they were on their way and Kayda's belly was blissfully full of pork rolls. Welsh had glamoured himself to look like a male elf with sharp cheekbones, shoulder-length black hair pulled into a low ponytail that covered the tips of his ears, and was dressed in a forest-green suit of crushed velvet. Shiny black shoes clicked smartly as he walked at a leisurely pace through Little Talonia, with Kayda and Henri flanking him. They had both put on a few of Welsh's glamoured items that he kept in the safe house for emergencies. Kayda had spiky blue hair, and the hoop nose ring she fastened onto a nostril had widened her face and nose. She donned mundane sunglasses to further obscure her face. Henri wore tinted shades that clipped over his glasses, and had changed his outfit to be more like Kayda's—all black. Kayda thought Henri was over-doing the macho thug walk he was employing, but when a guy was that big and fueled by unwavering determination, most people got out of his way even if his expression made him look mildly constipated.

Welsh kept an eye on the map, and confirmed the dot was still at Yogurt Town. Maybe the young elf worked there.

When they reached the pastel-colored frozen-yogurt shop, Welsh pushed open the front door and strolled in as if he owned the place. The few patrons sitting at bubblegum-pink and seafoam-green tables glanced up in wonderment at this elegant elf and his sunglasses-wearing entourage.

The shop was one of those self-serve places with one wall lined with yogurt-dispensing faucets, and the other with tubs of toppings. There was one person behind the small counter, and given his very wide-eyed expression and rapidly pounding heart, Kayda knew instantly he was human. And a few seconds from peeing his pants.

A young girl came out of a back room beyond the yogurt fountains with a cordless phone in her hand. "Hey, Randy, do you—" She came up short when she spotted Welsh standing in the middle of the small shop. Slowly raising the phone to her ear, she said, "I'll have our manager call you back." Ending the call, she swallowed hard. She peered around Kayda, presumably to silently plead for help from Randy. When she found no aid, she stood straight again, turning the cordless phone over and over in her hands. "Can I help you find your perfect flavor today?"

Kayda almost laughed. But she recognized this shy girl as one who had her arms stretched wide to the heavens last night, chanting in a foreign tongue in an attempt to open a portal to another world. Her blond hair was stuffed into a baby-blue baseball hat, which hid her pointed ears. There was no rule, no stigma about being an elf. The fact that she'd kept her ears covered last night at the bar—that all of them had made a point to keep them covered—was the odd part.

The girl had a tall, gangly frame that she would grow into eventually, giving her that classic long, elegant look that all elves seemed to have. In this moment, in her too-big yellow work shirt and light blue shorts, she looked every bit her age. Her name tag said "Snowdrop."

"Is this the one, Ajax?" Welsh asked, turning to Kayda.

Kayda was glad for the sunglasses, because her brow smashed together. She recovered quickly. "That's her, boss," she said in her gruffest tone.

"Please come with us, Snowdrop," Welsh said. "We have a few questions to ask you."

"W-w-what is this about?" Snowdrop asked.

Welsh shot a pointed look at Randy, and then took a step closer to Snowdrop. Very discreetly, he brushed back his hair on one side, revealing his pointed ear. Snowdrop's body went ramrod straight. After concealing his ear, Welsh resumed his regal posture. "I would rather not discuss your ... extracurricular activities while at your workplace. I could, if you prefer, bring this matter to your manager. I—"

"No!" Snowdrop said, then went scarlet. "No," she said

softer. "I can speak to you. We can go through the back office and into the parking lot. It's quiet back there."

"Very well." Welsh broke formation to approach Randy at the counter. Kayda heard the boy's heart rate take off at a gallop. "Snowdrop is taking her lunch break. We are not to be interrupted. If you can keep this meeting discreet, there's a reward in it for you."

Randy swallowed hard and nodded.

"Good chap," Welsh said, then strode back toward Snowdrop.

Kayda trailed after Welsh, and Henri brought up the rear. They moved through a small, cluttered office, where Snowdrop placed the phone back in its cradle, and then out the back door into the bright light of late morning baking the asphalt. Yogurt Town shared the small lot with a dinner-only restaurant on one side and a massage parlor across the way. A lone massage employee stood with his back against the brick wall of the building; he only had eyes for his phone as he slowly smoked down a cigarette.

Welsh expertly backed the nervous girl into a corner made by the connecting walls of the yogurt shop and the restaurant. Kayda and Henri flanked Welsh.

While there was a full foot of space between Welsh and Snowdrop, she cowered. Before the elf girl could get a word out, Welsh produced the ring from his pocket and held it between them.

Snowdrop's mouth dropped open. Her eyes snapped not to Welsh, but to Kayda. When the dark plastic of Kayda's sunglasses offered no information, Snowdrop's searching gaze skated over Kayda's arms and hands folded in front of her lap. Did the girl recognize something about Kayda from the night they'd fought over the coyote carcass?

"I ... I bought that legally."

Welsh chuckled. "We're not here about the ring itself. We're here because we need to know why you let three feral vampires into the city."

Snowdrop tried to bolt, but Welsh was too quick and shot out a hand that landed palm-splayed on the brick. "Why ..." She cleared her throat and fought the quiver in her voice. "I don't even know who you are. Why should I tell you anything?"

Welsh turned his back on the girl to have a quiet chat with Kayda and Henri. They mostly whispered nonsense at each other and nodded a lot, to make it appear that they debated how much to divulge to the terrified girl. Turning back to Snowdrop, he said, "I'm a co-owner of a business that operates in the Industrial District, the location of the incident. We export ... certain goods. Goods of a ... very sensitive nature. Goods that, if they were to fall into the wrong hands, could cause untold problems. Not to mention that I have very wealthy financial backers who will not hesitate to retaliate if their budding shipping enterprise is disrupted. The incident with the feral vampires was most assuredly a disruption, as the Collective sent out a band of were-cats to assess the area shortly afterward. They'd sensed the disturbance in the veil.

"If Ajax and Fergus here hadn't already been in the area that night on an unrelated job, they wouldn't have been able to dispatch the ferals and dispose of their bodies in time. If the werecats had gotten there any sooner, they could have declared the area unsafe, reported it back to the Collective, who then would have shut down the entire operation. My partners and I would be out the money our backers have already paid us, and when debts to these people are not paid in a timely manner, limbs and extremities are forcibly removed, families and friends are threatened, and eventually people wind up dead."

Snowdrop gasped and clapped a hand over her mouth. She looked like she was ready to try fleeing again.

"Now," Welsh said, "we don't want to do this, as it will make life harder for us, but our backers are hearing rumors about the dangers of doing business in Luma. We need information to assuage their fears that what happened wasn't an isolated incident. If you don't cooperate, I have enough evidence to use against you that the Collective would be obligated to bring you in for a … thorough questioning. This ring alone could be tied back to you. Truths about your life—your hobbies—could easily be extracted from it. If I was able to find you, the Collective surely could. This will be a lot less painful for you if you speak to me instead of them. Less painful for me, as well. I'd rather keep them out of it." He paused. "I even know about the ritual you participated in at the abandoned zoo last night."

The elf scratched the side of her nose, crossed her arms, then uncrossed them. A few beads of sweat dotted her hairline.

"This isn't only about saving your own hide, you know. If you're called in for questioning, how do you think your friends and your illustrious leader will fare when you're forced to be truthful, hmm?" Welsh asked.

Snowdrop had gone so still now, Kayda would have believed she'd been turned to stone.

"You tell me what you were doing," Welsh continued, "and under whose orders, and we'll let you get back to your day. We may even return your ring."

It took her a few long seconds, but then she asked, "What … what do you want to know?"

"Why did you part the veil like a curtain to let ferals into the city?" Welsh asked.

Chewing on her lip, she looked from Welsh, to Kayda, to Henri, and back again. "Have you heard of the Shades?"

Kayda hadn't. She detected the slightest shake of Henri's head and wondered if he'd known he'd done it.

"Please enlighten us," Welsh said.

"Umm ... okay, so, there was an elf thirty years ago or so named Lachlan Shade, who figured out how to open a portal back to the fae realm," Snowdrop said, a hint of reverence coloring her tone. "He planned to tell the fae about it—to let them know he'd figured it out and that they could go home. But the Collective—" She eyed him warily. "Are you, like, really pro-Collective or anything?"

Kayda was amazed that a girl this young had gotten caught up in something so big.

"I am not," Welsh said. "And the two behind me are loyal only to me. So don't concern yourself about them."

"Umm, so ... the Collective decided a long time ago that they like Earth better, and that they'd never be as powerful in the fae realm as they are here. Before Lachlan Shade could tell the fae about the portals, the Collective sent mercenaries after him. They have sorcerers whose whole job is to detect portal magic and close portals so that the fae are trapped here forever and the sorcerers can stay in power." She stood straighter, bolstered, perhaps, by the rapt attention of her audience. "The mercenaries found Shade and his portal, then pushed him through it, closing it after him. They banished him from Earth 'cause they were scared of him and what he could do."

Welsh cocked his head slightly. "And you and your group are trying to re-create what Shade did?"

Snowdrop vigorously shook her head. "The mercenaries did something to the portal before they pushed Shade through, and he ended up in a different world. It took him years, but he made it to the fae realm, and then he made contact with Earth from there! He can only keep the portal open on his side for a couple minutes, and the magic is too unstable to send living things through yet, but he's sent letters with directions on how to open a portal on Earth. We're going to open one here, and he's going to open one there, and when they're both stable, any fae who wants to go home—to our real home—can. You can come too, sir. The more elves the better."

Welsh offered a noncommittal grunt in response.

Incorrectly perceiving this as waning interest on Welsh's part, Snowdrop added, "He's made it his life's work to free us from the prison the Collective has created. They don't care about the fae. They just care about being in charge."

The words sounded rehearsed.

Silence descended on the group. Snowdrop's chest quickly rose and fell, as if winded by her passionate tale about Lachlan Shade.

Welsh said, "You have yet to say why you let ferals into the city."

"That was a mistake, honestly," Snowdrop said, wringing her hands. "We've all been given challenges to prove we have what it takes. Only elves with strong magic will be chosen to open the portal. My challenge was to manipulate the veil. Veil magic is basically supercharged illusion magic."

"A common skill set for us," Welsh agreed.

Snowdrop nodded. "There's been some rumors about ferals getting through in the Necropolis since the veil magic is weaker there. I chose a stronger spot to prove I had the skills to do it, and because I didn't think ferals would come up that high." Her voice grew soft and distant. "They must have sensed it though, and got in."

Memories of that night flitted through Kayda's head. She couldn't imagine how badly things could have gone if those ferals had decided to venture into Luma Proper. The destruction the monsters could have wrought on so many innocent people ...

Snowdrop's wide, panicked eyes shot to Kayda. "Did I hurt you? With the wind spell, I mean? I used that ring to juice up the power. I'd never used it before and it got so crazy so fast. I heard a crash on the other side, but I couldn't see what happened. That's why I wanted to get rid of any evidence of what I did and needed to take the coyote body back with me. If I hurt you, I'm really, really sorry. I swear I didn't mean any of it. It got so ..." Her eyes welled with tears and she furiously shook her head. "I ... I hate Earth. Hate it. I don't fit here. I want to go back to where we belong. We're not trying to hurt anyone, I swear. That's why we go all the way out to the preserve to practice. No one lives there. We just want to get home. That's it. If I messed up your business, mister, I'm sorry about that, too."

Goddess help her, Kayda almost felt sorry for her. She was a bit of a naive idiot, but Kayda had gotten in plenty of idiotic messes when she was a teenager. Hells, given where she was right now, it continued to happen.

And hadn't Kayda herself had all these same thoughts last night? Kayda didn't hate Earth, but a not-so-small part of her did wonder if she'd thrive in a world she was actually from—a world she was meant for.

"Thank you, Snowdrop," Welsh said, holding up the ring. "I'm going to keep this. After what you've told us, I'm not sure it's prudent for someone as untrained as you to have it."

Snowdrop's lips puckered, making her look like a petulant child, but she didn't argue. Kayda had no doubt the ring had been purchased with many, many saved wages from grueling hours at Yogurt Town.

"Get on inside," Welsh said, jutting his chin at the door.

Snowdrop didn't need to be told twice. She scooted sideways, her back against the brick, until she'd blindly made contact with the knob. Yanking the door open, she disappeared inside without a backward glance.

"Had you heard of any of that before?" Kayda asked after the door had closed behind Snowdrop. Even the smoking masseuse across the parking lot had gone inside.

"It was all news to me," Welsh said. "We should go. I can process this better if we eat something."

"Again?" Kayda asked.

"Yes, again. I already told you: I need calories to maintain this level of magic use. Do you need me to say it again slower … so … you … can … understand … me?"

Kayda's lip curled.

"Oookay," Henri said, forcibly taking Welsh by the shoulders and pointing him toward the exit of the lot. "Let's take care of the hangry problem first, and if he's still b-b-being a dick after that, Kayda, you c-can punch him."

"Aw, thanks," Kayda said, smiling.

"You two are gross," Welsh said.

Henri gave him a shove.

Letting the two men get lost in a volley of suggestions about where to eat, Kayda replayed the conversation with Snowdrop. The main issue she had with the elf's story was that it would be hard to verify. What if Snowdrop had made up the name Lachlan Shade?

Yet, the elf had seemed completely terrified. It was harder to maintain a lie while stressed. The elf's racing heart, shuffling feet, and shallow breaths had all been further proof she'd been scared. So she was either telling the truth or she deserved an Academy Award.

A few minutes into their hunt for food, Kayda spotted a public phone booth. She slowed. If there was anyone she knew who would have heard of Lachlan Shade, it was Felix Turner. He worked for the Collective, for Goddess's sake. She didn't know how much interaction bounty hunters had with the ruling sorcerers, but it was significantly higher than anyone not employed by them. Even if he didn't know all the details, the name had to have come up in passing conversation a few times, right?

"Hang on!" she called out as she reached the box, then stuffed herself inside.

She gagged on the urine smell. She couldn't tell if it was fresh, or if the heat had heightened any lingering aromas. She hadn't heard from Felix in a while. Had something happened to him? She hoped he didn't change his cell number as often as Welsh did.

Checking her cell phone, she pulled up his unprogrammed number from her text threads, then called the number from the public phone. Thankfully, he answered right away.

"This is Felix."

"Kayda."

He heaved a breath. "Hi. Dammit. I still owe you that phone, huh?" In an exhausted tone, he asked, "Are you all right?"

"Depends on your definition of all right, but I'm alive, so yes." Kayda didn't harbor any squishy feelings for the guy, but couldn't help being concerned about how worn out he sounded. "Are you all right?"

There was a swell of voices on his side of the line, then what sounded like a door closing. She pictured him hiding out in a stairwell or loitering in a parking lot. "Yeah, I'm fine. Just busy."

"Sounds like the kind of busy that not even a long weekend vacation would fix," Kayda said.

"Honestly? I'm getting worried. I'm on bounty runs nearly every night. I swear ever since Low and her pals put the Collective on blast, people have gotten a lot bolder about evading the law. I've got mundane police and EMT buddies, and they're seeing a rise in Bliss-related crimes and death. More humans are ending up in the hospital from too-high magic levels from charmed items. Can't even blame that last one on Caspian Blackthorn, 'cause he's not even in Luma to sell this shit to people. We can't figure out where the stuff is getting smuggled in from, or if there's a massive underground operation going on here that none of us can find. The city feels like a powder keg right now and I'm bracing myself for an explosion."

Kayda hadn't considered how different Felix's view of Luma would be given his job. It was easy to discount him because he worked for the Collective, but deep down she knew Felix wasn't a bad guy. He saw the worst of the worst in a lot of ways, and what he didn't see for himself, he had friends who did. She almost felt bad about calling him now. He needed a stiff drink, not more to agonize over.

"So what's up?" he asked, trying to sound upbeat and helpful.

"Random question, but have you heard of Lachlan Shade?"

Felix was silent for so long, Kayda wondered if the call disconnected.

"Hello?" she tried.

"Uh, yeah. I'm here. Why ... why are you asking about Lachlan Shade?"

She gave him a watered-down version of Snowdrop's story, as well as the elf's involvement with the ritual in the preserve.

"Man ..." Felix said, sighing. "There's been a lot of that shit, too. The Collective has a branch called Portal Relations. That's actually on public record if you know where to look. That's all those sorcerers do: track down portals and close them. There's a reason why they're closing them—other than what Snowdrop said—but I can't tell you what it is. As in, I'm physically incapable of doing so. I hope you can figure out what that means faster than Low did."

She had no idea what in the hells he was talking about, but she'd figure it out later.

"Anyway, the Shades are more of a nuisance than a full-blown problem. The bigger issue is that there have been so many reports in other hubs about portal magic fluctuations that our Collective started sending out sorcerers to help. With the Collective more short-staffed than usual, the veil breaches in the Necropolis seem to be increasing. The few werecats I've talked to say it's not related, but one, I don't fucking trust the cats to ever tell the truth, and two, how could they not be related? Maybe it's an ego thing, and they refuse to believe ferals are getting through on their watch."

Had Snowdrop been telling the truth? Had she let the ferals in by accident? Or was something else going on here?

"Is the Portal Relations branch aware of the Shades being in Luma?" Kayda asked. "Aster said everything in that preserve—including the trees—felt the pull of magic when the elves got the portal open for a few seconds. Seems like the Collective would have shut that down if it was happening in their city, wouldn't they?"

He started to say something half a dozen times, then sighed again. "There's only so much I can say. But the Shades here aren't strong enough to open one more than a few inches." He struggled with uttering partial sentences before finally saying, "The Collective might not be able to sense the elves' portal magic as well as they claim to. I've heard about the Shades for years, but I didn't think they were in Luma. Not enough for them to be performing rituals, anyway. If you get a chance to talk to that pixie again, give her my information. Pixies are a pain in the ass, but they're excellent informants if you can get a reliable one. They always know more than you think they do. Maybe I can tip off a few trusted people on my end to check things out down there."

Kayda kept the comment to herself that she thought Felix was stretching himself in too many directions. He'd always been the care-taking type—always making sure everyone else was taken care of. Which was why him abruptly leaving Harlow had been such a gut punch—it went against who he was at his core.

To Kayda, that made him a spineless coward. Harlow, however, had managed to convince herself it was a reflection of her worth —that she wasn't enough to keep him around. Kayda still considered him a coward, but she hated him less for it. Not that she'd ever tell him that.

"Damn, I gotta go. Stay in touch, yeah?" he said.

The call disconnected before she could remind him about the phone. She'd have to try Welsh's again.

When she emerged from the phone booth, she stared in astonishment across the street at Henri who had Welsh trapped in a choke hold. Welsh's nose was scant inches from Henri's armpit.

"What happened?" she asked once she'd crossed to their side. Behind the men was a toy store, and several wide-eyed children of a variety of species had their faces pressed to the glass.

"H-h-he's very annoying when he's h-h-hungry and I got tired of listening to him complain," Henri said. "So n-now he's eating armpit hair."

Kayda bit down on her bottom lip to keep from laughing, if only because Welsh might swap her next glamour tonic for something else and turn her into a slug in a cowboy hat or something. "There's a pizza place down the street. Let's eat there."

Welsh started to protest, so Henri wiggled Welsh's upturned face even closer to his armpit. Kayda waited it out. Eventually, Welsh slackened in the hold and angrily tapped out.

Henri abruptly let him go and Welsh hit the ground, breath whooshing out in a rush. Kayda stood over him, hand out. Welsh slapped it away. Kayda held it back out. Fuming, Welsh took it. Once on his feet, Kayda threw an arm over his shoulders and guided him to the pizza parlor.

"I may hate you two more than I ever hated Fletch," Welsh said, rubbing his neck.

"Felix confirmed the Shades are a legit fringe group who are obsessed with opening portals," Kayda said, adding in what Felix had told her about the growing sense of unease among the first responder community, as well as the possibility that feral breach numbers were increasing in correlation to a dwindling number of Luma sorcerers thanks to an uptick in abused portal magic across the country.

Welsh's surliness had faded by the time they were seated and three deep-dish pizzas were on their way. He remained quiet when the food arrived. When Henri and Kayda reached for slices, Welsh didn't immediately help himself—he just stared into space.

Kayda glanced at Henri over the top of the upraised pizza dish and he shrugged helplessly.

If Welsh wasn't eating, things truly *were* dire.

Chapter 29
HARLOW

A far corner of the warehouse had been outfitted with cots. A few privacy screens had been erected around the area in a futile attempt to block out the constant hum of noise from what was essentially a command center. Fingers typed away on keyboards. Quiet, muffled conversations were had in small groups, or over the phone. Every once in a while, an SUV would leave the warehouse or return to it. Sleep came piecemeal. Caspian lay on his back on a nearby cot, his hands behind his head and his ankles crossed. The sword lay next to me, its hilt near my elbow.

My mom had gone back to work.

She'd told me that she wasn't an official VHoA member and was more like a freelance agent, traveling to where she could offer help based on her experience as a PI and a Collective bounty hunter with an expertise in vampires. She seemed to know a little about everything, her contact list populated by humans and fae alike—inside hubs and out.

Caspian and I had eaten leftover pizza Soren warmed up for us while my mother joined us at the table. She'd regaled us with stories about some of her recent jobs and talked about her travels. A knot of concern had coiled in my gut the longer she talked. I got the impression that she'd turned into a workaholic. Whether that was borne out of a desire to stay busy, or a desire to stay ahead of her own demons, not letting herself idle for too long, in case they caught up with her, I couldn't be sure. My instinct said it was the latter.

I must have fallen asleep because what felt like moments later, someone gently shook me. Groggily, I peeled open one eye, then the other.

Caspian stared down at me. "You've got a call." He held the phone in front of my face.

The first thing I registered was that I'd somehow slept until two in the afternoon. The other was that the accepted call on the screen, the time ticking away, was from one Zeef Wellington.

Kayda!

I grabbed the phone and swung myself into a seated position. Pressing the cell to my ear, I said, "Kay?"

"Goddess above! Finally!"

My eyes welled up at the sound of her voice. "Oh, Kay ..."

"Girl! Don't you start crying on me yet."

I sniffed hard. "One sec."

Lowering the phone from my ear, I mouthed a thank-you to Caspian. He nodded, then left the sleeping area. A quick scan of the space revealed I was the only one who had been snoozing other than the six-year-old the sword had been playing with yesterday. I had no idea where the stabby menace had gotten off to now. Peeking between two privacy partitions, I spotted Caspian as he sat in the kitchen-slash-dining-room area. Soren, my mom, Caspian, and a man I didn't know were huddled around a picnic table covered in notepads and open books. Perhaps Caspian had pulled them into the curiosity that was Margaret Fengast.

Tiptoeing into a far corner so as to not rouse the dozing kid, I said, "Okay, hi. How are you?"

"Do you have any idea how utterly furious I want to be with you?"

"Want to be? So you're not?" I asked. "I got myself into such a pickle—"

"A pickle?" Kayda asked, snorting. "You've been spending too much time with that stuffy sorcerer."

I laughed. "Probably. But, honestly, Kay. I know it was shitty of me to ghost you. You're my favorite person on the planet. I couldn't let anything happen to you. And then ... it sounds like trouble found you anyway. Someone broke into your apartment?"

"Goddess. That feels like a million years ago."

Kayda told her about the break-in and running through the casino carrying Grayson Ipram like a baby while avoiding were-cats chasing them down. I told her about Margaret's journal, and that Grayson's many-great-grandfather had been a royal douche canoe. Kayda relayed her adventures with Henri as Angel and Damon, the feral attack in the Indie, and how Henri had kissed her.

"He. Did. What?" I shrieked with such alarm it startled the sleeping kid. She wailed like a banshee. I apologized profusely to her father who had run over to check on her. "Oh, that guy hates me so hard right now," I whispered into the phone as he carried his weeping child away. I redirected my attention to the conversation. "I need all the details. Wait. How did this suddenly happen? Oh my God! Have I been a clam block all this time?"

"Excuse me. A what?" Kayda asked.

"You know. Not a cock block, but a clam block."

"Yeah, that's not a thing," Kayda said. "But also kind of? He said we're very intimidating as a pair."

"Huh. Then I no longer feel bad about going radio silent on you if it means it finally gave that boy the courage to slide his lizard tongue down your throat."

"You're so awful," she said laughing. "Also, I know you still feel bad."

"I really do."

The hush that fell over us was charged.

Sighing, I said, "Just say it."

It took her a moment. "I get that two of the most important people in your life—Felix and your mom—bailing when things got hard gave you abandonment issues. And I get that when it came to dealing with something as big as all this, you bailed because you haven't had the best role models for sticking around. But, you and me? We don't do this. We don't skip out on each other. We're sisters."

My eyes welled. "I know. And me keeping you out didn't even shield you from it. You'd have been more prepared for dealing with everything if I'd talked to you. I promise I'll never bail on you again. You've been my rock for so long and you deserved better than me ghosting you."

"Thank you," Kayda said, and if I hadn't known better, I'd have said she was a little weepy, too. Kayda did not get weepy. "All that said, I get why you did it now. Your paranoia might have driven me nuts, but I honestly wish I'd listened to you more. It's not a conspiracy theory when you're right." She paused. "Did Welsh tell you about the elf kid we've been following?"

"Only that an elf let ferals into the city, which is so wild my brain rejected it."

Kayda told me about the young elf named Snowdrop who was part of an elfin group called Shades who wanted to open a portal back to their homeland with the aid of their elf savior, Lachlan Shade.

She seemed to suddenly remember something. "Oh, hey. When I called yesterday, Caspian said some big thing happened and you were too caught up in it to talk. What was it?"

I hadn't blurted out that I'd been reunited with my mom in part because it didn't feel real. Once I said it, it was out there. Maybe I was worried that if I breathed life into the reality, it meant I could lose her again. How could I consistently have her in my life and live in Luma—a city that had exiled her? I'd be my usual paranoid self every time I talked to her on the phone, scared someone had found a way to hack into the call and listen in. Even now, two states away, I feared that.

I told her about Cody the troll being murdered by the sword in Marley's Diner. About the run-in with Sweeney the sorcerer in our room when he tried to steal back the loot Caspian had paid Domino fair and square for.

"We got out of there alive because ..." I said slowly, "my mom rescued us."

Kayda was quiet for three long beats. "Oh. Oh shit. Low! Are you serious? She's alive? How are you just now telling me that part!"

"I'm still processing it! I thought the last month had been crazy. The last week has been batshit."

"A-fucking-men, girl."

We fell silent. I was exhausted, my throat dry. I wasn't ready to say goodbye to her yet. Plus, I could tell there was something more she wanted to say.

"Are you ... coming back?" she asked in the smallest voice I'd ever heard from her. "I was already thinking you might not, but now that you're back with your mom ..."

"I want to," I said. "I just don't know if I can. I don't know if they've banned me like they banned her. But I don't plan to stay gone forever. I promise."

Kayda heaved a long, relieved breath.

"Speaking of leaving ... how tempted were you by the idea of a portal opening back to the fae world?" I knew she was curious about her ancestors, and how much seeing charmed items like the sword broke her heart, knowing that parts of her history literally lined hilts and jewelry.

Kayda chuckled darkly. "Of course you'd ask me that."

I shrugged. "I know you better than you know yourself."

"Very tempted," she said in a rush. "I don't think I'd want it to be permanent. But the possibility is ... like you said, tempting."

"If Snowdrop and her Shades aren't lunatics and get a portal open, I'll understand if you want to go. You have to promise you won't leave before saying goodbye. In case you don't come back. Which is ironic as fuck coming from me ..."

"I promise," she said tightly. "Sorry, but I gotta get going. Welsh is being dramatic because he wants his phone back."

"Tell that grumpy asshole I say hi. And hi to *Henri* too." I batted my eyelashes solely for my benefit.

She laughed. "I will. And to your mom from me. That's so wild, Low."

Understatement.

"How does she feel about you smashing a sorcerer, by the way?"

I squawked. "Excuse me?"

"Are you telling me you and the stuffy old man aren't partaking in adult nap time?"

This time I spluttered. "First of all, he's not old. He's thirty ... something."

"Thirty hundred."

"That's not a number! Second of all, I'm not smashing or partaking in Cas. He thinks I'm a dramatic child."

"I mean—"

"Rude!"

Kayda yelped on the other line, then her voice was replaced by Welsh's. "If I have to listen to one more minute of this asinine conversation, I will implode."

The call ended.

It said a lot about me that one hostile sentence from Welsh had given me the warm squishies for him.

Shoving Caspian's phone in my pocket, I headed across the sleeping area. Kayda was okay and only slightly mad at me. I could live with that.

Stepping out from the barrier of the privacy partitions, I noted that nearly half the fleet of black SUVs was gone, along with a large swath of the team. Perhaps I'd slept so long in part because the place was much quieter now than it had been last night.

I slid onto the bench seat beside Caspian. My mom was on his other side. Soren and a dark-skinned man in his fifties were seated across from us. He introduced himself as Arturo.

On the table were Margaret's journals, a map of Washington, a couple of Caspian's rune textbooks, open notebooks, and scribbled-on legal pads.

Conversation had stopped when I'd joined them, and my mom leaned forward while Caspian leaned back. "How's Kayda?" she asked.

I gave them the gist of Kayda's adventures, spotlighting the feral breaches, as vampires were this lot's bread and butter. My mom had just taken a sip of her coffee when I said, "Oh, and there's a group of elves who are trying to open a portal to be reunited with their Elf and Savior, Lachlan Shade."

She did a literal spit take, spraying a fine mist of coffee over her notes and Soren across the way.

"Robin! Jesus criminy!" Soren yelped, though he was laughing while he ran a hand over his face.

Mom was on her feet a second later and came over to straddle the bench beside me. "Did you say Lachlan Shade?"

I instinctively scooted back an inch, my backside bumping into Caspian's thigh. "Yeah? You've heard of him?"

"What did that elf girl tell Kayda happened to Lachlan?"

I recounted the story to the best of my ability.

"Well, that's mostly right. But they left out the part where Lachlan kidnapped a fae girl and was bleeding her dry to open that portal. I'm not opposed to the fae finding a way home if that's what they want, but bloodletting a sixteen-year-old girl isn't the way to do it."

I stared at her. "And how do you know that? It supposedly happened thirty years ago."

"Twenty-nine," my mom said, placing a hand on her stomach. "I'd been hired by the fae girl's family when she went missing. I was pregnant with you while I watched a Collective sorcerer push Lachlan into the portal. The sorcerer said a portal opened with blood magic needs a sacrifice to close it. So he sacrificed Lachlan."

I blinked in rapid succession. "Where did the portal send him?"

Mom shrugged. "The sorcerer said portal magic is unstable at the best of times, and Lachlan's method could have opened a portal to anywhere."

"Well, wherever he is, he's made contact with this realm. That's why the elves are obsessed with the guy. He claims he can get a portal open on his side and ours, so if fae wanna flee this world, they can."

Mom didn't look convinced. "People can change a lot in three decades, but ... I don't know."

Arturo spoke up for the first time. His Spanish accent was a little heavy, but his English was perfect. "Caspian was showing me the pictures of the runes on that coyote. That is some very complicated spell work for a teenager to have mastered. Either someone else provided the runes for her to draw, or someone left the coyote and the young one was told to collect it after it died."

Kayda had said she could tell Snowdrop had been fearful, and I didn't question her ability to hear the biological sounds of that fear. But maybe what the elf had been scared of was getting caught. Which could mean she'd lied about why she'd parted the veil.

I pulled out Caspian's phone and sent Welsh a text.

Me: *Don't trust Snowdrop is telling you the full truth.*

Zeef Wellington: *Your cryptic warning has been noted.*

I cocked my head at Arturo. "Are you a sorcerer?"

"Eh. I tried the academy when I was about your age. Gave it up after a couple of years. It sucks the joy out of magic and strips you of your personality, that schooling." He offered an apologetic shrug to Caspian. "No offense."

"None taken. Harlow takes advantage of every opportunity to call me a lifeless automaton," Caspian said, deadpan.

"I've never said lifeless."

Soren snickered.

"I muck around with it from time to time," Arturo said, smiling. "Haven't practiced it so much as studied it. It's like learning a language—if you abandon it completely, you have to start over. Plus, every once in a while—like now—it comes up."

"Have either of you made any sense of the runes on the coyote?" I asked.

"Can you open the picture again?" Caspian asked me while grabbing a book.

I keyed in his password and got into his photos, selecting the clearest photograph of the four. Placing two fingertips on the screen, I drew them away from each other, zooming in on the blood-painted runes. Up close, it was evident fur had been shaved off the front leg, providing a smoother surface to add the runes. Had they drugged the poor animal to keep it immobile while they went through the painstaking process of applying them, and then carried its deadweight body to the spot in question? I hadn't seen Snowdrop, but Kayda kept talking about how small and slight the teen was. Would she have been able to carry a twenty-to-forty-pound body by herself? Had she driven it to the veil on the other side and hefted it out on her own?

It was possible, I supposed. But my gut kept telling me there was something more going on than a test of magical talent.

"So my first idea," Caspian said, having found the right page in his book, "was that it had to be a rune array for passage. Allowing one thing to pass into another—as in from one side of the veil to the other." Taking his phone from me, he placed it on his book and peered at the image, zooming in and out, sliding the picture this way and that.

"That there, though ..." Arturo said, leaning forward. "The third one down. That's the ancient variation of 'forward movement,' isn't it?"

Mom and I must have had identical expressions of utter confusion, because Caspian said, "It's like the difference between 'walk' and 'stride.' One is more general, while the other is precise. This older variation of the rune is a more precise label of the motion."

"Correct," Arturo said. "But the more precise label now gives the entire array a different meaning."

Caspian grinned at him. "You, sir, do more than muck around. Mrs. Flet—Robin. Could you hand me the journal by your elbow?"

Mom did as he asked.

I chewed on my bottom lip as Caspian flipped through

Margaret's journal. "Ah! Now, this array here ..." He placed the journal in the middle of the table so we could all peer at it, even if the majority of us had no clue what we were looking at. "This array is one Margaret was experimenting with for passage through the upcoming storm, hoping it would allow them through. But she talks here not of the ship advancing through by force. It's an array for forcing the storm to part to allow passage. So it's not an array for passage through the storm, but rather for the storm to grant passage. Two very different spells. The latter being more difficult."

"And that array is similar to the one on the coyote's leg?" I asked.

"Very similar," Caspian said. "This array is to make the veil grant passage. Someone with knowledge or access to ancient rune magic crafted these."

I thought of the map of Kensey that Felix had sent me ages ago, back when our grand plan had been for Caspian to perform countless experiments on the veil and chart data points. "I don't condone this method of getting around veil magic, but you have to admit it's far more efficient than the plan we started out with."

Caspian nodded. "Though if this method is reliant on having access to ancient magic, perhaps not."

"Who would be likely to have access to magic like this anyway?" I asked. "Most, if not all, the texts from way back when wouldn't have traveled with the marooned fae during the Glitch. The only way there would be ancient texts on Earth would be from scholars who ended up here and put the knowledge in their memories down on paper. The reason we have any of Kensey's writings is because she moved a whole damn island with some of her research on it." I looked at Arturo, Soren, and my mom in turn. "Have any of you been to Kensey? Are there museums with her writings on display or anything?"

Arturo shook his head. "Nothing like that. There's one museum in Kensey that's got an exhibit year-round devoted to her, but if any of her writings survived, they're locked up. My guess is they're in the Collective's tower. It's possible that a Collective sorcerer could have stolen or copied some of the ancient texts of Kensey's and then gotten it to the Shades, and that knowledge eventually made it to Snowdrop in Luma, but that all sounds pretty convoluted, doesn't it? And to what end? To open the veil for a few minutes?"

I agreed that it sounded like a lot of work. But perhaps Snowdrop's dangerous hijinks had been an experiment to see if this array would do what they'd hoped. Maybe her letting the ferals in had been the tip of the iceberg as far as nefarious elf plans went.

Something was missing. I didn't know if we were trying to make connections that didn't exist. Maybe it was a case of Occam's razor: the simplest answer was the most likely. Which was that Snowdrop was a scared teen nervous about getting in trouble for recklessly using old magic she didn't understand, and in the process accidentally letting in ferals who could have killed a lot of people.

I sighed, my brain tired. "Where is everyone, by the way? Seems like half the people here left while I was sleeping."

"Suspected feral horde near Chelan." Soren shoved a few things aside to reveal the map spread across the table. "Central Washington seems to be a vampire hot spot—maybe because it's more rural. We knock out a nest and another one springs up overnight. We got a call at 4 a.m. about a dozen of them ripping through a herd of cattle. The poor farmers around here used to call the cops when some crazy-ass beast that couldn't be taken down by bullets started raising hell, but then the cops would call us, so the farmers know to ring us up directly now."

"Four a.m. and they aren't back?" I asked.

"Last we heard, they took 'em all down by six," Mom said. "They're still celebrating."

She sounded casual enough about the whole thing, but I was unnerved. "Has there been an uptick in ferals lately?"

Mom, Soren, and Arturo exchanged shrugs.

Arturo said, "In the past month or so we've gotten a call almost every night. But activity usually picks up in summer. It's like the bastards are in hibernation and come crawling out as soon as the weather warms up."

Soren and Mom laughed knowingly. I tried to tell myself I was overanxious. I currently felt safer outside the veils even with a brand on my wrist, loosely tying me to an orc mob boss. But was Kayda safe? Were Felix, Welsh, Jo, and Grayson?

And if they weren't, would I even be able to do anything to help them?

Chapter 30

KAYDA

Shortly after Kayda's conversation with Harlow, Henri got a phone call from his mother telling him he'd missed family game night that week and if he missed family dinner night too, he was disowned. He and Welsh had been trapped at the park across the street from the pizza place they'd had lunch in while they'd waited for Kayda to wrap up her call.

Welsh clearly could tell Henri wanted to invite Kayda to dinner, but he shut it down. "We've been able to keep under the radar for now, but we don't know if anyone has figured out that you and Kayda have been spending a lot of time together recently. I can almost guarantee werecats or mundane police have been by the casino by now asking questions about Kayda. I presume your coworkers will have noticed that Henri hasn't been in for a few days either. There are probably cats positioned outside her old place, waiting for her to come back; at Henri's place to see if you two are together; and at the homes of your families. The last thing you want, Henri, is a bunch of werecats busting down your mom's door to tear Kayda out of the house, right?"

Henri deflated. "R-R-Right."

"Some time apart is good right now. She can stay with me. She'll be fine," Welsh said. "You won't perish if you're away from each other for a couple of days."

"Aren't you supposed to be less cranky after you eat?" Kayda asked.

Welsh frowned. "I only had one pizza."

Henri took Kayda by the hand and led her away. "If you n-need to kill him tonight, I'll h-h-help bury his b-body."

"That's very sweet of you," Kayda said, laughing.

Henri placed a chaste kiss on her mouth that devolved very quickly into a make-out session against a tree that Kayda very much enjoyed. The pair of teen mundanes who had been walking away from the park after playing tennis, given their cutesy tennis skirts, gym bags, and zipped-up tennis racks, had been mildly horrified, given their disgusted shrieks.

"Ew, get a room!" one of them said, sunlight glinting off the metal of her braces. Her nose was scrunched up as if she'd smelled something rancid.

Kayda, coming out of her fog, discovered that one of her legs was wrapped around Henri's. And his hand had slipped up her shirt and under her bra. Goddess, when had that happened? She glared at the girls over Henri's shoulder and let loose a menacing growl from her diaphragm. The girls ran screaming toward the parking lot. That cleared away the rest of her post-kiss high, yet managed to leave her feeling jubilant.

They disentangled from each other.

"S-Stay safe," he said, backing away. "Avoid murdering Welsh if you c-c-can help it."

She pressed fingers to her mouth to keep herself from calling him back. Watching him round a corner, she deflated. Now she was stuck with Welsh the Grouch the rest of the day.

Trudging over, she found him sitting on a park bench,

tearing off large chunks of a giant homemade pretzel. The two wrappers sitting beside him suggested this was not his first.

"Finally ready, are we?" Welsh sounded less grumpy, at least. "Grayson is due to call in an hour, so we need to get back to one of my places soon. I was thinking the uptown spot. I'm itching to cook. Haven't had a chance in a while, running around with you two goons. I need to restock the fridge with leftovers."

Kayda had almost forgotten about Grayson. "Do you promise to make more of that sauce?"

He stuffed the last large chunk of pretzel in his mouth and stood. "Promise."

Maybe missing family dinner at Henri's place wouldn't be a total loss.

Before grabbing a cab into uptown, Kayda and Welsh walked a few blocks to a busy shopping center. She loitered outside one of the public restrooms, getting weirder looks than usual. When she caught a glimpse of her reflection in an ice cream shop window, she saw why: she was still glamoured to look like one of Welsh's draken bodyguards. The spiky blue hair was growing on her, she had to admit.

Welsh had walked in as the posh elf who had scared the crap out of Snowdrop, and strolled back out as Bosworth Hemmingsley. If anyone noticed that she'd arrived with one man and left with another, she couldn't tell.

Within forty minutes, they were inside his swanky apartment in the Sarq. They'd just sat down at his dining room table, a notepad and pen in front of Welsh, when his phone rang. He hit accept, put it on speaker, and placed the cell in the middle of the table. Welsh kept up the Bosworth outer appearance but used his most recognizably Welsh voice.

"Hello, Ipram. I've got Kayda here, too. Our mutual collector friend found some information for you as well."

"You've spoken to her then! Good, good." Grayson cleared his throat. "Sorry, again, for taking so long to get back to you. I—"

"Was butthurt that I insinuated you didn't have any legitimate evidence that this infamous pirate captain was actually related to you?" Welsh asked. "Yes. I know."

Kayda stared at him, incredulous. She didn't know why Welsh kept insulting the overpressurized fire hydrant of a water elemental.

"You're a dick. You know that, right?" Grayson asked.

"I bet you dug hardcore into every avenue you could find since you were mad, though. Wanted to prove me wrong and shower me with evidence that you've got genuine pirates among your distinguished lineage," Welsh said nonchalantly. "Nothing motivates an elemental more than indifference and skepticism."

Grayson grumbled under his breath, implying Welsh had been right. Kayda truly couldn't tell if there was a method to Welsh's madness. It seemed like he was a raging asshole most of the time and somehow things kept working out in the end—as opposed to him being motivated by wanting good results and not caring what methods he used to get them.

In a much cheerier, friendly tone, Welsh asked, "What'd you find out?"

"Tell me what you found first," Grayson said, clearly trying to get back some control of the situation.

Welsh dramatically rolled his eyes but gestured at Kayda to proceed.

She sighed. How was she supposed to let the guy know that

Captain Ipram had been the worst? Directly, she supposed, because she was rarely good at nuance.

When Kayda was done recounting what she could remember of Harlow's discoveries in Margaret Fengast's journal, Grayson was silent. "You there?" she asked.

"Yeah," he said, sounding miserable. "None of that is really a surprise after what I found in my research, but it's a bummer the guy clearly sucked." He sighed. "What I had in storage was mostly newspaper clippings and old manifests and stuff. So ... like Welsh said ... I went deeper."

Welsh offered a dramatic "Like I said!" flourish of his hand.

"My grandma is in a retirement community about three hours from here. She lived in Washington most of her life, but she came down to California for the warmer weather and to be closer to me and my ma—but even my ma can't stand her and moved to Florida. I hadn't talked to her in like ten years because she's meaner than a snapping turtle. She put most of her stuff in storage, last I heard," Grayson said. "I asked if I could look through her things. She made me come to bingo night one night and a really whack art class before she'd agreed to let me. She spent the whole time telling me I needed to get married and that my hair was too long. Her best friend in there kept propositioning me. But I finally got access to that damn unit.

"One of her diaries from when she was a teenager was in a box. I bet the old bat didn't remember that because she'd never want me to read it. But her entries are short and rude, like her, so they don't reveal that much." He coughed awkwardly. "Anyway! She was Captain Ipram's daughter, and was about fourteen when the ship went down. Your Fengast lady was mentioned a few times."

"Really?" Kayda asked, perking up.

"Yeah. Give me a sec. I'll read you the ones she was mentioned in ..."

It took much longer than "a sec." The sound of pages flipping and harried muttering went on long enough that Welsh gave up to go chop vegetables.

"Okay! Ready! I'll read it. *It's been three months since we've heard from Father. A woman came to the door today, saying her name was Margaret Fengast, and that she's very sorry, but the ship my father was on capsized and she's the lone survivor. I do not believe her.*"

Welsh wandered back over, biting down aggressively on a carrot stick like a rage-fueled rabbit.

"Another one says," Grayson continued, "*The Fengast woman came back today with an ivory comb that had belonged to my father. She claims to have found it among the wreckage, but I do not believe her about this either. Father took sorcerers and elementals like him on the journey. I do not know which one she is. I pray she is not a witch sent here to curse our family. I buried the comb in the garden.*"

"Is your grandma a water elemental too?" Kayda asked, wondering how often that retirement home was under threat of flooding if this lady was as ornery as Grayson made her sound.

He snorted a laugh. "Nope! Skipped her generation. I like to think the Goddess saw how bad things could go if that nasty lady had magic at her fingertips. I think she's so hopping mad partly 'cause she doesn't have any powers." A few more flipped pages. "The other times Fengast gets mentioned is in the diary from when Gran was sixteen. Lots of boring stuff about her cotillion or whatever. Boring, boring. Not this one ... ah, here we go: *It was confirmed today that Papa's ship really did sink. That Fengast woman has been in the papers flaunting how she survived while everyone else perished. I'm unconvinced that she didn't curse the ship and the whole crew.*

"Then a few weeks later: *Fengast was at the market this morning. I should say Mrs. Rex now, I suppose. She flaunted her wedding in the paper. Her whelp Bernard was on her hip. It's unfair that she gets to go about her life while my father is lost to the sea."*

Kayda couldn't imagine how crotchety Grandma Ipram was now, when she already sounded like a curmudgeon as a teenager.

"I can look for any mentions of Bernard Rex in the diaries, but I don't remember his name coming up again," Grayson said.

"Don't sweat it," Welsh said. "Good work, Ipram."

Grayson didn't say anything for a couple of seconds. "What, no insult?"

"No. I meant it. I also appreciate you braving your odious grandmother to get this information," Welsh said, with complete sincerity.

After a long pause, Grayson asked, "What does it say about me that I still want to find treasure that might have belonged to him? It might not be a great history, but it's mine."

"That I can understand," Welsh said. "Learning where you came from can help make sure you don't end up on the same path as those before you."

Kayda eyed Welsh, wondering what kind of monsters lounged in the branches of *his* family tree.

Twice while making dinner, Welsh got sidetracked by phone calls. Kayda had to swoop in as his sous chef, him barking orders at her to ensure sauces didn't burn and meats weren't overcooked. The meal itself was interrupted once by yet another phone call. As Kayda did dishes, Welsh dashed off to meet with a client, came back looking world-weary, then left again twenty minutes later.

While he was out for the second time, she swapped her

spiky blue hair glamour for a black bob, grabbed some cash from her bag, and walked from uptown to downtown to purchase a new burner phone. At Welsh's insistence, she'd been keeping her old one powered off most of the time, but it made her feel better to have an entirely new one not attached to any records. She programmed Felix, Welsh, Henri, and Jo's numbers into the new one, then casually dropped her old one into a storm drain.

She loitered outside the Sarq for half an hour until Welsh came back, looking worn out. He needed to rest, and to be able to be in his own space in whatever form he wanted, without catering to her. She'd officially overstayed her welcome.

Even though she hadn't said anything, Welsh must have sensed she was planning to skedaddle, because in the morning, there was a case of glamoured items on the counter with a note that said, "Help yourself."

The only clothes she had at the moment were the ones on her back. She had a bag of them at Henri's place, but it was probably unwise to go back there yet. Welsh was right: if the werecats were keeping an eye on Kayda's likely haunts, someone could easily assume her and Henri's absence from work was related. He needed to get back to his usual routine, at least for a little while. Adventuring was exciting and all, but it wasn't conducive to having a normal life.

Throwing her filthy clothes in the washer nestled into an alcove next to the kitchen, she took a long shower, going over her options. By the time she was done, dressed in warm-from-the-dryer clothes, and had donned a shoulder-length black wig she happily pulled into a ponytail, she'd come to the same conclusion Welsh had proposed days ago. Kayda was going to see Marisol and seriously consider joining the vampire hunters.

The piece of paper Liam had given her before the VHoA meeting was on Welsh's coffee table. Kayda dialed the number, fairly certain the guy who answered was Liam.

"Can I speak to Marisol?"

"Who's calling?"

"The draken who helped kill one feral and chase away another."

"Ohh shiiit, dude!" He laughed. "You were a beast. Did you kill the second one too?"

"Nah, it slipped through the veil. But I've got an idea of how they got in and I figured Marisol would want to know."

"Yeah, yeah. For sure, for sure. Let me give you her direct number. This is mostly a hotline for noobs."

She thanked probably-Liam, disconnected, then called Marisol.

"Mari speaking."

"Hi, Mari. It's Kayda."

"Ah, so you *were* glamoured," Marisol said. "Thank God. I was wondering where Fletch had met such an ... optically challenged individual. How are you? Welsh said you got pretty banged up during the feral attack. I told him to tell you, but he probably didn't: thank you for saving our asses. The triplets are coming along nicely in their training, but we were outnumbered."

Liam, Ollie, and Ben were definitely not related, but Kayda figured they were inseparable, hence the nickname.

"Just glad I was there to help," Kayda said. "Did Welsh tell you about the coyote?"

"Uhh ... no?"

"It's probably best to show you. I'm in uptown right now but could meet you anywhere that's convenient."

"I'm at VHoA. You can meet me here."

After getting the address, she texted Welsh from her new number.

Kayda: *Angel's new number. Need coyote photos.*

Welsh: *Incoming. Don't get wrapped around any more trees.*

The pictures popped up a few seconds later, and then she headed out, her newly acquired ponytail swinging. She wore the sunglasses again, simply because she liked them.

The VHoA headquarters was in the Necropolis, because of course it was. Kayda took a cab most of the way there. As she strolled up the sidewalk of the residential street the house was on, she hoped she didn't stand out too much in this human neighborhood. Unlike a lot of the fae, most people could pick out a draken on sight, solely based on size. The street was crammed with too-close-together houses and lined on both sides of the street by cars, but it was mostly quiet at this hour. It was a middle- to low-class area, so most people would be at work. Still, dogs barked, traffic whizzed past behind her, babies cried. It was probably raucous with life at night, like Luma Proper.

As instructed in a recent text, Kayda slid the rolling gate open when she arrived, and walked up the long driveway. A small house sat to her left, with another one ahead. The property in back was where Kayda was headed, the front door swinging open before she reached it.

"I definitely prefer you as a draken," Marisol said in greeting. "C'mon in."

The front room was a sparsely furnished living room, with a door positioned directly opposite the one Marisol had just closed. Beyond it, Kayda could hear chatting voices, fingers clacking on keyboards, and the humming of computers.

"Let's chat in here," Marisol said, motioning to a saggy brown sofa. "Of those of us who are left after the Fresno Fiasco, several are still jumpy, and the rest are too green. If this is going to freak them out, I'd rather have a heads-up."

Kayda felt like her knees were up her nose when she sat on the low couch.

Marisol flopped next to her, one leg propped up on the cushion. "All right. Hit me."

Kayda showed her the coyote photos, telling Marisol about Snowdrop and the supposed reason why she'd let ferals into the Indie. "The people Harlow's with don't think we should believe the elf is being honest. I interacted with the kid and even I don't know what to believe. I figured VHoA would have some ideas about a possible elf and vampire connection. So ... let's run with the scenario that the elf kid lied to our faces. Can elves control the ferals like hybrids can?"

Marisol hadn't said a word since Kayda began speaking, her eyes glued to the screen as she flipped back and forth between the four pictures.

"Mari?"

"And this happened the same night we were attacked by the ferals?" Marisol asked, subdued, as if she hadn't heard Kayda's question. Without waiting for an answer, phone in hand, she scrambled off the couch and crossed the room to the inner door. "Through here."

By the time Kayda had extricated herself from the tiny couch and walked into the next room, Marisol was hunched near a guy at a computer. The room was even more sparsely furnished than the room Kayda had just vacated. All that was inside were two long tables pressed together longways, with six computers on them—three on each side—and a pair of free-standing metal tool sheds against a wall. Most of the half-dozen spots were occupied. Heads bobbed up to check out the newcomer, most offered a smile or wave, then they were right back to work.

The guy beside Marisol had pulled his headphones off his head, the headband resting against the back of his neck. He had the phone in his hand and was swiping through the pictures even faster than Marisol had been. He turned in his seat to look up at Kayda.

"I saw one of these too," he said. "An animal with runes on its body, I mean. The one I saw was a pig—it was a wild one, though, not like one that escaped off a farm. Coarse brown fur, mean-looking tusks. The runes on that one were on its stomach and side. The hair had been shaved off a lot of it. We'd taken out five or six ferals that had slipped through at one of the usual Necropolis hot spots. I spotted the body, at first thinking a wounded feral vamp had run away from us and had collapsed on this side, falling halfway through the veil.

"When I got closer, I realized it was half a hog covered in runes. Some real ritualistic shit, you know? No one else was nearby. I didn't have my phone so I couldn't take pictures of it. I swear I thought I'd hit my head and was hallucinating. I turned away for a second to call for my buddy, turned back to the hog— gone. Those damn things can weigh up to 400 pounds. How does something like that just disappear? I almost didn't tell anyone I'd seen it because I wasn't sure *I'd* seen it."

Kayda asked, "When did this happen?"

"Same night as the attack in the Indie," he said. "Most of the team is in the Necropolis at night because there have been so many breaches lately. That's why only Mari and the triplets were at the recruitment meeting you were at. We couldn't spare anyone else."

Marisol said, "If you hadn't been there, there's no telling what would have happened."

"Were there any other animals found that night?" Kayda asked. "Any other breaches in weird places?"

"Not that I know of," Marisol said.

"Like I said, though," the guy added, "I almost missed spotting the hog. There could have been other attempts at the same thing, but since we can't keep track of the perimeter of the entire city—who knows. The cats patrol out there, too. They might have seen something, but it's not like they'd tell us."

True enough.

The guy handed Kayda's phone back and she shoved it in her pocket.

Snowdrop might have been able to move the coyote carcass on her own, but a multi-hundred-pound hog being moved in a split second? Even if those slight elf teens had moved the hog's body when it died to "get rid of evidence" as Snowdrop had said, at least two of them, if not more, would have needed to be there. Maybe a single one could have managed it if they had a charmed ring like Snowdrop did that granted strength. In either case, for two incredibly similar events to happen on the same night implied this had been a group effort, even if there had been more than one group.

Kayda could believe Snowdrop had let the ferals in by accident, since ferals were less likely to be on that side of the city. But to tear open a sliver of the veil in the Necropolis where it was prime feral territory? That one hadn't been a mistake. Not to mention how dangerous it was for someone to be on the other side of the Necropolis's veil. The person who pulled the hog's body away could have been killed by ferals themselves.

"Could the ferals have anything to do with this portal ritual the Shades are trying to do?" Kayda asked.

"That I don't know," Marisol said.

Kayda sighed, feeling antsy with pent-up energy. "Need help on your patrols tonight? I need to hit something."

Without a word, Marisol strode across the room to the metal storage units. She unclipped a set of keys from her belt and unlocked one of the boxes. Kayda joined her, gaping at the small collection of what she instantly knew were charmed weapons. Magic lightly hummed inside the metal box, but all the pointy bits were covered by magic-dampening hoods. These hoods clearly weren't as well-made as Jo's if Kayda could feel the magic. Harlow bought hers exclusively from Jo, and Kayda couldn't remember even a tendril of magic wafting out of those.

"Seeing the damage you did with a fire extinguisher, I know you'll kick ass tonight, but want to go out back to practice?" Marisol asked. "You can try as many of these as you like. I'll talk you through a few feral-slaying techniques."

Kayda cracked her knuckles. "Thought you'd never ask."

Chapter 31
HARLOW

Sometime last night, Welsh had contacted Caspian with information Grayson had found in his grandma's diaries. Apparently, Margaret had had a son after surviving the ship-wreck that had killed the crew of the *Element of Surprise* and deposited her treasure chest of journals and magical items at the bottom of the sea.

We still didn't know if it had been Margaret who had crafted the sword. If she had, had she done so while onboard the ship? Had some of the magical items bobbed to the surface after the wreck or washed ashore with her along with Captain Ipram's ivory comb? She'd have needed access to those items in order to make the sword. Since her journals had remained intact inside the watertight treasure chest, had she needed to re-create her runework from memory? Maybe she'd found comfort in the act, following in the footsteps of her hero, Frederica Kensey, who had lost most of her research to the Glitch.

I didn't know how to answer any of these questions. So, while Caspian continued to pore over Margaret's journals, I commandeered one of the VHoA computers and started investigating. All I had were names and vague locations. Fengast had been Margaret's maiden name before marrying a Mr. Rex. Mr. Rex and Margaret then had a son named Bernard. I didn't know what year it had been when Margaret wrote her journals, but I did know she was a second-generation fae. The Glitch, according to Mom and Arturo, had been in 1913. Soren was adamant that it was 1914. Caspian claimed, according to his "exemplary schooling" at the academy, that it had been 1910. I wondered if the ever-manipulative sorcerers were responsible for the discrepancy. The date wasn't documented in any mundane resources. The whole point of the hubs was to allow trapped fae to live a life as close to normal as they could in a foreign land. Which meant whole chunks of history had been scrubbed—whether that was in written form or from humans' minds. And by now, there was an exceedingly small number of people alive who had experienced the Glitch firsthand. History was easier to tweak when those who lived it were long gone.

Either way, it had been at least 100 years ago, which gave me something to work with. The golden age of piracy had long since passed before Captain Ipram set sail, but those golden-age pirates might have thrived a lot longer had they had magic on their side, as Ipram had. I searched for references to "Margaret Fengast" and "Margaret Rex" in the years between 1910 and 1950, finding two obscure mentions of her in 1940. I didn't know if Margaret had been scrubbed from public record as much as the Glitch had been, or if the world had been so preoccupied with the Second World War that something as inconsequential as a woman surviving a shipwreck never would have made front-page news anyway.

Grayson's grandma had claimed that Margaret was boasting in the papers about her miraculous survival, but the bitter woman had either been greatly exaggerating or those articles no longer existed. At least not in any places I could readily find while digging through layers of the mundane internet.

Bernard Rex I was able to find, though only the very basics. Married in 1960. Deceased in 1998 by way of a heart attack. He left behind his wife Caroline, and their two children, Rhonda and Kenneth Rex. Kenneth passed away in a car accident when he was twenty-three. Rhonda married a Mr. Thomas Winchell and went on to have two kids of her own, born in the late '80s. Which gave me two possible living descendants of Margaret Fengast. Both were in their mid-to-early-thirties.

First was Vanessa Winchell, thirty-three, unmarried. Her social media revealed she was living in Boston, but not much else, as she had everything else locked behind a privacy wall.

Second was Shane Winchell, thirty-five, married with no children. He lived in Washington, in Klickitat County. A website was pinned to the top of his profile along with a note that read, *"Click here for more information about our restored historic forge!"*

My eyes widened. I sprang out of my chair, intending to dash to Caspian, who was hunched over his books on the picnic table. I had to give one of my legs a good shake first though, as my foot had fallen asleep. Blinking rapidly, I let my vision adjust to the light of the room instead of the bright computer screen. I had no idea what time it was. It looked like a lot of people were passed out on cots, including my mom. I checked the time stamp at the bottom of the computer screen I'd apparently been staring at for hours. Two a.m.! Yikes. I was turning into Caspian.

Bleary-eyed and bowlegged, I hobbled across the warehouse. "Cas!" I whisper-hissed.

His head popped up, equally bleary-eyed. "What?" he hissed back.

"Jackpot discovery maybe!"

Caspian didn't move, so I slapped him lightly, but very enthusiastically, on the shoulder half a dozen times.

"Up! Up, up, up!"

The sword was at my side an instant later, its blade glowing bright red.

"Did I wake you?" I asked it. "Sorry. But I found something. A thing that might get us closer to figuring out who made you."

The blade instantly cooled, then poked its hilt into Caspian's side repeatedly.

"Fine! Ow, cutlass! Stop it."

The sword zipped back over to me with a buzzy anticipation that matched mine.

Groaning, Caspian unfurled himself from his hunched position and angled his arms above his head, stretching. I poked him in the middle of the stomach, earned an "Oof!" in response, and then hurried back to my computer, the sword trailing after me.

"You're like a puppy," Caspian said as he took the seat next to me. "Both of you."

The sword inverted itself and tapped on the cement once, then resumed its position beside my head.

"Woof," I agreed, then pointed at my screen. "This is Margaret Fengast's great-great-great-grandson!"

Caspian's expression brightened. "Really?"

"Mm-hmm. See here? He's a local historian. He lives in his 'ancestral home' and has a forge on his property that dates back to the 1940s. Which is super recent compared to stuff from Old West historical towns or whatever, but Margaret Fengast was a second-generation fae bladesmith, so her family wouldn't follow the same patterns as a family who *started* on Earth."

Caspian leaned forward, which was how I knew he was intrigued. "It looks like he gives tours of the property, as well as classes for blacksmithing."

I nodded vigorously. "Maybe ancestral means it's

Margaret's old house. Maybe something in that forge will give us another clue. At the very least, we can suss the guy out and if he's cool, we can show him the journals. As a historian and a relative of Margaret, I'm sure he'd love to see them."

"By cool, you mean a sorcerer?" Caspian asked.

"Yes. If he's got no idea he's got fae heritage, we'll have to tailor our conversation." I swiveled to the sword. "And you need to pretend you're a regular sword. No tapping or humming or vibrating or—"

The blade went molten.

I pointed a finger at it. "Or that! We'll have to check the guy out before we say or do anything that's going to completely freak him out."

The blade slowly cooled then dropped to the ground, tapping once.

"Agreed," Caspian said.

I searched for directions. It would take us roughly four hours to get there. It felt strange leaving so soon after I'd been reunited with my mother, and when things were so up in the air as far as the rising feral threat went.

But we'd gone on this wild adventure at least in part to help the sword, who had done so much to keep us alive. It wanted to know where it had come from. And I wanted to understand it better for my own sake. The more I understood it, the safer I'd be in the long run.

Glancing over at the sleeping quarters, I told myself I wasn't leaving forever. It was a short trip to help out a friend, as odd as that label was for a sentient sword. We could technically drive there and back in a day.

"Leave bright and early in the morning?" Caspian asked, sounding far too chipper for what amounted to yet another road trip.

"Yep."

The sword took off, presumably to curl up on my cot again, and Caspian went back to his books. He promised he was "just going to clean up." I knew him better than that. I'd give him half an hour, then I'd make him go to bed, too. He needed rest.

We had a big day ahead of us.

A cheerful Caspian and a blue, glowing sword woke me at 6 a.m. I was decidedly less cheerful. Mornings were not meant for cheer. They were meant for grouchiness and asking for five more minutes. But an excited sword was actually worse than an excited puppy, and after getting poked in the stomach, back of my thigh, and a butt cheek half a dozen times, I finally got up.

My mom was already awake and making coffee in the small kitchen area. She said good morning but kept her back to me as she fussed with the coffee maker.

"Caspian told me your plans," she said, still not looking at me. "You can take the same SUV I picked you up in. That way you don't have to move the mystery treasure chest."

"Thanks. Look, Mom—"

She turned then, hand up. "You don't owe me an explanation. You don't have to ask permission. Do I want you to leave when you're not familiar with life outside the hubs? No. But it's not my place to tell you what to do either. This is new territory for us both, okay?"

My stupid eyes welled again. "Okay."

After loading up with mugs of coffee, a few packaged muffins, and a long tight hug, Caspian, the sword, and I left the warehouse. We programmed my mom's number into Caspian's phone, too, in case we ran into feral trouble along the way. She assured us that was unlikely, especially during the day, but these were weird times.

Shane Winchell's website said he was holding a class today for Beginner's Blacksmithing at 3 p.m. We made good time, stopping for a bathroom and snack break once, and were due to arrive by 10 a.m. When we were an hour out, I called the number listed on the site.

"Good morning. Thank you for calling Winchell's Forge. This is Alice speaking," a woman answered. "What can I do for you today?"

"Hi, Alice. I was hoping to speak with Shane," I said, then spewed the lie Caspian and I had settled on. "I'm writing a book about the area and believe I've come across a few items that would be of interest to Shane. It's very likely that they belonged to his great-great-great-grandmother, Margaret Fengast."

The woman gasped softly. "Oh, my. One moment. Let me get my husband."

I put the phone on speaker, shrugging over at Caspian who had glanced at me with a raised brow. I sat cross-legged on the passenger seat. One of my feet bobbed up and down, up and down, my big toe tapping out a restless rhythm against the underside of my knee.

"Hello?" came a man's voice a couple of minutes later. "This is Shane Winchell."

I sat up straighter. "Hi, Shane." I went through the same spiel I'd given his wife.

"And what kind of items are we talking about here?" Shane asked, sounding far more skeptical than Alice had.

"We acquired a treasure chest off the *Element of Surprise.* Inside were what we believe are pages of Margaret's journal," I said.

There were about a dozen loose-leaf pages that had been stuffed into the journals. One of them was a sketch of a dress, complete with infinite-depth pockets. She'd signed her name in a bottom corner. If Shane was pure mundane with no knowledge of his sorcerer heritage, he would likely think the "infinite-depth" part had been hyperbole instead of literal. Most of the other loose pages in the journals were covered in runework. We couldn't risk showing those to Shane yet.

Shane was quiet for a few long seconds, but there was a hint of excitement when he said, "I would love to see these."

"We're about an hour away. We saw you have a class this afternoon. We'll be out of your hair by the time you have to deal with students," I said.

"Sounds great," he said. "There are a few buildings on the property. You can come to the main house. Won't be able to miss it—it's the biggest one."

"See you soon."

I ended the call and turned in my seat to peer into the back. The sword lay on the pristine, black leather seats. I needed to get it a new duffel bag. It lay on top of the journal that had the fewest spells in it. It was the one Caspian had burned the midnight oil over the most, and was the one he'd be most willing to give up if we found out Shane actually knew he was descended from fae.

Addressing the sword, I said, "Remember you've got to stay in here when we're meeting Shane until we give you the signal."

It didn't respond right away.

"Sword ..."

It hummed, but it was a short, quick sound. Sword-speak for *"Fine!"*

The property Winchell's Forge sat on was in a remote area of Klickitat County. The scenery was lush and gorgeous, helping to calm my nerves about this meeting. The sky was a perfect cloudless blue, interrupted periodically by small birds winging by. There weren't places like this in Luma. The forests of pines created a thick wall of a deep green hue I'd never seen before.

Now that I was here, I could see why, after the Glitch, the half a dozen wooly beasts who'd gotten marooned on Earth—and who eventually got roped into the Bigfoot rumors—had settled in the Pacific Northwest for a while. They could easily live a secluded life in these woods. Last I heard, though, they'd moved to the Alaskan hub to get away from the constant stream of Sasquatch hunters. Maybe Caspian's parents, who were stationed in Alaska, knew the creatures.

Caspian turning onto a bumpy road knocked me out of my musings and back into the present. On either side of the road were wide stretches of grass dotted by the occasional big leafy tree. From the road, three buildings were clearly visible, and the main house was indeed the largest, the road leading us directly to it. To the right of the road, a bright red barn stood on the well-tended lawn. A brood of chickens pecked and scratched at the ground near the open doors, and an old hound lounged on its side in the late morning sun. To the left of the road, much farther out, was the corner of a smaller building. It looked more rustic than the house or barn. A wild patch of blackberries grew nearby, their white flowers bright against the thick woody branches and worn wood of the small building. Was Margaret's old forge in there?

As Caspian pulled into a gravel parking lot to the side of the main house, a man and woman stepped out the front door. I peered at them through the side mirror, trying to get a read on them from a distance. My research had put Shane at thirty-five, but if I had met him blind, I would have pegged him as younger. They were both fair-skinned, brown-haired, and sported wide, friendly smiles. Shane was a little on the heavy side, and when he raised his arm in greeting, it revealed a sweat stain on his blue polo shirt. Maybe he'd been working in the barn before we arrived. I'd looked up a few pictures of blacksmith shops and forges last night, and the whole thing looked ... sweaty. What with all the hammering and the open flames needed to heat metal to cherry-red temperatures.

Alice was just as sweaty, but that was because it was summer and she was exceedingly pregnant. She was all smiles, but both her hands were pressed to her lower back.

As Caspian got out to offer cheery hellos to the Winchells, I opened the glove box to pull out the two pieces of yellowed paper from Margaret's journal.

I turned in my seat one last time. "Stay. Put."

Hum.

With the sheets in hand, I climbed out of the SUV and joined them on the porch. I shook each of their hands in turn, and then Shane led us inside.

It was a nice, tidy house with a rustic feel to it. Wood floors, wood walls, wood table surrounded by wood chairs. Shane led us across the creaky floorboards to the table, where white-and-blue checkered cushions were tied to the seats. A wooden bowl full of red apples sat in the middle of the table, though their waxy shine said they weren't for eating.

Caspian and I sat on one side of the table, with Shane on the other. His wife brought over a pitcher of lemonade and four glasses, placing each full glass on a white-and-blue-checkered coaster. She groaned and muttered to herself with every step.

"Honey," Shane said, cautiously. "Don't you—"

"If you tell me to sit down one more time, I will throttle you," she said, then kissed him on the temple. She offered Caspian and me smiles. "My feet are swollen and my back aches but sitting makes me cranky. Standing also makes me cranky. I'm just cranky. Sorry in advance."

Then she waddled off, continuing to mutter.

I wondered why she'd poured herself a glass of lemonade only to flee the scene, albeit slowly, but I decided not to make the cranky pregnant lady any crankier.

"Alice is due in two weeks." Shane shrugged. "Whatever she says goes. Even if she contradicts herself in the same sentence."

"I heard that!" came a shout from the kitchen, followed by the sound of slamming cabinets.

Shane leaned forward and whispered. "She's also developed super senses. It's the freakiest thing. And she feeds me five times a day. I've gained twenty pounds!"

We chuckled politely.

I took a sip of my lemonade, choking on it when Shane said, "It's sweet you two have matching tattoos."

Caspian handed me a napkin he'd plucked from a holder positioned beside the bowl of fake apples. I dabbed my chin and the front of my shirt, discreetly offering my inked wrist a death glare.

"What do they mean?" Shane asked. "What language is that? Japanese?"

Runes didn't resemble any human language I'd ever seen, but when presented with foreign things, human brains were very determined to try and make sense of what they didn't understand. It was almost instinctual, this need to slot things into neat boxes and categories. Which meant Shane had probably never seen runes before.

"Yes, Japanese," Caspian said stiffly. "They mean ... devotion. Always?"

"You're not sure?" Shane asked.

Caspian struggled to reply, so I steamrolled over their conversation and changed the subject. Thankfully I hadn't sprayed lemonade all over Margaret's drawings. "This was what we wanted to show you."

Shane had been casting curious glances at the two folded pieces of paper in front of me since we sat down.

While Caspian went into teacher mode and recounted a heavily redacted version of the events that resulted in us sitting in Shane Winchell's dining room, I casually studied the room. If Shane was a sorcerer living in the mundane world in secret, it was unlikely that the barn would be full of sorcerer paraphernalia, since I guessed that was where he taught his classes. He'd be more likely to keep that stuff in the main house, wouldn't he? But I didn't even know what I was searching for. It wasn't as if I knew what a typical sorcerer house looked like. I'd only ever been in Caspian's house, and that one had been his extra house, not his primary residence.

Plus, sorcerers weren't the flashy sort, so Shane probably wouldn't flaunt his magical proclivities for any rando to find. I supposed that might not be true in the mundane world, where sorcerers didn't get training so rigorous that it "strips you of your personality," as Arturo had put it.

"I'm no handwriting expert," Shane said now, peering down at one of the sheets, "but this signature looks identical to the one on the picture we have framed in the old forge building."

I straightened. "Is that something we could see? The picture and the forge, that is."

Shane shrugged. "Sure. Can I keep these?"

"All yours," said Caspian.

"Excellent," Shane said. "The forge is that small building you might have seen on your way in. We restored it some, but have done our best to keep it as true to the way Margaret would have." He stood. "Honey? I'm going to show them the forge!"

"Fine! I'll just be here slaving away making your lunch!"

"Do you want me to—"

"No, Shane! I do not!" Alice snapped.

Shane stood rigid, clearly not sure which direction the wind would blow next.

"Do you want a pulled-chicken sandwich or leftover tuna?" Alice hollered, sounding perfectly agreeable.

"Pulled chicken sounds great!"

"Good choice, my love. It'll be ready in twenty minutes."

Shane nodded and slowly started slinking toward the front door again, as if he were afraid of waking a sleeping bear. There were a few more slammed cabinets in the kitchen, but otherwise Alice seemed appeased.

The trek to the forge building took a few minutes, the way marked by a path of coarse sand that crunched underfoot. I eyed the car in the near distance, making sure all the windows were intact. A wink of light shined beyond the tinted windows, and I imagined the sword leaning on its hilt and watching us go, like a forlorn dog left behind while its owners went shopping.

The building had a small wraparound porch, wide enough to fit a chair or two. Taking a short step onto the porch, Shane pushed in the unlocked door and stepped inside, sliding over a waiting rock with his shoe to prop it open.

It was a small space—maybe 200 square feet—and crammed full. There was enough room for a few people to weave through the decor, but in a single-file line. We stood clustered inside the entrance. Against the far wall was what looked like a brick chimney, but because of the flat surface that was about waist height, with a metal hood poised above it, I guessed that was where Margaret would have done her forging. The tiny space was already hot as hell *without* a smoldering fire.

The forge was currently clean, but I imagined it covered in burning coals, Margaret standing before it with her metal of choice held in the grasp of a pair of metal tongs, waiting for it to get red hot. An anvil stood in the middle of the room atop a stand, putting that at waist height as well.

Wooden crates, small tables, and freestanding shelving units dotted the room, many of them covered in tools—hammers, chisels, tongs, and various types of metals. Farming tools like rakes, pitchforks, and shovels hung from a wall near the forge. A giant stone disc attached to a metal stand was in a corner with a small stool before it. I figured that was for sharpening her blades.

"The framed picture I mentioned is over here," Shane said, skirting a table covered in tools and rounding the side of the anvil. Caspian and I stood on either side of him, staring at a detailed drawing of an ax. The handle of the ax was lined with small guitar pick-like shapes. The drawing had been done with colored pencils, each of the small shapes shaded in with hues of purple, blue, and green. Exactly like the sword's hilt. If I leaned forward and squinted, I could make out what looked suspiciously like etched runes along the cheek—the curving line that ran from either pointed corner of the ax head.

Behind Shane, Caspian and I shared a wide-eyed look.

"What made you frame this drawing?" I asked.

"This particular ax is very ... special to the family. The physical weapon has been a prized possession for generations."

I took a few steps forward, and Shane shuffled over to make more room for me in front of the drawing. Hovering a finger above the glass, I traced a finger along the runes. "Are these markings on the physical ax as well? Based on some of our research of similar weapons, they've been revealed to have hidden etchings that become visible when the metal is heated."

Shane turned abruptly, and I instinctively retreated to where I'd been before—closer to Caspian. My heart rate had ticked up for some reason—my sixth sense telling me to be on extra alert. I just wasn't sure why yet.

"Where did you say you were from again?" Shane asked.

"Luma," I blurted, mentally kicking myself for not being a better liar under pressure. "It's—"

"A hub in California," Shane finished.

"Oh, thank goodness," I said, sagging. "So you know Margaret was a—"

"Sorceress? Yes." He regarded the drawing, pointing to a set of runes near the ax head's cheek. "I believe these here are part of a dystilian chain."

"Aha!" Caspian said cheerfully. "So you practice the discipline then?"

"Eh. Not really," he said.

Caspian deflated.

"I know enough to recognize many runes on sight. Like the ones on your wrists. They mean you're bonded then?" Shane asked.

To a mob boss, yes, I wanted to say. "Something like that."

"Is Alice a sorceress?" Caspian asked.

"Oh. No. She's a descendant of a fire elemental. She's got enough command of it that she can help keep my forge fires hot. It seemed like kismet—a blacksmith falling for a fire witch."

"Well this is a relief. We actually have an entire journal for you," Caspian said. "It's full of runework, so we wanted to keep the truth of it under wraps before we potentially opened a can of worms."

Shane stared at us in turn for a long moment. "That trunk you purchased was really hers, then? From the shipwreck?"

I nodded. "Yep. We came here in part to give you a piece of your history back. It's kind of what I do back home." I eyed the drawing. "So ... uhh ... how special is this ax?"

Without a word, Shane put two fingers in his mouth, inhaled, and issued a series of three whistles. I shied away from the piercing, abrupt sound, then reached out to grab Caspian's arm. I needed something to ground me. My gut told me what was about to happen.

Something sprang up in my peripheral vision. My gaze whipped toward the open doorway.

Sunlight winking off its iridescent handle, was a floating ax.

I stared, my mouth agape. "*Oh* boy ..."

Caspian chuckled softly, but I couldn't tell if he was amused or troubled. "It would appear the cutlass has a sibling."

Chapter 32
HARLOW

I was still staring dumbstruck at the floating ax when glass shattered in the distance. The ax took off in an instant, presumably to investigate. The three of us shared a quiet moment of mutual confusion, then we dashed out of the forge building and onto the lawn.

As I suspected, the sword had broken its way out of the car, a pile of broken black glass glittering in Shane Winchell's parking lot. Hopefully VHoA wouldn't be too upset about needing to replace the window when we got back.

The sword and the ax were poised halfway between the car and the forge building, pointiest ends facing each other as they slowly circled one another in the air like lions from rival prides.

"Huh," Shane said, arms crossed. "You have one, too."

He said it as if the "one" he referred to was something normal, like a goldfish.

"How many of these things did Margaret make?" I asked, bewildered.

"Wait, what?" Shane asked, more confused by this question than by the existence of more than one sentient weapon. "Margaret didn't make these."

My brow furrowed. "But ... the drawing in the forge ..."

"She's purported to have claimed, all her life, that the captain on the ship she'd been on said there was a way to make weapons that could give the user heightened powers," Shane said, watching the circling pair of animate objects. "She supposedly had figured out how to do that before the ship capsized but lost all her work and had to recreate her theories from memory. When her son, Bernard, was old enough, she sent him to the sorcery academy in Kensey—the best one in the nation."

Caspian grunted, clearly offended at the implication that he'd gotten his schooling at an inferior academic institution.

Shane either didn't hear him or was ignoring him. "After he graduated, he came back here and he and Margaret worked on the project together."

"In her journal, she sounded horrified by what her captain had asked her to do," I said. "Do you know why she wanted to keep working on it?"

Shane shrugged. "She had witnessed the killings of many fae animals during her time aboard the ship. Their deaths haunted her for even longer than the trauma of the shipwreck. She wanted to do something with the bits of their bodies that she'd been able to find—to make their deaths not be in vain."

The sword and the ax suddenly barreled forward and clanged their metal together. What the hell were they doing? It wasn't like they could fight to the death.

The brief contact must have caused some reaction in them though, because they stopped posturing. They got into the inverted position across from each other, hung there motionless for five full seconds, then flew over to us as if nothing had happened. The sword took up its position by my shoulder, while the ax lingered beside Shane.

"I feel a bit left out," Caspian said, glancing between the two floating weapons.

The sword hummed and glowed blue.

"Whoa," Shane said, cocking his head. "Mine's never done that."

"Has it gone off on its own mission and come back coated in blood?" I asked.

Shane's brows smashed together. "*What?* Mine has never even tried to leave the property."

Either mine was unique or it was dealing with repressed trauma from whatever had caused it to end up in stasis. It had woken up in Haskins's basement, confused and furious. It clearly had gone through some shit that the ax hadn't.

"So it was *Bernard* who made the weapons?" I asked, trying to get us back on track.

"Oh, right. Yes, it was Bernard. Margaret came up with the designs and the basic rune arrays, and Bernard—a fully trained sorcerer by then—helped her bring the vision to life," Shane said.

Caspian asked, "Was it only the two?"

The front door banged open. "Lunch is ready! There's enough for everyone. If you say no, I'm going to be so offended that my granddad will roll over in his grave!" The door banged shut.

"Follow me," Shane said and strode for the house, his ax trailing obediently.

My sword, however, launched ahead of us, then shot upward through an open upstairs window. I sighed. "Don't break anything, you fool sword!"

Shane didn't speak again until we were all seated at the table, pulled-chicken sandwiches dripping with barbecue sauce alongside small piles of potato chips, already waiting for us. "Does your sword not ... listen to you?"

The ax drifted behind Shane.

"Oh, do tell it to stand down," Alice said, lowering herself into a chair.

"Dismissed, ax," Shane said, without even looking at the weapon.

It flew away to hang itself on a wall beneath the stuffed head of a deer. Its handle went from a shimmer of iridescence to a plain wood. I'd skipped right over the ax when I'd been scanning this room earlier. It looked perfectly ordinary now.

"It listens," I said, picking up my sandwich. "It just doesn't always cooperate. Sometimes what it wants overrides what I want and then it goes off and murders people."

Shane stared at me with his open mouth poised to take a bite of his sandwich. Alice peered at me over the lip of her lemonade glass.

"If it's any consolation," Caspian said, "it seems that the cutlass strictly murders those who have personally done it harm, or who threaten Harlow. They have 'no murder' and 'no maim' rules that the cutlass mostly complies with. She only lifts the ban when we're faced with something particularly nasty."

Alice placed her glass back on the table and pursed her lips. "It was a consolation until you started using words like 'it seems' and 'mostly complies.'"

As if on cue, something crashed from upstairs.

"Sword!" I bellowed. "What did I tell you about breaking things? Everything good up there?"

A long pause, then a muted thud. Which I guessed was from the sword thumping its hilt against something in response.

"That means yes," I said, wrinkling my nose. "Probably."

"As you were saying outside, Shane?" Caspian asked, his sandwich untouched. His body was angled toward Shane across from him, signaling that he was very curious about what Shane had to say. I wondered if I'd be able to steal his sandwich without him noticing. "Did Bernard only craft the two weapons?"

Shane and Alice shared a silent, married-couple conversation.

"What's your interest in them?" Alice asked. "You aren't the first to come sniffing around with supposed information about Margaret. But it always turns out that they're treasure hunters who've come here looking for riches, or clues to lead them to riches. You two are the first to have actual evidence from that ship. But these weapons have brought out the worst in people. How can we be sure that you're not treasure hunters of a different kind, searching the country for more of these unique weapons?"

The sword must have sensed my growing unease because it came hurtling into the room from who knew where. It came to a halt over the table so abruptly it made my head spin. I registered a moment later that its tip was angled at Alice. The blade slowly grew redder and redder.

I gasped. "Sword! Don't you dare threaten a pregnant woman! Those are on the 'no' list under all circumstances."

The blade cooled, but it still pointed itself at Alice, whose mouth had formed an O of surprise.

I shoved my face into the sword's line of sight. I went cross-eyed with the proximity but I held my ground. "Knock it off!" I hissed at it. "These are very nice people and you're being incredibly rude. They're allowed to ask us our intentions, especially since now they know you have a tendency to murder people."

It quickly inverted itself and tapped its hilt on the table.

"Yes, what?" I asked. "You're agreeing that you murder people?"

Tap.

I rolled my eyes and sat back down. "Don't be a jerk."

The blade went red again, vibrating.

"If you can't handle my honesty, then you can go wait in the car!" I snapped.

It hung there, "staring" at me. Suddenly, it swung in a wide arc and knocked one of the wax apples across the room, then lay itself on the other side of the bowl. A sliver of its hilt was visible.

Now it was sulking? I shook my head. I needed to find the thing a hobby.

Turning back to everyone at the table, I found Shane and Alice regarding me with complete stupefaction.

Out of the side of her mouth, Alice said to Shane, loud enough for Caspian and me to hear, "Either they have a routine they rehearse or they're telling the truth. I almost don't care if it's the first one. I'm fascinated by this dynamic."

I gave them a rundown of my situation as far as the sword was concerned. "We can communicate, but we're limited. The better I can understand its motivations, the better I can control—"

The sword vibrated so hard that the wax apples quaked in their bowl.

"The better we can *coexist* ..." I amended. "And lessen my worries about it stabbing someone else."

The sword calmed.

Shane stared at me for a while longer. "The story goes that Bernard created the ax first. The goal was to start small. The rune arrays were to grant the user strength—to aid in things like chopping down trees. They went through many iterations and it supposedly took them a year to get it to work. But it wasn't until the final array was etched onto the blade that Bernard discovered a rune phrase had been drawn incorrectly. That one mistake gave the *ax* strength instead of the *user* of the ax."

I glanced over at the sword to find that it was floating above the wax apples now, clearly paying attention.

"It took them a while before they could make more like it, as they had a limited supply of things like dragon scales and orc tusks. Over the next few years, they worked on farm tools, adding rune arrays to items they already had. Every farm tool had the 'accidental' array etched into metal or wood to grant the tools a kind of autonomy.

"Word spread in the area about tools that helped out on the farms that were prevalent here. A dagger could help a cook peel potatoes at three times the speed while she worked on another task. Shovels to dig, rakes to clear away debris ..."

I tried not to laugh at the idea of a sentient rake.

"Without the magic in things like scales to hold and replenish magic, though, the autonomous tools went dormant fairly quickly if the runes weren't redrawn often. And even then, you can only carve and re-carve into wooden handles for so long before the material weakens," Shane said. "Based on Bernard's contacts within Kensey, he and his mother slowly acquired the magical items needed to make the weapons they'd first sought to make."

"How many?" I asked.

"Five," Shane said. "This sword must have been one of the last ones created, given how advanced it is."

The sword glowed blue.

"It appreciates the praise," I said.

Caspian asked, "Are there more like the ax on the property?"

Alice sighed, shaking her head. "That was part of the reason for my questions earlier," she said, warily eyeing the sword who had been hovering over the wax fruit bowl for a while, but much less menacingly. "There had been many accounts of a mysterious man in town in the 1960s who asked around about the weapons. One by one, the weapons would disappear. It's believed an alloy powder had been used to subdue many of them."

I nodded, familiar with the powder. Caspian had even used it on my sword. So far, that stuff had been the only thing to keep the sword down—other than when it reluctantly agreed to heed my requests.

"Like before," Shane said, "Bernard and Margaret would share their creations with friends and neighbors. What better source of security was there than a sentient weapon? Each weapon was spelled to have an owner, for lack of a better word. And that weapon would then treat that property as theirs, doing perimeter checks, investigating odd sounds, and defending their owner against threats."

"So the mysterious weapons thief had to be someone with magic then," I said.

Shane nodded. "My guess was that it had been a wind elemental. A person who could create a wind current they could control, add the powder to that current, and sneak up on an unsuspecting weapon. There were never reports of seeing the man creeping through yards at night. Guard dogs didn't bark. But every few days or weeks, a weapon would go missing overnight. Margaret and Bernard were the only ones targeted by the thief who were sorcerers—everyone else had been mundane. The Rexes' protective runework around the property, which they reinforced often, must have been enough to repel the intruder. Eventually the reports of the mysterious man stopped, and life went back to normal."

"Did they make more weapons after that?" I asked, but I already knew the answer.

"No. They realized how dangerous their experiments were," Shane said. "Margaret continued journaling up until her death. She always wondered where her and her son's other weapons had ended up. It's sort of incredible that over ninety years later, one would return."

I eyed the sword. "Does being here bring you any memories?"

It inverted itself and tapped twice on the table. It burned red, then tapped twice more. It was frustrated that it couldn't remember.

Then it abruptly cooled and went completely motionless. Which meant it was thinking.

"*Sword* ..." This was why I needed to know more about it. When a murder sword gets an idea, and you don't know what that idea is, it makes it very difficult to know what to do next.

It flew toward Shane. Thankfully it was in the inverted position, and not in the "I'm going to disembowel you" position. The speed that it employed to beeline for Shane made him raise his hands in defense. The sword quickly pressed itself into one of Shane's palms, his hand instinctively closing around it.

Shane frantically shook his hand, and while I knew he was trying to get the sword out of his grip, it looked like he was angrily preparing for battle against an oncoming horde. I'd experienced this phenomenon once myself.

"It's okay!" I said, hands out in placation. "It sometimes does this thing where it pulls information out of you."

Alice had her hands pressed to her mouth as she warily eyed her husband. "Is it hurting him?"

Turning his wrist so the sword was parallel to the table, Shane opened his hand and gave it another violent shake. The hilt remained fastened to his palm. He was more dismayed about the sword being stuck to his skin than he was about anything the sword might have been doing to him.

Caspian chuckled awkwardly. "Don't fret, Alice. One of the spells on the blade is for 'insight into one's opponents.' It's not that the cutlass views Shane as an opponent, but it allows the cutlass to acquire information useful to it."

I suspected Caspian's crisp, matter-of-fact explanation did nothing to mollify Alice, but at least she didn't fling herself at the sword.

One more hard shake and the sword dislodged itself. It halted its own descent toward the table, hovered there for a moment, and then shot through the space between Alice and Shane's heads. It flew to the ax resting below the mounted deer head and pressed the tip of its blade against the ax for several long seconds. We waited in silence.

What could possibly be happening now?

When the ax started to shift on its hooks, the sword flew away from it. It floated in the living room, the air around it shimmering. Caspian and I sprang to our feet at the same time.

"What's going on?" Alice asked, a touch frantic.

"Often when the cutlass does this, it takes on the form of someone," Caspian said. "It's an easier way for it to let us know what it wants."

It also does this, I added silently, *when it has another person on its hit list and using the illusion of a body attached to a sword rather than a floating weapon makes murdering more convenient.*

What if the sword learned Shane was a serial killer and there were bodies buried under the barn?

It was indeed an image of Shane that appeared, holding the sword aloft. Like most of the sword's borrowed bodies, the expression on this one was murderous. It pointed a finger at me, then at the door behind him.

Grabbing the last of my sandwich off my plate, I said, "I know you can't talk, so demanding gestures is the best you can do, but you could at least smile when you do it."

The Shane image bared all its teeth.

"Never mind," I said, shoving the sandwich piece in my mouth and striding for the door. At least it was asking me to open the door rather than bashing through it. Maybe we were making progress.

I opened the door and out went the sword and the ax. Shane's image dissolved like smoke as it went. "Let's go see what fresh hell these two have in store for us."

Chairs scraped along the wood floor behind me as I jogged across the porch. The weapons were headed for the forge building rather than the barn, but that did little to assuage my fear that Shane could have bodies hidden somewhere.

Caspian caught up to me and we jogged side by side down the coarse sand path. The weapons had already disappeared through the still-open door. When we reached it, we loitered on the small porch. If those two were going berserk in there, I didn't want to go in after them and get sliced to ribbons. When we didn't hear anything for a few long seconds, I slowly tiptoed forward. Movement out of the corner of my eye told me Caspian was gearing up a spell.

Peeking inside, I found both weapons floating in the middle of the room. The sword was wearing Shane's form again and was pointing at the anvil. I didn't move. Again, it pointed at me, and then the anvil. A hysterical voice in my head screamed that the sword had finally snapped and it wanted me to bend over the anvil so it would be easier to decapitate me. I inched forward, looking from the anvil to the sword and back. The third time I glanced over, the Shane image made a shoving motion with his hands.

It wanted me to *move* the anvil?

Standing in front of it and its metal base, I gave the thing a tentative push. No movement at all. The thing had to weigh at least a couple hundred pounds. As curious as I was about what the sword had seen when it touched Shane that had led to this, I didn't want to destroy Margaret's many-decades-old belongings at the behest of a diabolical sword.

"Step ... aside ... Harlow ..." Caspian said, walking into the room while his hands worked in a frenzy.

His go-to spell was a concussive air blast. It would be an efficient way to clear a path, but it was definitely a more destructive option. Before I could protest, he hunkered in front of the anvil's base, his glowing rune array hovering in the space between his chest and the anvil. Just as Shane—the real one—reached the doorway, Caspian released his array, sending the transparent circle of runes outward.

I braced myself, expecting to be blasted off my feet and thrown into the pointy things hanging from the walls. The sound of scraping stone made me crack open an eye. The anvil and its base slid across the floor. I supposed Caspian had never needed to gently shove something out of the way before this— he'd always needed this particular spell when we were in deep trouble.

He moved the anvil several feet, then shakily stood. A trap door hadn't been revealed for all his efforts, and I sagged in disappointment. With the toe of my shoe, I tested the various floorboards, waiting for one to be loose and swing upward like a seesaw. But that didn't happen either.

The image of Shane moved to the spot where the anvil stand had been, given the lighter circle of wood unmarred by dirt and time. I took a step back to stand beside Caspian. The real Shane lingered in the doorway.

"Sword, what are you—"

The sword flipped itself so the blade faced down and slammed into the floor. I yelped. The moment the sword pulled free, the ax flew over and came down hard on the same spot. Caspian and I backed up farther.

Stab. Thunk. Smash. Chop.

Wood splintered. The sword used itself to fling broken pieces of wood aside so the ax could keep hacking away unimpeded. A layer of cement was revealed below the wood floor and I figured that would be the end of it, but the ax kept going. Blessed by whatever sorcery and magical items Margaret and her son Bernard had used to craft the thing, within three hard chops, the cement split. The sword went molten, and the ax did, too. And then they were back at it again, switching off as they laid waste to the floor.

Caspian and I pulled the larger chunks of broken cement out of the widening hole and carried them outside. Shane was finally shocked out of his stupor and joined in.

Within a few minutes, both layers of flooring had been chopped through to reveal a metal box surrounded by dark, moist earth. It was a decent-sized hole. Caspian and I squatted there, staring into the opening.

Shane cautiously stood on the other side of the hole.

Glancing up at him, I asked, "Did you know this was here?"

Wide-eyed, he shook his head. "How ... how did the sword know?"

I shrugged. "Sword works in mysterious ways and all that. Do we have permission to take the box out? It's your property. I guess I should have asked about smashing through your floor, but the weapons didn't discuss the matter with us first."

Shane snapped out of his daze. "Yes, of course."

Lying flat on my stomach, I reached into the hole, my fingertips reaching the top of the cold metal. I scootched forward a bit more and slipped my hand between the damp soil and the short side of the rectangular box. Wiggling my fingers blindly, I felt a thin, cylindrical piece of metal on the side.

"It has handles!" I said.

Caspian dropped to his stomach too, mimicking what I'd done on the other side. Once he assured me he had hold of his side of the box, we lifted it straight up on his count of three. It had been impossible to tell how deep the box was before we started moving it. The forge was dark and the hole was darker.

The box ended up being five or so inches deep, and at least thirty-five across. There was a definite heft to it—whether that was from the metal it was made of, what was inside it, or both, I couldn't be sure—but we managed to free the box from its prison without extra help.

We thunked the metal onto the wood floor.

"There's a padlock on this side," Caspian said.

Shane said, "I have bolt cutters!" and ran out of the building.

Thinking that this padlock might be spelled like the last one we'd had to contend with, I suggested we take the box outside. If the lock took offense to being forced open, and one of us got flung aside like a child's toy, I would rather land on grass than a wall lined with old farm tools. I wasn't up-to-date on my tetanus shots.

Shane and Caspian each tried a few basic spells on the lock, and both determined it wasn't bewitched. Even still, when Shane went after the box with his bolt cutters, I might have hidden behind Caspian.

"I can't decide if I'm insulted that you're using me as a meat shield," Caspian whispered.

"It's because you're such a big, strong man and I'm a delicate flower."

One of his rare guffaws made an appearance at that. I had a feeling which part he'd thought was so funny. I was delicate, dammit.

A shift in my peripheral vision drew my focus toward the bramble of blackberries. My brows scrunched together, my sixth sense tingling. I regarded the thick ropy branches, and the ivy-choked trees and bushes behind them.

The padlock fell harmlessly to the grass, redirecting my attention.

Shane, holding his bolt cutters in front of him like a weapon, said, "Go ahead. It was your discovery, after all."

I gave Caspian a gentle push. "Open it."

"Oh, you're both chickens," Caspian said.

Shaking out his arms, he stepped forward and stooped by the box. The dark metal was rusted in the corners and around the hinges. I braced myself, one eye squinted shut, as Caspian flipped the clasp open and lifted the lid. It thunked against the grass.

He whistled.

Curiosity would be my downfall. I hastened over to peer inside.

A sword identical to mine lay in the box atop a bed of white paper. Same iridescent hilt, same curved blade. I bet when heated, runes would appear along its fuller.

When nothing happened, the sword drifted toward its twin and pressed its blade against it, as it had done with the ax. Was it passing on information? Communicating with it? Issuing the sword equivalent of "wakey, wakey, eggs and bakey"?

Nothing.

"Perhaps it's something to do with you, Harlow," Caspian said. "You woke up the cutlass in that basement. Perhaps you can do the same with this one."

Like I wanted two of these things following me around!

Sighing, I stood to full height. Caspian did too, offered me a reassuring shoulder squeeze, then moved to stand with Shane.

I ran my sweaty palms down the front of my pants, but my attention was pulled to the bushes near the forge building again. I cocked my head, almost sure there was something inside the blackberry brambles staring back at me. I blinked several times, and the maybe-thing I thought I saw was gone. If anything threatening was out here, the sword would have reacted to it by now, right?

I stared at my sword. "If this one comes after me, you'll stop it, yeah?"

The blade glowed red and vibrated, insulted by the question.

I held my hands up in innocence. "Sorry, sorry."

Before I could talk myself out of it, I grasped the hilt, held it out at arm's length, and braced myself. Seconds ticked by in silence. "You guys see anything?"

"Not a thing," said Caspian.

This time when my sixth sense tugged at me, it was accompanied by a slight rumble beneath my feet. "Did you feel that?"

The men looked at each other and shrugged.

"You're the one holding the sword," Shane said.

I stared down at my feet. God, what if a sinkhole was going to swallow me up thanks to the sword and ax smashing up the forge building's foundation?

My sword and the ax suddenly flew off together, back toward the car. I spun, turning my back to the blackberry bushes. My heart rate picked up when the slight rumble came again.

I gave the new sword a hard, panicked shake. My nerves were on the fritz all of a sudden, my chest tight—and our two weapons had abandoned us. "Awaken!"

Shane snorted a laugh, then tried to cover it with a cough.

I glared at him. "Don't be rude."

"What I find rude ..." came a booming voice.

My breath caught and I slowly turned once more toward the blackberry bushes. A hand materialized in the air several feet away. A very large hand that ... waved at me. While I was processing this very confusing sight, a large swath of the air rippled—like it had gone liquid. I registered that it was a rather dome-shaped ripple just before the whole thing fell away, revealing a thin, fair-skinned woman, three trolls, and an orc.

The trolls and orc were in their natural form, their huge, muscled arms corded with bulging veins on full display. They had sickly gray or deep green skin. The trolls' ears pointed away from their bodies; while those bodies were mostly hairless, their ears were lined with peach fuzz. I guessed the woman with them was a sorceress. Caspian didn't seem to recognize her, but that didn't mean anything. Domino could have sorcerers from any number of hubs on his payroll.

With the useless sword held out in front of me, I took several steps back until I was huddled with Caspian and Shane. The ax and my sword returned. I noted with no small amount of horror that they were bloody.

"What I find rude is that we had a perfectly clear agreement, Harlow," Domino said, his green skin fitting in rather well with the scenery here. "If you found another sword like yours, you were duty bound to alert me." He reached into his pocket to pull out his phone, making a dramatic show of swiping at the screen. "Alas, no messages from Harlow."

I turned my wrist slightly, frowning at the runes inked there. "We just found it. You didn't give us enough time to contact you."

"You were going to sell us out?" Shane whispered incredulously.

"Tsk, tsk," Domino said, rubbing one pointer finger across the other, pouting dramatically. "We knew you had no intention of honoring our agreement, so we've been following you since you fled that motel." His eyes shifted to my right, presumably toward the ax. "And to think you've actually found two for me! I'm quite pleased. But since you did disrespect me, I'm going to take all three of them."

My sword darted in front of me, tip facing Domino and his entourage.

When their personal veil had dropped, none of them had advanced. There was a few hundred feet of space between us, but I'd already seen how fast a troll could move regardless of their size. Domino was no doubt even faster. Caspian would be limited in how much he could throw at them before he was depleted, and these beasts were built like tanks. Shane had even less access to magic. And who knew what kind of power the woman with them had. We were vastly outnumbered, even with two sentient weapons.

I gave the one in my hand another shake, hoping my panic would travel into its hilt, waking it up. Nothing. Turning quickly, I shoved the sword at Shane, who took it instinctively.

Knowing I was going to regret the hell out of this later, I said, "Sword, you ready?"

It inverted itself and hurtled backward into my open palm. The moment my fingers circled the hilt, its magic poured into me. My mind was dizzy with it. I felt taller and stronger in an instant. Widening my stance, I stared Domino down. "If you want it, you'll have to come get it."

Domino roared. "Go!"

Chapter 33

HARLOW

The trolls barreled forward. Just before the trio reached us, the sword's magic yelled *"Duck!"* in my head a moment before Caspian did.

Two of the trolls got out of the way of the air blast in time, but the one pelting for me didn't and was shot backward, landing in the blackberry bushes. The plethora of cursing implied it hurt. One of the trolls went for Caspian, but the ax hurled itself at it and embedded into the troll's skull. Caspian yanked it free with a sickening crunch and held onto it.

To the right! the sword's magic said, and I started running before my brain knew it was going to happen. A troll had come around the back of the forge building in an attempt to surprise Shane, who stood holding the sword I'd given him, his eyes wide and unblinking. He might have been from a line of sorcerers and bladesmiths, but he'd never faced a troll before.

My sword had sensed the troll's movements before I had, and I blindly followed the commands now, outmaneuvering the troll.

Pivot right. Slash down. Thrust up. Duck.

The troll, its throat and back of a thigh sliced through,

collapsed in a bloody heap at Shane's feet before he'd registered that he'd almost been a pancake. I grabbed the sword's hilt with both hands, turned the blade over, and plunged the sword deep into the troll's back, the metal slicing through flesh and bone with ease.

I glanced up at Shane long enough to note his face was covered in a spray of blackish blood, and his chest rose and fell entirely too quickly.

My enhanced hearing picked up the soft pat, pat, pat of someone on the move. I yanked the sword free and spun, clocking the woman sprinting forward, leaving only the orc in the group's original spot. Her blond hair snapped out behind her like a banner, revealing the tips of pointed ears. An elf?

"Leave the girl," Domino said, and the elf managed to avoid me despite the speed I'd put on to intercept her before she reached Caspian. Sunlight reflected off the pair of daggers in her slender fists. I came up short as the elf whizzed out of my path like a streak of light.

Metal clashed behind me. Caspian grunted. Hopefully the ax was able to share some of its power with Caspian because I couldn't help him. The sword's magic didn't *want* to help him. It was us against the orc now, and that was where our focus needed to be. The sword had a sense of self-preservation after all. It wasn't scared per se, but it didn't want to end up at the orc's beck and call. It would rather shatter into a million pieces than hang at his belt.

"Just you and me, girlie." Metal bracers ringed Domino's massive forearms, and shin guards protected his legs. He'd shown up anticipating a fight.

He charged.

My instincts told me to sprint in the other direction, but they were immediately squashed by the sword's. I took off toward Domino, me a measly five eight running full speed toward an eight-foot-tall monster with a chest as wide as a truck.

Right. Slash. Block. Parry. Duck. Feint left.

I let the magic fill every cell in my body, giving my trust fully to the sword to control me in whatever way would keep us both alive. The fight stretched on and on—the sword and the orc too evenly matched. He had a counterstrike or dodge for everything we threw at it. My sword clanged off Domino's metal bracers time and time again.

It wasn't long before my mundane energy, as coursing with magic as it was, started to flag. My legs burned. My chest ached. My arms strained from the impact of the orc blocking our attacks. The sword absorbed most of the hits, but I got knocked aside enough times that by the fifth, I struggled to get back up.

Soon our attacks were solely defensive. I scuttled under his legs and tried to attack from behind, but even being two seconds ahead, Domino kept up. More than kept up.

I feinted right, only to have the orc's monster-sized fist clip my hip, sending me spinning away from him like an out-of-control top. I rolled my ankle, tripped, hip-checked the back bumper of the SUV, and lost my hold on the sword. It clattered to the ground. Its magic leached out of me with such force I vomited. I heaved, doing all I could to stay conscious. I swayed dangerously on my hands and knees.

I could vaguely hear the sound of Caspian and the elf still fighting, but it was simply a matter of time before Caspian weakened, too.

The sword lifted itself like a drowsy fly, its magic waning for the first time since I'd met it. But it still managed to drift in front of me, ready to defend me till the bitter end. Was its magic depleted? Had its hilt been irreparably damaged?

"I probably wouldn't have bothered to kill you if you'd stuck to the bargain," Domino said, slowly striding for me. I had enough of my wits about me to note the way he favored his right leg. "But this way is more fun. I may even keep you too, girlie. You're small and feisty. Cody missed his chance with you, but the others wouldn't mind a go."

I tried to crawl backward, to get on the other side of the SUV to use it as a barrier between me and Domino, but I was so weak, the gravel of the parking lot biting into my palms and knees, that I made very minimal progress.

"Why an elf?" I called out to Domino in a futile attempt to stall him.

The sword, poised in front of me, jutted itself at the orc, but its energy wasn't back to normal.

"Why not an elf?" Domino asked. "They come in handy when I need access to veil magic."

The battle between Caspian and the elf raged on. Out of the corner of my eye, I could tell she was gaining the upper hand, calling on her apparent earth magic to make vines and roots erupt out of the ground.

My vision went murky and I gave my head a clearing shake. "Is she a Shade?"

Domino stopped walking long enough to throw his head back and laugh. "She's no idealistic fool. She doesn't believe in fairy tale saviors. We fae will save ourselves."

Whatever the hell *that* meant.

A root shot out of the ground near Caspian, whipping toward his ankles like a cobra. He swung the ax at it with an efficient grace he usually reserved for casting spells. Tears in his clothes, cuts on his face and arms, and the sheen of his brow all told me he wasn't going to be able to fend the elf off much longer.

I had even worse odds. Domino had lost interest in our conversation and was fifteen feet away from me now. Ten.

A battle cry rang out.

Domino bellowed, his head whipping to the side. The sword's twin was embedded in Domino's torso. He pulled it free and tossed it away, apparently forgetting that the sword was one of the reasons he was here. But an orc's rage was second only to an elemental's, and this orc was well and truly furious. With his fists balled by his sides, his veins bulging in his neck and arms, he let loose a bloodcurdling roar. Blood oozed from his side.

I silently thanked Shane for shifting Domino's attention, but he was in serious shit now. And he knew it, given his high-pitched screech before bolting for his house.

A door banged open before Shane could reach his porch. "What's going on out here?" Alice had spotted Domino hauling ass after her husband. She took several waddling steps forward. "Who—and I can't stress this enough—the *fuck* are you? I'm trying to nap, you ogre!"

"I'm no ogre, human!"

"Don't give a shit about semantics," Alice sing-songed. "You're big and green and ugly, like an ogre."

"Honey! Get back inside!" Shane wailed, frantically waving his arms.

Domino laughed. "Ah! A pregnant one! Two for the price of one. Maybe I'll tear the little one from your womb. They taste better fresh."

Alice went down one step, then another. "Get the fuck out of here! This is my property!"

Domino loped faster. "So many mouthy bitches here who don't know their place."

Alice, her chest heaving, clenched her jaw. Her fists opened and closed. I staggered to my feet. My sword streaked toward Domino. The orc wouldn't actually murder a pregnant woman, would he?

Shane finally reached the porch. To my astonishment, he

didn't grab his wife to run inside with her. He shot right past her and dove for cover.

Alice thrust out her hands when Domino was a mere ten feet away. As if that would stop him.

A fireball the size of a beach ball materialized out of nowhere and slammed into Domino's chest. He was airborne for what felt like an eon, then hit the ground with such force it left a trail of torn-up grass in his wake.

Domino, his chest a smoldering mess of singed clothing and ruined flesh, tried to get up.

Alice wasn't done. "Come to my fucking house and threaten my family." She hurled another fireball. "Disrespect myself and my guests!" Fireball. "Fuck. *You!*"

I shielded my eyes when a veritable inferno poured from her hands. Domino screamed in agony, but the sound died quickly. As did he. I gagged on the stench of burnt flesh.

During the distraction, my sword had beelined for the elf who had sent another root whipping out of the ground toward Caspian. The sword, having regained some of its energy, sliced through the root and then hurled toward the elf.

"Wait!" I cried.

The sword stopped inches from her throat. The ax yanked itself from Caspian's hands and poised itself at the elf's back. Given the way her breath caught and her upper body stiffened, the ax's blade must have made contact.

She wasn't going anywhere unless she had a death wish. I staggered over. Caspian remained upright, but he had his hands on his knees. I didn't know if the ax poured its magic into him the way the sword did with me, or if he was exhausted from fighting off the elf for so long.

"You," I said. "Elf."

She rolled her eyes in my direction, keeping her head

stationary lest any sudden movements should result in a torn-open throat.

"What do you know about the Shades?" I managed. Every inch of me hurt. I hurt on the inside. I had remembered that the last time I'd fought using the sword's magic that the aftereffects had been horrible. I didn't remember them being this horrible. My stomach churned and I swallowed back the flood of saliva that poured into my mouth. I willed myself not to hurl again.

"Just because I'm an elf doesn't mean I'm versed in every aspect of elf culture," she said. "I'm not a spokesperson for my entire species."

"Sure, but Domino knew your opinion on the matter. He said you're not an 'idealistic fool.' What did he mean?"

The elf sighed, albeit very gently. "The Shades believe Lachlan can do the impossible. He opened a portal by accident to the wrong place and got punished because of it. There's been no proof he's coming back. The sole chance for us to have a life worthy of our species is the Restoration."

"What's the Restoration?" I asked.

"The meaning is in its name," she said, managing to sound imperious despite being trapped between two sentient weapons.

"What, is it a new business venture? You're all going to start restoring old furniture?" I asked, mostly because I knew it would annoy her.

"Don't worry about it," she said, the corner of her mouth quirking up. "Mundanes aren't allowed."

A rustling sounded behind me, followed by pounding footsteps.

"The last troll is escaping!" Caspian shouted, staggering forward a few steps.

The ax tore off after the troll, who started screaming as soon as he registered he was being followed. He'd almost made it to the road leading out, but had his head lopped off for his efforts.

Poor bastard.

I choked on a gasp, hands flying up to my throat suddenly wound tight with ropy vines.

In the same instant that Caspian yelled my name, the sword sliced through the vines. I sucked in deep breath as the elf expelled her last, the sword buried in her sternum. It pulled itself free and the elf collapsed into the grass.

Caspian helped me pull the vines from my neck and I heaved again, spewing bile onto the gravel. I barely missed his shoes. I staggered a few feet away, sank to my knees, then flopped onto my back in the spongy grass.

Caspian hobbled over, hands on his knees as he peered down at me. Up close, he looked even worse than he had in my previous assessment. His skin had paled, his lips an almost ashy color, and sweat soaked his shirt and hairline. But at least he was alive. Holding up an arm, he revealed his unblemished wrist.

Good to know our bond to Domino didn't stretch beyond death.

"Are y'all gonna want to eat again before you head out?" came Alice's disembodied voice, somehow not the least bit winded or fazed despite roasting an orc on her lawn. Shane was going to need to revise his claim that while pregnant, Alice had "developed super senses." Her senses weren't the only things that were heightened. "I got some really tasty turkey from the deli this week!"

Caspian and I stared at each other a beat, then burst into delirious, relieved laughter.

Chapter 34

KAYDA

Kayda's first night working veil perimeter patrol had been equal parts terrifying and exhilarating. Hitting shit really always had done wonders for her soul. Her father might not have understood her on a deep level, but getting her into high-contact sports from a young age had been a blessing in disguise. The fact that her love of hitting things also meant she could protect her city had helped even more.

Had Welsh sensed that in her? Had he known that doing this—working with VHoA—would spark an interest in her that she hadn't even known she needed?

One day she'd figure that guy out.

The front house on the VHoA property was a residence, where any of the members could crash if they needed a place to stay. The sleeping quarters were cramped, with people taking any available space they could find. But, after a night spent slaying feral vampires together, Kayda already felt a camaraderie with the group, even if she couldn't remember everyone's name.

Kayda awoke early, as usual, despite having been up past 2 a.m. The house was relatively quiet with ten people dozing in various parts of it. Someone else was awake though; she could hear them puttering in the kitchen.

She gently swung her legs off the couch, where her feet had somehow ended up in the lap of a guy who slept sitting up, his head angled back toward the ceiling and his mouth agape. She gave him a gentle nudge and he tipped onto his side on the couch cushion. He issued a whimper but remained asleep. Shrugging, Kayda crept toward the kitchen.

Marisol was in the process of making a large pot of coffee and had pulled things out of the fridge to make breakfast. Deep bags hung under her eyes, her hair was up in a wild bun on top of her head, and her socks below her high-water pajama pants didn't match. She still managed a smile for Kayda.

Without a word, Kayda familiarized herself with the kitchen and scrambled two dozen eggs while Marisol popped frozen waffle after frozen waffle into the four-slice toaster. People slowly started to wake up and stumble into the kitchen for breakfast. It was the smell of sizzling bacon that woke up the rest.

The table in the small dining area seated ten semi-comfortably. Two others ate while standing in the kitchen—the division of the two "rooms" marked by one arm of the C-shaped kitchen counter.

Utensils clinked against porcelain, forks sliced through the crunchy crust of waffles, lips smacked. But no one spoke. Kayda got the impression it wasn't due to the early hour.

"There was another animal-sacrifice-related breach last night," Marisol finally said, her eyes downcast as she pushed a wedge of waffle around her plate. "It was technically in Montclaire—not far from the border between it and the Necropolis. The team went after the ferals while Annie and I searched for the animal, since we know what to look for now." She looked up long enough to offer Kayda another small smile. "I stabbed the coyote to close the curtain, but another feral got through before it closed and ... Annie didn't make it." Tears tracked down Marisol's face. "She just got married last month. Somehow I have to tell her husband that she's gone."

A woman excused herself from the table and retreated into the bathroom. Kayda didn't need enhanced hearing to know the woman was crying.

There was a hollow pit in Kayda's stomach. Bashing in feral heads with the charmed spear Marisol had lent her last night had actually made Kayda feel like she was making a difference. But if the ferals kept coming, and kept slowly picking off VHoA members faster than Marisol could recruit them, were they really holding back the tide, or just plugging up a leaky dam?

"Aren't the werecats supposed to protect the perimeter?" Kayda had bent her fork clean in two. She dropped the mangled metal onto her plate.

Marisol sniffed, wiping her eyes with the too-long sleeve of her sweatshirt. "As much as I'm all about bitching about the cats, they've been helping out."

Several heads bobbed in agreement.

"Not as much as we'd like, but the problem has gotten bad enough in the past couple of weeks that even they know these aren't isolated incidents anymore," Marisol said. "After I killed the coyote, I pulled it through the veil onto our side. It was a werecat who helped me kill the last feral, actually. We just didn't take it down before it got Annie. I told the cat about the breaches and she took the coyote back with her. I don't think the cats had known about the animal sacrifices before last night."

That mollified Kayda somewhat. Chasing that first feral down, taking pictures of the coyote ... that had helped move the needle for VHoA. The knowledge hadn't managed to save Annie, but it had probably helped save others, since Marisol had been able to stop the breach before more had slipped through. If the werecats were taking this more seriously, it would mean VHoA wouldn't get decimated as quickly.

Her thoughts strayed to Harlow. How overrun was the outside with these things? Or were they swarmed at the border of the Necropolis, like a horde of zombies in a movie, scrabbling and clawing at each other as they probed for a weak spot to grant them access to the city?

Suddenly Kayda felt too boxed in. This house was too small and there were too many people in it. She was currently wedged into a corner with a person on either side. Her nervous fidgeting was enough to get the person to her left to get up. Kayda sprang for the opening between bodies.

"I gotta go," she said, rubbing the back of her neck. "I'll be back tonight. I'm sorry about Annie, Mari."

Within a minute, she had her shoes back on and had grabbed her bag, phone, and keys off the coffee table in the cluttered living room. She shouted an anxious goodbye and let herself out.

As she walked down the sidewalk, she took in great pulls of air. Being in a human neighborhood in the Necropolis had her less concerned that someone would recognize her, yet when she reached a shopping center a few blocks away with a sandwich shop, laundromat, and a liquor store, she dipped inside the laundromat to use the restroom. Inside her bag were the small glamoured items she'd gotten from Welsh. She hadn't wanted to risk losing them while fighting monsters last night. Having the ponytail back lightened her mood a bit.

The laundromat was deserted at this hour other than an old woman sitting on a stool with her back against a dryer, her eyes closed. Perhaps the steady *whomp, whomp, whomp* of her tumbling clothes had lulled her to sleep.

Kayda walked a few more blocks, heading west through the Necropolis, without a destination in mind. The fresh air had cleared her head and had loosened the knot of anxiety in her chest, but she was restless. Kayda had never done well with being idle. She needed a job, a project, a goal to work toward. It was why she liked gaming so much. There was always another level to achieve, a raid to complete, a boss to defeat.

She'd been happy with her new job as feral exterminator until she'd heard about Annie. Being an exterminator wasn't enough. It was treating a symptom, not the cause.

She stopped.

She had an idea of where to go.

The walk from one side of the Necropolis to the other took about an hour. When she was almost there, she slowed her pace to a casual stroll. Now that she was close, she'd started questioning the wisdom of this decision. Mostly because—

"You again!"

Kayda came up short and curled a lip involuntarily. "Hi, pixie."

Aster put her tiny hands on her tiny hips and arched her tiny eyebrows. Before Kayda could say anything else, several other pixies appeared, flitting behind Aster. The amount of tiny fluttering wings this close to Kayda's face was giving her a headache.

"You lost?" asked one of the pixie ladies in Aster's gang.

Kayda gusted an annoyed sigh, accidentally sending three of the pixies tumbling away end over end, screaming curses all the while. She would have laughed had she not been sure the tiny things would chew through her Achilles tendon if given enough reason. "I came here to talk to Aster, actually."

"Oh ho!" Aster said cheerfully. "How the tables have turned."

She rolled her eyes. Yep, this was a stupid idea. "Never mind," she said, and turned to leave, coming up short when Aster was directly in front of her once more.

"Will talking to you help me with that, erm ... thing we talked about?" Aster asked.

"It wouldn't hurt," Kayda said, then did her best to sound as agreeable and friendly as possible. "He's been very busy lately, but I could give him another nudge if you'd be willing to chat."

Aster crossed her arms and tapped her foot in the air as she stared at Kayda. "Yeah, all right." She zoomed above Kayda's head. "It's fine, girls. She's a ... business associate."

There was a smattering of snarky commentary about a bakery being "a stupid idea" and that Aster was "too wild" to run her own shop.

"What's a draken gonna do for you, Aster?" one of them squeaked. "Gonna hire her to work security so no one steals your cupcakes?"

The gaggle of pixie ladies chuckled, the sound redolent of leaves crunching underfoot. Weird.

"Yeah, yeah! Get on out of here." A moment later, Aster was back in front of Kayda's face. "We can go across the street to the park. Less chance the girls will be eavesdropping."

"Don't want them to know about your ... request?" Kayda asked, cocking her head, resisting the urge to point out that her friends sounded like jerks.

"Nah. They wouldn't understand. They usually don't," Aster said, then zipped away.

Kayda waited for traffic to clear, then crossed the street after the pixie. Her new "business associate" waited below a metal archway Kayda hadn't noticed before. The metal had been painted brown, matching the wood fencing lining a pathway.

The fencing lined a curving stretch of asphalt that ran along the backs of several homes. The tops of the weather-worn boards were a smidge shorter than Kayda was, and she peered into yards as she followed the pixie. The asphalt ended at another metal archway, and beyond that was the park, the asphalt giving way to a cement biking path.

Aster alighted on Kayda's shoulder and it took everything in Kayda not to flick her off like an insect. She wasn't scared of pixies so much as creeped out by how small they were. Any wrong move and she could snuff a life out with her boot—like accidentally stepping on a snail, but so much worse. Kayda kept her hands tucked behind her back.

"So what'd you wanna talk about, draken?" Aster asked right by Kayda's ear.

Kayda wasn't sure how much to divulge to the pixie. It wasn't that she didn't trust her—okay, that was a big part of the reason—but she also didn't want to be responsible for causing widespread panic in the pixie community by revealing too much. Though, Felix had said pixies could be great informants if you could find a reliable one. Kayda had to guess that was because they went unnoticed or were easily dismissed, making them excellent spies.

"Is this about the elves again?" Aster asked.

"Kind of," Kayda said, then gave Aster a very brief explanation of the recent veil breaches.

Aster whistled. "I bet my sister-in-law would know more about this. The one who lives in the preserve. Wanna ask her some stuff?"

"That could be helpful. I—"

"Give me ten minutes!" Aster took off in a blur.

The preserve was clear across the Necropolis. A pixie could get there and back in ten minutes?

Kayda flopped onto a park bench to wait. She debated calling Henri. She mostly just wanted to hear his voice, but she believed Welsh was right and that keeping their distance for a while was a smart move.

The buzz of wings pulled Kayda out of her musing. A

moment after she'd registered the sound, there they were, bobbing before her. There were four of them now.

"Kayda, this is Iris," Aster said, motioning to a black-haired pixie with a gorgeous face. She wore a pretty dress made of soft-pink rose petals and no shoes. "These are her siblings, Ash and Basil." One girl, one boy. They were equally elegant and sophisticated. Kayda's gaze ping-ponged from the polished trio, to the rough-and-tumble Aster, and back.

"It's lovely to meet you, Lady Draken," Iris said, bowing demurely.

Ash and Basil did the same behind her. Aster discreetly rolled her eyes.

"Asteria here tells me you have questions about some of the events we've witnessed in the preserve?" Iris asked, smiling softly. "We came right away when Asteria informed us that she's in debt to a draken. I apologize on her behalf, and extend that apology from our entire frollick, for whatever untoward offense she waged against you, my lady."

Aster's wings glowed red for a brief, bright spark of color. "I already told you I didn't do anything *untoward*," she hissed at Iris.

"It's true," Kayda said.

Iris smiled sweetly. "You cannot blame me for double-checking, Asteria. You tend to get into trouble with those ... friends of yours." She toyed with the wedding ring on her hand. "Family means the world to me. Now that we are trying to conceive, I have to be extra cautious, don't you see? If you're getting into trouble again, I—"

"Look, *Iris*," Kayda said, cutting her off. "Aster is helping me because she's a nice pixie. She asked you here to help me. All *you're* doing is making me mad. Not sure you and your hoity-toity siblings want to be on the shit list of a draken ..."

Said siblings clutched their invisible pearls. "*Iris ...*" they sing-songed in unison.

Iris pursed her lips. "Fine. What do you want to know?" She hiked her button nose in the air.

Aster chuckled delightedly, then perched herself on Kayda's shoulder once more.

"Tell me everything you can about the rituals you've seen in the preserve," Kayda said.

"I do believe Asteria told you the most significant thing I witnessed: when the elves tried to open a portal," Iris said. "But in the last month or so, elves have been in the preserve not for the ritual, but for hunting. Many wild animals live in the preserve and cross in and out of the veil freely. The elves have been tranquilizing the animals with blow darts and then carrying their unconscious bodies away. Many pixies are nocturnal, and a few were hit by the darts when the elves first started hunting in the preserve. At least two that I know of died from being struck."

What a terrible way to go: taken out by a weapon the same size as yourself.

"That was why so many of us started spying on the rituals when they started, unsure of what was happening in our home," Iris said. "A few pixie representatives have attempted to get an audience with law enforcement, but no one ever follows up."

"I'm sorry to hear this," Kayda said, frowning, pushing down the guilt about her own pixie aversion. "Anything else strange been happening in the preserve? Even something you might think is irrelevant could help me figure out what's going on. Anything connecting the elves to ferals, by any chance?"

Iris's siblings gasped in unison, their hands clasped now. Upon closer inspection, Kayda suspected they were twins. They bent their heads together and whispered furiously to one another. The pixies talked too fast for Kayda to understand them; it sounded like nothing more than high-pitched mouse squeaks.

Iris huffed and stomped a foot in the air. "Will you two stop it?" she snapped. "Tell the woman what you know."

Ash and Basil, flushing from head to toe, abruptly stopped chatting.

"Basil knows more than I do," the girl twin said, pulling her hand free from her brother's and shoving him forward.

Kayda recoiled when Basil ended up a few centimeters from her nose.

Basil's shriek said he hadn't enjoyed this development either. He coughed delicately as he fluttered back a couple of inches. "Okay. So." He shot a glance over at Iris, whose pretty little face was pinched. "During the summers, there are these ... parties we go to. Moonshine soirees."

"You *still* go to those?" Iris asked, horrified.

"You went to them in high school too!" Ash added, coming to her brother's defense even while hiding behind Iris.

"Anyway!" Basil said. "The soirees are usually in the preserve, but sometimes we go to the old rail yards because Juniper has been cultivating winterberries in one of the old train cars. They grow better in dark places and the train car is perfect for that."

Kayda blanched. Winterberries were wildly hallucinogenic even in very small doses. Just three of the berries had been enough to send Henri on a trip so traumatic he swore off anything over Level 2 magic. It seemed like a single winterberry would flat-out kill a pixie.

"We don't eat them raw!" Basil said, clearly having read Kayda's expression. "He distills them and makes the most incredible wine that's totally safe to drink—though it will get you drunk very fast."

Iris appeared scandalized by every word.

"We were at a soiree last night," Basil said. "The vampire hunters were out there doing their thing. We sat on top of the train car, drank our winterberry wine, and waited for one of the ferals to come through. We make bets on how fast the hunters can kill them. It's like watching for shooting stars. Ferals usually come in ones or twos, and not that often. Lately, it's pretty much guaranteed that we'll see at least a few when we're out there, though.

"Anyway, around 6 a.m., I woke up on the roof of the rail car. A bunch of us were asleep up there or inside. The feral flood stops by morning, and the last of the hunters were gone, too. I went to take a leak, and while I was doing that, I saw the veil open like a freakin' curtain. Wildest thing I'd ever seen! Thought I was still drunk. It didn't open very wide, but it was enough that three human-like people were able to stroll right in. A fourth one walked through and turned back to the veil, did some kind of spell, and then the veil closed. I assumed it had to be sorcerers because who else can do that to the veil, right? They start having a conversation, and since I've never seen an academy-trained sorcerer up close, I had to know what they were saying, obviously. So I flew over there."

Kayda instinctively leaned toward him, but he didn't flinch away that time. "Were they sorcerers?"

Basil shook his head. "Elves. Every single one of them. I stayed low and out of sight. They were talking about 'the kids' and were comparing notes on how successful they were at manipulating the veils. At first I thought they meant 'the kids' were the ones letting the ferals in. But ... I don't know ... it seems like they were testing the kids on how good they were at parting the veils. They were saying the ferals have been a good distraction, but that it's also a relatively harmless test since every night, the vamp hunters are already expecting ferals to come through. One of the elves said a few of the kids were getting too cocky, though, and were parting the veil near high-population places where the magic is stronger—to really prove how good they are—but that it got someone killed last night."

Kayda wondered if that had been Annie. As bad as she felt about Annie—this vampire hunter she didn't even know—she hoped Annie had been the only one to die last night at the claws of the ferals. "Anything else?"

"Uhh ... let's see. Oh! There was one woman in the group, and she said her last batch of kids were the most promising they've had, and that they'd be ready by the full moon to complete 'the real thing,'" Basil said.

Great.

"Does any of that help?" Basil asked. "It didn't make a lot of sense to me."

"Very helpful, actually," Kayda said, strangely relieved that what Snowdrop had told her was true: her letting ferals into the Indie had largely been an accident.

"Sweet!" Basil glided back behind Iris to get into another squeaky-mouse conversation with his twin.

Iris scrutinized Kayda's face. "Are you ... an officer of some kind? Asteria said you're investigating what's been happening in the preserve. I have to admit I was pretty skeptical that a draken would be assigned to a case about pixies. I came here partly out of curiosity."

As snooty as the pixie was—and clearly very judgy—Kayda supposed she could understand the newlywed with dreams of a family being apprehensive about the kind of world she might bring a child into. The preserve might have been considered an abandoned wasteland to most citizens of Luma, but a large swath of the pixie population called it home. Other lesser fae must have lived there, too. The elves' curious behavior was threatening that. Between the animal attacks and the portal magic that made everything in the preserve recoil, Kayda supposed if she were a pixie, she'd be uneasy, too.

She didn't want to give Iris false hope, though.

"Private investigator," Kayda said. "I have connections with bounty hunters, witches, and sorcerers. They're all aware of the growing problems in Luma and I'm working to gather information from as many sources as possible to get to the bottom of it. I promise that I'll pass on your concerns to as many people in power as I can."

Iris offered her a genuine smile at that, then shifted her gaze to a spot near Kayda's ear. "I'm sorry I thought you unscrupulous, Asteria. Please come to dinner this weekend. We'd love to have you."

Without another word, the trio of pixie siblings took off, leaving a faint streak of blue in the air before it disappeared. Aster was in Kayda's face a second later.

"You made Iris Grendowel-Loam apologize to *me*!" Aster howled with laughter. "Incredible! That's almost even better than that other thing."

Kayda crossed her arms and studied the pixie. "Why do you want that glamour tonic anyway?"

Aster frowned. It took her a while to finally say, "You ever mess up so bad you want to be someone else?"

She hadn't. "Sure."

"Figured it would be nice not to be me for a bit. To be near people who know what I did and have them look at me and not see that," Aster said.

"They wouldn't see you at all," Kayda said. "Look, I'm not good at talking about feelings or whatever, but speaking from experience, you'll get some freedom from being someone else, but it always fades. And then you're right back where you were and you might even feel worse. You gotta be comfortable in the skin you've got."

Aster sputtered a laugh. "That was so cheesy."

Kayda smiled ruefully at her. "I don't know what you did and you don't have to tell me. But it looks like Iris is willing to give *you* another shot, not someone else. So try it as you and see how it goes."

Aster wrinkled her nose.

"I'll make you a deal. If you go to this dinner and it's absolutely fucking terrible because Iris gets mad you didn't use the right fork or something, you come find me and tell me all about it. Bring over a bottle of winterberry wine, get drunk, and pass out in my sink."

Aster sniffed. "Yeah?"

Kayda shrugged. "Yeah. You're not so bad."

"You either," Aster said. "Catch you later."

Then she was gone.

Kayda sat on the bench for a while longer, listening to the gentle breeze in the trees, enjoying the nice moment before she tossed herself back into reality and ruined it.

Pulling out her phone, she searched for details on the full moon. Every month's full moon had a name, and she easily found the one for July. The Buck Moon was to shine bright in the sky in two days. The image of the brown-robed Moon Children popped into her head, one wearing the head of a deer. Moonrise would be just before 9 p.m. She suspected that peak full-moon viewing would also be peak portal-opening time. She recalled the way Snowdrop had held her hands to the sky, her upturned face awash in the blueish light of floating orbs. Had the orbs been meant to mimic moonlight?

She called Welsh.

"How's vamp hunting treating you?" he asked, clearly having guessed where she'd disappeared to when she'd left his apartment yesterday. She didn't know how he seemed to be right about a lot of things a lot of the time, but she found it annoying. Smug bastard.

"The Shades are going to try to open that portal in two days," she said.

All smugness fled his voice. "Well, shit."

Chapter 35
KAYDA

Kayda walked back to VHoA, where Welsh said he'd meet her. The rational part of her knew she should be leery of portal magic—not because of what she'd been taught all her life, but because of how Iris had said the preserve itself had reacted to it. Elves possessed nature magic, and if the magic they used made nature itself shy away, that fact couldn't be ignored. As much as Kayda craved the idea of visiting her home world, of seeing a place where her people had come from, she had to maintain a healthy level of skepticism.

She called Marisol along the way to tell her what she'd learned that afternoon. "I don't know if it's any consolation," Kayda said, "but the elves overseeing this lunacy probably didn't mean for anyone to get hurt. It sounds like they've been opening tears in the Necropolis knowing that it will result in ferals getting through, but also knowing VHoA are on the other side ready to kill them."

"Then why not do their tests during the day when ferals are less active?" Marisol asked.

Kayda figured the answer to that was obvious: if the elves were trying to keep their extracurricular activities a secret, doing it under the dead of night where they were less likely to be spotted made the most sense.

"And why all the secrecy?" Marisol asked, as if she'd heard Kayda's thoughts. "They're either planning to only offer a Get Off Earth ticket to elves, and not all of fae—or they're not actually doing what they claim they're doing."

A sense of betrayal tightened Kayda's chest at the idea of it being elf-exclusive.

Marisol let out a bone-weary sigh. "I can't shake the feeling that we're not seeing the whole picture. Like we've got an entire jigsaw puzzle finished, but one of the pieces is missing."

Kayda mulled that over for the rest of her walk.

Welsh was already at the house by the time she let herself into the back unit. She surveyed the room, but didn't see Marisol anywhere. There was an excited buzz of energy, and Kayda caught snatches of conversation about Marisol bringing in a special guest.

When Marisol entered the main room a few minutes later, Kayda instantly knew what kind of special guest it was. Not because Kayda could sense the feline grace of a werecat on sight, but because she recognized her.

"Officer Magnan?" Kayda said, cocking her head at the too-pretty officer she'd talked to that Sunday a million years ago, when Kayda had pinned the handsy draken Reynard to the ground.

"You can call me Jasmine," the werecat said. "I guess I shouldn't be surprised to see you here—the vigilante type, eh?"

"Since when are you friends with cats, Mari?" a man finally asked, sounding none too pleased.

Marisol addressed the group. "Hear me out. If you don't like what I say, be mad *then*. Last night during the feral attack that killed Annie—Jasmine is the werecat who helped take that feral out. I'm not sure I'd be here if she hadn't jumped in when she did. She also took that carcass back to the Collective."

"And?" someone else called out.

"And," said Jasmine, "the Collective is pulling a lot of cats off their regular duties to help with veil patrol until we get this problem resolved."

A few bitter chuckles rippled through the room.

Grouchy Guy asked, "Where have you been before this, huh? Why has it been—for years—a group of volunteers who've had to train ourselves? No one gave a shit but us until now."

"For what it's worth, there are a lot of us who have been trying to get this threat taken more seriously, but we're in the minority," Jasmine said. "Frankly, the Collective is stretched too thin, and that's only gotten worse in the last few months, especially the last few weeks. I completely understand that this is too little, too late—but we're still here to help."

Grouchy Guy harrumphed but didn't say anything more.

"We're anticipating that between now and the full moon, things will escalate," Jasmine said.

So the Collective *did* know.

The Glitch had started a series of events that eventually resulted in werewolves being wiped off the planet. The full moon had only affected them—no other fae. And there was nothing "special" about this full moon, as far as significant celestial events were concerned, either. It wasn't a lunar eclipse, or a supermoon, or a once-in-a-lifetime strawberry moon that coincided with the summer solstice. It was a run-of-the-mill full moon that happened to be chosen as the day by a bunch of elves who wanted to get the hells off Earth.

"Ah, I get it," Kayda said. "The Collective doesn't *actually* give a shit now. They're sending their cats out to help with pest management while the sorcerers deal with the bigger issue of the Shades trying to open a portal to be reunited with their leader."

Jasmine's mouth slightly dropped open. "Uhh ... yeah. That."

Mutters filled the room. Clearly Marisol hadn't fully briefed her crew on what they were up against. Marisol shot Kayda an aggrieved look, then addressed the group again to fill them in.

As Marisol was peppered with questions, Welsh nudged Kayda, angled his head toward the door, then walked away. She offered a "they were going to find out eventually" shrug to Marisol, then followed Welsh, closing the door behind her.

Once they were in the small living room, Welsh said, "I talked to a contact who's a linguistic scholar in fae languages. The Elfin those kids are chanting? It isn't Elfin."

Kayda cocked her head. "What is it then?"

"He's not sure. There are roots of Elfin and Goblish—which is one of the oldest fae languages. But as far as languages that would have been brought to Earth after the Glitch—whatever those kids were chanting, Elfin wasn't it."

Kayda didn't know what to make of that.

"Caspian says the runes on the carcasses are an ancient variant," Welsh said. "I get that Snowdrop could be a world-class actress and she's more with it than we're giving her credit for, but from what I know about how long it takes to master runework, it seems very unlikely she even has any idea what those runes mean. My best guess is that these kids aren't being trained so much as groomed. For what, I don't know."

It wasn't a comforting thought.

Veil perimeter patrols typically began at dusk. Vampires could be out in the sun, but like many apex predators, they were most active at night. The ferals were no exception. VHoA liked to be in place at least an hour before it got full dark, which felt even more important lately since at least some of the breaches were due not to the whims of deranged vampires but young Shade trainees. Trainees who could throw the city into complete turmoil if they decided to pull their stunt at high noon and set loose a pack of rabid vampires on the lunch crowd in Luma Proper. Kayda shuddered at the idea. Even if the majority of people who lived in Luma Proper were fae, it didn't mean they were battle-ready.

It would be a slaughter.

So as much as this whole situation was a shit show, Kayda was glad the trainees weren't straying from their MO.

Kayda was assigned to one of the southernmost sections of the Necropolis, which naturally was one of the biggest hot spots for feral activity. The rail yards were behind her, the rusting cars slumbering in the coarse sand. VHoA and werecats were spaced twelve feet apart, with VHoA armed with weapons pulsing with magic. Several of the werecats had shifted into their feline forms already and were pacing, muscles bunching and coiling beneath sleek fur.

Shortly after sunset, a shout went up off to Kayda's right. Whoever had yelled was too far away for her to see, her view blocked by the corner of a dilapidated stone building. She could hear them, though. The sound of snarling feral vampires was burned deep into her memory. Goose bumps broke out across her skin. She readjusted her grip on her spear, the wicked-sharp tip sizzling with red-tinted magic that seared flesh on contact.

A pair of ferals slipped through to her left. The triplets were ready for them. Liam clocked one in the temple with his electricity-laced baton, stunning it long enough for Ollie to slice off its head with a spear very similar to Kayda's. Ben brained his feral with a metal baseball bat outfitted with sparking spikes.

The feral's skull crunched and the monster went down in a heap.

They came in ones and twos for the next half hour. Kayda heard more than she saw, only needing to take out one herself so far. Marisol was a few feet away, her walkie-talkie crackling. VHoA teams in other parts of the Necropolis, the Indie to the west of the city, and Montclaire in the east were in constant contact in case there was another breach in an unexpected location. They all hoped the activity would keep to the Necropolis, like usual.

Jasmine had said that a few teams of werecats would be stationed outside Luma, too. They were attempting to figure out where the ferals had been coming from. VHoA had been doing this for years themselves, but with the hit the Luma chapter had taken to their membership numbers last month, they'd been forced to restrict most of their efforts to keeping the ferals out, rather than determining how they were getting in.

An hour after the ferals had started their nightly assault, Marisol's walkie chirped with an alarming message. *"We've got reports of two breaches in Montclaire! One near the border with the Necropolis and one in the middle of the district!"*

A fresh wave of ferals slipped through the veil near Kayda after that. They hissed and growled, the magic of the veil zapping them like an electrified fence, though never strongly enough to stop them. All it seemed to do was assure they'd be even angrier by the time they were on Luma soil.

Marisol's walkie crackled.

"Breach in the Warehouse District! Mari, we need anyone else you've got. We've got two werecats here and they called for reinforcements, but—shit—"

Kayda sidestepped the necrotic claws of a feral that had swiped for her midsection. She swung out with her spear, catching nothing but the tattered rags of what might have been a dress. The feral stopped on a dime, spun, and lunged for Kayda again. Her next swing was wilder, sloppier, and the feral dodged the blow, leaving Kayda gasping with her back exposed to the monster. A snarl and the pungent scent of burning flesh erupted behind her. By the time she turned back, the feral was dead at her feet. Liam's chest heaved, but he wore a bright smile.

"Now we're even, Angel!" he said, jogging back to his original spot.

Kayda huffed a laugh, her heart beating too fast. "Thanks, kid."

Marisol plucked her walkie-talkie from her belt. *"Diane? How are you doing in Warehouse?"*

No answer.

"Diane?"

"I'm here! We found another one of the animal sacrifices. Three werecats ran through the tear in the veil and told me to close it after them. I don't know if they're okay. Eight ferals got through before I closed it. Eight, Mari. What the hell is going on?"

"It's hectic here, too. Have there been any more breaches up there? I don't know if I can spare any more here," Marisol said.

As if on cue, another three ferals ran through the veil. Marisol hooked her walkie back on her belt and stabbed a feral in the chest in a matter of three seconds. The triplets took out the other two before they reached Kayda. She sagged, heart continuing to hammer out a frantic rhythm. The night was young. What if there weren't enough of them on this side to hold back the tide?

"Another breach in Montclaire!"

Kayda lopped the head off a feral.

A subdued, exhausted male voice reported in. *"Animal sacrifice found in the Indie. Three civilians lost before we could kill the animal and close the veil. Jameson is critically injured."*

A scream went up to Kayda's right, followed by a cacophony

of hisses and chittering. Her instinct told her to run that way, but another four ferals came barreling through her section of the veil. She raised her spear, the red magic glitching.

By the time the beasts were dispatched, the magic in her spear had gone out entirely. She wasn't sure if the magic was forever depleted or just needed to be recharged. Either way, the ferals kept coming. There would be a lull for ten minutes, maybe fifteen, and then more would arrive. Ben had a gash in his chest that was bleeding far too much. Yet, he had his spear held at the ready in defiance of the injury. Ollie and Liam flanked him—protecting their friend.

"Massive breach in Warehouse!" a voice shouted over the walkie-talkie. *"Send everyone you've got. We found three animal sacrifices. Twenty ferals are inside the city. A pack is running down Larkspur Lane. The club is in that area tonight. Cops, werecats, and hunters are already on their way, but we'll need more. We'll—sonofabitch."* A snarl sounded, then the walkie went dead.

Kayda wanted to be under the covers of her bed, not be out here fighting a losing battle. It had been bad last night on her perimeter patrol but not this bad. Her ears rang. She was losing her grip. Her senses were getting overloaded. She could hear everything. And all of it was too loud.

Something was wrong. Something other than the obvious. Kayda's chest was tight with it. Her breath was shallow.

A tiny pinprick of a buzz sounded right in her ear. Sharp and persistent, it cut through the veritable wall of sound that was trying to drown her.

Somehow she knew who it would be before she turned her head. Aster, her wings as bright red as Kayda's ill-fated spear had been, flitted there, her fist closed around a single white hair. Kayda's hair. The one she said she could use to find Kayda if she wanted to.

Aster said the words Kayda already knew she'd say. "The ritual has started. The preserve is *quaking*. That's what Iris said."

This swarm of ferals was popping up all over the city the night *before* the full moon. The Shades wanted the police, the werecats, and the hunters to be so caught up defending the city that everyone's resources would be spread too thin. Felix had said the Collective's numbers in Luma were down. Jasmine had said the ones who were left were already swamped.

If this truly was a matter of getting a few elves back home to their home world, would the Shades be risking this many lives? Snowdrop said they hadn't been trying to hurt anyone, that the breaches were an accident. Maybe she'd been telling the truth, but whoever her handlers were, whoever Basil had overheard talking, wanted this portal opened so badly, they were willing to let people die.

What if the Shades weren't successful tonight? Would this keep happening until the ferals so overwhelmed Luma's defenses that there would be no one left to fend them off?

It had to stop.

Kayda ran to Marisol. "The Shades are doing this tonight. I have to go."

The pounding of massive cat paws told Kayda that reinforcements were arriving. And just in time, too, because it made her feel slightly less guilty about bailing. She couldn't ask Marisol to leave now. The people best trained to take care of this were here.

Kayda pulled out her phone, dialed Welsh, pressed the phone to her ear, and then took off at a sprint, passing a pack of werecats going the other way. Aster kept up in Kayda's peripheral vision.

"Thank the Goddess!" Welsh answered. "I can't get anyone

from VHoA to pick up their phones. What the fuck is going on?"

"Get to the preserve. The Shades moved up the timeline. Call whoever you can."

He cursed and hung up.

Chapter 36

KAYDA

The preserve was clear across the Necropolis. It wasn't the district Kayda wanted to be in alone, especially with a weapon that was nothing more than a pointy stick now, but she didn't know what else to do. Maybe she could run in and punch the shit out of the assembled elves while they had their attention honed in on summoning Lachlan. At the very least, if something went horribly wrong during the portal-opening, she could be a witness. Assuming this little excursion didn't kill her, of course.

"What's the plan?" Aster asked, her wings still glowing a panicked red.

Kayda would have felt a lot better about this if she had a sentient sword of her own by her side, rather than a pixie the size of her pointer finger. She knew beggars couldn't be choosers, but she'd earned the right to be choosy in this situation. "I don't ... really have one."

"Excellent," Aster deadpanned.

When Kayda was at the start of the long, curving dirt road that led into the preserve, she slowed to a stop to catch her breath. It was quiet here. Even the animals weren't making their usual scrabbling sounds in the brush. Kayda couldn't see the run-down parking lot from this distance. Shielding herself behind a tree, she made another phone call.

"Welsh?" came the harried reply.

"Uh, no. It's Kay."

Henri gusted a sigh so deep she had to pull the phone away from her ear. "F-Finally. You c-c-changed your number on me. I didn't know if y-y-you were okay."

Yeah, yeah. She was a hypocrite.

It registered then that Henri sounded like he was on the move.

"You haven't gone in there yet, right?" he asked. "Into the preserve, I mean?"

She cocked her head in confusion. Then it clicked. "Welsh already talked to you."

"Yeah. He said you needed help. I'll be there in fifteen."

"Did he even tell you what I needed help with?"

"Well, no. But it doesn't matter. If you need help smashing in h-h-heads, I've got my handy-dandy flashlight. If y-you need a getaway v-v-vehicle, I've got the motorcycle. That sh-should cover everything."

Said motorcycle rumbled to life.

Goddess help her, she was fairly certain she was falling for this boy.

"Henri, I—"

"Sh-Shut up, Kay," he said, somehow making it sound endearing. "If you're going to try to convince me not to c-c-come, I'll hang up. You calling sort of ruined my plan to sh-show up like a w-w-white knight on a horse—or a draken on a motor-cycle. I sh-should make a joke about h-horsepower, but I g-got nothin'. If you're going to ap-apologize, you can just m-m-make it up to me l-later. Hopefully r-r-repeatedly."

Kayda flushed to her hairline.

"S-S-See you soon."

The call ended. She silently begged Welsh to get here first so she could sock him in the throat and then hug him. Or maybe the other way around. She didn't know which order she preferred yet.

The flutter of Aster's wings was one of the few noises in this deathly quiet place.

"You have any ideas?" Kayda asked her.

"Not yet," Aster said. "Finding you was the main plan. Possibly the whole plan."

"Excellent," Kayda deadpanned, and Aster grinned at her.

Welsh did in fact show up before Henri, but Kayda was so stressed out of her gourd by then that she didn't want to waste her energy on him. The side door of his minivan trundled open and Kayda wordlessly climbed in. Aster landed on Kayda's shoulder and grabbed a fistful of her collar. After tossing the still-dormant spear onto the floorboards, she'd just started to pull the door closed when Welsh hit the gas and the lumbering vehicle lurched forward.

Kayda's eyes quickly adjusted to the dark interior of the van. Welsh was in the driver's seat in his twenty-something form, Josephine was in the passenger seat, Grayson was in the back seat with Kayda, and in the back sat a very sour-looking Erik, of all people. Kayda involuntarily curled her lip at him. He mirrored it.

With a hard yank, Kayda got the door closed.

"Please continue, Mrs. Fletcher," Welsh said, bouncing in his driver's seat as he semi-successfully maneuvered the van around the potholes.

Mrs. Fletcher? As in Harlow's mom?

"Hello, Kayda," a familiar voice said from Welsh's phone propped up in a cup holder on the dash. The voice brought up goose bumps, as if Kayda were hearing from the dead. "Harlow would say hi too, but she's not back from her own adventure yet.

And don't ask me what the adventure is, because I don't know. Something about the sword and a treasure chest. They left this morning."

"Hey, Mrs. F," Kayda said, barreling right past the information about Harlow. "Glad you're not dead."

Camila laughed. "Me too. Anyway ... I wanted to tell you all something I remembered from the time I interacted with Lachlan Shade decades ago. When I figured out that he was going to open a portal, I asked him if he wanted to open it to go back to his people. He said he wanted to open it to allow his people to join *him*. He was on the Collective's radar well before my interactions with him in Sacramento. We don't know what kind of private success he had with portal magic before all this. For all we know, he'd made contact with the fae realm way back then, and him getting pushed through the portal ruined a long-standing plan. A plan that Lachlan was a cog in, rather than the mastermind. We don't know. All I do know is that when I met him, he wasn't doing this for altruistic means and had no problem slowly bleeding a fae girl dry to get what he wanted.

"Three decades is a long time. Maybe the guy has changed his life's mission, has made it back to the fae realm, and wants the same for the elves here. But my gut tells me he wants the portal open to let things out. And if he never actually made it to the fae realm, and he's still in whatever world he was pushed into thirty years ago? Lord knows what he might be trying to bring with him."

This all reiterated what Kayda was already feeling: this ritual needed to be stopped, as did the people who were trying to make it happen. She assessed her companions, wondering how this ragtag group was going to accomplish that.

"We're trying to make as many calls to our contact lists as possible," Camila said, "but we're getting word about breaches in multiple hubs tonight. Nothing about animal sacrifices as far as I know, but the number of ferals forcing their ways through veils has definitely gone up."

"Are Shades trying to open portals in multiple hubs?" Grayson asked. "What if we're on the brink of another Glitch if too much portal magic is in use at once?"

"I don't think so," Kayda said. "I think the Shades have been setting up this large-scale distraction for a while. Aster's sister-in-law said the elves have been hunting in the preserve for wild game for at least a month."

"Who the hell is Aster?" Welsh asked.

The pixie in question flew across the van and floated by Welsh's ear. "Me."

Welsh yelped and swerved. "Dammit, pixie!" Once he recovered he said, "You're the one who wants a growth tonic, right? Since you seem to be one of the rare helpful pixies, if we don't all die tonight, you and I can talk."

Aster's wings went a shimmery silver.

"But if you scare me again, I'm going to pop your tiny head off your shoulders."

Aster was back by Kayda's side in an instant.

Josephine's dark arm reached across the space between her seat and Welsh's. She shook a bag of peanuts at him. "I assume this is one of the hangry times you warned me about? Eat this, you brat."

Welsh took them with a grunt, managing to drive, get the bag open, and dump several peanuts into his mouth without crashing. "Ugh! They're unsalted!"

Jo tsked at him but said nothing more. Kayda wondered if Jo had any idea that grumpy Welsh and charming Bosworth Hemmingsley were one and the same.

Camila chuckled again. "For what it's worth, I think Kayda's theory makes the most sense. Lachlan has likely been planning this for years. He doesn't want anything to go sideways this time. Distracting the Collective, bounty hunters, VHoA, and the werecats all at the same time is a good way to minimize getting interrupted. As well as changing the date it's happening. He wants everyone to be scrambling."

There was a long, tense silence.

"If it looks like blood magic was involved," Camila said, "the way to close it is a sacrifice. Ideally one of you can knock his ass back into whatever portal he opens. I don't envy you. I'll keep making calls. Hopefully someone can get down there to help. And, Kayda, for Harlow's sake? Don't get killed."

"No promises," Kayda said, her leg bouncing.

Camila sighed. "Good luck."

By the time Welsh's minivan reached the broken-down gate of the old zoo, Henri had arrived as well. Several cars were parked in the lot, moonlight shining on their hoods and windshields. Welsh and Henri both parked outside the lot, to aid in an easier escape should they need to get out quickly.

Kayda had even less of an idea of what in the hells they were supposed to do to stop an elfin ritual years in the making, but it was too late to back down now. They piled out of the minivan. Henri sidled up next to Kayda and offered her a shaky smile. He was nervous, she knew—for himself, for her, for Luma.

Welsh addressed the group. "We have to assume we're on our own tonight. I've got a couple of charmed weapons in the back of the van for anyone who doesn't have magic. Hells, even if you do have magic, you might want one. Do what you can to keep that portal from opening. And, you know, don't die."

Henri pumped a fist in the air. "R-Rousing speech, Welsh. G-Go team!"

A smattering of awkward laughter erupted from the group of seven. Even Welsh managed a smile.

After Welsh, Henri, Kayda, and Erik grabbed weapons, they

headed out. Kayda and Henri took the lead since they knew where to go. Her spear hadn't come back to life, so she wielded a battle-ax now, which she was sort of in love with already. She rested the handle on her shoulder, the hood-dampened blade by her ear. Aster flitted ahead often to check for anything nasty waiting for them on the path. Kayda kept her ears peeled for the sound of hungry ferals and the chants in an ancient language that Welsh's fae contact couldn't identify.

They had just passed the central tree when Kayda felt it. It felt like the sound of TV static. A buzzing that she could feel in her teeth, in her bones. It made her jittery, like she'd downed ten espressos. Was this the "quaking" Iris had claimed to feel? If Kayda could feel it, how terrible must this be for someone as tiny as a pixie?

Aster had been flying ahead of them when Kayda walked into the wall of fritzing magic, but she hadn't returned. She hadn't left Kayda's line of vision for more than a few seconds before this. Had she flown off to check on her family?

Jo moaned miserably. "Oh ... this is not good." Her breath caught on a sob. "Goddess, every living thing in here is terrified. The wrongness of it ..." She sniffed. "We must stop this. It's as if the life energy is being sucked out of everything—the plants, the animals, the very air. The natural magic is pushing against the portal magic. I don't know how much longer it can fight it. This isn't an opening of a door from one place to another. Permission wasn't granted. This is magic fueled by force. The portal is being *torn* open."

Aster rushed toward Kayda's face and Kayda came up short. The pixie was talking so fast, Kayda could hardly keep up. "Kay. Kayda! Hurry. Come. The portal. It's partially opened already. You can see something beyond it. Red rocks. White-blue sky. Desolate. Not like a desert. Deserts have life. This place is barren. It wants the life here." Then she took off.

Kayda and Henri shared a look of alarm, then broke into a run. The others quickly followed. The odd cadence of at least two of them behind her said someone was probably helping an unsteady Jo keep up the pace. If Welsh's glamour magic had been enough to set Jo's sensitive nature magic on edge, what the elves were doing had to be ten times worse.

The greenhouse building had just come into view when Kayda heard it. Snarling. She came to an abrupt halt.

"Henri!" she hissed, and he mercifully ran back to her.

She played with the dials of her hearing to assess how many there were. Ferals had turned, well, feral by drinking too much fae blood. Currently, everyone in attendance in her band of misfits was fae in one way or another. They were more in danger than all the humans battling the vamps, in a way, because the ferals were more intoxicated by the blood of fae than mundanes.

Which made Kayda question again how the elves had remained unscathed around the ferals for this long. Being outside the veils to lay their animal sacrifice traps was risky at best, suicidal at worst. And now there were ferals inside the preserve with a gaggle of elves nearby.

The rest of her group caught up. With the whole party unmoving, Kayda could more clearly make out the distant sound of chanting. She wasn't sure why she hadn't heard it sooner, but sound didn't seem to travel normally right now. Jo had said the air itself was being sucked dry of energy. The abandoned remains of the overgrown zoo weren't helping to offset the creepy factor.

The ring of beached boats that had once been a ride for kids was off to her right. She hoped that the family of raccoons she'd seen last time was long gone now. This was no place for them. This wasn't even a place for her and she had a charmed battle-ax.

When the ferals grew louder, she removed the magic-dampening hood from the blade. The metal gleamed in the snatches of moonlight that filtered through the canopy of leaves. A few seconds later, the blade gleamed with a different kind of light—blue magic rippled around the edges of the double-bladed beauty like a halo. She longed for a lightning spell, like the one in Welsh's preferred dagger, but she'd take whatever she could get. The magic rolling off this thing had to be at least a Level 5. It would surely kill a human just by coming in contact with the spell. Which meant it would fry an undead quite nicely.

The most unsettling thing wasn't that she could hear the ferals—it was that while the snarling grew louder, it didn't grow closer. In her albeit limited experience with the monsters, once they were near a potential kill, they charged after it like a rabid dog. There had been an intelligence in the one she'd seen on top of the construction van in the Indie, and it had watched her with a quiet, murderous calculation. But it had come after her almost immediately.

Were these ones watching them now, trying to suss out which in the group could be picked off the easiest? They were huddled together on the path like sitting ducks, their backs to each other as they formed a haphazard circle. Magic glowed from weapons and hands alike, at the ready for what might be coming. The ferals' rumbling seemed to echo—bouncing off the trees and dilapidated walls. Possibly off the air itself.

"Where are they?" Welsh growled.

Better yet, where was that damn pixie when Kayda needed her? "Aster!" she whisper-hissed.

Red-tinted wings fluttered in her face. "What are you doing! We need help! We—oh." The pixie's eyes were wide, her head whipping from left to right.

"Can you figure out where they are?" Kayda asked.

Aster shot straight up and out of sight. It was like she was high on uppers. She was back seconds later. "Four of them. Two straight ahead, one coming your way from near the big tree, and the last one ..." Aster's eyes and a single pointer finger were angled upward.

Kayda heard the creak of a branch a moment before the feral made its move. "It's above us!"

The group scattered, narrowly avoiding the feral, who landed on all fours on the spot they'd just been standing in. It cocked its head, skittering forward a few steps toward Kayda and Jo. The feral's unnaturally jointed shoulders rolled and bunched as it assessed them, its head cocked curiously. This one was bald, and its tattered clothes did little to reveal what the vamp might have looked like before the necrosis had really taken hold.

It chittered twice then lunged for them. In the same instant, a string of foreign words poured from Jo in a beautiful lilting tone, almost a song. Kayda had never seen Jo's defensive magic in action before. The ground fissured beneath the feral's feet, throwing it off-kilter. In three quick strides, Kayda had run forward and lopped the monster's head off with a wild swing of her battle-ax. Her rotator cuff issued a twinge of protest. The weapon was borderline too heavy, and she wondered who the massive thing had been made for. Her steady workout regimen had kept her skin in the game a lot longer than she would have lasted otherwise, but when this was all over, she'd need much better training. Brute strength and sheer will could only get her so far.

Monstrous chittering in the distance reminded her that there were three more ferals to contend with. Henri and Grayson were squaring off against a feral that didn't look nearly as necrotic as the last one had. Maybe this was a relatively new turn. When Grayson let loose a blast of water that sent the feral hurtling backward into a brick wall, Kayda bolted for the pair of monsters circling Welsh and Erik.

Welsh had his lightning dagger in hand, swiping at the feral that kept lunging for him. Welsh had excellent aim when it came to throwing the weapon, but hand-to-hand combat was something else. Erik, armed with a spear, waved his weapon in panic, as if trying to shoo away a wild animal.

Why had Jo brought him along? Kayda knew he was well-skilled at having a terrible attitude, but wasn't sure how that would help them tonight. He was going to slow them down. Maybe he'd forced his way into the van, determined to protect his "Lady Josephine" even if he was useless in a fight.

"Stow your fear, Erik!" Jo called, running alongside Kayda. "Try the spell we practiced last week."

"I'm freaking out, Lady Josephine!" Erik screeched, then ineffectually jabbed his spear at the swiping feral. Gone was the overly proper witch who had tried to get in the good graces of Bosworth Hemmingsley. "I can't do this if I'm harnessed!"

What in the world did *that* mean?

Ten more steps and Kayda would be able to help the weasel, but he had to hold it off until then. Welsh wasn't doing much better, the lightning spell on his dagger doing more to keep the vamp away than his swings were.

Jo's lilting voice mingled with the nightmarish growls of the monsters, working up another spell.

Five more steps. Erik cried out as the claws of the feral caught his forearm and tore flesh. As much as it probably hurt, it spurred Erik into attacking rather than weakly fending off impending death. He jabbed his spear at the feral, successfully piercing it in the chest. The magic in the tip seared its flesh, which didn't drop the feral, but stunned it long enough that Jo was able to command the branches of a tree to snake down and wrap their fibrous limbs around the vamp's neck, yanking it upward. Kayda finally reached them, swinging her battle-ax up in a diagonal arc, severing the vamp across the middle. A splash of blackened gore hit the path. The stench was horrendous—like rotting meat soaked in ammonia. Kayda was surprised by how little gore there was, though. Of the organs there were, which plopped onto the ground, they were no longer recognizable as anything Kayda knew of human anatomy.

Erik's voice rose behind Kayda and she spun just as he heaved both arms into the air. Ivy that had been choking the wall of a dilapidated building suddenly shot out like whipping snakes. Tendrils of ivy encircled the wrists, ankles, torso, and neck of the remaining feral and yanked him back toward the wall with such force, it broke bone. Erik shouted another spell and shot his arm out sideways. The vine around the feral's neck cinched tight enough to snap its neck.

Jo stepped in front of Erik, blocking his view of the feral he had strung up on the wall. The pinch of his brow eased when he saw her, and his arms dropped to his sides. "Release your hold," she said gently.

Erik gusted out a breath.

The vines released the feral and it dropped to the ground with a wet thunk. Erik stooped under the weight of so much attention on him. There was a ball of fury residing in this man— fury that fled when he wasn't actively controlling magic.

"You did well, Erik," Jo said. "Every day is a day closer to gaining control. I wouldn't have brought you along if I believed you were a liability. We have much to do, but I'm deeply proud of your progress. You should be, too."

"So touching," drawled a voice from somewhere in the darkness.

Kayda was unnerved that she hadn't heard anyone else out here. She didn't know if that was a result of the elves' magic messing with the natural energy of the preserve, or something else. If she had hair on her arms, it would have stood on end. The voice stirred some primal fear in her that she didn't like one bit.

She pushed her way past the group, putting herself between them and whatever thing lurked in the dark. Gripping the ax handle in both hands, she hoisted it, the blade's magic rippling by her ear.

The chants of the elves sounded in the background, a constant droning reminder that the thing Kayda and her friends had come to stop was still happening. For all they knew, the portal would open to a different timeline and dinosaurs would be pouring into the preserve at any minute.

"I find it very impolite that you killed all my pets," the voice drawled again.

Kayda scanned every inch of the dark preserve in front of her but couldn't make the shadowy patches materialize into a recognizable shape. Nothing crouched behind bushes or trees, no eyes watched her from behind buildings, and nothing hid in the branches above her either.

It was when she focused forward again that the shadows shifted. Not the shadow of a tree moving as the physical leaves themselves were shuffled by the breeze. These shadows moved independently. They oozed forward like a slick of black tar, slowly morphing into the shape of a person. The shadows slipped off until what was left was a man in a white suit and hat. His outfit would have made more sense on a person strolling the humid streets of Havana, not a dilapidated zoo. The theatrics already told her what he was; the wrongness of his existence setting off that primal fear in her confirmed it.

Jo whispered, "Vampire."

It wasn't a pure one, as he had swirls of black swimming in the whites of his eyes. The swirls moved as independently as the shadows had earlier. This was what Marisol had said hybrid vampires looked like—trapped in an in-between place of vampire and feral.

A vampire, hybrid or pure, most assuredly shouldn't have been on Luma soil. The solitary reason ferals could get in on their own was because they'd lost what had remained of their humanity. This guy was undoubtedly human, albeit an undead one.

Kayda eyed the greenhouse building in the distance. Moonlight glinted on its grimy glass surface. Chanting echoed faintly. They had time. Kayda just didn't know how much.

The off-kilter energy in the air grew thicker. She knew the portal was wider, even if she couldn't see it. She felt it. And this asshat stood in her way.

From behind her, in a tone so soft even her draken hearing might have missed it, she heard, "Don't move."

Two things registered at once. First was that it had been Welsh's voice. Second was the whoosh of a dagger bright with lightning whipping past her head.

The hybrid vampire with his hands in the pockets of his white linen suit saw the dagger coming. He clearly noticed the blade sailing toward his neck with deadly accuracy. The vampire didn't make an attempt to dodge the dagger. He simply pulled a necrotic hand free from his pocket and gave a flick of his wrist.

It was a gesture Kayda had seen witches and sorcerers employ when using magic. But vampires didn't have magic. Superior senses, sure. But magic? No.

In a blink, the vampire was gone. Kayda's posture straightened, her brow creasing. The dagger sailed through the spot where the vampire had been, parting what looked like a wafting cloud of undulating black ink. The dagger thunked into a tree. A blink later, and the vampire was back, one hand still in the air.

A breath hitched behind Kayda. "Shadow magic ..." Jo said, tone caught between awe and horror.

"Dark magic," Welsh added. "Magic that requires so much blood, most witches can't master it without having willing assistants who basically become glorified blood bags. The blood has to be as fresh as possible."

"But vampires can't *do* magic," Kayda said, dumbfounded, feeling as if she were stating the obvious.

"There is a lot to be said for tailoring one's diet to achieve the life you want," the vampire said, channeling the spirit of an infomercial salesperson. Then in his usual drawl, he added, "As they say ... you are what you eat."

Goddess above ...

The vampire craned his neck in an attempt to see past Kayda, then delicately sniffed the air. "I smell at least three more witches I could add to my blood bag supply."

Kayda readjusted her grip on the ax's handle and kept a soft bend in her knees, not sure what to expect next. "Like you said: we killed all your pets. There's one of you and six of us. I like our odds better."

The vampire stood stock-still for breath, then thrust both arms above him in a V, reminding Kayda of Snowdrop during the ritual. The hybrid disappeared in another swirl of black, only for the cloud of ink to jerk toward Kayda and her companions in tendrils. It was as if someone stood behind a wall of oil and then had thrown tennis balls at it. Oil-slick globules shot out of the main mass of black, broke free, and then coalesced into vaguely humanoid shapes. There weren't eyes or features—except for mouths of sharp white teeth that gleamed in the imps' dripping-wet faces. Imps made of undulating black tar.

A dozen of them sprung from the spot where the vampire had been, and they wasted no time charging straight for Kayda's group. She awkwardly swung downward with her ax, missing the pair that sprinted for her ankles. They snapped at the air, swiping blindly with their taloned hands. The ax missed again; they were too fast. She frantically stomped her boots, worried the damn things really were going for her ankles. But she couldn't see them anymore. A hissing cry made her jerk her head up and she got her ax back into the air with a wild swing to stop the tar imp that had launched for her face. It sailed over her head without being struck.

She rotated to the left, swinging her ax at the sound of another one by her head, then to the right at the one by her knees. She swung and kicked and spun, her heart hammering. Her companions' yelps of surprise and confusion mingled with her own. With her lungs burning and her mind wild with fear, the distant, logical voice in her head told her she didn't hear any of her friends make contact with the imps. She wasn't a perfect fighter with this ax, but she had good enough aim that she should have hit one of the buggers by now. One of them would have been able to sink teeth into a leg or arm when she was facing the wrong way, but not one of them had touched her.

The moment she figured out what was happening, she heard Erik cry out. The sound snapped her into focus. She pivoted, ignoring the jumping, snapping imps and found Erik a hundred yards away, pinned on the ground as he fought off the hybrid.

Kayda broke into a sprint. Her tunnel vision-fueled anger got her there in seconds. The ax was already swinging before the hybrid registered someone was after him. He disappeared in a cloud of black ink just as Kayda's ax passed through the spot where the vampire had been. Luckily Erik hadn't tried to get up right away, otherwise he would have lost something vital.

"Where are you, you sonofabitch?" Kayda yelled, ax hoisted up by her head again, eyes sweeping the area while keeping close to Erik. "Everyone, stop fighting! The imps are only shadows. He's after the witches!"

Her voice had broken through to some of them, and the sound of ragged breaths around her calmed somewhat. Henri moved beside Jo, then clicked on the industrial flashlight he actually had brought with him. The bright beam of light sliced through an imp thrashing at his feet, dispelling it like smoke on the wind.

The group spun in slow circles, searching for the vampire while Henri cast his flashlight beam in sweeping arcs.

Jo and Erik started spells at the same time, creating two orbs of glowing light. The two witches held the light orbs aloft, where they bobbed above their palms. Kayda shied away from the one Erik held beside her, temporarily blinded as her eyes adjusted to the sudden brightness.

Welsh yelped in surprise somewhere ahead, followed by a crash.

Half-blind, she stumbled forward. "Welsh! Where are you!"

No response.

She rubbed a fist against her eyes, trying to get the phantom glow of Erik's orb light to fade.

"They're going back the way we came!" Henri said. "Welsh is unconscious and the vamp's carrying him off."

As if on cue, the elfin chanting increased in volume. She didn't know where to go: toward the portal or toward Welsh.

Jo grabbed Kayda by the arms. "Leave Welsh to us." She rounded on Erik. "For this situation alone, I'm taking off the harness. You are granted permission to use your magic to its full extent. Do whatever you must to that vampire to save Welsh."

The smile that crossed Erik's face gave Kayda the willies. He took off at a speed that would make an Olympic sprinter proud.

"He's a scary young man," was all Jo said before she ran after him.

Henri stopped in front of Kayda long enough to kiss her, shrugged, and then took off after the witches.

Kayda cut a glance at Grayson. "And you?"

"Let's stop this ritual, yeah? I'll flood the place. You smash in the heads of whoever doesn't drown," he said casually enough.

She cast one last look toward the direction the others went, sent a prayer to the Goddess that they'd get to Welsh in time, and then she and Grayson ran for the greenhouse.

Chapter 37

KAYDA

This time, Kayda opted for the front entrance of the building rather than peeking in through the side windows. She and Grayson hunched low and trod quietly.

With the dials of her hearing adjusted, Kayda was fairly certain all the elves were inside. If any more shadow-magic-wielding hybrids lurked nearby, Kayda wouldn't be able to hear them. And then she and Grayson would be royally fucked. So she decided to go with the glass-half-full outlook: there were no more hybrids, they were going to stop the ritual, and Welsh was going to be fine.

The greenhouse building had a smaller lobby-like area just inside the front entrance. The glass was mostly intact here, but there was debris everywhere—shards of pottery, broken glass, dried plant material. One wrong step on any of it, and it could give them away.

The open doorway of the lobby led into the main room where the elves were, their voices echoing off the enclosed space. The elves were far enough into the room that Kayda couldn't see them from her spot huddled behind the tempered glass. There were far more of them this time. Was that a dozen voices? Two?

She listened for footsteps heading her way. When she didn't hear any, she peered around the open doorway. A cursory glance told her all she needed to know and she pulled back.

Eighteen young elves stood in a circle, their arms to the sky and their eyes closed as they chanted. Floating in the center of them was a swirling vortex of energy. Kayda's nerves were frayed being this close to it. The soul-deep fae part of her recoiled. A blond woman—the one who had been with the teens last time—was here as well, slowly walking around the circle of chanting elves. It seemed as if she were offering words of encouragement, but Kayda couldn't be sure.

The vortex reminded Kayda of an old vanity mirror: oval with ornate edging, the center revealing an image. As Aster had said, it showed a desert-like scene.

Would Grayson blasting the group with a tsunami be enough to disrupt the ritual, making the vortex close before anything could come out? Kayda figured they'd have to try it; she didn't have any better ideas. Casting a glance at Grayson on the other side of the doorway, she gave him an encouraging nod.

Color rose in his cheeks. "It'll work best if you make me mad."

She'd recalled all the things Welsh had said to tick Grayson off, and even the implied things his grouchy grandmother had said to him. Kayda needed him pissed off and quick.

She had it.

She stared at him for a long beat, then fiercely whispered, "Captain Ipram might have been an asshole, but at least he made a name for himself. What have you done? You're a washed-out has-been. Actually, you're a washed-out never-was." Then she lunged at him and slapped him square across the face.

There was too much force behind it, possibly because she

felt genuinely terrible about saying any of that. It knocked him on his ass. Kayda scrambled back to her side of the lobby. When Grayson righted himself, the rage that thrashed in his expression made her consider running in the other direction. She couldn't see storm clouds brewing in his eyes, and his expression wasn't literally thunderous, but it was close.

Steam wafted about him, undulating above his skin like fog on a lake. She genuinely hoped she hadn't pushed his buttons so hard that he turned that fury on her. He finally swung his murderous gaze toward the lobby, and she let out a relieved breath. When he rose to his feet and stalked forward, Kayda took that as her cue to run into the room, ax held high and a battle cry on her lips.

The blond woman holding vigil swung around, her hands already whipping about in the air. Kayda knew now that elves had a powerful hold on nature magic. Even with Kayda's size and a magicked battle-ax, she was no match against magic, so she dove out of the way as Grayson released his torrent of water at the woman.

The elf had magically taken hold of the vines snaking over and through the glass walls, and had commanded them to grab the metal shelving units, yanking them into the middle of the room. Metal scraped across the cement with a horrendous screech that scratched Kayda's nerve endings. Grayson's water magic slammed into the haphazardly constructed barrier, which took the brunt of the attack. Water gushed across the cement floor, soaking the shoes and pant hems of the assembled elf teens. If they noticed, they didn't show it. Their chants hadn't slowed from what Kayda could tell, either.

While Grayson and the woman geared up for another magical showdown, Kayda slunk along the right side of the room, ducking behind and under the scant amount of furniture. She tried to stick to the shadows, made more prominent by the moonlight filtering in through the broken panes in the roof.

Scanning the teens, Kayda finally found Snowdrop. She wore a plain T-shirt and jeans, nothing fancy, but these clothes fit her, somehow making her look older and more confident than she'd looked in the ill-fitting uniform from Yogurt Town. She was in her element here.

Kayda froze. A person—an elf—stood inside the portal. A strikingly handsome elf at that. Kayda couldn't guess how old he was, what with his ethereal elfin nature. He had short jet-black hair, well-defined cheekbones, and his eyes were an icy blue. The determined pull of his brow and his pinched mouth, however, twisted his pretty features into a mask of unchecked fury that made him decidedly less attractive. Scary, even. Kayda had to assume this was Lachlan Shade. If Harlow's mom had known him, he had to be in his fifties at least, but with a face like that, he looked closer to thirty.

She didn't know how much he could see from his side of the portal, but she tried to stay low and out of sight. He currently only had eyes for the teens doing his bidding.

Another blast of water hit the makeshift barrier, sending it to the ground with an almighty crash. The female elf got out of the way in time, but barely. A small wave of water, littered with plant debris, broken plastic containers, and trash, sloshed around the teens' feet. That got Lachlan's attention.

"Blythe!" he bellowed.

Kayda was unnerved sound could travel through the portal even though it wasn't fully open yet. She could currently see half his torso, but as the spinning vortex slowly opened wider and wider, more of Lachlan and his surroundings were revealed. The world behind him still looked bleak.

"Blythe, what on earth is happening over there?" He chuckled darkly. "I suppose I mean that literally, don't I?"

Blythe was too busy to reply, using her magic to throw whips of vines at Grayson. He used his magic to knock the grabbing tendrils away, even managing to freeze some of them, which crashed to the ground and shattered, bits of leaves and twigs caught in small shards of ice. But his energy was depleting rapidly, and Blythe looked like she was just getting started.

Lachlan angled his head to the side. "Is that an elemental? Oh, oh! Add him to the mix, Blythe. His energy will help hasten this along."

"I'm *trying*," Blythe ground out, her arms a frenzy of movement as she kept up her relentless attack on Grayson with her commanded vines. She reminded Kayda of a lion tamer at a circus.

Kayda studied the circle of teens, knowing her efforts needed to be concentrated there. She knelt behind a stack of plywood propped against a shelving unit. The dim lighting would aid in keeping her shielded, but as soon as she made the decision to attack, she'd be out in the open.

Lachlan grew frustrated with the battle Blythe waged, and took a few steps back. "Too much time has already been wasted. It's only a matter of when more will show up to try and stop us. I will take the first one."

"It's too soon!" Blythe shouted.

While she was distracted, Grayson threw a volley of golf-ball-sized chunks of ice at Blythe. They hit her more than they missed. Blythe howled, stumbling away, arms shielding her face.

Lachlan threw his head back, his arms in the air, offering a chant similar solely in cadence to the unending one pouring from the teens. Though Kayda had no idea what they were saying, she'd heard the chant droning in the background long enough now to know that what Lachlan spoke was something else. A few of the words sounded familiar in an abstract kind of way. Was this a spell spoken in the unidentified language?

Perhaps the language of the people who lived in the bleak world Lachlan had been trapped in for nearly three decades ...

Bright streaks of white-blue magic erupted from the central portal, each one hitting a teen. The teens didn't seem to notice. The volume of their chants increased, as if the magic had given them a jolt of energy.

Blythe let out a furious scream, spinning toward Grayson. Red welts dotted her arms, and the skin around an eye had purpled. He stood, panting and woozy, clearly seconds from passing out from overexerting himself. A great gust of wind slammed into him, lifting him off his feet, across the room, and through a section of glass. He landed in the front lobby area, out of view.

Kayda's heart lurched into her throat. *Oh, Goddess!*

She tried to pick out the sound of him groaning or shifting among the broken glass. But either he wasn't moving or she couldn't hear him over the cacophony of voices. Her heartbeat thrummed in her ears.

Blythe had her hands on her knees, worn out from her last assault. "Hurry it up, then!"

Lachlan shouted something from inside the portal. His eyes were open, one hand angled toward a teenage boy. The streak of magic that linked the boy to the portal glowed brighter than any of the other seventeen tendrils of magic. Another stream of not-Elfin poured from Lachlan's mouth.

A glowing orb of magic encased the boy, as if he were caught in a giant hamster ball. Lachlan raised his arm slowly, and with it went the boy, his arms stretched to the sky, chant matching the tone and cadence of the others, as if in a trance.

Kayda, in her heart of hearts, held onto the hope that Lachlan truly wanted to bring these elves home. That he'd found a way and wanted to share his discovery. That all the secrecy was because this was an elf-only mission, leaving the rest of the fae population behind.

That hope died when Lachlan gave another shout, the magic orb glowed to a blinding brightness, and the boy's back arched. The boy was no longer chanting. His mouth stretched wide in a silent scream. His body hit the ground with a thud, passing through the hamster ball of light. The orb of magic yanked itself into the portal. The vortex abruptly widened a couple of inches.

The very air around Kayda shuddered. It felt heavy on her skin, like humidity. Even her battle-ax seemed off, the rippling blue magic glitching erratically.

A scrabbling sounded above her. She caught the eye shine of some wild animal near the roof. It had probably been lured here by the curiosity of what was causing the off-kilter magic. She wanted to wave it off. Every living thing with legs or wings needed to get the hells out of here.

Lachlan gave another shout. Bolstered by his success, Lachlan selected two teens at once. They lifted into the air, encircled by orbs of light. Arched backs. Silent screams. Twin thuds. Magic was slurped into the portal like liquid through a straw. The portal grew.

Shit!

Her ax issued a bright burst of magic, then went dark altogether.

Camila had said portals made with blood magic required a sacrifice. Was that what was happening here? Lachlan didn't plan to bring these kids through to his side. Lachlan wanted to get out. *He* was coming *here*. And he planned to murder eighteen elf teens to do it.

Worst savior ever.

The totality of Kayda's plan was to charge into the fray, screaming. Disrupting the circle of teens had to at least slow this down, right? Though now that Lachlan had started sacrificing the kids, having fewer of them chanting hadn't made a difference. The portal actually appeared to continue widening even between the sacrifices.

Getting a firm hold on the handle of her now-dormant ax, she got into a sprinter's lunge, ready to dart forward, only to come up short when Aster appeared in her line of sight.

"Not yet," Aster said. "Your friend with the water is alive. We gave him some herbs to wake him up and get his magic replenished faster. He's going to hurt like hells in the morning, but he's okay for now. He's waiting for his cue."

Kayda stared dumbly at her. "What cue?" she whispered.

Aster held up a tiny finger, her head cocked.

A whistle—soft yet high-pitched—made its way to Kayda's ears. Lachlan didn't appear to have heard it. But he did hear the flood of sound that came next. Tapping, scratching, thudding, fluttering, clawing, screeching. Bats and insects poured through the roof like a cloud. Foxes, raccoons, and opossums crawled in through the broken panes in the walls. Fae creatures came too. Gnomes with pointy hats on their heads, and sharp objects clutched in their fists. Furry beasts who ran on two legs and had the angry look of a gremlin about them. And hundreds upon hundreds of pixies.

"That cue," Aster said, beaming.

Blythe shrieked as she was attacked from all sides. She wildly thrashed with magic and flailing arms.

Kayda sprang out of her hiding place, running toward the portal. She had no idea what she was going to do when she got there, but she couldn't let Lachlan succeed.

The problem was, while chaos had descended on the greenhouse, Lachlan had increased his efforts. Eight elf teens remained. The portal had opened wide enough that the elf had been revealed from head to knee. Did it have to open wide enough for him to walk through effortlessly? She picked up the pace, diving for Snowdrop, calling the girl's name in a futile attempt to break her of Lachlan's hold. Kayda was mere inches from the girl when something ensnared Kayda's ankles and yanked her backward. She hit the ground hard on her stomach, losing the ax. Wind knocked from her lungs, black spots swam in her vision. The taste of copper flooded her mouth and she suspected she'd bitten her tongue.

Groaning, she flipped onto her back, finding her ankles enveloped in thorn-covered vines. Before she could pull them free, more circled her wrist, yanking her arm sharply to the side.

Then she was hoisted off her feet entirely. She was trussed up and hung upside down from the ceiling, blood rushing to her head. The thorny branches dug through her clothes and into her skin. Her arms were pinned behind her as she spun slowly in her stabby cocoon, her view angled away from the fight. She craned her neck, finding four newly arrived elves. One of them had strung her up. She supposed she'd been deemed the worst threat, and they got her out of the way while they fended off the easier target: the herd of smaller creatures. Except these smaller creatures were downright vengeful. The elves quickly found themselves fighting against swarms of biting pixies, swooping bats, stinging insects, and nipping wild animals.

"About damn time!" Blythe called out to her fellow elves, fending off a wild boar who charged at her, tusks seeking flesh. "We have to keep them away from the kids!"

Where the hell was Grayson? Aster said he was awake.

"Grayson!" Kayda screamed as loud as her lungs would allow. "Get your bitch-ass up!"

A battle cry rang out. Kayda slumped in relief. She thrashed in her bindings, getting herself twisted toward the front entrance in time to see a pair of coyotes lope into the building in front of Grayson. Thankfully he'd determined the attacking animals had Blythe occupied—especially when a maniacal gnome scaled up her back like a spider monkey and clapped its hands over her eyes. While she thrashed, a fox wound itself about her ankles, making her lose her balance. She hit the ground hard.

Oh, they were going to tear her to pieces. Kayda looked away.

Grayson sprinted past Blythe, hands already whipping about as he went. Five teens remained. The portal revealed Lachlan from head to shin.

The four newly arrived elves had more energy at their disposal, but they were losing the fight. Nature had turned against them. Grayson turned a gush of water on the teen nearest him, knocking the girl off her feet and washing her across the cement floor. The water had done its job to pull her from her trance. Unfortunately, the thing that had stopped her momentum across the room had been the body of one of her friends. She screamed bloody murder.

Instead of distracting Lachlan, this pissed him off. He locked eyes on Grayson, shouted something, and shot his hand forward. The same tendril of magic that had been attached to each of the teens attached itself to Grayson now, pulling him forward as if by an invisible rope. An orb of glowing white light engulfed him and he passed out, suspended in the air. Lachlan cackled triumphantly, pulling the orb toward the portal and placing him in the position vacated involuntarily by the still-screaming elf girl.

"Shut her up!" Lachlan bellowed.

One of the elves broke away from the attacking animals long enough to cross to the girl and backhand her across the face. The shock of it cut off her tears. "You get back into formation or I'll put you there!"

The girl shakily got to her feet.

A trio of gremlins launched at the slap-happy elf, one of them sinking its needle teeth into the elf's neck. The girl screamed again, but this time she had the sense to run from the melee. She skirted the battles and sprinted out the front door. Well, that was one saved, at least. Kayda prayed the girl would tell whoever she could that Lachlan Shade hadn't opened a portal to save anyone but himself.

There were three teens left, including Snowdrop. Kayda wiggled and squirmed, making the thorny branches cut into her even deeper. The blood rushing to her head wasn't helping matters, her vision blurring.

Now that Blythe was down for the count, the animals and fae creatures who had contributed to her demise swarmed across the cement toward the remaining elves.

"Aster!" Kayda yelled.

It took the pixie a few seconds to find her. "What you doing up here? We need you down there! Grayson is in real trouble. C'mon!"

She flew away.

"Aster!"

The pixie reappeared. "I think the portal magic scrambled my brain." She giggled.

Thorns suddenly poked painfully into Kayda's arms, as if the vines had shifted into the coiling body of a boa constrictor, slowly squeezing her to death. She did an upside-down crunch to get a better look at what was going on at her feet. Dozens of pixies had covered Kayda's body, like flies on honey. It took her a moment to realize they were chewing through her bonds. And it was a few moments after that that she realized the magic-drunk pixies had forgotten about gravity sand that Kayda didn't have wings. The vines gave way. Kayda managed to flip herself in the air so she was falling feetfirst instead of headfirst. A shelving unit broke her fall, the sturdy plastic buckling and snapping under her weight. Something in her foot snapped. She'd heard it as much as felt it. The ankle on the other foot rolled.

She stumbled out of the debris, woozy from the blood rushing back into the rest of her body. Her stomach lurched from both dizziness and the excruciating ache in her feet. She willed herself to give in to the pain later. Finding her battle-ax on the ground not far from where she landed, she hobbled over, snatched it up, and staggered into the chaos.

Bats and pixies swooped and dove around the portal like a tempest, obstructing Lachlan's view. The bats couldn't cross the portal and Lachlan couldn't get out, but they were doing enough to stall Lachlan on siphoning the magic from the teen elf boy he had in the air. Grayson hung unconscious in the orb of light while Snowdrop, entranced, repeated the chant for the umpteenth time.

The elf who had been taken down by the gremlins was being absolutely slaughtered by a pack of furious gnomes armed with pitchforks. They were arguably scarier than the ferals.

The remaining gremlins, a few foxes, three gnomes, and a blood-soaked wild boar rounded on an elf. She was covered in scratches and her hair was a wild mess—a chunk of it ripped from her scalp. Blood leaked from a gash in her temple. Her magic had kept most of the animals at bay until now, and the evidence of the slain creatures lay at her feet. She weakly flicked a wrist, tapping into her last reserves of magic to fend off the beasts.

When nothing happened, she simply held her hands out, placating. "Please ..." she begged, a sob catching in her throat. The pack of animals advanced a few paces as the elf stutter-stepped away, backing herself into a darkened corner. "We didn't mean any harm."

The boar shook its massive head. The foxes yipped. A

raccoon launched off a windowsill, landing on her back, claws out. The animals descended on her. Kayda looked away from this one too, knowing there was nothing she could have done to save the elf anyway. The elves had violated the preserve for the last time: the residents had had enough.

Though the bats and pixies had done what they could to stop Lachlan, a boy was drained and dropped to the ground like all the others. All that remained were Snowdrop and Grayson.

"Draken ..." Lachlan said, craning his neck to see past the spiraling wings and limbs.

She knew this monster had left these two for a reason. Although he'd been considerably busy murdering teenagers, Lachlan had figured out that these were the two who meant something to Kayda. What did he want to do now, negotiate?

"Pixies ..." Kayda said, her breath labored, "you can ease up."

It took a few seconds, but the pixies and bats eventually dispersed. The pixies flanked Kayda on either side while the bats moved upward, winging erratically in the moonlight pouring in through the roof.

Lachlan was revealed from head to ankles now. He gave Kayda an assessing appraisal. "I only need one of them to get through. You won't have time to save them both. You make a choice, and then you and I can have a chat in person, hmm?"

Kayda tightened her jaw and the hold on the ax's handle. Her boots squelched in the muck beneath her. Blood, viscera, flesh—she couldn't be sure. The tang of blood and the musk of wild animals was thick in the air. The pain radiating from her feet clawed up her legs. "What do you want?"

"Chat later," he said. "Choose now. I'm rather curious which one you'll select. The young, innocent elf who had no idea what she had agreed to? Or your friend the elemental?"

Kayda eyed Snowdrop to her right, chanting away like the

dutiful disciple she was, and then Grayson to her left, suspended unconscious in midair.

"Teenagers are so susceptible, aren't they?" Lachlan asked, head cocked. "I do like working with teenagers. They all feel so misunderstood. They don't fit in anywhere. Boo-hoo. It was easy to convince so many of the awkward ones that there was a place where they belonged. A secret club full of elves just like them who would get to experience life as they were meant to. My poor sister has been my liaison between this shithole of a world the Collective banished me to, and Earth. She's been working tirelessly to get as many of these young, innocent elves on our side so I could tap into their raw power to feed to the portal. Your little elf friend had no clue she was destined to be sacrificed for me. It's still a beautiful, selfless act even if she was unaware of it, don't you think?"

Kayda's gaze flitted between the two. He'd deliberately used the word "innocent" more than once. Lachlan was doing this so that no matter who she chose, she would be gutted by the loss of the other.

"Tick-tock, draken," Lachlan snapped.

He shouted the same word he used before every sacrifice started. The tendril of magic linking Grayson and Snowdrop brightened. He was going to pull the magic from them both at the same time. She had to decide. Now.

She really hated this asshole!

On ruined feet, she ran.

Chapter 38

KAYDA

Kayda tackled Grayson to the ground. Her twisted ankle throbbed in time to her heartbeat. They'd landed in a heap, Kayda half on top of him. She hoped she hadn't crushed the guy.

He groaned. Alive! He was still alive.

As she scrambled onto her feet, her stomach roiled. She shook her head. Pain later. She turned toward the portal, keeping Grayson to her back. Snowdrop hung in the air, encased in the orb of white-blue magic. Injured or not, Kayda knew she couldn't get there in time.

Snowdrop's back arched, her mouth stretched wide in a silent scream like all the others just before Lachlan siphoned their life force. Kayda was debating running for it anyway when a ball of light nearly as large as the one Snowdrop was in hurled through the air. It slammed into Snowdrop, knocking her free from her enclosure and into the muck on the floor. The ball of light burst apart, revealing hundreds of pixies, their wings shimmering with a silver light. Their triumphant giggles reminiscent of tinkling wind chimes.

Lachlan howled in frustration.

Thank the Goddess ...

Kayda sank to her knees, relieved and exhausted and a little delirious. She crawled over to Grayson, who lay on his back. Bloody, muddy water soaked into the back of his pants, his shirt, and his long ponytail. But his chest rose and fell steadily. She didn't know how badly he'd been hurt. She needed to get him out of here—possibly to a hospital. If there had been any pain-killing properties in the herbs the pixies had fed him earlier, he was going to be in a world of agony when they wore off.

The air gave another great shudder. The bats squeaked, the gnomes chittered, and the foxes yipped. A swell of excitable pixie chatter set Kayda's nerves on end.

A furious roar—that hadn't come from one of the animals.

Kayda watched in horror as Lachlan threw himself at the portal shoulder first, as if he intended to crash through it like it was a plate-glass door. A stream of not-Elfin poured from him as he did it. The portal had started to slowly close again once the last of the sacrifices had been removed. Kayda could only see him from head to shins.

The edge of the oval-shaped portal undulated and pulsed like the frothy waves of a turbulent sea. It suddenly flared so bright, Kayda had to shield her eyes. Even with her vision blocked by her own arm, she could tell the room illuminated to the point it chased away the shadows from every corner.

Lachlan screamed again—some mix of determination and anger.

Kayda's breath hitched when she heard what sounded like something splashing into a puddle. She unshielded her face. Lachlan, halfway on this side of the portal, pulled his head and torso out of his old world. The portal magic clung to him like plastic wrap, but he shucked off the filaments. The portal grew smaller and smaller by the second. Maybe it would slam shut and sever him down the middle.

Kayda managed to get to her feet, her knees threatening to give out. She scoured the area for the battle-ax, finding it in a stinking puddle nearby. She was covered in small cuts, something was seriously wrong with one of her feet, and her stomach was sick from the cloying smell of murky blood coating the floor and her clothes. She couldn't imagine how many types of bacteria were burrowing their way into her wounds.

She staggered forward a couple of feet, got a firm hold on the ax's handle, and steeled herself. Channeling a shot-putter, she spun a few times, and once she got enough momentum, hurled the ax at the portal. The ax might not have been as crackling with magic as it had been at the start of this, but it was still wickedly sharp. Something inside her foot shifted, issuing a stomach-churning crunch. She collapsed to a knee, watching as the heavy ax rocketed away from her, its path true.

She held her breath, hoping the ax would kill Lachlan while he was distracted, but one of his hands shot up at the last second and a gust of wind knocked the ax off course. It sailed over the portal and crashed into unseen debris.

"You didn't actually think that would *work*, did you, draken?" Lachlan asked, not even deigning to look at her.

The air gave another heave, like a dog shaking its fur of water. The portal closed faster now. The animals and fae creatures that remained had begun inching toward the vortex. They were as tired and weary as Kayda was, but they'd stay to fight.

Lachlan moved faster, continuing his stream of spells uttered in not-Elfin as he struggled to pull free from the portal magic that attempted to keep him in his prison.

His torso and head were out. The portal was no wider than a beach ball now. His other leg came free. He shouted the spell, frantic, unable to pull away from the clinging magic. It was as if something on the other side had him by the wrist, playing tug-of-war. Kayda prayed it would wholly suck him back in.

She was out of her depth when it came to magic. She hated feeling this helpless. Camila had said a portal opened by blood magic needed a sacrifice to close it. Kayda highly doubted she could just chuck an unsuspecting raccoon into the portal to end this. What she needed was a sorcerer. All she had was one elf teen, a nearly unconscious wind witch, a handful of preserve residents, and her own strength—which waned by the second.

Even though she could barely stand, she'd help the animals and fae creatures take Lachlan down if the portal magic didn't do it for them. That was the best she could do, as much as it pained her to admit it.

Lachlan switched languages. His arm and fingers carved shapes in the air that fused and formed into a circle. A glowing ring of runes. Lachlan had been trained in sorcery? He shot his free hand into the air, sending the glowing circle of runes upward, like tossing a translucent coin. The branch of a tree slammed through the glass ceiling. Kayda grabbed Grayson by the shirt and hauled him backward with her. A glass shard the size of her head crashed point first where Grayson had been, shattering on impact.

The branch wound around Lachlan's waist and bodily yanked him out of the grasp of the portal. Lachlan let loose a howl of agony. The vortex slammed shut. Lachlan's arm from the elbow down was gone. Kayda saw no blood.

Kayda ran for him. The elf forcibly raised his remaining hand, sending a rune circle at her.

How in the hells did he cast that so fast—while one-handed? was all she could think before the runes hit her square in the chest, sending her careening backward and over the body of a dead teen. The elf's eyes were stuck open, her mouth wide in a scream.

"I've had years to do nothing but practice, draken." Lachlan's confident words were belied by his exhausted, weak tone.

As she struggled to sit up, shaking off the liquid of unknown origins from her arms and hands, Lachlan scanned the room. He cocked his head at Kayda. "Did you dispose of my vampire as well? Blythe said he'd sensed witches in the zoo and went to investigate. Foolish man and his cravings. They're like potato chips, he says: can't have just one."

"Yes," Kayda said, not knowing if that was true. For all she knew, all of her friends, even Henri, were dead. The hybrid vampire with his unholy shadow magic could be on his way back right now, his phantom shadow imps bounding around his feet.

"Ah, you're not sure then. I'll hold out hope that my oldest friend made it through," Lachlan said.

"What about your *sister*?" Kayda asked, briefly eyeing the ruined corpse that had once been Blythe.

"I appreciate her hard work all these years," he said, clutching his severed arm to his chest. There was an unhealthy sheen to his forehead, which hopefully suggested internal damage as well. "She kept the vision alive while I was trapped. Our blood bond allowed me to make that first connection through a portal. She worked so hard to recruit these young elves to sacrifice their lives for my return."

"You lied to us!" a choked voice cried.

Snowdrop was alive then.

"Omission isn't technically lying," Lachlan said, then pursed his lips. Maybe he'd pass out and Kayda could hobble over there and sever a few more limbs with her ax, should she find a reserve of energy to wield the bulky thing.

She froze, a new sound reaching her ears. A sound she silently implored Lachlan not to hear: the rhythmic *thump, thump* of dozens of cat paws. The werecats had finally arrived.

They'd be here in under a minute. Kayda had to keep him occupied until then. It seemed fitting that he'd done everything he could to come to Earth, and then would wind up in a different kind of prison. He wiped his hand across his sweaty brow. He didn't look too good. Perhaps the delirium of pain would keep him talking.

"Your oldest friend is a vampire?" Kayda asked.

"Oh yes. Well before my banishment. The best friendships are ones built on mutual goals, don't you think?" Lachlan asked, his eyelids drooping as he listed slightly. "He'll be fine, I'm sure. He's even more integral to the Restoration than Blythe was, Goddess rest her soul."

Thirty more seconds and the cats would be here.

"What's the Restoration?" Kayda tried.

But Lachlan wasn't listening, his head cocked like a curious dog. "Ah! Draken, you try to distract me while the cavalry arrives! Nice try. Let's see here ..."

With his severed arm clutched to his chest, he shouted the words of another spell. Words that started lackluster and then gradually rose in pitch and volume.

"Oh no ..." Snowdrop moaned, confirming Kayda's suspicion that this one had been in Elfin. Snowdrop covered her head, curling into the fetal position.

She clearly knew what was coming even if Kayda didn't, so Kayda braced herself.

Wind whistled through the broken panes in the building, filling the greenhouse with what sounded like the howls of anguished ghosts. The wind turned gale-force, kicking up the water, tossing the fallen bodies of fae creatures, wild animals, and elves like debris in a tornado. Because that was what this was: a localized tornado whose wind whipped with such force, it lifted shelves, trash, and bodies. Lachlan stood in the eye of it, twirling his good arm in a slow circle by his head. He looked even weaker and paler than he had before, but the fact that he could conjure this much magic while in this state said a lot about how much he'd been "practicing."

The wind whipped at Kayda's clothes and she threw herself over Grayson, partly to have something solid to hold onto, and partly to keep him from getting lifted into the air.

"Tell your Collective that Lachlan Shade has done the impossible, draken!" he shouted over the furiously whipping winds. "And tell them that I will do it again when they least expect it. They will pay for what they did to me."

He suddenly jabbed his fist toward the ground rather than spinning it by his head. His tornado responded in kind, carrying him up toward the ceiling. The bats that had been circling and swooping were long gone. The spinning winds took Lachlan through the broken roof and to locations Kayda couldn't even guess at.

The howling wind abruptly stopped, the silence ringing in Kayda's ears. Bodies and debris splashed back into the water. Once everything settled, the remaining animals and fae creatures sensed the approaching werecats and began to scatter. They scurried up walls and out the front entrance. Kayda wanted to call out a thank-you, but exhaustion had slammed into her. Cold dirty water soaked into the butt of her pants. She shivered.

Bodies littered the ground. The adult elves with their torn-apart torsos and tattered faces. The sixteen elf teenagers who lay silently screaming. Kayda hoped the escaped elf girl was okay.

The eighteenth elf slowly made her way toward Kayda now, sidestepping friends, enemies, and the creatures of the preserve who had died protecting their home.

Snowdrop was alive now because Lachlan had sensed the connection, no matter how tenuous, between the elf girl and Kayda.

That chance encounter in the forested area of the Indie, when they'd fought over that coyote carcass, had ultimately saved Snowdrop's life. Given the way sobs wracked her body, tears cutting lines through the dirt and grime on her face, Kayda wasn't sure Snowdrop was happy to be left standing. Survivor's guilt was sure to be a debilitating problem for her in the days, weeks, and months to come.

The werecats barreled through the front entrance just as Snowdrop reached Kayda. Most of the guards stayed in cat form, but a few seamlessly shifted from feline to human, stalking toward Kayda, Snowdrop, and Grayson, correctly sensing that the trio were the sole survivors.

Snowdrop sobbed, wringing her hands as she told the cats about Lachlan's successful portal-opening, as well as which direction he'd gone. Half a dozen cats sprinted back out of the building.

Kayda and Grayson helped each other to their feet. He swayed dangerously to one side and a werecat caught him before the elemental hit the ground again, as Kayda was in no position to help anyone. She stood there, going numb all over as she took in the horrible stench and sight of the place.

Someone was talking to her. A werecat, maybe. She was going into shock, she thought. Some protective mental place her body was sealing herself inside to protect her from the reality that she hadn't been able to stop this. Sixteen elf teens were dead because she couldn't figure out what to do. The ache in her feet was making its way up her legs again, seizing muscles in her thighs and quads. She'd collapse soon.

And there was the note of disquiet that had been in the back of her mind, clawing its way to the surface now: her friends might be dead. She was too scared to ask anyone. Because that would be her fault, too.

"K-K-Kayda?"

She spun toward the sound so quickly, she was woozy.

Stumbling into the room, looking absolutely awful, were Erik, Jo, and Henri. Henri had Welsh in his arms.

Welsh looked the worst of all of them, blood caking his shirt. A bandage encircled his neck, bright red blood slowly seeping into the fabric. The vampire must have bitten him.

Her hands shook and she clasped them in front of her to stop their trembling. Her friends made their way toward her, which she was grateful for, because she couldn't move.

"You good, witch?" she asked when the bedraggled group reached her own.

"Mostly," he croaked, sounding like a man with a lifetime habit of smoking a pack of cigarettes a day.

"The vampire nearly choked him to death," Jo said. "We're lucky we reached him when we did." She cast a horrified look about the greenhouse. "As horrific as our experience was, I believe you had it worse."

"I owe a life debt to Erik," Welsh managed. "He might be the most ruthless fighter I've ever met."

Kayda studied the small-statured man with his vaguely punchable face. His usually detestable demeanor was gone though, and shining behind his brown eyes was a calculated malice she'd never seen in the man before tonight.

Erik took a couple of steps forward and held something aloft, his expression triumphant. Kayda stood corrected: it wasn't bloodthirsty gnomes who were scarier than ferals. It was Erik. Because in his fist was a handful of thick black hair. And below that was the severed head of the hybrid vampire.

Lachlan Shade wasn't going to be happy about that.

Kayda chuckled softly, then giggled, then was laughing so hard she got a stitch in her side. She was vaguely aware of Henri putting Welsh down, who leaned on Jo for support.

Henri was suddenly standing before Kayda, his arms out. Her laughter slowly dried up, and her bottom lip trembled. She fiercely threw her arms around Henri's middle, burying her face in the crook of his neck. She grabbed a fistful of his shirt, pressing her knuckles against his back. He smelled like blood and wet earth and something tangy and stomach-curdling, but notes of his scent were there too. Her shoulders relaxed, the tight ball of tension in her chest loosening.

And then for the first time since her grandmother died, Kayda Verdan wept.

Chapter 39
HARLOW

It took a long while for me to be able to get up without feeling like I was going to vomit. The sword's magic was no joke, especially when coursing through my non-fae body. Caspian told me that the ax had done the same thing for him as the sword did for me: shared its magic and gave him insights into his enemy. It helped keep him two seconds ahead of the elf who had done everything in her power to take Caspian down. Letting the ax go had left Caspian woozy too, but since he was magic-touched, what equated to magical withdrawal hadn't been as bad for him.

Once I'd been stable enough to be upright on my own, and my brain started working again, I remembered something. As I made my way across the Winchells' ruined lawn, I pinched my nose and covered my mouth to minimize the intake of the foul odor that was Domino. Sidestepping his body, I found what I was looking for a few feet away. And mercifully it hadn't been incinerated by Alice's inferno: the metal box the sword's twin had been in. The bottom of the box had been lined with white paper. I wanted to see if anything was below it.

Caspian and the sword waited as I examined the box. The

white paper was softer than I expected, and it hadn't merely been a cushion for the sword. Unfolding the large rectangle, I stared down at a beautifully hand-drawn map—with Bernard's signature in the corner.

I glanced up at Caspian, grinning. With a grin to match mine, he held out a hand and hoisted me to my feet. Leaving the now-empty box in the grass, we hurried back to the house. Well, the sword hurtled, Caspian hurried, and I stagger-walked like a drunken sailor.

Caspian had gotten good at figuring out when I needed coddling and when I needed to be left alone. Currently, I was in my stubborn "I'll just walk it off" mode, and he knew it. If he had tried to offer me a piggyback ride into the house, I would have slugged him.

He already had the map laid out on the dining room table by the time I hobbled in. The sword's still-dormant twin lay on the table, too. I wasn't sure when someone had brought it in. It had been wiped clean of orc blood, at least. Shane and Alice's half-eaten turkey sandwiches sat on the table. I hoped their baby arrived soon if only so Shane didn't have to keep eating ten times a day. Welsh would be in heaven here.

Caspian popped his head up from where he'd been hidden behind Shane. He cocked a brow in question.

I waved him off.

He returned his focus to the map.

"So what are we looking at here, exactly?" I asked, coming around the other side of the table to stand beside Alice. She looked miserable and sweaty, but I resisted the urge to pull out a chair for her, because if I did, I'd be the one getting slugged.

"It appears to be part of a reservoir in Paso Robles, California," Caspian said. "Grizzly Bend, Dry Creek, and Christmas Cove are all labeled. 'Lake Nacimiento' is at the top here," he added, pointing to the neat all-caps handwriting.

Shane grabbed his phone off the table. "Can you spell Nacimiento?"

Caspian obliged.

A few seconds later, Shane whistled. "The nickname for the lake is the Dragon." He turned his phone to show us.

My brows arched. The aerial view most certainly looked as if a dragon had been cut into the earth. The creeks Caspian had named resembled a swooping tail and back. Two large creeks made up the dragon's pair of hanging arms, while a lake, dam, and marina that all bore the Nacimiento name made up the dragon's curved head.

On the drawn map, near the start of the dragon's tail, a large red question mark had been placed near "Oak Shores."

"Can we keep this, Shane?" Caspian asked.

"I tell you what," he said. "If you leave that journal here, you can keep the sword, too. Frankly, if it mysteriously wakes up and is as ... volatile as yours, I'd rather not have it here with a baby on the way."

My sword, hovering above the bowl of wax apples, buzzed softly in response. I supposed it agreed that it wasn't baby-friendly. That, or it knew something about its twin that we didn't. If that was the case, I didn't want to know. Not yet, anyway.

"Deal," I said.

We stood on the porch, staring out at the absolute mess on the Winchells' lawn. Because of his connection to Kensey due to being an almost-alum of the academy, Shane suggested he call the hub's hotline designated for "fae cleanup." He was sure he could get someone by to help without them asking too many questions. I wasn't so sure.

"I have an idea," I said, and pulled out my phone, selecting a number from my recent call log.

The woman answered with a cautious, "Hi, Harlow."

"Hey, Fiona. Remember when you gave us information on how to track down an orc mob boss and you felt real guilty about telling us anything and then instructed us not to die?"

Fiona hesitated. "Yes?"

"Well, I have good news for you!" I said. "Not only are we still alive, Domino isn't."

She spluttered a laugh. "Holy shit. Felix wasn't lying when he said you were more than capable of taking care of yourselves."

I decided to leave out the fact that we would have been quite dead and/or turned into troll love slaves had a cranky, pregnant fire elemental not saved our asses. "Got any suggestions on how we can get rid of the bodies of an orc, an elf, and three trolls? Preferably by three p.m.? Several mundanes will be descending on this place soon for a class."

"Crap. I completely forgot about that ..." Shane muttered.

Fiona whistled. "We need to meet up for drinks sometime so you can tell me this story."

"Only if you promise to tell me any embarrassing stories about Felix," I said.

"Oh, I've got tons of those," Fiona said with a laugh. "I can get a cleanup crew there in an hour. Since it's Domino, I'm pretty sure we can make sure the bodies and the paperwork disappear. He's been a thorn in our sides for years. I'm a little scared about which scumbag is going to take his place, but I'm not sorry to hear he's gone."

"You're welcome?"

A smile was evident in her voice when she said, "Text me the address and I'll get it taken care of."

I thanked her, disconnected the call, and then texted her the address to Winchell Forge. "All done," I said. "Bounty hunters and maybe a few werecats will be here soon."

"I wonder if I have enough time to prepare a thank-you pot roast," Alice mused.

Shane grimaced but morphed it into a supportive smile when his wife looked at him for approval.

In addition to handing over Margaret's journal, I gave the Winchells a few dragon scales. Alice made us take a couple of turkey sandwiches. We promised to keep in touch, exchanged contact information, hugs, and well-wishes for the new baby, then we piled back into the SUV. My sword and the ax touched blades in farewell before the sword flew into the back seat through the busted-out back window. I placed the sword's twin on one of the back seats. With any luck, my sword wouldn't hang its blade out like a panting dog on the drive and get us pulled over.

I felt bad leaving them with such a mess, even with help on the way. Alice had assured me that if the cleanup crew took too long for her liking, their sentient ax could "hack up the corpses" and Alice could set them on fire.

I'd offered Shane an alarmed frown at that, but all he did was shrug.

We passed yet another body on the way out, his large green feet sticking out of a bush. Which explained why the weapons had come back covered in blood after that first perimeter check at the initial hint of danger.

It was almost 8 p.m. by the time we got back to the VHoA warehouse. We'd stopped twice along the way. Once for the restroom, and once for food. We'd gotten a large pizza to go and had sat in a park to eat. We'd done what we could during the first stop to freshen up a bit. Which mostly consisted of washing off my face, neck, and arms in the grimy gas station sink. Upon first washing, the water swirling down the drain was a murky reddish-brown. I wrangled my sweaty, dirty curls into a bun, but couldn't do much about my clothes. My tank top was splattered with spots of dried blood of various shades. Luckily it was a black tank and not a white one, otherwise someone might have informed the police.

I was sore all over by then, once the adrenaline had finally ebbed. I tried not to fidget in my seat too often, as every movement elicited a twinge of pain. Caspian didn't seem to be faring much better, but he complained far less than I did.

We'd examined the sword during the lunch break. Caspian couldn't find any obvious damage to the dragon scales on the hilt or the runes on the blade. It turned out that the sword had a finite well of energy after all, just like we did. After some rest, we'd all be back in tip-top shape.

The VHoA warehouse was packed, and the energy of the place was nearly palpable as I climbed out of the SUV. My sword's twin was still dormant, so we left it in the back seat.

Phones rang and buzzed with messages. People clacked away at their keyboards. A large group, my mom and Soren among them, stood around a map spread out on the picnic table we'd been sitting at last night.

My mom sensed our approach and waved us over. She pursed her lips as she took in how disheveled we were. I'd called her on the way back to give her a rough estimate of our arrival, but I hadn't gone into any details about the afternoon. "When you said you'd run into trouble, I was imagining a flat tire."

I offered her a deliberately overly wide smile. "What's all the fuss about?"

That got her attention back on the task at hand. "Well, the news from Luma is that Lachlan Shade is trying to open a portal tonight. Kayda says hi, by the way."

I blinked at her.

"Elsewhere, we're getting reports from all over the country

about veil breaches by ferals. None as bad as whatever is happening in Luma, but enough to stretch resources, which I'm guessing is the point."

"Do you think Lachlan can do it?" I asked, remembering the elf back at the Winchells' who had said the elves' future lay not with Shade, but the Restoration.

"The fact that he got as close as he did thirty years ago says it's a real possibility," my mom said, mouth pinched. "Isolation can either drive you mad or give you ample time to hone your skills."

"With our luck, it'll be both," I said. "Is there an increase in feral attacks outside of the hubs too?"

My mom sighed, crossing her arms. "The attacks we've been seeing for weeks out here have alarmingly ... stopped."

I shuddered at the idea that the uptick in activity had been some kind of training for tonight. "Can we do anything?"

"For now, we're collecting information," my mom said. "Kensey's an hour out. A group of our VHoA headed that way already. They'll report back if we're needed. But so far, it sounds like Kensey's veil is holding a lot better than Luma's." She offered me a tight smile. "There're showers you can use to get cleaned up. All we can do now is wait."

Reluctantly, Caspian and I both showered. We ate Alice's sandwiches. We paced. We checked our phones. We listened in on conversations.

Welsh wasn't answering his phone. We didn't have Kayda's new number.

When the sixth call of the evening to Welsh went right to voice mail instead of ringing, my anxiety shot through the roof. I wandered out into the warehouse parking lot to pace out there instead. The sword divided its time between checking on me and Caspian, and the goings-on inside. I'd escaped outside partly to get away from its antsy energy. It was hard to describe the feeling of being around an antsy sword, but all I can say was that it kicked my survival instincts into overdrive. Being outside made those lizard-brain fears lessen a tad.

I pulled out my phone for the millionth time that evening and this time sent a text to Felix. He wasn't answering my calls either, but he also hadn't returned the one from days ago. Given the chaos of the evening, I figured he wasn't going to be checking his phone any time soon.

Me: *I hope you're okay. I have some news! I found my mom! She tells me you already knew she was alive, but couldn't tell me because of the Soul NDA. I suppose I can forgive you for that one since you didn't have much choice, and because you calling in a tip about where we were headed made sure she intercepted us before we became troll food.*

I hit send. The air was warm, but a slight breeze swept past every once in a while, bringing with it the scent of dust from the construction company next door—their open-topped truck beds piled with gravel and sand.

My phone buzzed.

Felix: *Thank God! Worst secret I've ever had to keep. Luma is in chaos right now. First time in my life I'm glad you're not here*

I frowned.

Me: *Stay safe*

Felix: *I'm trying*

He started to type something else, then stopped. Started

again. The dots vanished once more and stayed gone. Sighing, I pocketed my phone.

I stared up at the yellowish light of a lamppost swarmed with tiny insects. The occasional bat would fly by, disrupting the cloud, only to have it re-form seconds later. It reminded me of the night I'd met Caspian—me creeping through the dark rail yards searching for Welsh's "chaotic evil" friend and finding my first feral vampire instead.

The sound of claws on metal sounded then and my heart nearly stopped. When I whirled around, it wasn't a feral I saw perched on top of a cement mixer. It was an eagle.

I cocked my head. It did the same.

"Cas!" I called out without breaking eye contact with the bird.

I assumed Caspian was playing the riveting game that was Word Jumbles for All Ages. A few minutes ago, from some corner of the lot, I'd heard, "*Palatable!* You sneaky game, you!"

He jogged over now, started to ask what was wrong, and then followed the trajectory of my pointed finger. "Oh!" He placed his hands on his hips. "Rory! Good to see you. Why are you skulking about up there?"

Normally I would have said something like, "You know he can't understand you, right?" But on top of courier animals going through rigorous training that included learning command words, Caspian seemed able to talk to his birds. Possibly something akin to telepathic communication, which I'd assumed was more of a druid ability—talking to animals. I didn't even know if druids existed on Earth outside of video games and novels.

"What do you mean you *intercepted* it?" Caspian asked his bird. "Is that code for defeathered? Because we've talked about this."

Rory screeched.

The sound grated on my nerve endings and I shied away.

"Come down here, then," Caspian said, arm out.

Rory launched off the cement mixer and alighted on Caspian's forearm. Its terrifyingly long talons dug into Caspian's long-sleeved shirt. I guessed the eagle was anywhere from eight to twelve pounds, as courier birds were often bigger than their run-of-the-mill counterparts. Perhaps the bulk of it was because of its fluffy feathers. Still, I was intimidated. Mostly because behind those beady eyes was a vow that he would defeather *me* if he could figure out how. Rory hadn't been this irritable the last time I'd seen him. Perhaps he was upset with me for taking his master away for so long.

"Sorry," I muttered, unsure of why I said it.

Rory flapped his wings a few times, his chest and head feathers puffed up before he resettled on Caspian's arm. I got the impression that Rory was at least temporarily mollified.

Caspian regarded me curiously, then focused on his eagle. "Now, what is this about an interception?" He paused. "A Collective courier! Really, Rory. This rivalry has gotten out of hand." He shook his head. "No, it's not the same thing." Sighing, he stared off into space for a few seconds as he presumably continued listening. "Well, that is distressing. Are you sure?"

Rory let loose a soft, indignant screech.

"All right, all right," Caspian said. "Do you have the note?"

Rory riffled in his chest feathers with his beak and slowly pulled out a small scroll of paper. Caspian took it, then rubbed his fingers along the front of Rory's beak. Despite any earlier hostility, Rory closed his eyes, appreciating the affection.

"Okay," Caspian said, nodding. "I don't approve of your methods, but I am glad to see you."

With a dip of his head directed at each of us in turn, Rory launched off Caspian's arm. The night swallowed him almost instantly.

I allowed the silence to linger for all of five seconds before I turned to Caspian. "We'll talk about the super weird telepathic avian conversation thing later. That message is from the Collective? And your bird stole it?"

Caspian carefully unraveled the tight scroll. "Rory, like myself, was destined to work for the Collective. I met him as part of my extra credit program while working in the Collective rookery. Most Collective couriers are magic-touched, though not as much as Rory. He's like a draken, in a way. He's a descendant of avian shifters, from an evolutionary branch that lost its ability to shift."

"Is he, like, *trapped* as a bird?" I asked.

Caspian shook his head. "Aeorci came to Earth during the Glitch. There were enough of them that they were able to procreate here. He's a bird with a humanlike consciousness. He's more bird than human, yet takes great offense at being treated as merely a bird—which was how he was treated at the rookery."

"But not by you," I said.

"Not by me. When I fled the academy and brought great shame upon my family, Rory decided to come with me. Collective couriers are, according to him, insufferably pretentious, mindless drones. They think he's a reckless abomination. So he harasses the Collective couriers as often as possible."

"I see why you two bonded." I jutted my chin toward the message. "What does it say?"

Caspian cleared his throat. "*Miss Fletcher, the Collective requires your assistance. Should you agree, all charges will be dropped.*" His brows hiked. "There's also a phone number."

Without hesitation, I pulled my phone out of my back pocket. "Read it to me."

Caspian did hesitate.

"I just want to see what they say." I shrugged. "Sounds like things have gone to shit in Luma. They've got too much going on for this to be a trap for little old me."

Caspian read off the number.

Once I had it dialed, I put the call on speaker and held the phone between us, screen facing up.

It rang twice. A female voice said, "We weren't sure if you'd received the message. Our courier falcon returned quite wounded. Its missive tube had been, dare I say, forcibly removed."

Caspian grimaced minutely but didn't say anything.

"What exactly do you need *assistance* with?" I asked.

"I don't know if you've heard, but Lachlan Shade successfully opened a portal this evening. He sacrificed many young elves to do it, and now he's loose on Earth. He's promised that he'll open more portals, implying that he seeks revenge on the Collective for his banishment."

"Sounds like a *you* problem," I said, unable to keep my snark in check.

The sorceress hmm'ed. "Be that as it may, we're going to need all the help we can get in stopping whatever he's got planned next. Portal Relations has been tracking uses of portal magic for decades. Not even we believed Shade would be able to pull this off. Our resources suggest that Shade has a network of elves scattered through the hubs who are loyal to him and his mission. The details of that mission continue to elude us. The whole of the hub system is in jeopardy now that he's been successful. If you harbor any love for Luma or the people in it, I assure you it's a *you* problem as well."

I smiled softly to myself. I kind of liked her.

She continued, "We also have reason to believe that the Shades have allied with the hybrid vampires. Which threatens not only the hubs, but humans at large."

Well, that wasn't good.

Caspian spoke up for the first time. "With all due respect, you haven't said what you need assistance with."

"Ah, hello, Mr. Blackthorn. I suppose it was your Rory who attacked our courier?" She didn't sound particularly upset. If anything, she almost sounded amused. "What we need from you, Miss Fletcher, is any information you can give us about your mother. Our research has us fairly confident she's alive, but she's slippery. If anyone would be able to catch her, it's you."

The anger was back. "It's your fault you lost track of her in the first place. People usually don't feel warm and fuzzy about being exiled."

"Ah," she said. "So you have been in contact with her then. Good. We must speak with her. She's had interactions with Lachlan Shade, and her extensive work hunting vampires could prove invaluable in planning our actions going forward."

This woman truly wanted my mom and me to just … forget how thoroughly the Collective had blown up our lives?

"I do understand your reluctance," the sorceress said in the same kind of flat affect Caspian had, making her sound the opposite of understanding. "All charges will be dropped, as the missive said. You and Mr. Blackthorn—"

"And the sword."

The sorceress offered a huff of annoyance, whether because of the stipulation or the interruption, I wasn't sure. "You *three* will be permitted to come back to Luma with clean slates. All we ask for is your mother's expertise."

She did expect us to go "no harm, no foul" and come slinking back simply because we proved useful now. The audacity.

"Take her off the exile list," I said.

"Done."

I pursed my lips. "Dissolve Felix Turner's Soul NDA."

She took longer to reply to that one. "That process is possible, but it can cause irreparable harm to a person's psyche. Mr. Turner would have to consent to that himself. Any other demands?"

I glanced up at Caspian for the first time since I started negotiating. His expression was nothing short of wary.

"Maybe," I said. "I have to talk to her first. There's no guarantee she'll agree. I'll call you back. Wait by the phone, yeah?" I hung up on her.

Petty, but satisfying.

Crossing my arms, my phone hidden from view, I stared at Caspian. "What do you think? Do we take the sorceress at her word that they'll let us come back without consequences?"

"Definitely not," he said. "But what if your mother really *can* help? She's essentially a traveling professor who gives lectures about vampires. She knows ... a lot about them. The detail in her notebooks is very impressive—which should tell you something, coming from me."

I managed a faint smile, but anger and fear were battling it out in my chest, so it pulled down into a frown shortly after. I had complicated feelings about the Collective. They had turned me into a fugitive, locked Felix into a Soul NDA, exiled my mother, and turned Kayda's life upside down. They'd shunned Caspian and spread rumors about his character when he'd left the academy for noble reasons. Their unwillingness to take the Bliss epidemic seriously had made my parents work outside of their protection, and my father had paid the price for it.

Margaret Fengast's journals implied very strongly that it was sorcerers who were ultimately responsible for the deaths of the ancients on Earth—deaths they then blamed humans for, all in an attempt to grab a foothold of power in this new world. It was even possible that sorcerers had been the ones who footed the bill for Captain Ipram's exploits, leading to such a horrific slaughter of fae creatures that it had haunted Margaret until her death. The result of that slaughter filled the boxes lining the treasure chest in the back of my mom's SUV. It felt wrong to trust this sorceress even when she claimed the Collective's actions were rooted in protecting Luma.

I knew this particular sorceress hadn't been one of the founding sorcerers who had manipulated and cheated their way to the top of the food chain. But she worked for the organization —their ideals and their history were hers by association. Caspian had seen the downside of power and had turned his back on it. When presented with those downsides, did this sorceress ignore them, combat them, encourage them ... cause them?

Siding, however temporarily, with the Collective might be the best chance that Luma—that all the hubs—had, but it still left me feeling uneasy. It was impossible to know if we were really on the same side, or if agreeing to help the Collective would result in some horrible scenario like the massacre that took place on that island.

Caspian cut into my thoughts. "If the hybrids are in cahoots with the Shades, and Shade just successfully did the impossible ..." He shrugged. "The Collective doesn't request aid unless it's urgent. If they're reaching out, the situation is even more dire than we think."

"Was anyone planning to talk to me about this?"

My mom stood a few feet away, the sword drifting beside her. I guessed it had gone to fetch her when it figured out where the conversation with the sorceress had been headed.

"How much of that did you hear?" I asked.

She strode over. "Enough to know that my services have been requested by my mortal enemy."

Caspian muttered, "I see dramatics run in the family."

We glared at him. He held his hands up in placation.

"One bonus to all this is that you can be smug as hell," I

said. "It's like hackers who get recruited by the government to hack for them. You eluded capture for years and you're back because they're groveling at your feet."

We all knew the Collective didn't grovel, but this was as close as we were going to get.

"I'd want the conditions in writing," my mom finally said. "Verbal agreements will get all of us in trouble."

I didn't doubt it.

My mom had worked for the Collective for years and even with half a decade of distance, her reluctance practically poured from her like a fog.

My gut twisted watching that reluctance furrow her brow—sorrow because of her evident torment and guilt at wanting her to agree to this anyway—so I turned to the sword instead. "The next clue on your Self-Discovery Tour takes us back to California anyway. You good with this 'saving the entire hub system and human race at large' thing before we try to figure out how to wake up your twin?"

The sword instantly hummed, glowing blue.

"Guess that settles it," my mom said, her forced smile shaky. "Call her back."

I did so, and we all huddled around the phone.

"That was quick," the sorceress said. "I barely had enough time to make tea."

"Hello, Rhiannon," my mom said.

I was surprised she could recognize the sorceress's voice after all these years—especially when it was such a plain, generically female voice. But at this point, I supposed I'd be able to pick Caspian's cadence out of a lineup. Perhaps that spoke to a long history between my mother and Sorceress Rhiannon.

"Oh," Rhiannon said, sounding genuinely surprised. I imagined her sitting up straighter. "Hello, Camila. It's good—"

"Don't," my mom said. "I'll only do this if we get all our demands in writing, written up by a lawyer of my choosing."

"Agreed," Rhiannon said. "I've already escalated the request to revoke your exile status. You'll be free to re-enter Luma within the hour."

"Fine," my mom said, then reached out to hit the "end" icon to disconnect the call.

Pettiness ran in the family, too.

There was a long tense pause before my mom said, "I can't make any promises about how I'll feel about Luma at the end of this. You and me, that's rock solid. We'll figure that part out. But it will be harder for me to reconcile with Luma. It's taken too much from me."

"That's fair," I said, resisting the urge to come to my city's defense. It wasn't the city itself that had done this, but the people in it. Perhaps it was easier to blame Luma, the place that held so many memories for her, like a grief time capsule.

"You can all stay with me," Caspian said.

I jabbed my thumb in his direction. "He's got a palatial estate. We could probably spend days wandering the place independently and never see each other."

"She's exaggerating, as always," Caspian said. "It's only a mansion."

My mom laughed, but the sound was strained. There was a haunted, distant look in her eye. I pulled her into a hug, unable to resist it any longer. She stiffened at first but hugged me back.

"We're going home?" I asked.

"You're going home." When I struggled in her grasp, confused, she squeezed me tighter. "I'm already there."

KAYDA

. . .

The first face Kayda saw when she finally opened her eyes was a very small one.

"Finally!" Aster cheered.

As the pixie prattled on excitedly about what had happened at the preserve after Kayda had blacked out and "collapsed like a felled tree," Kayda glanced around, disoriented. There was a familiar groggy feeling weighing her body down, and she knew Welsh must have given her another sleep-slash-healing tonic. She was in his Bosworth Hemmingsley apartment in uptown.

Welsh must have been growing soft if he let a pixie in here. Maybe the near-death experience with the hybrid had changed the witch.

"How long was I out?" Kayda asked, her throat scratchy and raw. She'd interrupted Aster's very spirited reenactment of herself and her fellow pixies forming a sphere using their shield magic to knock Snowdrop out of Lachlan Shade's magical grip.

Kayda hadn't even known pixies had shield magic. She had a renewed sense of guilt over how often she'd discounted the little pests.

Fat lot of good it did. Shade had gotten out. Goddess knew where he was now.

"Only a few hours," Aster said. "You had a busted ankle and a shattered foot. Shattered. Welsh said if he shook it, he would have heard the bone shards rattling around in there."

"Leave the patient alone, pixie," came a voice from somewhere beyond Kayda's view, sprawled out as she was on his couch. She groaned as she got herself onto her elbows. There was no immediate pain anywhere, only the heavy fog of the sleep tonic's last dregs.

Welsh stood at the mouth of his kitchen, streaks of flour

splattered across his apron. "Feeling better? If so, call your boy. He's at work now, but he calls at every break."

Her boy. Henri.

"That's the goofiest smile I've ever seen on a draken," Aster commented.

Kayda swatted her away. Aster easily dodged Kayda's hand, laughing all the while. Sitting up, Kayda asked, "What are you doing here, anyway? Decide to get that glamour tonic after all?"

"Nah!" Aster said. "Something even better. I'm super close to opening my bakery, but I've been struggling with the menu. Welsh offered to help."

"It's extremely challenging figuring out the measurements for baked goods the size of a penny," Welsh said, but he sounded agreeable enough.

Kayda got to her feet, cautiously testing out the strength of her shattered foot. It felt fine, but both her ankles were stiff. She took her time shuffling toward the kitchen. "It's going to ruin your street cred if it gets out that you're baking cupcakes with pixies."

He pointed a finger dotted with red food coloring. "Then it better not get out."

Over the next few hours, Kayda got up to speed on the state of things in Luma and beyond. Thanks to insider information provided by Snowdrop, Kayda learned that the Shades and hybrids had been working together for months, if not longer, preparing for the night Lachlan Shade would come through a portal. The teenage elves, who'd been sacrificed just as much as the wild animals had been, were chosen because of their raw power. The hybrids, who could control ferals like attack dogs, had made a pact with the Shades, granting them immunity from the ferals' attacks, allowing the breaches to occur without fear that the elves would get slaughtered in the process.

No one knew where Lachlan was, but he obviously had a

vendetta against the Collective. It was simply a matter of time before he came back. Kayda assumed the Collective would attempt to exile him as they had with Harlow's mom, but Kayda had her misgivings that they'd be able to do it.

And the best news: the sword, Caspian, Harlow, and Camila were returning to Luma. Maybe life would feel less unstable once Kayda had her "sister from another mister" back.

She called "her boy" that night, and talked long enough that Aster left, and Welsh retreated to his room. They spent very little time talking about their ordeals in the preserve. Instead, they talked about normal, everyday things. Henri's stutter had even calmed down a bit by the end of the conversation.

By the morning, armed with the assurances she'd gotten from the werecats last night that she was no longer under surveillance, Kayda returned to her apartment. The place was largely a disaster and smelled stuffy, but there was a check on her counter to help her pay for the damages. She could replace her gaming console and then some.

The money wouldn't replace all that was lost last night, though. Sixteen elfin families had just learned about the death of their teenage children. Several wild animals, two gnomes, and a dozen pixies perished in the fight, too. Not to mention the hybrid and the adult Shade elves, including Lachlan's sister. Not that Lachlan had shed many tears over the loss.

Kayda pushed thoughts of last night away. There was something very significant happening this afternoon and she needed to be in the right headspace for it. It had been a long time coming. Henri had made the suggestion last night, and she smiled to herself at the further proof he wanted her in his life as more than a coworker and friend.

Yes, these thoughts were much better.

By the time she'd showered and put on fresh, clean clothes, she felt mostly draken again. She didn't linger at home for long.

She set out, her head held high, not bothered about who might be watching.

When she reached her destination, she took a few calming breaths and wiped her hands on the sides of her dress. It was the same one she'd worn to the farmers market—the delicate cream-colored dress with the dainty flowers. Henri had said she looked pretty in it.

She wasn't sure why she was so nervous. She'd met his family before.

She knocked.

The door swung open and Kayda looked down into the blue-spotted, confused face peering at her.

"Umm ... Henri isn't here."

"I know," Kayda said. "I'm here for you."

Libby blinked rapidly.

"I promised to teach you how to protect yourself, didn't I?"

Libby squealed and pumped a fist in the air. "This is going to be the best day ever."

Trouble was on the horizon for hubs everywhere, and potentially even the unaware mundanes living beyond the hubs' invisible veils. Kayda was downright terrified of what the future might hold.

Libby gestured Kayda inside with a dramatic sweep of her hand.

Today, Kayda wasn't going to worry about the future. Today she was going to teach an impressionable young lady how to knee a guy in the junk.

Kayda and Harlow are back in Unholy Magic in 2023!

Also by Melissa Erin Jackson

Thank you for reading *Wicked Treasure*! If you enjoyed this story, please consider leaving a review. Reviews mean the world to authors. Reviews often mean more sales, and more sales means more freedom to write more books.

If you'd like to read a **free** short story about how Camila Fletcher and Lachlan Shade first met, you can find *Veiled Threats* at: https://melissajacksonbooks.com/the-charm-collector/veiled-threats

Next up in Harlow and Kayda's adventure is *Unholy Magic*. If you'd like to be notified when new books are released, you can join my newsletter at melissajacksonbooks.com.

If you're looking for a ghost-filled paranormal tale, consider *The Forgotten Child*, a haunting mystery starring a reluctant medium.

The dead can speak. They need her to listen.

Ever since Riley Thomas, reluctant medium extraordinaire, accidentally released a malevolent spirit from a Ouija board when she was thirteen, she's taken a hard pass on scary movies, haunted houses, and cemeteries. Twelve years later, when her best friend pressures her into spending a paranormal investigation weekend at the infamous Jordanville Ranch—former home of deceased serial killer Orin Jacobs —Riley's *still* not ready to accept the fact that she can communicate with ghosts.

Shortly after their arrival at the ranch, the spirit of a little boy contacts Riley; a child who went missing—and was never found—in 1973.

In order to put the young boy's spirit to rest, she has to come to grips with her ability. But how can she solve a mystery that happened a decade before she was born? Especially when someone who knows Orin's secrets wants to keep the truth buried—no matter the cost.

Also available as an audiobook!

If you're interested in a lighter story, try *Pawsitively Poisonous*, the first book in a complete, five-book paranormal cozy mystery series starring a secret witch.

Every town has its secrets, but no one has a secret like hers.

Amber Blackwood, lifelong resident of Edgehill, Oregon, has earned a reputation for being a semi-reclusive odd duck. Her store, The Quirky Whisker, is full of curiosities, from extremely potent sleepy teas and ever-burning candles to kids' toys that seem to run endlessly without the aid of batteries. The people of Edgehill think of the Quirky Whisker as an integral part of their feline-obsessed town, but most give Amber herself a wide berth. Amber prefers it that way; it keeps her secret safe. But that secret is thrown into jeopardy when Amber's friend Melanie is found dead, a vial of headache tonic from Amber's store clutched in her hand.

Edgehill's newest police chief has had it out for Amber since he arrived three years before. He can't possibly know she's a witch, but

his suspicions about her odd store and even odder behavior have shot
her to the top of his suspect list. When the Edgehill rumor mill finds
out Melanie was poisoned, it's not only the police chief who looks at
Amber differently. Determined to both find justice for her friend and
to clear her own name, Amber must use her unique gifts to help track
down Melanie's real killer. A quest that threatens much more than her
secret …

Also available as an audiobook!

Acknowledgments

Phew! This book and I struggled a bit in the beginning. I was burned out for a good chunk of the year, and this book had big plans for itself. Thank you, as usual, to my writer buddies and first readers. I got this sucker done quite close to release day and y'all happily jumped in to read it for me. I appreciate all your time with my stories.

Thank you, Mom, Jennifer Laam, Lauren Sprang, Garrett Lemons, Cecilie Schulze, Cynthia Sandusky, Emilie Vecera, Holly Starkey, and John Parker.

Thank you again to Danielle Fine for these covers. I've been wanting covers with POC on them for a long time, and I'm glad I stumbled on your group. You're so talented. Thank you to the artists at Etheric Tales for the drawings of the ship, talisman, and dragons. Thank you to Tomasz Madej at Fictive Designs for the beautiful city of Luma map that keeps getting more detailed with each book.

Thank you to Greg Likins for jumping in to proofread for me on a tight deadline.

Sam, thank you as always for managing my neurotic writer issues when I'm drafting, and for all the plotting conversations. I get so many good ideas from our chats! I love you lots.

And, of course, thank you to my readers—especially if you'd never read an urban fantasy before but were willing to give it a shot because it was one of mine.

I hope you'll join me and the Luma gang in *Unholy Magic*!
slinks back into the writer's cave

About the Author

Melissa has had a love of stories for as long as she can remember, but only started penning her own during her freshman year of college. She majored in Wildlife, Fish, and Conservation Biology at UC Davis. Yet, while she was neck-deep in organic chemistry and physics, she kept finding herself writing stories in the back of the classroom about fairies and trolls and magic. She finished her degree, but it never captured her heart the way writing did.

Now she owns her own dog walking business (that's sort of wildlife related, right?) by day ... and afternoon and night ... and writes whenever she gets a spare moment. She alternates mostly between fantasy and mystery (often with a paranormal twist). All her books have some element of "other" to them ... witches, ghosts, UFOs. There's no better way to escape the real world than getting lost in a fictional one.

She lives in Northern California with her very patient boyfriend and way too many pets.

You can find out more about her upcoming books and join her newsletter at: https://melissajacksonbooks.com

www.ingramcontent.com/pod-product-compliance
Lightning Source LLC
Chambersburg PA
CBHW030655190726
48286CB00001B/40